Praise for *The Heart* [of a King]

"Smith uses poetic intervals to infuse [the] sensuality and beauty of the ancient cu[lture.]

*Booklist*

"*The Heart of a King* was an intriguing, gripping look into the life of one of history's most famous kings."

*Interviews & Reviews*


Praise for the Daughters of the Promised Land Series

"Readers will appreciate that Smith infuses this well-known story with emotional depth and a modern sensibility not typically seen in historical novels."

*Publishers Weekly* on *A Passionate Hope*

"*A Passionate Hope* is a wonderful novel rich with historical detail about real people who suffer the heartache that comes from stepping out ahead of God, and the miracle of grace that comes when we cry out to Him."

Francine Rivers, bestselling author of *Redeeming Love*, on *A Passionate Hope*

"Smith's fresh retelling of the story of Ruth and Naomi portrays these strong biblical women in a thoughtful and reflective manner. Her impeccable research and richly detailed setting give readers a strong sense of life in ancient Israel."

*Library Journal* on *Redeeming Grace*

"Rahab's story is one of the most moving redemption accounts in Scripture. *The Crimson Cord* perfectly captures all the drama of the original, fleshing out the characters with care and thought, and following the biblical account every step of the way. Jill's thorough research and love for God's Word are both evident, and her storytelling skills kept me reading late into the night. A beautiful tale, beautifully told!"

Liz Curtis Higgs, *New York Times* bestselling author of *Mine Is the Night*, on *The Crimson Cord*

# Books by Jill Eileen Smith

### THE WIVES OF KING DAVID

*Michal*

*Abigail*

*Bathsheba*

### WIVES OF THE PATRIARCHS

*Sarai*

*Rebekah*

*Rachel*

### DAUGHTERS OF THE PROMISED LAND

*The Crimson Cord*

*The Prophetess*

*Redeeming Grace*

*A Passionate Hope*

*The Heart of a King*

*Star of Persia*

*Miriam's Song*

*When Life Doesn't Match Your Dreams*

*She Walked Before Us*

# Miriam's
# Song

## Jill Eileen Smith

Revell

a division of Baker Publishing Group
Grand Rapids, Michigan

© 2021 by Jill Eileen Smith

Published by Revell
a division of Baker Publishing Group
PO Box 6287, Grand Rapids, MI 49516-6287
www.revellbooks.com

Printed in the United States of America

All rights reserved. No part of this publication may be reproduced, stored in a retrieval system, or transmitted in any form or by any means—for example, electronic, photocopy, recording—without the prior written permission of the publisher. The only exception is brief quotations in printed reviews.

Library of Congress Cataloging-in-Publication Data
Names: Smith, Jill Eileen, 1958– author.
Title: Miriam's song / Jill Eileen Smith.
Description: Grand Rapids, Michigan : Revell, a division of Baker Publishing
    Group, [2021]
Identifiers: LCCN 2020019551 | ISBN 9780800739706 (casebound) | ISBN
    9780800734725 (paperback)
Subjects: LCSH: Miriam (Biblical figure)—Fiction. | Moses (Biblical leader)—
    Fiction. | Exodus, The—Fiction. | Christian fiction. | GSAFD: Bible fiction.
Classification: LCC PS3619.M58838 M57 2021 | DDC 813/.6—dc23
LC record available at https://lccn.loc.gov/2020019551

Unless otherwise indicated, Scripture quotations are from the *Holy Bible*, New Living Translation, copyright © 1996, 2004, 2007, 2013, 2015 by Tyndale House Foundation. Used by permission of Tyndale House Publishers, Inc., Carol Stream, Illinois 60188. All rights reserved.

Scripture quotations labeled NIV are from the Holy Bible, New International Version®. NIV®. Copyright © 1973, 1978, 1984, 2011 by Biblica, Inc.™ Used by permission of Zondervan. All rights reserved worldwide. www.zondervan.com. The "NIV" and "New International Version" are trademarks registered in the United States Patent and Trademark Office by Biblica, Inc.™

This is a work of historical reconstruction; the appearances of certain historical figures are therefore inevitable. All other characters, however, are products of the author's imagination, and any resemblance to actual persons, living or dead, is coincidental.

Published in association with Books & Such Literary Management, 52 Mission Circle, Suite 122, PMB 170, Santa Rosa, CA 95409-5370, www.booksandsuch.com.

22   23   24   25   26   27       7   6   5   4   3

*To Keaton and Jade.*
Gramma loves you.
This story is for you.

# PART ONE

Then a new king, to whom Joseph meant nothing, came to power in Egypt. "Look," he said to his people, "the Israelites have become far too numerous for us. Come, we must deal shrewdly with them or they will become even more numerous and, if war breaks out, will join our enemies, fight against us and leave the country."

So they put slave masters over them to oppress them with forced labor, and they built Pithom and Rameses as store cities for Pharaoh. But the more they were oppressed, the more they multiplied and spread; so the Egyptians came to dread the Israelites and worked them ruthlessly.

Exodus 1:8–13 NIV

# PROLOGUE

## 1526 BC

Hatshepsut peeked through a slit in a curtain that allowed her to watch her father in his audience chamber and listen to his magicians and advisors speak to him. She had escaped her servants and tutors as she often did to watch Pharaoh Thutmose I in his jeweled clothes, his crook and flail crossed before him and the sign of the cobra on his head. One day she would wear that crown, she promised herself. It was a big dream for a young girl, but she had never wanted anything more.

It was all in fun, she'd told her mother when she scolded Hatshepsut for her daydreams. But in her heart Hatshepsut knew better. She *would* wear her father's crown, and since she was the only child of his first wife, she knew, even in her seven years on earth, that she held a highly favored position. She let the curtain fall back into place lest she be seen but sat quietly, straining to hear the men.

"My lord," one said, "the Hebrews only grow stronger, despite the added work we give them. They breed like cattle even when we beat them with whips and rods. What can we do?"

Silence followed the desperate question. She peered again through the slit and held her breath. If she were caught here, her father would ban her from the audience chamber. But she had to know. What did her father plan to do with the Hebrews?

"You have sent them to the fields and forced them to make their own mortar to go with the bricks?"

"Yes, my lord. We have upped their quotas and put them in rocky fields and forced them to make the land smooth. Nothing works," the man said.

Hatshepsut released her breath as quietly as she could. They had to be cruel to people who could oppress them. That's what her father had said many times. She watched him stroke the fake beard he wore on his normally smooth chin. His eyes were slits, painted with kohl, and they narrowed even more now.

"Then we will have to resort to harsher means," he said. "Call to me the Hebrew midwives."

Hatshepsut scrunched her brow, mimicking the surprised looks on the faces of her father's men. What were midwives? And how could they help against so fierce a people as the Hebrews?

"Yes, my king," two or three men said at once. They retreated backwards from the pharaoh's presence, and Hatshepsut leaned on her heels and placed both hands around her knees. Her father would not wait long for these midwives to appear before him. No one resisted a summons from the pharaoh.

So she would wait. And learn. She wished she could ask her mother or her servants what a midwife was or why her father wanted to speak to them, but she would figure it out if she could just sit here quietly and not be discovered. Her stomach growled, and she almost rose to hurry to the palace cooking rooms to coax the cooks for a treat, but she didn't want to miss whatever happened next.

❦

An hour passed and Hatshepsut grew tired in her cramped position, but still she waited. At last the big doors swung open, and two young women slowly walked the length of the audience chamber. They bowed before Pharaoh, their faces to the ground.

Hatshepsut studied them. They wore woolen robes over linen or woolen tunics, with no ornaments in their hair or jewelry on their arms. They were slaves like the rest of the Hebrews. Suddenly Hatshepsut didn't see them as people to fear. Why, they were no different from her servants, only poorer. As they lifted their heads at her father's order, she saw that they wore no makeup to enhance their plain features.

"Tell me your names," Pharaoh barked, making her jump.

The women still knelt, eyes looking again at the floor. "Shiphrah and Puah," one said, her voice shaking. They were obviously afraid of her father, and she felt sorry that the women had been forced to come here at all. Why did her father want them?

"You are the heads of the Hebrew midwives?" Pharaoh's voice carried unquestioned authority.

"Yes, my lord."

"Look up," he said. "I want to see your faces when I tell you this."

They both lifted their heads, and Hatshepsut read fear in their eyes.

11

"When you are helping the Hebrew women during childbirth on the delivery stool, if you see that the baby is a boy, kill him, but if it is a girl, let her live."

Her father's words echoed in the hall, and a heavy silence followed. A shiver rushed down Hatshepsut's spine. A midwife must be a person who helped deliver babies.

"If you see that the child is a boy before the mother completely delivers it, kill the child before it sees the light of day," he added. "Now go. See that you do not disobey my orders."

The two women backed from the pharaoh's chambers without a word, not even an acknowledgment that they would do as he said. Shock filled their faces, and Hatshepsut felt the same.

Her father wanted to kill the Hebrew babies because the Hebrews were becoming too strong for him. Even a child could understand that. But why not just let the Hebrews move away? Send them out of Egypt and ban them from coming back.

She saw the tiniest hint of movement in her father's quiet sigh. His shoulders slumped. Her father was afraid. Was it true, as her mother had hinted when she didn't know Hatshepsut heard? Was the pharaoh of Egypt, the grandest nation on earth, weak?

# ONE

"Ohhh!" A woman's cry woke Miriam with a start. She pulled the light blanket from her shoulders and tossed it aside. The sky was still dark. Had she been dreaming?

"Ima?" she called out, leaning on an elbow and rubbing her eyes.

"Go back to sleep, Miriam. Marta's baby will be here soon."

"Please, dear God, let Hava's ima have a girl." Miriam pulled the covers over herself again as she prayed for her best friend's mother. She squeezed her eyes tight, trying to block out the fear. Everyone knew that a boy baby would be sacrificed to the river god.

*A girl, O God. Please let it be a girl.*

When Miriam awoke later to the *croo-doo-doo* of a laughing dove, she strained to listen for Marta's cries. Instead, she heard the soft whimper of a baby.

Miriam jumped out of bed and hurried to where her mother stood by the curtained window and watched the rising sun color the sky in pink predawn light. She touched her mother's round stomach with one hand. Her father came and stood behind them, stiff and silent, his robe warm against her back.

"The head taskmaster knew Marta was in labor, poor girl," Ima said, her voice soft and sad.

"It was a boy?" Miriam whispered against her mother's side and felt her father's arm touch her shoulder. She glanced back at him and caught the tears flowing down Ima's cheeks. Abba nodded.

Ima turned from the window and pulled Miriam to sit beside her on a low stool. "They will come for him, won't they?" Miriam's throat hurt as she voiced the words.

"We can pray that they won't. But no boys have survived since Shiphrah and Puah refused to obey the pharaoh's orders."

Tears stung Miriam's eyes, and she swiped at them with one hand. "Can I go to Hava?"

Abba came and knelt at her side. Her little brother, Aaron, rose from his cot, pulling his blanket with him. "Hungry," he said, as though nothing awful had just happened.

"I prayed, Abba. Why did God give them a boy instead of a girl?" She was crying now, though even at five years old she knew crying wouldn't change anything. Her gaze turned from her father to her mother, who would give birth to another baby soon.

"We don't know the ways of our God, my daughter." He shook his head.

The sound of horses' hooves pounded the pavement outside of their little hut, shaking the earth and the walls along with it. They all stilled, even Aaron, though he climbed onto Ima's lap.

"We will speak of this later," Abba whispered.

Miriam crept from the table to peek through the curtain again. Bare-chested soldiers dressed in red and white skirts stood beside their captain, who hopped off his horse and pounded on Hava's door with his fist.

The door creaked open.

Miriam heard shouts, then a baby's wail.

"Don't take my baby!" Hava's ima screamed.

But the soldiers marched out of the house, carrying the newborn boy by his legs, and mounted their horses. Miriam watched Hava and her father run after them, leaving her mother sobbing in the house.

When the soldiers had disappeared from view, Ima slipped quietly from the house to comfort Hava's mother.

"Can I go with you, Ima?" Miriam stood at the door, longing to run after her friend. But her father, who now held Aaron in his arms, pulled her back. She turned slowly to face him.

"You must protect your ima now, Miriam. Only God can comfort Hava's family, and we must pray that He does the same for us."

Miriam looked at him, her eyes widening. "What if Ima has a boy?"

Abba held a finger to his lips. "Do not speak of it, child. You must keep our secret. Not even the taskmasters know of your ima's condition. And when the baby comes . . ." He paused, his gaze traveling toward the thatched ceiling. "When that day comes, we must trust our God."

⁂

Several weeks later, Miriam awoke to the soft mewling of a newborn. She threw off her blanket and padded quickly across the floor to her mother's side. "What is it, Ima?" she whispered, bending close.

Her mother opened the blanket to show her.

Miriam sighed. "He's beautiful!" She put a shaky hand to her chest. "But what about the soldiers . . . the river god?"

"There is no river god, Miriam. There is only one God, and He alone can keep your brother safe." Ima's voice was soft, barely above a whisper. "We will keep him quiet, and we will tell no one of his birth. Not even Hava." She looked at Miriam with sternness in her gaze. "Do you understand, Miriam?"

A tear slipped down her cheek, but she nodded. "I won't tell anyone." She reached one hand to touch her baby brother's creamy soft skin. He had a head of thick black hair, and his black eyes were wide with wonder. His mouth opened and closed, and he sucked on Miriam's finger as though he thought it was food.

Miriam coughed, forcing back the urge to laugh. A moment later, she remembered Hava's brother. "Why does the king take the boy babies, Ima?"

"The king is afraid of us, my daughter. He throws our boys into the river because he thinks we will grow too powerful and rise up against him."

Ima placed the baby's mouth to her breast, leaned against the cot, and closed her eyes. What would she do with him when she was expected to work in the fields?

"I could take your place in the fields today," Miriam offered, wishing she were bigger so she could truly help.

Ima opened her eyes and smiled. She shook her head. "No, my sweet girl. You will come with me as you always do. I will feed your brother, and then we will go."

"But you just gave birth." Though Miriam was young, she knew that women needed time to heal after birthing a baby.

"I worked the fields after Aaron's birth. I will do the same now." She stood with the sleeping baby in her arms. She placed him in the large lunch basket she always carried and covered him with a blanket, then placed bread and cheese on top.

"Our God sees what the king is doing to us, Miriam. He will not forget His people forever. Someday He will send a deliverer. And no river god, or any other god, will stop Him."

Eight days later, Miriam's father planned to circumcise the new baby after a long day of working on one of Pharaoh's cities. He did not call the elders to join him but took the family to the river, where the sound of lapping water might drown out the baby's cries.

Miriam clasped Aaron's hand as they knelt beside their mother. Their father quickly cut off the baby's foreskin along the banks of the Nile. "What shall we name him?" he asked Ima.

She shook her head. "I cannot name him yet. He will be our *tikvah*, our hope. When he is old enough to go unnoticed, then we will name him."

Miriam stared at her baby brother, her mouth agape that he had not cried. Her mother had been quick to cover and soothe him and put him to her breast. Miriam let out a relieved breath as she watched her mother tuck the baby into her robe, blocking all view of him.

They stood slowly and moved back to their hut by the light of the moon. When they were settled inside, Miriam led Aaron to his pallet and told him a story while her parents sat at a small table, her mother still nursing the baby.

"He is an unusual boy," her father said softly. "There is something about him . . ."

"Do you see it too?" Her mother's voice held awe. "I sensed it even before his birth. This child has a future ahead of him. God has surely set him aside for something. Perhaps he is the answer to all of our prayers."

Miriam listened to her father's agreement and their talk of a deliverer. What would it be like to live in a place other than Egypt? To be free of taskmasters and guards who threw boy babies into the river? Could her brother be that person?

She tucked Aaron into bed and touched his soft hair. What would it be like to be considered special by God? She had thought about Him ever since her parents began to teach her of Him when she was no bigger than Aaron.

What was God even like? She pondered the thought as she lay down on her own pallet beside Aaron's. Maybe someday she would know. For now she was simply glad that her baby brother was safe for one more day.

# TWO

wo weeks later Miriam held Aaron's hand again as they walked beside their mother toward the fields where she worked digging up stones and carrying them to the edge of the field. The work was hard, the day long, and Miriam did all she could to lift the stones and watch Aaron at the same time. She couldn't let her mother be distracted when she was trying to keep their tikvah quiet.

As the sun rose higher in the sky and the people groaned beneath the heat of the day, the sharp sound of a whip cracking caused everyone to jump. An old man screamed, and Miriam whirled around. Three rows from where her mother worked, a taskmaster stood beating a weeping man who could not lift the heavy boulder at his feet. Welts appeared on his bare back, and with every scream, the taskmaster shouted, "Get up, you lazy slave! Pick up your load and do your part, or I will feed your body to the crocodiles."

Miriam grabbed Aaron's hand and ran to stand behind her mother. She put her hands over Aaron's ears and hid them both against the length of her mother's skirts. But she couldn't block the man's screams from her own ears, and she feared the baby would hear and begin to cry himself.

*Please, God, make it stop. And keep our baby quiet.*

The whipping ended as the man attempted to lift the boulder, but the weight was too heavy. It fell on his foot, crushing it. His screams ended when the taskmaster ran him through with a sword.

Miriam could not stop her silent tears, but she managed to hush Aaron's soft weeping. She pointed toward home. "We will leave soon," she whispered. Surprisingly, the baby did not make a sound. He was not in the basket where her mother usually tucked him but strapped to her body beneath her clothes, nursing.

Miriam glanced at her mother, who looked worn. Neither of them could keep the horror from their eyes. "Keep working," Ima whispered. "All is well. We will talk when we are home."

Miriam nodded and led Aaron back to the small section they were trying to clear. Aaron could carry barely more than the size of a small rock, but Miriam managed some twice as big. The Egyptians had picked this rocky field to make life harder for the women and the older people. And now she saw that they would not even care that the work was too much for them.

Egyptians were cruel. Miriam had known that from what happened with Hava's baby brother, but now she felt the fear creep up her spine. They were not safe here or anywhere in this awful land. No one was safe.

How long until their baby was discovered and her parents suffered for hiding him? What would happen to her and Aaron then?

⤜⤚

Hatshepsut walked through the halls of her father's palace, trailed by her serving girls. She wanted to escape to the river, but a commotion at the front of the audience chamber made her turn. She motioned to her maids. "Come," she said. Even at her young age, she had learned quickly to command those older than she was.

She led the girls to climb the steps to an antechamber that overlooked the audience hall. No need to give up her hiding place behind the curtain. Besides, she was allowed to watch when the chamber was open to people besides her father's advisors. And the sight of the two Hebrew midwives approaching the pharaoh now made her sit tall and lean closer to the railing to better hear them.

Pharaoh's narrow eyes turned to slits, his gaze as hard as his tone. "Why have you done this? Why have you let the boys live?"

Hatshepsut's eyes grew wide. Her father had known of these women's disobedience for months and had sent his soldiers to toss the babies into the river. She had heard him from her hiding place when he was first given the news.

"My lord," one of his advisors had said, "it is said that the Hebrew midwives you sent for have not done as you asked. Hebrew boys are allowed to live, and they are coming faster than they were before."

Her father said words she did not often hear him speak, and they made her curl tighter into herself and cover her ears against his raised voice.

"Then *we* will kill them," her father said. "Have the taskmasters keep watch over the pregnant women. When their time comes to give birth, watch their houses and send soldiers to check. If it is a boy, toss it to the crocodiles."

The memory of that awful day came back to her now. How could her father order his men to kill innocent babies?

Her thoughts turned back to the midwives as one of them spoke.

"Hebrew women are not like Egyptian women, my lord. They are vigorous and give birth before the midwives arrive."

Hatshepsut looked from the women to her father. He remained silent. Did he believe them? Would he have them killed too? She held her breath and squeezed her eyes shut. No. *Please don't kill them too*. They could be telling the truth.

But when she looked again at the women, she wondered. She had never seen a baby born, or even a Hebrew woman except these two midwives. What did she know of what they said? What did her father know? Men did not attend the birthing of Egyptian babies.

"You have defied my order," her father said, his tone menacing. "So I will repeat it again. If you *do* happen to get there in time to help these women give birth, which it seems you should—why else would they need a midwife?—you will obey me, or I will take away your privileged place and put you under hard labor like your fellow Hebrews."

Hatshepsut let out a long-held breath. The midwives bowed and backed from the king's presence. Hatshepsut watched them go and felt a deep sense of relief that her father had not punished them. It was not like him to give them a second chance. He was not known for kindness or leniency. And yet he had allowed them to leave unharmed.

Hatshepsut moved down the steps to head toward her rooms. Something was not quite right, but she didn't know what. Mostly, she was thankful that the women would be spared. If only her father were as kind to the baby boys.

# THREE

Miriam stood at the table where her mother sat working at her basket weaving, late as it was. She saw Ima's slumped shoulders and her tired eyes. But she continued to weave the papyrus reeds into the shape of an oblong basket, in and out, over and through.

"Why are you making this, Ima? You should sleep. Please let me help you." Though Miriam had never made a basket, she knew she could do it. Following Ima's example didn't look hard.

Her mother shook her head, her smile worn, the lines around her mouth deeper than they usually were. "We have to hurry, Miriam. It is for your brother."

Miriam gave her a curious look. "But why? No one has found him yet. Surely God will keep him safe."

"That is my hope, little one. But our little tikvah grows bigger by the day. Soon I will no longer be able to hide him from the taskmasters. He will bulge under my skirt, and they will know. They are always looking for signs of women who are carrying a child. They will know."

"But . . ." Miriam wanted to say that wouldn't God hide the truth from their eyes? Instead she simply nodded. "Can I help you?"

"You can stir the pitch I have waiting in the bowl over there." Ima pointed to a wooden bowl on the floor, where a black, tarry mass filled it to the top.

Miriam did as she was told. She took a wooden stick and stirred, though it took both hands and all of her strength to make the sticky mixture move.

Her father came and lifted the bowl. "You did well. It is enough." Though she had not made even a full circle in her stirring.

Her father took the bowl to her mother and set it on the table, where the basket now stood finished. Miriam glanced at her brothers, both sleeping on pallets.

"Hand me that wide stick, Miriam," her mother said. Miriam hurried to get it.

Her mother took the object and dipped it into the pitch. She coated the basket inside and out, then took another bowl filled with tar and did the same. "It will dry overnight," Ima said as she set the little ark, for that was what it looked like, on the floor near her pallet. "We will bury the bowls, for there is no time to clean them well." She glanced at Abba. Bowls were scarce, and it would take time to make more. But it would be easier to make new ones than try to clean the old.

"We will manage," Abba said.

"Miriam, you must listen to me now." Ima took Miriam's hand and guided her to her pallet near Aaron, farthest from the door. "Tomorrow we will swaddle your brother and place him in the basket and put a papyrus covering over him so he can breathe. I will put the basket in the water near the bulrushes along the Nile, where the princess comes to bathe. I want you to stand near, out of sight, and watch to see what happens to him. To see whether God is going to answer our prayers."

Miriam stared at her mother for a long moment, trying to take in what she had just heard. Put their baby in the Nile? That's where the boy babies went to die. Would their baby be safe in the little ark? For how long? Would God protect him? Was there no other way?

But she simply nodded. "Yes, Ima. I will do as you say."

Her mother patted her hand. "That's my good girl. If the princess finds him, and if she looks on him with favor, you must not be afraid. You must go to her and offer to bring a nurse for the baby. Then you will come and find me."

Miriam nodded again. Did her mother expect this to happen? What if the ark drifted away from the reeds and out into the Nile, away from the princess? But again, she did not voice her fears. "I will, Ima."

Her mother smiled, but Miriam saw the sadness in her eyes. Her mother wanted to believe that this baby would bring them hope. Wanted to believe that God would spare him. But she didn't know that for sure. No one did. Miriam thought on that long into the night.

~∽~

The next morning, Miriam's mother touched her shoulder before dawn had fully risen. She nodded toward the basket and the door. Abba and Aaron still slept, but soon Abba would have to leave, and Ima couldn't wait and leave Aaron alone.

Miriam quickly pulled her small cloak over her shoulders and followed her mother in silence as they hurried through the semi-dark streets of Goshen on the long walk to Memphis, where the pharaoh's palace stood. The sun began to brighten the sky in gray and pink bands. Soon it would rise and make them visible to all. Miriam ran to keep up with her mother's longer strides.

At last they reached the banks where the young princess was known to bathe or relax with her feet in the water. Here no crocodiles ventured, as the waterway was narrow, making a safer place for the baby and the princess.

"Here," Ima said as she found a spot that seemed secure. "This should hold the ark in place and keep it from floating away. When he awakens and cries, as he will surely do, let us pray it is when only the princess will hear him." She touched Miriam's shoulder. "Remember what I told you," she whispered.

Miriam nodded, then bent to kiss the baby's forehead as her mother did the same.

"God go with you, my little bundle of hope. May His plans for you be good." Ima lowered the basket into the water and secured the lid with a little woven clasp. The reeds were strong here, and while the basket swayed, it did not leave the bank.

"Ima?" Miriam asked as her mother turned to hurry home.

"Yes, child." She bent low to look Miriam in the eye.

"If no one comes to rescue him, shall I bring him home again tonight?" The question had come to her as they walked this long road.

Her mother tilted her head as if she was thinking. "If no

one comes today, yes. Bring him home and we will try again tomorrow. But leave the basket here. You will not be able to lift it with him in it."

"I will hide him under my cloak," she said, already thinking how she would do whatever it took to protect him. "Don't worry, Ima. I will watch over him."

But as her mother slipped from view, Miriam worried. How would she keep him quiet all day? Should she wait until sundown when no one would see? She would need to find a place to hide the basket until tomorrow. And he would need feeding and changing. She had nothing with which to help him.

Suddenly she realized that she wasn't big enough or strong enough to truly protect their baby. Her mother was right. She would stand watch, but she would have to wait to see what God would do.

*Please, God, help our baby. Help me too.*

―――※―――

Hatshepsut rose earlier than normal, feeling restless. She could not shake the thoughts of her father's fear of the Hebrews. Or his cruelty to them. Nightmares had troubled her, and she rubbed sleep from her eyes as she stumbled toward her private chamber. Her maids dressed her in her day robe, and another carried her ointments and oils and soaps to help her as she washed herself in the Nile.

It would feel good to be clean and wash away the feelings she could not shake of ill will against her own father, her own people. If she were queen, she would have compassion on the Hebrews' suffering. She would not be afraid of people who had never done them any harm. Had they?

Why were the Hebrews even living in Egypt? She should have her tutors search the history of her people and find out why, but now all she wanted to do was bathe. Perhaps Ra would bless her with peace and she could forget about the Hebrews.

She stepped through the door to the patio that jutted out into the Nile. The cool morning air touched her face and lifted her hair from where it hung to her shoulders. She would have to wear it up soon enough and wear wigs, as all women of Egypt did, but she was young. She was still free to do as she pleased most of the time.

"The water is warm today, mistress," one of her servants said, smiling.

"Good." Hatshepsut hated a cold bath, but this time of year Egypt grew hot and the waters of the Nile remained warm along with Ra's rays.

She walked to the edge, sat on the end of the limestone dock, and dangled her legs in the water. A tingling feeling ran up her body as she plunged into the water and came up laughing. She raised her arms to the sun's rising. She dunked again and again as her servants walked along the river's edge to watch for any onlookers. When they were satisfied that they were alone, she allowed her maids to scrub her body with soap and wash her hair. Hatshepsut dipped beneath the surface to rinse, then hopped onto the dock to allow the maids to rub fragrant oils into her skin.

In the distance, she heard muffled cries. "Hush," she commanded her servants, for she couldn't be sure above their chatter if the noise was her imagination. But the cries came louder now. She had not imagined them. She looked toward the reeds, where she saw something floating. "Rashida, go

28

and see what is in the water and where that noise is coming from."

The servant bowed. "Yes, mistress." She jumped into the water and walked toward the reeds, where the crying grew louder. She returned moments later with a heavy basket in her arms and brought it to Hatshepsut.

Hatshepsut pulled the basket beside her, undid the clasp, and opened the lid. "A baby!" Of course, that was what it had sounded like. "Pick it up." Another of her servants did so and held the baby out to her.

Hatshepsut looked at it, trying to decide what one did with a baby. She had seen her father's younger children in the harem, but she didn't actually touch them. When she saw this one's face pucker and more tears slip down his cheeks, her heart stirred.

"This is one of the Hebrew children. Check for me. It is a boy, yes?"

The servant undid the baby's swaddling clothes and nodded. She folded the clothes around him again.

Hatshepsut held out her arms and took the baby, holding him close. His crying quieted, and she knew she could never allow her father to kill him.

"I must protect him," she said to her maids. "I will raise him as my own son."

"But you are not old enough to be a mother," one protested.

Hatshepsut looked at the maid, silencing her. "Nevertheless, I will raise him. He *will* be my son."

"Yes, mistress."

"And you will all support me."

They all nodded in silent agreement.

A moment later, rustling sounds caused them to turn. There before them, on the king's patio, stood a Hebrew child of about five. "Shall I go and call you a nurse from the Hebrew women to nurse the child for you?"

# FOUR

Miriam straightened her shoulders and looked the princess in the eye. Her stomach felt strange, but she tried not to let her feelings show before these Egyptian women and this girl who was holding her brother. The girl was not much older than Miriam. She wanted to adopt him? Had God sent this princess to save her brother?

"You are Hebrew," the princess said.

"Yes." Miriam bowed her head. Was she supposed to fall on her face before a princess? But she remained standing and clasped her hands in front of her.

"You can find me a woman to nurse the child?"

"Yes." Miriam studied this young girl who held her brother close to her heart. Miriam's own heart pinched at the sight. Would the girl allow her to get her mother? Would she suspect?

The princess studied her in return. "You are brave for one so young. To enter Pharaoh's palace alone."

"Yes," Miriam said again, wondering whether she would be allowed to go or have to keep standing here answering

31

yes to everything. She held back a sigh and the desire to run to get her mother.

"Go, then. Bring me the Hebrew woman who can care for my son until he is weaned." The princess turned her attention from Miriam to her brother, so Miriam whirled about and ran off.

Had she done the right thing? Should she have waited for some other command? But the girl had said to go, so Miriam ran toward the field where she knew her mother would be anxiously waiting.

She stopped when she reached their hut. She was so thirsty! It wouldn't be good to stop for a drink, but what if her mother waited inside instead of in the fields? Would she have risked being missed?

Miriam wiped the sweat from her forehead and ran to the house. Just a quick drink from the cistern outside and she would head to the fields. She lowered the wooden dipper into the water, blew on it to push the gnats away, and drank greedily. One more ladleful and she turned to head toward the fields.

The door opened. "Miriam. I thought you were someone else in need of a drink."

"Oh, Ima, you're home!" Miriam hugged her mother. "You must come at once. The princess found our baby and I asked her if she wanted me to get someone to nurse the baby for her and she said 'Go' and here I am." She was nearly out of breath, feeling as though she was still running.

"Calm down, my daughter," her mother said as she grabbed her shawl and closed the door. She took Miriam's hand as they walked along the path. "There is no need to run. Catch your breath and then tell me everything."

They slowed their pace, and Miriam took in great gulps of air. A moment passed until she felt able to speak again. "I watched, like you told me to. And after a little while the princess and her maids came out to the water. Her maids walked along the river, and then they washed the princess. She is young, Ima. I thought she would be a woman grown, but she is not much older than me. But the older servants did everything she said, and they brought the baby to her and she knew he was Hebrew. But she didn't drown him. She held him close and said she would raise him. She wants to keep him, Ima!"

Her mother nodded, her smile sad. "It is God's will, then. Your brother will live, but he will not stay with us forever."

Miriam fell silent, still holding her mother's hand. What would happen to her brother when they had to give him back to the princess? "But you will be able to nurse him for a few years, won't you?"

"Yes. I think so. We will find out soon enough." She picked up their pace and at last pointed up the road. "Look. We are here."

"The princess bathes behind the bulrushes. I will show you." Miriam's heart beat faster and her skin tingled. Surely the princess would still be there waiting.

They turned a corner and walked along the Nile to where the path to the palace touched the eastern bank. They moved along the wooden dock until their feet touched the base of the marble steps. There beneath an awning sat the princess and her serving maids, while Miriam's brother, who was crying loudly now, was walked about by one of the maids.

"You are back," the princess said. "He began to wail again soon after you left and hasn't stopped."

"He is hungry," Ima said.

The princess nodded to her servant, who brought the baby to Ima. Miriam watched her brother calm at the sight of their mother, and Ima wasted no time in putting him beneath her tunic and letting him nurse, right in front of the princess!

"What is your name?" the princess asked.

"Jochebed, wife of Amram of the tribe of Levi." Ima shifted the baby but did not take her eyes off the princess.

"I am Hatshepsut, daughter of Pharaoh Thutmose I. This is your son, isn't it?" She looked at Ima with wide dark eyes and a knowing, even vulnerable gaze.

Ima nodded.

"You put him in the basket and set him among the reeds. Did you hope that I would find him? For if I had not come today, the boy would have fallen prey to something in the river, if not the river snakes then the crocodiles."

"Our God watched over him. I knew He would protect the boy." Ima looked so calm, but Miriam inwardly shuddered.

Hatshepsut gave Ima a curious look but did not say anything against her for what she had done. "Take this child away and nurse him for me," she said after a lengthy pause, "and I will give you your wages."

Ima bowed her head. "I will do as you say."

"Good," the princess said. "When he is weaned, I will call for him. You will keep me informed."

"Yes, my lady."

"And your daughter may collect your wages. You will no longer need to work the fields. I will make sure of it." Hatshepsut crossed her arms as if to prove she had such power.

"Thank you, my lady." Ima's eyes shone, and Miriam thought she saw tears there.

"You may call him Moses, because I drew him out of the water." Hatshepsut placed her hands on her knees. "I know you may think me young, but I am Pharaoh's daughter. My father will not know of our arrangement until the child is weaned, but if he should find out somehow, I will protect the boy and you. My father will listen to me." She looked deeply into Ima's eyes as though she needed to convince her.

"I trust that you will do as you say," Ima said. "And I will keep the boy safe for you. When you are ready, when he is weaned, we will bring him to you." She bowed slightly. "Thank you, Princess, for looking kindly on the boy."

Hatshepsut's face softened. "If I could, I would do it for a thousand Hebrew boys." She looked about. "I wish this was not a concern for you. I wish your people were treated differently."

"Thank you, Princess. As do we. But we are most grateful that you have shown us such great kindness." Ima bowed again, and this time Hatshepsut stood.

"Let me see the boy once more." She stepped closer, and Ima pulled Moses from beneath her tunic. Hatshepsut touched his soft hair and cupped his infant cheek. "He is a beautiful boy." A soft smile lit her face. "He will be great in Pharaoh's house someday."

Ima nodded.

Hatshepsut stepped back and dismissed them both. "Go now, before you are seen. Be sure to send the girl to me each week when I come here to bathe. I will pay you then."

Miriam carried the basket a servant handed her, and the three of them headed back toward home. When they were far from the palace, she glanced at her mother. "Our God really did protect our baby."

Ima smiled. "We need not doubt Him when He leads us to do His will."

"But how did you know, Ima? Hava's brother was not spared. How did you know Moses would live?" Miriam could not understand her parents' faith. "Why didn't God spare all the boys?"

Ima stopped and held Miriam's gaze. "I did not know, my daughter. I only hoped. Your father and I both believed this child was chosen of God for some reason. That is why we hid him as long as we could. But we could not know for sure what God would do. That is why we placed him in the river and waited and trusted. But we did not know if God would answer our prayers the way we wanted Him to answer."

"Then why . . ." She shook her head. "I don't understand."

"And right now you do not need to try, my sweet girl. One day, when you are older, you will learn to trust our God. But we cannot control Him. We can simply ask Him."

Miriam fell into step with Ima again. She knew Ima had great faith, something she wished she had too. But she couldn't forget Hava's baby brother. She was happy for her own, but she wasn't sure she would ever stop feeling sad for her friend.

# FIVE

Miriam woke with a start and a sense of confusion. Where was she? She blinked hard and looked about her. She was in her own bed in her own home, but the day was all wrong and backwards.

She rose quickly, grateful to see that both of her brothers still slept, but Ima sat at the table folding Moses' little clothes.

"I can't believe the time has gone so quickly. And the princess even gave us more than enough time for him to be weaned." Miriam sank down next to her mother and sipped from the cup of water her mother handed to her.

"Yes, I expected her to ask for him sooner. He could have weaned two years ago." Ima leaned her elbows on the table and sighed. She looked so tired. How hard it must be to be a mother and have to let your child go to live somewhere else.

"We still have today," Miriam said, hoping it brought some comfort. But by nightfall, they would walk with Moses to the pharaoh's palace, and he would not return with them.

"I think he will remember," her father said, coming to join them. "I taught him of our God and of our ways every time we were together and when he walked beside his brother and me to the houses of the other Levites. He was too young to go, but it was important to me."

Miriam looked at her father. "You did well with him, Abba. And today we will remind him again of all the lessons our God taught our forefathers. We will remind him to never forget where he comes from."

"I only hope that he is able to remember once the palace tutors fill his mind with Egyptian history and culture." Her mother held a tunic to her face and sniffed the scent of her son. "It can be hard to remember the truth of your childhood when faced with a culture far different, one that will surely offer him riches and pleasures beyond anything we can imagine."

"I have seen the palace many times, Ima. I have told you of it when the servants allowed me to glimpse a few of the rooms. I do not think our Moses will find it appealing after he has been so used to living with us." Deep down, Miriam prayed that Moses would miss them and never forget his people. But five was so young. Did she remember much of her own fifth year? But of course she did, for that was when she watched the basket in the water and met Hatshepsut, the boy babies stopped being killed, her mother was able to stop working the fields, and her father was no longer forced to make bricks or build the cities for the pharaoh. They'd enjoyed food in abundance, something Ima insisted they share with their neighbors, and worked to help those less fortunate. Miriam learned to weave for her family and neighbors, all while talking to Moses and Aaron as their mother prepared food.

38

They'd had a good life these past five years, despite the slavery. Would everything they had known now come to an end? With Moses leaving them, how would that affect their future in this foreign land of their groaning?

"I won't forget you, Ima." Moses stood at the side of the table, rubbing sleep from his eyes. Aaron rose from his pallet and joined him.

Ima turned to face Moses and cupped his cheeks. "Today is the day I told you about, remember? You will go to live in the palace, and your new mother will adopt you as her son. You will no longer be called the son of Amram but the son of Pharaoh's daughter." She touched his hair and then pulled him into her arms. "You must remember all of the things we have taught you about the God of Abraham and Isaac and Jacob. Remember the stories of how our God called Abram out of the land of Ur to the land of Canaan, and how Isaac was born to Sarah when she was ninety years old, and how Jacob fathered the twelve tribes of Israel as we are today. Remember that our God promised to give us the land of Canaan and that one day He will bring us out of this land of Egypt. Do not become too attached to the things you see in your new home, my son."

Miriam wondered if her brother understood. But surely he was as bright as she had been at his age, even more attentive.

"I won't forget, Ima." He kissed her cheek. "I'm hungry."

Everyone laughed, and Miriam went to get bread and cheese and dates to set before them. She poured goat's milk into clay cups and handed one to Moses and another to Aaron before she gave some to her parents and herself.

They ate, all talking at once in happy tones, but underneath, Miriam could not shake the sense of confusion and loss she had awakened with. How could they leave him with Hatshepsut, kind though she was? She was Egyptian. She would know nothing of their God, even though she had come to visit a few times and heard them speak of Him.

No, Moses would now learn of the many gods Egypt worshiped, of their history, of their conquests. He would learn to speak their language and write with their strange symbols.

Miriam looked long at her little brother, wishing she could follow him and protect him in that place. She had watched over him since her youngest days, and she would continue to do so if she could. But this was a time that Ima had spoken of—a time when they would have to trust their God with things they could not control.

Miriam knew her mother was right, but she wasn't sure she could do what she said.

⌒⊗⌒

The sun had begun its descent into the west when Miriam's father led the five of them down the road from Goshen to the palace of the pharaoh in Memphis. They passed buildings still in the process of being built, the work ended now, the slaves returned to their homes. Night sounds came from the nearby Nile River, and they slowed their pace the closer they came to the gleaming royal palace.

Miriam walked beside her mother, who carried Moses in her arms as though she needed these last few moments to hold him close. Aaron held tight to Miriam's hand.

Words were few as they walked. They had shared all they could during the day, so now what else could be said? He was leaving and he wasn't coming back.

"It's just around that bend," Miriam said as the lights

from the palace blazed to the surrounding area as though to keep the night at bay. "I don't think they like the darkness here." Why she noticed that just now, she could not say. "The princess said to meet her at the side door of the palace, not the usual place where she would bathe. We will have to use the standing barge to cross."

"At least we don't have to walk into the river." Aaron's comment nearly made her laugh except for the serious tone of his voice.

"We would surely be food for the creatures that live there." Miriam shuddered as she looked to her mother, who had stopped now and clung tightly to Moses. Miriam carried a basket of his things in case he wanted them, though she wondered if Hatshepsut would allow him to keep them.

They stepped onto the barge, and her father used the long pole to move them to the palace doors.

"We are here, my son," Abba said, turning to face Ima and Moses. "Remember us always. And if you can visit us, please, come as often as you can."

"But you must not ask," Ima said. "Only if your new mother allows it." She nearly choked on the word "mother."

Miriam stepped closer to touch Moses' arm, still holding on to Aaron's hand. They had prayed over Moses at the house, but her father spoke again quietly before they moved another step.

"The Lord bless you, my son. May He keep you always in His care. Never forget that He has saved you for this time and place. One day you will understand why." He kissed Moses' head. Ima kissed his cheek and then lowered him to the ground.

Moses hugged Miriam and Aaron, and Miriam led the

way to the place the servants had told her Hatshepsut would meet them. The door was large and ornate, and the gold gleamed in the light of the rising moon.

A servant opened the door at their knock and ushered them inside. A moment later, far more quickly than Miriam expected, Hatshepsut appeared. "You are here."

"Yes, my lady," Ima said. She placed Moses' hand in Hatshepsut's. Moses stared at the princess. Though he had met her a few times, he acted as though he did not remember. "This is your mother, Moses. She drew you out of the water, and we have cared for you until you were old enough to live with her."

Ima released her hold, and Miriam saw Moses' lip pucker for a brief moment, but he did not cry. He allowed Hatshepsut to keep hold of his hand while Ima and Abba backed away.

Miriam handed the basket with his things to a servant, and then she joined her family moving closer to the door.

"He will be well cared for," Hatshepsut said. "In a few years, I will marry, and he will have a father as well." She looked at Ima and Abba. "But do not fear. I will not allow him to forget you. And when he is older, we will arrange for a visit now and then."

"You are most kind," Ima said.

Hatshepsut smiled slightly. "I appreciate all you have done for my son. Do not fear that you will return to the fields and the slave labor you did before you cared for him. I will still provide for you all of your days, as long as it is in my power to do so."

"Thank you," Abba said, and Miriam wondered if her words were a relief to him. Her parents were not young, and she feared the taskmasters might kill them one day.

"It is nothing. I do what I can. Please do not allow it to be a burden to you. I do not wish to cause jealousy among your people. The gods know there is enough of that right here in this palace." She shrugged as though they should know what she meant, then smiled. "But never fear. Your son will be mine, and no one can hurt him here."

"We thank you again for the privilege of caring for him."

They moved closer to the door, and Moses turned to look longingly at each one of them. For a moment, Miriam thought he might run after them, but Hatshepsut had a good hold on him. When Miriam and her family slipped back into the night and crossed the river, they heard no cries coming from inside the palace.

"He will be all right," Abba said. "The God of our fathers will watch over him."

"We have done all we could." Ima leaned against him once they walked again on dry land, and he wrapped his arm about her shoulders.

Miriam held tight to Aaron's hand. Life was never going to be the same again without Moses. Whatever would they do now?

# SIX

Miriam carried the jar of water on her head and walked with
Hava toward home. Dawn had barely risen, but Hava had
to work in the fields, and Miriam was needed to care for her
mother. Though Hatshepsut had singled them out from the
rigorous labor of the other slaves, there was always too much
work. And now her mother could no longer do the things
she once did. How long would Miriam have her?

"At least the air is cooler today," Hava said as she lifted
her other hand to steady the clay jar on her head. Miriam did
the same with her jar, as the terrain was more difficult here.

"Yes. The days shouldn't be so extremely hot as autumn
approaches. I hope the cooler air helps Ima." She couldn't
stop the sigh that escaped her.

Hava glanced at Miriam, her round face wreathed in concern. "I'm sorry you are facing this, Miriam. I do hope Jochebed recovers quickly."

"As do I." They walked a few steps in silence. The sound
of the Nile at their back never failed to remind Miriam of

Hava's lost little brother those many years ago. "Do you think of him still?"

"My brother?" As the path smoothed out, Hava lowered one hand and touched her heart. "He is here and here." She touched her head. "It is impossible to forget. Not with Ima's sadness that slips out often. Her smile is never very warm, and she rarely laughs as she used to." She stopped and faced Miriam. "We groan under the weight of this slavery, Miriam. I know you do not face the work as your parents once did because of Moses living in the palace, but the work does not grow lighter. I wonder how we will survive this. We used to rejoice over a new birth or a wedding. Now we are afraid to assemble and laugh and sing for fear of the Egyptians. They have stolen everything from us. Especially our joy." She searched Miriam's face a moment, then turned and began walking again. "I don't fault you for the special treatment. I just want you to know how hard it is for the rest of us."

"That is why my mother has always tried to share what we've been given, to help those who have less than we do." Miriam felt her defenses rise a little, but she tried to keep her tone even. "I only wish we could do more." She stepped around a large boulder.

"I know." Hava kept her gaze on the road. Their houses were a short distance away now. "I just wish . . ." She lowered her voice. "I wish our God would get us out of Egypt and that we could raise families without fear. What if we marry and have children and a new pharaoh comes to power and snatches our children from us? Do you never fear this?"

Miriam didn't, because she felt protected with Moses in the palace. But what might change if something happened to him? "Maybe Moses will come to power and release us all," she said. "Ima believes Moses is our tikvah."

"She thinks your brother is our hope?" At Hava's incredulous tone, Miriam wished she could retract her words.

"It is what she thought when he was born. Now that he is in the palace, we rarely hear from him. We hope, but we don't know if the Egyptians are teaching him to trust their gods over ours. If he becomes like them . . ." She let the words die. He couldn't become like them! Not after all she and her parents had taught him when he was young. *Please, Adonai, do not let my brother fall into the trap of the Egyptians and their gods.*

Hava touched Miriam's arm. "I will pray that he does not. Perhaps our God will use Moses to set us free. Perhaps that is why he was spared."

"You are very kind, my friend. Thank you. I do wish your brother had lived as well." Their gazes met, and Miriam sensed sadness but acceptance in Hava's eyes.

"Next time, let us talk of other things. Did you hear that Hatshepsut is to marry the crown prince, Thutmose II? She's not much older than we are! Does that mean Moses will become Thutmose II's son?"

They had reached the door to Hava's house, where she set the jar in a niche in the ground. Miriam lowered her jar before taking it to her house next door.

"I guess so. I heard from one of the palace servants who speaks with me sometimes that Hatshepsut should become pharaoh, but since she's a girl, Thutmose II is marrying her to secure his rule. He's only thirteen and she is fifteen. But her father would never agree to choosing her over his son, even though she is the firstborn of his primary wife."

"But thirteen is barely a man! Can you imagine marrying a child?" Hava shook her head. "I just hope this new pharaoh will be kinder once their father dies. They say the father is not well."

Miriam thought again of her mother. "No, he is not." What would life be like with a boy her age ruling Egypt? "I better get home to Ima. She needs more care these days."

Hava put a hand on the latch. "I hope she improves. I know my ima grieves, but I cannot imagine life without her."

"Nor can I." Miriam bid Hava farewell, for her friend needed to get to the fields to work. Miriam returned to her home, set the water down, and stepped inside.

Her father met her at the door, his face ashen. "She is worse."

Miriam looked at him, his words hitting her hard. She rushed past him into the room, where light coming from the windows illuminated her mother's face. "Ima." She knelt beside her mother's pallet.

Ima's breathing had grown shallower since she left for the water. "Ima," she said again. But her mother's eyes did not open.

She felt her father's presence behind her. She rose and faced him. "Has she awakened at all?"

He shook his head. "I found her this way when I awoke. She will not be roused." Sorrow knit his brows, and Miriam felt as though someone had punched her.

"She seemed better yesterday." She took his hand and pulled him to the window, where the people of the village were busy carrying their tools to work the fields and quarries.

"Sometimes the end surprises us." Her father's voice sounded strange, far away. "She is older than I, but she has always been strong."

"Ima never takes ill. This is not like her." Miriam tried to understand. The rest of the family had remained well. Only her mother had succumbed to whatever it was that made her take to her pallet. "Perhaps it had to do with helping some of the poorest people in the village. I think some of the children were ill."

"She has helped sick children and mothers before." Again her father's voice sounded as though he were talking to someone else. He did not look at her, only stared out the window.

"Do you think . . . ?" Miriam stopped. She could not ask it. Her mother's time could not come yet. They needed her. Aaron was only eleven and she thirteen. She would need Ima's help to find a suitable husband in a few years. How could her father help her with that? Though he might be the one to approve the betrothal, everyone knew it was the mother who helped the daughter choose.

"I do not know how we will manage without her." Her father looked at her then, his graying hair and haggard expression a testament to the hard life he had lived before Moses' birth. "We will need you now more than ever, my daughter."

Miriam nodded. "I do not plan to go anywhere, Abba." Though she did hope to marry one day. "Not as long as you need me."

Her father looked out the window again. "You will marry one day."

"And I will still care for you. But who knows? Ima may improve yet today." She moved back to her mother's pallet and knelt again at her side. Her breathing had grown even shallower, if that was possible. "Ima?" She touched her shoulder and tried to rouse her, but her mother continued in her strange state of sleep.

Miriam remained at her mother's side until her brother awoke. She rose to feed him and her father and ate a little food herself, then returned to her spot. Her father remained staring out of the window, something that concerned Miriam almost as much as watching her mother fade away.

*Are you dying, Ima?* She had not watched anyone die, though she had heard a dying man's screams and seen a few men fall over in the fields from beatings. She had watched her mother wash many wounds. She had been at her side to help women give birth and to give some of their food to the hungry. But she wasn't ready to live without her strong mother.

Why was this happening? Why now when they needed her so much? She wanted to look up and ask God the questions, but she couldn't, for she knew there would be no answer. Her people had been asking God for a deliverer from slavery for years. And yet nothing changed. Moses was still a boy of eight, far too young to lead anyone. And she wasn't ready to marry, to have a husband's help. She needed her father as well as her mother. But if they lost Ima, would she lose Abba too? He might live, but would he remain her abba, the man from whom she sought help and advice?

Miriam placed a cool cloth on her mother's brow, though Ima had no fever. She needed to do something! Fix something. But she knew with a sinking heart that this burden was too big for her, and there was nothing she could do.

# SEVEN

efore the sun set the next day, Ima's funeral procession made its way to a common burial cave far from the village. Miriam walked beside her father and Aaron, moving but not feeling, as though she were one of the dead. The entire village had come to walk with them, despite their exhaustion from the day of hard labor. Jochebed was well loved, and the mourners' cries broke through Miriam's numbness.

The men carrying the bier placed her mother's body into the cave, and someone spoke a few words that Miriam barely heard. Tears streamed from her eyes, but no bitter cry would escape her lips. She could not get her voice to work even to speak to Aaron or her father. Every attempt only caught on a hoarse whisper.

The crowd did not linger long, and soon Miriam felt herself caught up in the throng headed back to the village. Darkness fell about them, the last rays of the sun falling below the horizon as if waving goodbye to her mother, to them all.

Silence descended on the people as they neared the village. Exhaustion accompanied grief, and these people had done more today than normal. For the slightest moment, gratitude filled Miriam for their kindness, but in the next breath, grief overtook it. *Ima*. Her heart felt like a piece of pottery shattered on the floor.

She gripped Aaron's hand tighter. Moses would need to know. But how to tell him? Her thoughts spun. She could meet with Rashida, Hatshepsut's servant. She had often been the one to pay Ima for nursing Moses, and now and then Miriam attempted to meet her, to hear how things were with Moses.

Suddenly another awful thought hit her. Should they have waited to tell Hatshepsut of Ima's passing? She would be offended that she had not been told. Miriam would have to find a way to explain . . . Her head began to pound. Why hadn't she thought of this earlier?

Hatshepsut held more power now that she was to marry Thutmose II. And since she was older than he was, she might be the greater power behind the throne once their father entered the Valley of the Kings to rest with his fathers.

Miriam considered that thought longer than she had the other day with Hava. Had that been only yesterday? She looked from Aaron to her father. Without Ima, she would need to take charge of the family. She could manage to do the work she had already been doing. But one glance into her father's distant gaze and fear took hold of her again. He had not been himself since Ima took ill.

She could *not* lose them both! She was too young to handle Aaron alone. While they might be able to live with an aunt and uncle, some might think it wiser to see her wed.

Her stomach knotted as dread snaked up her spine. She did not want to wed a stranger, and there were no young men of their tribe who interested her in the least. With the work they were forced to do, she rarely saw any enough to know them, and if she wed, would she be forced back into a life of slavery? Would Moses' presence in the palace keep her husband from working the fields or making bricks for the pharaoh's cities? When Thutmose I died, would the work continue or would Hatshepsut put a stop to their slavery?

Miriam's eyes closed briefly, but she opened them again to watch the path when she nearly stumbled on a rock. She must stop this. No one knew the future but God, and she would have to be the one to trust Him now. Her father trusted Him, but Ima had been the one with the stronger faith. She needed that faith now. She needed Ima, but Ima was no more.

Miriam walked alone toward Pharaoh's palace the following week. She wanted to go right away, but her father had bid her to wait. Now she asked herself whether such advice had been wise, but she wasn't going to disobey her father.

She kicked a clump of grass near the Nile's bank, careful not to get too close to the edge. The palace grew larger as she boarded the waiting barge and crossed the short distance. She entered the back door where she often met Rashida. A different servant met her.

"Is Rashida here?" She had learned to speak Egyptian almost as soon as she had learned Hebrew, for her father had wanted his children to be able to converse with their captors should the need arise. Goshen was cut off just enough to keep most of her people separate in everything, including their language, but four hundred years of overbearing taskmasters had caused them to understand more than they wanted to. And Miriam had wanted to learn every word she could.

The servant disappeared, and a moment later Rashida moved through a side door to meet her. "Miriam! How good it is to see you." The servant stepped closer, though she did not touch her even in greeting. It was not their way.

"Rashida, I am sorry to have been so absent. Is there any way that I can see my—Moses?" She had almost called him her brother. She could not make that distinction here. But her heart pounded as anxiety took hold. What if they denied her?

Rashida took her measure. "You know the princess is mourning the death of her father."

The news came as a blow. Miriam's eyes widened. She shook her head. "No. I had not heard. Did this just happen?"

Rashida nodded. "This morning. The trumpets have yet to sound, but the embalmers have been called. There will be days of preparing his body for burial. Our nation will be in mourning for months, but in the meantime, Hatshepsut and Thutmose II must wed so he can ascend to the throne in place of his father. I'm afraid Moses will be in mourning with the rest of the palace, more so since the pharaoh was his grandfather."

Miriam stared at this servant who was like a friend. Dare she trust her with this information to pass on to Moses? But how could she do any less? "There is no way to see him, then, even to offer my condolences?"

Rashida shook her head. "No one is allowed near the royal family except the servants." She assessed Miriam. "Even if I dressed you in Egyptian clothes, you look Hebrew." She gave

Miriam a sympathetic smile. "Is there something you want me to tell him for you?"

Miriam studied her feet. Would Moses be torn between two families if he knew? He would not be allowed to visit his mother's grave when his adoptive mother was about to wed and his grandfather had just passed into the underworld, or whatever they called Sheol.

A deep sigh longed to escape, but Miriam held it back. She looked up and met Rashida's gaze. "No. It can wait. In time he will want to know, but I see I have not come at the right time." Perhaps things would have been different if she had come right away as she'd wanted to. Why had her father implored her to wait?

"You are sure? You don't normally ask if it is not important." Rashida tilted her head, her dark eyes holding deep concern.

"I'm sure. It is important, but it can wait. Let them mourn. When that time has passed, please send for me. Then I will tell you—or him—if I can."

"If you are certain."

"I'm certain."

Miriam thanked the servant and left the way she had come. Had she done the right thing? Moses should know about Ima. But in that moment she knew everything had changed. Hatshepsut would be queen and a new pharaoh would reign. Moses would have even less access to his people, especially if the queen wanted to prepare him to follow in Thutmose's footsteps. Moses would not be allowed to mourn his true mother or father. He was shielded from everything Hebrew in the halls of that gleaming palace.

Grief hit her all over again. She not only missed Ima, she

missed the brother she did not have time enough to know. Now it was just her and Abba and Aaron. And God. But God seemed far away, and sometimes she wondered if He saw them or the plight of their people.

Did He still care for the people of His covenant?

# EIGHT

Miriam stood at the table, kneading the bread for the evening baking. Aaron had gone with Abba to the fields to help their fellow Hebrews, though her father was really too old to do much work. Fear always followed Miriam when they walked out the door. They had no need to help in this way, for nothing had changed since Hatshepsut had become queen. But Miriam could not stop her father, stubborn as he was.

They would be home soon though, which lightened the loneliness in her heart. She still missed Ima, more each day. She shaped the loaf of bread and slid it onto the coals in the courtyard of their small home.

A knock on the door startled her. No one called during the day. Hava had married and moved away to another part of the village, and most of the women worked the fields.

Her pulse quickened as she moved slowly toward the door. Had something happened to Moses? She looked through the window, relieved to see the man standing there was not Egyptian. She opened the door.

"Miriam, daughter of Amram?" The man's beard was long, but he had a young face and eyes that looked at her with kindness.

"Yes. And you are?" She suddenly realized how alone she was.

"Jephunneh, the Kenizzite of the tribe of Judah." He clasped his hands behind him and looked at his feet.

She studied him a moment, her mind whirling. "Is something wrong?" She heard the tremor in her voice. He was handsome, but this was not the time or place for her heart to betray her.

"I have come to get you. Your father needs you." He met her gaze.

"What happened? Is Abba hurt? Or Aaron?" If something had happened to Aaron, Abba would have come. If Abba, then Aaron. Why would they send a stranger to get her?

"Your father . . . he is hurt." Why was he so hesitant? "Aaron stayed with him, which is why I am here." He blushed as if he were embarrassed to speak to her. Or perhaps he also realized how alone they were.

"Let me pull the bread from the oven and grab my cloak." She hurried into the house, frantic. What could possibly be wrong? Why wouldn't the men have just brought her father home for her to tend? If he was injured, she could help him here far better than in the field.

She closed the door and nodded at Jephunneh. "Tell me what happened." She would not show up to a surprise. She had to know.

Jephunneh fell into step with her and led her toward a different field than she'd expected. "I was tending sheep." He looked at her. "Your father and brother came in our direction, but on the way, your father fell. I fear he broke his leg. Some men are making a way to bring him to you now, but I thought you might want to tend to him before we move him."

Miriam stopped. "Why did you not tell me this? I would have brought my herbs." She turned around and ran back to the house before he could stop her. She rushed inside and searched the ceiling, where herbs from the garden hung to dry. She snipped off several, grabbed her mortar and pestle, and ran back out the door. Jephunneh closed it behind her.

They half ran toward the field. *Abba*. How could this have happened?

She was out of breath, but she managed to ask, "Did he fall into a hole? Trip over something? How did he fall?"

"I didn't see him fall, but there was a dip in the ground nearby. Aaron thinks he tripped. The accident shouldn't have caused a break, but your father is frail. And your brother is trying to be strong, but he is young."

"He is not always able to handle difficulties," she admitted. "He fears sometimes, especially since we lost our mother."

"I'm sorry. I knew of it and was there at the grave, but I did not know your family."

"We were in no mood to speak to anyone that day." She slowed as they neared the rise where the sheep grazed. She lifted a hand to shade her eyes.

"He's over here." He pointed to the right, and she followed his longer strides with effort.

"Abba!" Miriam saw him lying on the ground, looking as gray as Ima had looked when she took her last breath. She knelt at his side. Took his hand in hers. How cold he felt.

"Miriam." The word came out in a tight whisper.

"I'm here, Abba. Let me look at your leg." She moved

down to where his robe covered him. She slowly lifted it and peeked beneath, almost fainting at the sight of his leg nearly snapped in two and sitting at an odd angle. He would never walk again. How could she care for him if he could not walk?

She moved back near his face. "It will be all right, Abba." She kissed his cheek. "Let the men help carry you home."

She could mix something to help with the pain, which he was obviously feeling by his pinched expression and his great effort not to cry out. But there was nothing else her herbs could do.

She found the willow bark and ground it down. She looked at Jephunneh. "Do you have some water?"

He pulled a goatskin bag from his side and handed it to her. She poured a little into the powder, then carried it to her father. She managed to get some of it into his mouth, but even after several moments, she saw no difference in the pain he felt.

She stood and walked a few paces away, where she saw Aaron sitting on a rock, head in his hands.

Jephunneh caught her arm. She turned as he released it. "It is not good," he said.

"No. He will not recover from this." To say so even in a whisper made her heart ache with hurt so deep she had trouble breathing.

Jephunneh crouched to meet her at eye level. He was a head taller than she was, and despite her whirling thoughts, she could not deny the way his dark eyes drew her, as though he wanted to hold and comfort her but of course wouldn't. "I have some experience in mending the legs of sheep, but to put the bone back in place and tie it tight will cause him great agony. I fear I must though, or we won't be able to move him."

Miriam nodded. "I should have brought bandages."

"We will tear a tunic and wrap his leg after I straighten it."

She didn't ask him where he would find a spare tunic. She simply nodded, fighting the desperate urge to weep.

"You might want to take Aaron and walk away. Far away. Home, even. He will not want to hear your father's screams." Jephunneh took her hand and held it briefly, holding her gaze. "I will do my best."

She nodded again, tears springing up and slipping unguarded down her cheeks. She had to be strong for Aaron. But the tears continued. She swiped at them, angry with herself, and straightened her spine, willing strength into each quaking limb.

Aaron still sat on the rock with his head in his hands.

"Aaron." She knelt beside him and touched his knee. "You must come with me."

He lifted his head, his expression one of great agony. "It's my fault, Miriam. I should have watched for dips in the ground. Abba doesn't see like he used to, and if I'd been a better son . . . if I'd watched out for him—"

She held up a hand to stop his words. "It is not your fault. No one could have known this would happen but God Himself. The break is bad, but Jephunneh said he could straighten it, so perhaps Abba will walk again. But we must go far from here lest we trouble Abba. He will not wish to cry out if we are near."

Aaron nodded and slowly stood. Miriam held on to his arm, and together they walked away, careful of the rugged ground, then hurried once she glimpsed her father's misery and Jephunneh's anxious look in their direction. He would wait for them to protect them, and suddenly she liked this strange man for caring about her father and their family.

But though Jephunneh waited until they could no longer see her father, it was not far enough away once he began to straighten her father's leg. She would remember Abba's animal-like, howling cries as long as she lived.

# NINE

Jephunneh's work on her father made the leg look as it should again, but Miriam saw little improvement in her father's health a week after they had brought him home.

She knelt at his side and stroked his head. "Abba? Won't you please eat something? You need to regain your strength." Fear pulsated through her, growing with each passing day. She was not ready to lose him too. She could not raise Aaron alone.

Her father's eyes fluttered open. "Moses," he said softly.

Miriam searched his dear face. "You want me to get Moses?"

His nod was barely perceptible. Miriam's heart sank. She had not been able to tell her brother of their mother's passing. How could she possibly get through to him now when he was shut away in Pharaoh's palace? And how could she leave her father to try?

Aaron entered the house at that moment and came up beside her. "How is he?" It was a daily question. "Jephunneh has asked every day, and I have nothing new to tell him."

Miriam motioned Aaron to the window a short distance from their father's pallet. "He asked after Moses." She met her brother's worried gaze. "But I had no success when I tried to tell Moses about Ima. I don't know what to do. I can't just leave him." Aaron was only thirteen, barely a man. While he might be old enough to marry, most men waited until they were closer to twenty.

"I will stay with him." Aaron's earlier timidity when their father was injured had lessened, despite the fear that lingered in his dark eyes. "You should at least try. Moses should know. If you can find a way to get word to him."

Miriam studied her brother. "It is a longer walk than it used to be. Remember how much time it took me when I tried to tell him about Ima? But you had Abba with you then. What happens if he . . ." She lowered her voice. "What happens if he passes while I am away?"

"I will send for Jephunneh then," Aaron said, crossing his arms and straightening as though he somehow felt he should be the man of the house now.

Miriam still lingered, hesitant, but at last she agreed. "All right. I will go now and see if Rashida can get me an audience with Moses. Two years might have made a difference."

*Or not*, she thought as she covered her head. She half ran, half walked the longer distance toward the palace, which had been moved to Thebes instead of Memphis, where Moses had first lived as a young boy. She glanced back at the house, her heart sinking. *Please, Adonai, allow me to gain an audience with Moses. And don't take Abba while I am away.* Would God hear her prayers? Last time they had done no good.

As she found herself at the now familiar palace door and saw Rashida enter the small room, her heart lifted at the servant's smile.

"Miriam! It has been too long."

Miriam smiled back. "It has been. I have missed you."

"You are here to see your brother."

Miriam nodded. "I know he is busy with his studies and he is not officially ours anymore . . . but I have news he would want to know."

Rashida tilted her head, considering her. "The queen does keep him busy with studies. She wants him to know everything there is to know about Egyptian history, and he is constantly practicing his writing on different forms of papyrus and even rock, as though she wants him to know how to chisel his name on a monument someday."

Miriam considered this. Would Moses become so famous that his name would be carved into the stones of Egypt? Something in her spirit denied that possibility. Was she just against it as impossibly awful, or was this different? Her heart twisted, and she felt a sense of something she had not felt before. Sudden fear for him. She could not allow such fear. *Trust God*, her mother would have said. But she had no one left to trust. She drew in a breath and pushed the feeling aside.

"I will see if I can find him for you," Rashida said softly. "He should be taking a break from his studies soon, and perhaps I can coax him to come. Stay here."

She disappeared before Miriam could respond. Moments ticked by, and Miriam paced the small room, wondering if a superior had waylaid Rashida or whether her brother was unable to come. She was about to leave the palace when footsteps made her turn.

Her heart stopped at the sight of him. This younger brother she hadn't seen in years stood before her as an Egyptian, not as the little Hebrew boy she had taught in their home.

"Miriam?" He stepped closer.

"Moses?" She laughed. "How good it is to see you!"

He touched her arm, but he did not embrace her. The Egyptians had already taught him well.

"Rashida said you have need of me?" How old he seemed for a boy of ten.

Miriam regarded him a moment, then nodded. "There are things I have needed to tell you, but when I came two years ago, they would not let me see you." She looked about her. "Is there somewhere more private we can go?"

Moses looked at her, concern etching his dark brow. He nodded and led her outside to a colorful garden courtyard. They walked closer to the edge, where the Nile came near enough to lap the shore and drown out their words.

"Tell me," he said, glancing back toward the palace.

"Ima, your birth mother, passed into Sheol two years ago . . . back when your mother Hatshepsut married Thutmose II and the pharaoh died. That is why they would not let me talk to you."

Moses frowned. "Such information should not have been kept from me."

Miriam held up her hands. "I know. But you were a child, and I didn't want you to hear it from a servant. I should have told you regardless. I'm sorry." She cleared her throat. "But now our father is dying. He asked after you. I thought you should know."

Moses' brows shot up. "What happened that he is dying? Is he so old, then?"

Miriam shook her head. "He fell and broke his leg. A shepherd straightened it a week ago, and I have tried to coax him back to health, but he will not eat. He was already frail—ever since Ima died. But it is as though he has given up."

"I must go to him, then." Moses turned back to the palace.

"Wait!"

He turned toward Miriam.

"Can you just leave?"

"Yes. But I must tell them where I am going. I would be missed."

Of course he would. How closely was he watched? Would guards accompany him?

"Wait here. I will be back soon." He disappeared into the palace.

She looked out over the Nile, reminded again of the day the princess had found Moses in a different palace along the same river—a river the Egyptians worshiped. Now Hatshepsut was queen, though Thutmose II held the title of Pharaoh. Would the Egyptians accept a Hebrew to rule over them someday as they had in the days of Joseph?

She turned at the sound of horses' hooves and many feet. Moses had returned in a chariot, a cloak over his Egyptian clothing, with another chariot and two guards behind him. "I cannot leave without them," he said, his voice apologetic.

"Of course not." She took his hand, and he pulled her up into the chariot with him, the noise of the wheels offering them a measure of privacy.

"Do you think he is truly dying?" Moses asked as the horse hurried its gait.

"It would seem so." She looked into his dark eyes devoid of Egyptian kohl, thankfully.

"What will you do—you and Aaron? You are not yet wed, are you?" His genuine concern warmed her. Perhaps he had not forgotten them.

"I am not yet wed. Aaron is only thirteen. He is not ready to wed."

"But you could."

She nodded. "Yes. But I have not thought of it since Ima passed."

"You will need someone to take care of you."

His comment grated just the slightest, for she had been the one caring for everyone else since Ima became ill. But he was also right. A woman alone in Israel was unheard of unless she was widowed. A virgin would be expected to marry and bear children. To "be fruitful and multiply," as God had commanded Adam and Eve.

"Do you have someone in mind?" Moses' question caught her off guard.

"Not really." Though Jephunneh's face jumped to her mind.

"You should think on it." Moses reined in the chariot at their home. He bid the guards to wait outside, entered with Miriam, and shut the door.

Daylight spilled into the room, but the corner where their father slept lay in shadow. Aaron arose from his side and greeted Moses.

This time Moses embraced both Aaron and Miriam. "It is not something Egyptians do, but I have missed you both terribly."

Miriam sighed, relieved. He had not forgotten. Perhaps

God did still intend for him to have a hand in delivering them from Egypt, as their mother had imagined.

Miriam led him to Abba's side, and they both knelt next to him, while Aaron stood at their father's feet.

"Abba? It's Moses."

Their father opened his eyes. "Moses?"

"Yes, Abba, I'm here." He touched his father's arm, then gripped his hand.

Their father rose slightly and wrapped feeble arms around his youngest son. "Moses. My son."

"Yes, Abba. I have not forgotten you." He held their father close, then laid him back against the cushions of his bed.

"Your mother is gone," Abba said softly. "I will soon join her in Sheol."

Moses did not speak, and Miriam fought the urge to weep.

"When I am gone, be careful not to follow the ways of the Egyptians," he said, his words quiet and slow. "Take care of your brother and sister. See that your sister marries a good man. Perhaps the man who straightened my leg. The shepherd is a good man, though he is of the tribe of Judah."

"Perhaps you will get well and live to see her wedding. I can have the Egyptian physicians come to help you." Moses' voice had taken on a tone of disbelief, of desperation.

Their father shook his head. "No, my son. I wanted you here to bless you and your brother and sister. All of you have a special role to play in the deliverance of Israel from this place. I cannot see what that means or when it will happen, but you must never forget the Lord your God. Walk in His ways and keep His commands. Be faithful to Him, even in this land where darkness rules."

Moses only nodded, as if he suddenly accepted his father's words over his own desire to fix the situation. Miriam wanted to beg Moses to do as he had said. Why hadn't she thought to ask him to bring physicians? But perhaps this was God's plan all along.

A sense of defeat settled over her as their father fell into a deep sleep. Moses kissed his cheek, and the three of them stood and walked to the small table where they used to eat meals with both parents.

"You were right," Moses said with far too much knowledge for one so young. "He knows he is dying. A broken leg can bring on infection, and even the Egyptians cannot always help such things."

"I've given him every herb I think will help, but nothing does. He just grows weaker and refuses everything except a little broth." The thought depressed Miriam even more.

"I think Moses and Abba are right about one thing, Miriam."

She looked at Aaron, surprised he had addressed her when he had so little time left with Moses.

"I think you should marry Jephunneh the shepherd. Abba approves of him, and I do too. We cannot manage on our own. And I will marry in a few years. You could stay with me, but you need a family of your own."

"You are the age my Egyptian mother was when she married," Moses said.

Miriam looked from one to the other. "Are you trying to decide for me right now? We should be thinking about Abba."

Moses shrugged. "I will send a physician today." He stood, walked to the door, and gave orders to the guards. One took the chariot and left, while the other stayed to guard Moses. "He will come," Moses said, sitting again. "But I think you should marry before Abba slips into Sheol. He would want to know you are in good hands."

"What if Jephunneh does not want me?" She had thought of him more than she should have since the accident. But she couldn't imagine that he would want to marry her. She was so young, and he was a man fully grown.

"He likes you," Aaron offered, his smile slightly mischievous. "I have overheard him say so."

Miriam felt heat creep up her neck. "Well, if you can work it out so that he seeks my hand while Abba is still here to approve, then be quick about it."

She hadn't meant for Aaron to leave in that moment, but at the look that passed between her brothers, she realized she had just agreed to accept this man if he would have her. Cheeks flaming at her own audacity, she turned away from their scrutiny to focus on her father.

Abba might live long enough just to know she would be settled. He was stubborn enough to hang on to life for such a purpose. But why not live long enough to care for them, then? Torn between mixed feelings of marriage and loss, she glanced at her brothers. Moses sat smiling at her, and Aaron slipped out the door, running off to find Jephunneh.

"You will be glad you did not wait," Moses said when it was just the two of them. "My mother did not want to marry her half brother, but it is what is done in royal circles."

"You will not marry an Egyptian, will you?" He was too

young to know his own mind, but she prayed he would not do so just to please his mother.

Moses hesitated and glanced at the door. He leaned closer to her. "I do not wish to. But I do not know if I will have a choice."

"Pray that you do," Miriam said. "And I will do the same."

# TEN

Miriam walked to the Nile, meeting Hava along the way. They set their pots on the ground and hugged. "How good of you to come," Miriam said. She had last seen Hava at the burial of her father nearly two weeks before. "Thank you."

"Of course. I would do anything for you." She smiled and touched her middle, where Miriam spotted the obvious growth of a child.

"You are several months along now, yes?"

Hava's smile turned shy. "If I counted correctly, the babe should be born before harvest." She looked at Miriam. "A year from now it could be you in this condition. Are the rumors true?"

Miriam nodded. Memories filled her of that last day with her father and Moses when Aaron had run off to find Jephunneh. She shook herself. Everything had happened so quickly. She still could not take it all in.

"Tell me about it." Hava lifted her jar, and Miriam did the same as they continued their walk to the river's edge, where it was easy to dip the jars and crocodiles did not roam close.

Miriam looked at the river road before her, wondering if her life would always be as winding. Nothing had been normal since Moses was born. Would she ever know a life of normal or of freedom?

"Abba was only hours away from slipping into Sheol when he asked me to get Moses. So I half ran to the palace and was pleasantly surprised when he came to meet me. He and his guards came to the house—he even sent for a physician—but the man did no more than I had already done for Abba." She drew in a breath. Every last thought of her father brought emotion, but she tamped it down. "While Abba slept, Moses and Aaron determined that I should marry right away. Aaron insisted that Jephunneh liked me, so he rushed off to find him. Moses stayed with me. When Aaron returned with Jephunneh, Abba roused enough to bless us."

"Didn't he first ask Jephunneh if this was what he wanted? Or did Aaron do that for you?" Hava lifted a brow, her expression a mixture of surprise and skepticism.

"He asked. Briefly. Jephunneh was quick to assure him."

"What of Jephunneh's father? Things were done so quickly." Hava looked off toward the bulrushes.

"Yes." Miriam felt her face grow hot. "Moses couldn't stay after that, of course, though he wanted to wait to see if Abba improved. I sent word when Abba slipped away, but he could not come to the burial. I don't think Hatshepsut wants him to have much to do with us, and he had tipped his hand when he sent for the physician."

Hava nodded. "I'm so sorry, Miriam. He is like a brother that is not a brother. At least you still have Aaron."

"Yes, but Aaron is a child." Though they were only two years apart, she was glad that she would have Jephunneh to help her. To take Aaron's advice or rely solely on him was too hard.

"So you wed Jephunneh tomorrow?" Hava lowered her jar into the water, filled it, then set it on the ground again.

"Yes. Abba managed to affix his seal to a ketubah he and Ima had waiting for me, and Jephunneh did the same. We are already wed, but tomorrow he will come for me. Actually, Jephunneh will move into our house rather than try to fit two more into the house of his father. It is better this way."

"You will be glad for the privacy. Except for Aaron, of course." Hava smiled. "Would you like me to invite Aaron to stay with us for a few nights?"

"Would you?" Miriam filled her jar, and they hefted the jars onto their heads. "I think Jephunneh would like that, though Aaron could go to stay with Jephunneh's mother and father."

"Aaron knows me better," Hava said as they began the walk back to their village. "But it is up to you. I'm sure he will be welcome in either home. A newly married husband and wife need some time alone."

"Yes." Miriam's cheeks grew hotter, and she faced her friend. "Was it . . . that is . . . Ima never told me what to expect. Is it terrible or wonderful? The gossips say it's both."

Hava laughed. "That all depends on whether or not you love him and he loves you. Of course, in most arranged marriages, love comes later. It is so rare for love to bloom before we come together." She touched her middle again, a soft smile on her lips.

"I respect him . . . as much as one can respect another they do not actually know. But I do not think I have any feelings beyond appreciation for him right now. I am grateful that he finds me pleasing to wed. He is older—he could have married years ago." A sudden feeling of fear swept through her. "What if no one would have him before now? What if he isn't what I expect at all?" Miriam's stomach clenched at the thought, then recoiled at the realization that tomorrow he would know her as no one ever had. *Oh, Adonai, help me.*

"You will come to know him in time," Hava soothed. "If he is kind . . . that's what matters most." Her gaze took on a distant look before she glanced at Miriam again. "Can you keep a secret?"

Miriam nodded. "Of course." Who would she tell?

"I didn't even like Doron when we first wed. My parents picked him. He is a cousin, so I knew him, but I did not think I could ever love him. I thought of him as rather spoiled." She laughed lightly. "But in time, he grew up, and once we could get away from living beneath his father's roof, even though we live right next door, he proved to be a most ardent lover." It was Hava's turn to blush. She again touched the place where the babe lay. "And soon we will be three."

Miriam smiled at her friend. If Hava could make such a marriage work to a cousin she hadn't even liked in the beginning, surely Miriam could learn to care for Jephunneh. He did seem kind. What other man would be so willing to take on a young woman and her younger brother with no parents? And yet . . . what if he was glad that she had no parents to protect her from him? What if he was secretly mean-spirited?

The fears would not abate, and she questioned what had come over her to make her give in to her father's dying wish and her younger brothers' promptings. She was a strong woman, young or not. She could have decided whom to marry in time. When she was ready. When Aaron was old enough to help her.

"You seem worried." Hava touched her arm, drawing her thoughts back to the present.

Miriam nodded. "I guess I am. A little. I have so many things going through my mind. What if he turns out to be someone I cannot trust or who has a temper? What if he does not love Adonai or doesn't allow me to continue to do the things I'm used to doing—helping the needy among us, selling my weaving to the Egyptians who will buy it?"

"You worry needlessly, my friend. I doubt very much that your father would have agreed to this man if he didn't see something good in him. Your father knew him, did he not?" Hava's gait slowed as they neared the place they would part ways.

"My father met him when he began to go to the fields of the shepherds. It surprised me that he picked a Judahite, since we are from the tribe of Levi. But I suppose the man can't be faulted for being from the wrong tribe." Miriam chuckled, hoping it would loosen the knot in her middle.

"The tribe of Judah was blessed of Jacob, my friend. You should not worry about that." Hava patted Miriam's hand. "You have nothing to fear. You will find your first few nights together strange, but you will soon come to appreciate marriage."

"I hope you are right." Miriam watched Hava turn to leave.

"I am." She followed the path to her home, leaving Miriam wondering if her friend truly knew of what she spoke.

⬿

The songs of the well-wishers wafted through the open window the following day, filling Miriam with excitement and dread.

"He is here," Hava said, beaming. A few of Miriam's cousins filled the small house, all giggling as they fought for a place at the window to watch for the bridegroom.

Miriam looked at her best friend, trying to hide her panic. Hava touched her arm. "It's going to be fine. You will see."

Jephunneh's parents had prepared a feast, such as they had, and by the sound of the crowd, she wondered if the entire tribes of Levi and Judah surrounded Jephunneh. "There are so many people." She risked a glance from behind her maids to see a long line of men and women coming closer. "How will they feed them all?"

"People will bring food to help. No one has much, so we share." Hava put both hands on Miriam's shoulders. "You are the strong one, my friend. Do not fear now."

Miriam met Hava's gaze, then glanced one last time at the house she had grown up in and the place she had made for Jephunneh and herself. A new pallet he had provided and cushions she had hastily made took up one corner of the room where her parents used to sleep. It all felt so different, so strange.

A knock interrupted her musings, and Aaron's voice could be heard above the others. She drew in a deep, calming breath. There was no more time to reminisce, as she'd been doing most of the day. She looked once more at Hava and her maids. "It's time," she whispered.

They all stifled giggles as she opened the door and smiled.

"I have come to claim my bride." Jephunneh looked good, his beard trimmed slightly, his clothes and hair washed.

Aaron stepped beside him. "And I am here to place her hand in yours." He reached for Miriam's hand, and she allowed him to do this honor.

Jephunneh's fingers closed over hers. His hand was warm, and he gently squeezed hers. "Come," he said. "A banquet awaits us."

She closed the door behind her and walked beside him, a thin veil pulled over her face, her robe clean but not new. There had been no time to make new garments. She'd been so busy caring for her parents the past few years that she had thought nothing of herself. But there would be time enough after the wedding.

They arrived after a brief walk, for the tribe of Judah was not far from the houses of the tribe of Levi. Lights spilled from the mud-brick house, and Jephunneh's father greeted them both with open arms. His mother, Temima, rushed forward to kiss her cheek. "Welcome, my daughter."

"Thank you, Mother." She would never be able to call the woman Ima as she had her own mother.

Inside, Jephunneh's father gave a short speech to them both, Jephunneh removed her veil, and they all filled clay bowls with lentil and barley stew brimming with leeks and garlic. The scents of date cakes and red wine filled the room.

Laughter flowed along with the wine, and Miriam's dread slowly slipped away as she found Jephunneh's father a humorous, welcoming host. His mother sat beside her briefly and whispered in her ear, "I have not had a daughter, so I do hope we will become friends." She patted Miriam's hand. "My son will be a good husband to you."

"Thank you," Miriam said, praying it was true. She swallowed a bit of date cake and sipped the wine. She had eaten little but found that despite the lessening of her dread, she had no appetite.

Jephunneh leaned close to her. "I am glad you came."

She looked into his eyes, seeing the same kindness that had been there the day she learned her father was hurt. "I am as well." And she meant it.

Life would not be the same from this point on. She did not know what marriage to Jephunneh would be like, but she would learn. And she would be a good wife to this man.

Her heart lightened as she felt him grasp her fingers after the last of the men and women had dispersed to their homes. Slaves could not celebrate long into the night. It was a wonder that his parents had been able to afford wine at all, but somehow they had had enough.

As Jephunneh walked her back to the home she would now share with him, she couldn't stop from asking, "How did your parents get so much wine for the feast? I know friends would have brought food, but the wine? It is not like slaves have that in abundance."

Jephunneh stopped in the road and touched her face. His own shone beneath the moon's glow. "Your brother provided the food and wine. He could not be here, for his mother would not allow it, but he sent what he could. It was his way of joining us."

"Moses did this? He is only ten! How would he even think of such a thing?" Most ten-year-olds she knew were still childish or working the fields. They would think only of filling their own bellies.

"Moses is being raised as royalty, Miriam. He is taught by the best Egypt has to offer. I am sure that means he sees what is expected at banquets and assemblies the pharaoh puts on for his people." He cupped her cheek, his gaze filled with longing.

Miriam could not meet his gaze for the sudden shyness that crept over her. "You are right, of course. He seems mature for ten. But I have barely seen him since we took him to the palace when he was five. How much time has changed him."

"And teaching." Jephunneh continued walking toward their home. "Moses will rise to greatness in the land, if my guess is correct. Of course, only Yahweh knows for sure what will happen in each of our lives."

Miriam's heart warmed to hear him speak of Adonai. "As only He knew that we would be wed so quickly."

He laughed softly. "Yes. Though your father knew that I have watched you from a distance since your mother passed. I did not think a woman as beautiful as you are would want a shepherd from Judah as her husband. Your father thought otherwise."

Miriam looked at him, stopping at the closed door. "He did? Why did he never tell me this?"

Jephunneh shrugged. "I do not know. Perhaps because he was not sure I was ready. Or perhaps because he did not wish to let you go."

"But we would still have cared for him."

"Of course we would. As we will care for Aaron until he weds." He reached around her to open the door, lifted her in his arms, and carried her inside.

His arms about her felt warm and strange and comforting and disconcerting.

He set her down and shut the door. "It is time, my love."

She nodded, unsure what to do next.

He lifted the veil from her hair, undid the belt that held her cloak shut, and placed them on a peg by the door. He removed his own cloak and hung it up, then came to her and took her hand. "Show me the house first," he said, as though he were simply here to inspect things. But Miriam sensed that he wanted to put her at ease.

"There is not much to show." She moved her arm in an arc. "This is where I keep the pots for cooking. The clay oven is outside in the courtyard. Those jars hold grains of barley for bread. Aaron sleeps in that corner, and the table is here." They were standing so close to it that to say so seemed silly. She met his gaze. "And our bed is there." She pointed behind him. "It is where my parents slept, but I had no other place to put it."

"It is exactly where it should be." He turned her palm up and kissed it.

Something within her melted at the tenderness in his touch. Her shoulders relaxed, and she did not move when he leaned closer to her. His fingers traced a line along her cheek, and slowly, gently, his lips brushed hers.

He pulled back, intertwined their fingers, and moved around the table to the corner, where the bed she had made awaited them. Her heart thumped in an anxious rhythm as she allowed him to remove her garments and release the combs from her hair.

He smiled as she lay among the cushions, and his fingers sifted through her long, silky strands. "You are more beautiful than I imagined," he said, his tone husky as though he held back emotion. His lips covered hers, and she slowly returned his deepening kiss.

As the night fell about them, Miriam realized the gossips who said the marriage bed was an awful thing were wrong. Even if she did not love him yet, her husband made her want to. His tenderness filled her with joy.

# ELEVEN

Elisheba opened the door of her parents' house to the sight of Miriam holding her young daughter's hand. "Miriam! Welcome." She stepped back, wiping flour from her hands onto the piece of linen tied to her belt, and allowed them entrance. Her mother and father were at work in the fields, and her younger sister, Gilla, stood a short distance away, chopping the few vegetables they had from the garden for an evening stew.

Elisheba stared at Miriam, this sister of the Egyptian prince Moses, and sensed she should say more, but no words would come. Why was she here?

"Thank you," Miriam said, setting her daughter on the dirt floor inside the house and handing her a small wooden object to occupy her. "May we sit down?" Miriam asked, her gaze now on Elisheba.

Elisheba nodded and pointed to a bench where she and her sister took turns eating meals in the small space.

Miriam grabbed her suddenly crawling child and sat

slowly. "I hope you don't mind the visit. I do not mean to keep you from your work."

Elisheba sat on the other end of the bench while Gilla continued to chop vegetables. Every now and then, the plopping sound of her dropping them into the water broke the awkward silence.

"It is no problem. I still have time before our parents return. I am grateful that your Moses has been able to make it so that not all of us have to work the fields. At least until we are older. I know my time to join my parents is coming soon, and my sister will do this work alone." She glanced at Gilla with fond sorrow. She would miss the time she had alone with her sister.

"I have come to ask you something." Miriam held her child's toy in one hand while the little girl tried to take it from her. "I know this is something our fathers would normally work out, and Jephunneh will surely come to speak with your father on Aaron's behalf, but I wanted to come first, to ask you if you would find my brother pleasing to wed."

Elisheba felt heat creep up her neck, her brows lifting. Miriam was forthright, of that there was no doubt. But the question caught her off guard. "I . . . I haven't given marriage much thought."

"You are of marriageable age though, yes?" Miriam's quick, assessing glance warmed Elisheba's cheeks.

"Yes. I am of marriageable age. My father and mother have not talked to me of it yet, though. They return from the work so tired that they eat and sleep. We barely talk."

Miriam's expression softened. "I am sorry to hear it. If I could help . . ." She let the sentence linger, for of course no one could stop the slavery or control what the taskmasters expected. Not even Moses' sister.

They looked at each other in silence a moment.

"The truth is, I am responsible for my brother Aaron, as I am his only close relative. He has confided to me that he is interested in you now that he is old enough to wed. But I do not want you to feel pressured to marry someone you do not want. While love can come later, as it has for Jephunneh and me, I would rather know that the woman I choose for my brother already knows she might be able to care for him."

Elisheba straightened. "I have met your brother a few times. Of course, without festivals or times when we often come together, I cannot say that I know him."

"But you have met him."

"Yes."

"And do you find him pleasing or displeasing?" Miriam shifted her daughter to another position on her lap. "I want you to be honest, Elisheba. I do not wish to have a sister-in-law who does not like my brother." She smiled, and Elisheba finally felt herself relax a little.

"Nor do I," she said, smiling slightly. "This is all just so sudden. But you are Levites as we are, and I know of no other Levite who would please me more."

Miriam nodded. "So if I send Jephunneh to speak to your father, you will agree?"

Elisheba knew Miriam probably needed to return to her duties, and holding on to a wiggly little girl could not be easy, but she was not used to making such hasty decisions. Especially one of such importance.

She looked from the child to the mother and nodded. What else could she do? "I will agree."

Miriam smiled, her look relieved. "Thank you. I will send Jephunneh within the week to speak to your father. If for any reason you change your mind, please come to me before week's end so I do not send my husband on a fool's mission."

Elisheba stood as Miriam did. "I will. But you need not worry. I will not change my mind."

Miriam's smile was genuine and warm. "I hope we will be good friends." She moved to the door. "We will work to make room for you and Aaron in our home, as there is little room for you to have a place of your own. I hope you find that agreeable as well?"

Elisheba nodded. Of course she would leave her father and mother to live with her husband's family. She only wished the homes in Goshen were larger as the families grew. But the Egyptians tried to confine them to a small area of the land, claiming the fields were needed for crops, which they took for themselves. Only the shepherds were free to roam beyond the area, for Egyptians wanted nothing to do with them.

Miriam bid her farewell, and Elisheba closed the door, her head spinning. "I'm going to be married." She walked closer to Gilla.

"I heard. And you are going to leave us." Her look displayed her displeasure.

"As will you when you are of age."

Her sister's mood did not lighten with that comment. "I will miss you."

"I know." She pulled Gilla into her arms and held her close. "I will visit often. And the wedding probably won't happen for a few months anyway."

"I hope it takes a year."

Elisheba laughed. "Perhaps it will." But she sincerely doubted it.

⁓

Miriam finished the date cakes and pulled the last loaf of bread from the oven. She wiped her brow with the back of her hand. How she missed her mother's help in times like this. She was not accustomed to hosting a feast, and she would likely never give one again. When Moses wed, they probably would not even be invited to the event. Hatshepsut had made the distinction between Moses and his birth family very clear.

Still, even once, the work of a wedding feast overwhelmed her. Fortunately, Jephunneh's mother had helped in the morning and would be back soon. Lysia slept peacefully, thank God for that! But the growing babe within Miriam depleted her strength, and she looked longingly at her pallet.

One glance at the sun's descent, however, and she knew she could not stop. Jephunneh had promised to return sooner rather than later, and Aaron with him. Elisheba would come with the well-wishers once the men went to get her. Her mother would help by then as well, but she could not get away from the fields to assist Miriam ahead of time.

*Curse these Egyptians!* Miriam bit her tongue at the unkind thought. *But oh, Lord, how long?* Her prayers had increased of late, perhaps because she knew her children would also be slaves in Egypt unless God did something to change their situation. But God seemed immune to their prayers.

Aaron was old enough to wed at eighteen, though barely.

She knew he needed to be on his own, and these past months, when they could, he and Jephunneh had worked on a makeshift addition to their home for him and Elisheba. They would have to share the eating quarters, but at least they would have a room away from Miriam and Jephunneh, a room of their own, especially important as the children grew.

She touched her middle just as the door opened. Her mother-in-law, Temima, came inside and closed the door. "The wind has grown in strength today," she said. "I do hope our men and women in the fields are not getting hit with sand in their faces and clothes. I was in a sheltered spot, but not everyone works in the same areas. They will be worn out if they have been fighting against the wind all day."

"Which means less of them will have the strength to come tonight." How had she not heard the wind in all of her work? She must have been too focused on hurrying to complete every task.

"Now don't you worry about that. People love to celebrate a wedding. They will come if they can walk. Our people are strong." Temima lifted her chin. "Now, what else needs doing?"

Miriam put her to work measuring the lentils to add to the already simmering stew. They had killed a young goat for the occasion, and Miriam had prepared it the night before to add to the stew, a treat for all.

At that moment Lysia awoke and called for her. Miriam excused herself and slipped behind the curtain to where their family slept. Privacy such as it was.

"While you are in there, go ahead and freshen up. The men will be here soon," Temima called from the cooking area.

Miriam sank onto the pallet and changed Lysia's linens, then pulled a fresh tunic over the two-year-old's head. She gave her a few blocks to occupy her while she removed her own stained tunic and pinched color into her wan cheeks. She should be pink from the heat of the room, but she felt only tired and worn.

She had sent word to Moses about Aaron's wedding, but this time there had been no word in return. He had not sent the extra food and wine as he had for Miriam's wedding five years before. Perhaps he was kept too busy becoming Egypt's prince.

Voices came to her from beyond the curtain. She quickly pulled her hair back and tucked it with the combs she had used for her own wedding. She was not the bride, but she must look the part of a good host.

"It smells wonderful in here." Jephunneh's voice came to her, calming her. She hadn't realized how nervous this day had made her. Perhaps that was why she was so tired.

"Don't touch that!" Temima said.

Miriam heard a soft slap and peeked out from behind the curtain. Aaron had tried to help himself to a date cake.

"But I'm the groom!"

"It matters not," Temima said. "Even the groom has to wait for the wedding. You will have your fill of food soon enough."

Lysia jumped up and ran to her father. "Abba!"

Miriam followed as Jephunneh scooped their daughter into his arms. "And how is my girl today?" He kissed her cheek.

"She just woke up. She will be full of energy tonight."

Jephunneh gave her a knowing look, which quickly turned

to concern. "But it appears you will not. Not unless you go and rest right now."

"I'm fine." Her protest sounded hollow.

"You're tired and with child. I will help my mother and be sure to wake you before we leave to get Elisheba." Jephunneh gently led her toward her pallet.

"Promise?" She didn't need convincing. Why was she this tired? She hadn't been this way with their firstborn, and she was only twenty—still plenty young enough to bear a child.

"I promise." Jephunneh kissed her forehead and retreated back to the cooking area.

The next thing Miriam heard was the sound of shouts and the song of the bridegroom in the streets. She jumped up and pushed the curtain aside. "Why didn't he wake me?" she asked Temima.

"He tried. You needed your sleep, my daughter."

She sighed deeply. "Yes, I did." But now she was rested and did a quick check of everything. The door opened, and Jephunneh, Elisheba's parents, Aaron, and a host of villagers entered. More people than she'd expected. And then she saw him.

Moses. Without his guards.

She ran to him and embraced him, Egyptian garb or not. "You came!" How she wished he could have done the same for her wedding. But he was here now.

"I had to sneak away." He kissed her cheek. "And I have a cart full of wine with me. Where would you like it?"

She smiled. This would be a very good night.

# PART TWO

Many years later, when Moses had grown up, he went out to visit his own people, the Hebrews, and he saw how hard they were forced to work. During his visit, he saw an Egyptian beating one of his fellow Hebrews. After looking in all directions to make sure no one was watching, Moses killed the Egyptian and hid the body in the sand.

The next day, when Moses went out to visit his people again, he saw two Hebrew men fighting. "Why are you beating up your friend?" Moses said to the one who had started the fight.

The man replied, "Who appointed you to be our prince and judge? Are you going to kill me as you killed that Egyptian yesterday?"

Then Moses was afraid, thinking, "Everyone knows what I did." And sure enough, Pharaoh heard what had happened, and he tried to kill Moses. But Moses fled from Pharaoh and went to live in the land of Midian.

Exodus 2:11–15

# TWELVE

Moses hurried from his rooms, down winding palace halls, and stopped outside of his mother's suite. The sound of weeping seeped beneath the closed door, and he hesitated. His servant had awakened him with the news that his mother's husband, Thutmose II, had died in his sleep, still a young man. What would happen now? Would his mother expect him to take Pharaoh's place?

He knocked once. A servant opened the door, and Moses moved slowly toward his mother's sitting room, where she sat on her couch, silent and stoic. The professional mourners stood in the corners and wept, but no tears or words came from Hatshepsut.

She looked up and smiled at his approach, extending a ringed hand. "Moses, my love. Come. Sit." She patted the place beside her on the couch, and he obeyed. She took his hand and held it. "He is gone."

"Yes. My servants told me." He looked into her eyes,

93

searching for some hint of grief. "You are not sad," he said when he detected no hint of sorrow there.

She shook her head. "The illness took him, but he had failed as a great leader long before his skin broke out with the rashes and cysts." She paused, leaning closer. "He was weak."

Moses squeezed her fingers. "I am sorry, Mother."

She looked beyond him, then turned and touched his cheek. "Thutmose had a son with a lesser wife. The people will expect him to rule, but I will rule with him. The boy is but an infant in arms." She paused. "And you are not ready."

"No, of course not. You will be a great pharaoh." Moses felt a sense of relief rush through him that she did not suggest he take Thutmose's place. Though he had been under Pharaoh's roof for seventeen years, even at twenty-two he had no desire to rule. With every day that passed, with every lesson in languages and writing and studying and public speaking, he only longed to return to his true people, to Miriam and Aaron.

"Thank you, my son," Hatshepsut said, interrupting his thoughts. "I knew you would understand. After I am gone, I will see to it that you take Thutmose III's place." Her voice trailed off, and Moses knew that she thought such a thing would appease him, but this infant would grow up and expect to take full control of Egypt once his mother rested in the Valley of the Kings.

"When that time comes, I will be ready," he said, for he knew she wanted to hear it. "But may God give you long life on the earth."

She tilted her head to better face him. "After all of the training in this place, you still call on only one god? Better that you should say, 'May the gods bless you with long life and prosperity,' my son."

"That too," he said. He lifted her hand and kissed her ring. "I wish you much success, Mother."

She smiled at that and released his hand. "Your sister will be here any moment. One day soon, you must marry her. That will strengthen your right to rule instead of that half-breed child of my husband."

Moses felt his stomach knot at the very mention of Neferure, daughter of Hatshepsut and Thutmose II. He had no desire to wed her now or ever. But everyone knew that Hatshepsut had no love for Thutmose's secondary wives or this son who would be crowned king though he was barely old enough to walk.

"There is plenty of time for that since you will be pharaoh for years to come." He kissed her cheek. "I support you, Mother."

She smiled again, rose, and ordered the weeping women from her chambers. "Enough of this mourning. We must bury my husband and declare my place beside his infant child of an inferior wife before the sun sets. Of course, the burial will take longer with the embalming, but my appointment as pharaoh must be immediate. You will come with me to the priests and stand at my side." She studied his expression.

"Of course." He stood and walked with her from her chambers to the audience hall just outside of the main audience chamber, where she called for the priests to join her.

"And bring Thutmose III," she told a waiting maid.

"Yes, my queen." The woman hurried off to the Household of Royal Children.

Moses waited beside Hatshepsut in the audience hall.

Soon the chamber filled with priests and courtiers and advisors to Thutmose II and a maid holding a squirming Thutmose III.

Hatshepsut sat on her husband's throne and took the crook and flail in her hands. Moses stood to her right, longing to be anywhere but here. He stood his ground nonetheless.

"I have called you here to announce, as you already know, that my husband is dead. The embalmers even now are preparing his body for the tomb in the Valley of the Kings. But in the meantime, Egypt needs a pharaoh. Unfortunately, my daughter is too young, and Moses, my son, is not of Egyptian blood."

To hear her say it to such a crowd caused a feeling of unease to sweep over him. Everyone knew it, of course, but she had never announced it publicly like this. He remained staring straight ahead, like one of her guards.

"My husband does have a son, Thutmose III, but as you can all see, he is not old enough to know his own name. Egypt will want a male pharaoh, so this is what I want you to do. Today we will name Thutmose III as Pharaoh, king of Egypt, and I, Hatshepsut, as co-regent. I will rule in his place until he is old enough to take the throne." She gave each man looking her way a stern glance. "If you have any objections to this, let me hear them now, or remain forever silent."

Moses watched as each man, priest, advisor, courtier, and servant standing along the wall bowed before her. Then the high priest of Ra stepped forward, took Pharaoh's crown, and placed it on Hatshepsut's head. The crown was too large for her, but he shifted it to fit until it could be adjusted or a new one made.

"Long live Pharaoh Hatshepsut," the priests shouted, followed by the rest of the men in the room. Moses joined the chorus of voices and saw the slight smile lift the corners of his mother's mouth.

She would enjoy this position. She had been the force behind her husband for as long as Moses could remember. In that moment, he wondered if she really wanted him to ever take her place. No, she would reign even when Thutmose III grew old enough to take over for her. He sensed by the gleam in her eyes that she would never step down. Not until she also rested in the Valley of the Kings.

# THIRTEEN

Miriam woke with a start, the dream vivid in her mind. She sat up, blinking several times. Darkness shrouded the house. The children slept, and Jephunneh snored next to her. She slowly lowered herself back onto the pallet.

Her mind replayed the dream. Moses was in Pharaoh's court, something that held no significance. He had been in Pharaoh's court for twenty-six years now, his adoptive mother still ruling Egypt along with her stepson Thutmose III. The child must be ten or eleven by now. So Miriam seeing Moses there in her dream should not have startled her awake.

But the dream seemed distant, not something that was happening in Pharaoh's palace now. Moses stood before Pharaoh, but not in Hatshepsut's audience hall. She had never seen Thutmose III, so perhaps the dream would come to pass after Hatshepsut's death. But Miriam was disappointed to realize that Moses was not sitting on the throne, since she had always hoped he would one day.

What was he doing there? He looked different from the

last time she saw him, which had been several years now. After Aaron's wedding many years ago, he had only appeared at her door twice. And both times he had done so in disguise. But since Hatshepsut had come to power, he had stayed away.

Miriam shifted onto her side, trying to recall the child princess who had rescued her brother. The woman, who looked like a man in her pharaoh attire, was said to be fearful of the people one day and a demanding ruler the next. Once when Miriam had sought out Rashida, she heard the rumors that Hatshepsut had carved "Now my heart turns to and fro in thinking what the people will say" on a monument in the Egyptian city of Karnak. Yet when it came to proclaiming the good traits about the pharaoh before her—her husband—as most pharaohs would do, she had nothing to say.

"She disrespects him in public," Rashida had said. Miriam could only wonder why, but she did not push the maid for more information.

Had Hatshepsut also become unhappy with Moses? Was that why he had not yet married? Everyone thought he would have by now. If he was being groomed to take Hatshepsut's place, he should have already married her daughter. But Thutmose III was the true pharaoh by most gossip accounts. What kind of upheaval did Moses live with behind those opulent walls?

She closed her eyes, seeing Moses again in her mind's eye speaking to the pharaoh, a man she did not recognize. Moses was older . . . much older than he was now, though his beard had no white or gray in it. Years had passed, but how many, Miriam could not tell.

*Are You trying to tell me something, Adonai?* Ima had always hoped that Moses would deliver them from slavery

in Egypt. But as the years passed, Miriam had nearly forgotten that hope. They were treated better than most, but
their relatives and neighbors were not. How long would this
oppression last?

And why would she dream of Moses when her last thought
before sleep claimed her had been how to teach her daughters
a better way to dye the thread for weaving?

She shook herself, knowing that such dreams could be
nothing but the ramblings of an overwrought mother's mind.
Still, she could not deny that she missed Moses more now
than she did in the early years. Knowing he was near and
yet so far was hard to bear. And fears for his future, as if he
were her own son, continued to haunt her, even when she
told herself he could take care of himself. But could he?

# FOURTEEN

### Nine Years Later
### 1486 BC

Moses slipped out of the confines of the palace and rode a chariot through the city of Thebes to Rameses to see the work his mother had done during the eighteen years of her reign. Monuments to her greatness stared back at him at every turn.

He looked away from the structures to the slaves who bowed low as his driver moved through the city paved with stone streets and buildings built on the backs of these Hebrews, his true people. The thought turned his stomach. *Why, Adonai?* He had not forgotten his people, but he could not understand why the God of their fathers had seemingly forgotten them. Thirty-five of his forty years he had spent in a place of privilege, while his fellow countrymen suffered at the very hands of the people who bowed to him.

He glanced to the right, where a group of slaves pushed bricks into place for yet another building project of his mother's. A taskmaster stood near with a leather whip.

"Slow down," he commanded. His driver quickly complied.

"Move faster," the Egyptian master shouted.

The slaves tensed, but most of them attempted to hurry. One older man could not move as quickly as the younger ones. The taskmaster raised his whip and brought it down hard on the back of the slave. "Faster, I said!"

The slave cried out, and Moses nearly jumped from the chariot and reprimanded the man. But what could he do? He did not have power to stop such treatment. It had been given to these Egyptians by several pharaohs before his mother.

And yet, why could she not see that saving him while continuing to enslave his people was the ultimate hypocrisy? If she wanted to make a difference in Egypt, she should have released the Hebrews and sent them away. But enslaving them was good for Egypt's coffers, and if nothing else, his mother loved gold and every material possession she could gather. Her clothing reflected the best linens, some of which were also made at the hands of slaves. But it cost her nothing to take from them what they could have sold in any marketplace in Egypt.

His jaw clenched at the thought. "Move on!" He could not bear to watch such mistreatment, and the sick feeling in his gut felt more like someone had dealt him a blow. When had he come to resent the woman who had saved him? She had rescued him from death and raised him to be her own. She had given him the best Egypt had to offer in education and wealth. But she did not know how to love. Not like the love he still recalled from the mother who had borne him.

Suddenly his missing her, missing his birth family, burned within him, a desperate ache. Tomorrow he would visit them. And then he would go to the fields and see if the Egyptians treated his people any better there. Perhaps God had given him all that He had so he could help his people. Perhaps he could convince Thutmose III to do something once Hatshepsut passed into the underworld. He could assure this half brother that he had no intention of vying to take his place and would only ask that he consider the plight of the Hebrews. But first he must see the scope of that plight.

He leaned close to the driver as they turned to head toward another city. "Take me back to the palace," he said, his mind whirling with how to handle these things. He could not let anyone know he was making these trips to Goshen and the surrounding cities where the slaves worked. He could not have guards following him to his sister's house for a visit. How long it had been!

He must plan, and the gardens of Pharaoh's palace were the place he thought best, where his mind could concentrate. One thing was certain. He had seen enough to anger him, and he was tired of sitting in the halls of Pharaoh and doing nothing. He was the adopted son of Pharaoh. He should have the ability to put his weight into seeking change. Surely God had put him here for this purpose. Now it was up to him to figure out how best to do just that.

～⤲～

Miriam worked the loom while Elisheba spun the thread Jephunneh and Aaron had shorn from the flocks they tended. Miriam's girls, Lysia and Janese, had homes of their own now, added on to the houses of their husbands' families. Elisheba and Aaron had been forced to seek another house near them for their two oldest sons, Nadab and Abihu, and their wives. Their youngest boys, Eliezer and Ithamar, would marry soon, in a year or two. All of the boys tended the flocks rather than work the fields.

"I'm glad no one has forced our boys into the same slavery my parents have known," Elisheba said as the colored wool took shape into thread in her skilled hands. "I'm not sure I could bear it."

Miriam nodded. "I am grateful our girls are allowed to weave garments, though the palace takes most of our goods without pay. It is still better than having a taskmaster standing over us." At forty-five, Miriam carried the strength and energy of her youth, but in the twenty-five years since she gave birth to her youngest daughter, she had never borne another child. Was Jephunneh to have no sons? The thought saddened her, and she felt a sense of failure sweep over her. She loved her girls, but every man needed a son.

She was not past the point of childbearing, but it seemed as though she was. She glanced at Elisheba, who had given Aaron four sons. How was that possible? She was fortunate the ruling against boys was no longer what it had been at the time of Moses' birth.

"Have you found a wife for Eliezer yet?" She had to focus on something other than self-pity. It did no good to wish for something that would never be.

Elisheba shook her head. "We haven't talked about it much. I know we need to, and I've had my eye on a few of the young women nearby. I want to stay within our tribe and clan, but I haven't had time to see the women long enough to choose one."

"They are working the fields with their mothers, no doubt." Memories of the days she'd helped her mother in the fields before Moses was born surfaced. Sometimes she still heard the painful cries of the man who had suffered the lash of the taskmaster's whip. She shuddered, praying again that God would give them a deliverer.

A soft knock sounded at the door, and Miriam set aside the shuttle, bringing her weaving to a stop. She looked at Elisheba, whose eyes were wide with fear. Who would be at their door at this hour? Everyone was busy. Had something happened to one of their men? Visions of her father's injury added to the memories of her childhood and the pain slavery brought to her countrymen. She moved slowly to the door and tried to see through the curtained window.

A man stood there, but she did not recognize him. She opened the door, heart pounding. "Yes?" Surely something had happened to Jephunneh or Aaron!

But when the man removed his false beard, she gasped. "Moses!" She flung herself toward him and pulled him into the house. "How long it has been! Why are you here? Is something wrong? Is your mother well? The men are not here right now—they are with the sheep."

Moses laughed and held a finger to her lips. "Slow down, my sister, and take a breath."

She did just that and released her grip on him. "What are you doing here?"

He smiled. "I missed you. Is that not reason enough?" He glanced beyond her to Elisheba. His brow furrowed until recognition eased the lines there. "Elisheba, wife of my brother, yes?"

She nodded. "Yes. Welcome."

He looked from one to the other. "I would have come when Aaron and Jephunneh were home, but as it is, I must sneak away when I can."

Miriam noted his Hebrew disguise. "I should have known the beard was not real."

He smiled. "We do not wear beards in Egyptian company, but I knew I would be recognized without one here. I am about to visit Aaron in the fields but do not know where they are keeping the sheep."

Miriam urged him to sit at the low table. "You cannot leave yet. You just arrived. Please, tell me how you are."

Moses sighed. "I am weary of Egyptian life, truth be told. I want to do something to help our people, but I do not yet know what that might be. I have come to talk with Aaron and see what he knows, and then I want to see how the slaves in the fields are treated. I have already seen enough in the cities they are building. I want a clear picture of this slavery to take to my half brother."

"Would you not take the news to your mother? Surely Hatshepsut has a kind place in her heart for our people." Miriam had always thought the princess to be kind, but the queenship may have changed her.

"My mother has become too used to the value of slavery and the gold it saves the kingdom. If we had to pay the Hebrews, Egypt would have no money left in its coffers. If Egypt released them—allowed them to leave our land—we would have no workforce. I must find a way to convince Thutmose that when he comes to power, he must do something. It is wrong to treat people so cruelly."

Miriam stared at him, feeling her mother's hope rising in her. Had her own dreams of Moses before Pharaoh predicted this very moment? Would he indeed deliver them soon from this awful oppression that caused many men and women to die too young?

"I will pray that the God of our fathers gives you the wisdom you need to do as you must. Ima knew you were destined to save us. And I think she was right." Miriam smiled, and he returned it.

"I do not know that I will be successful, but I will try my best. For now, I need you both to tell no one of my visit. Just tell me where I can find Aaron."

"They are in the pasturelands north of Goshen. They are not allowed to travel far, even in search of food for the animals, but the area is large enough that we have not lost any to lack of grazing land," Elisheba said.

Moses stood. "Thank you. I will go in search of them now. Tomorrow I will visit the fields to assess what is going on. I will try to let you know what I discover."

Miriam walked him to the door, wishing he could stay longer. She touched his arm. "I will pray for you."

"As I hoped you would." He kissed her cheek. Then he slipped out of the house and moved quickly toward the pasture.

Miriam turned to Elisheba. "Perhaps our prayers are finally about to be answered!" She could not help the joy that filled her. At Elisheba's smile, she clapped her hands and laughed.

# FIFTEEN

Moses moved cautiously through the crowded streets of Goshen, appalled by the sparse living conditions and the obvious poverty of his people. While the mud-brick walls of the cities his people were being forced to build stood tall and strong, here their houses were crumbling in places and too close together.

His chest grew tight as though a weight had landed on it. Why had God allowed this? Worse, why had God allowed him to live in wealth and splendor while the children of Abraham suffered such violence and hardship?

He moved swifter now, no longer able to take it all in. His resolve to do something grew with each step, but first he must speak to Aaron and Jephunneh. They would be able to tell him more accurately what was truly happening to the Israelites.

He broke free of the houses and continued toward the pasture beyond the fields. He moved along the edges of the land, away from the workers. He had no desire to reveal himself or be mistaken for a slave and given no chance to prove otherwise.

But should he prove otherwise? Could he allow himself to live among his people?

The thought troubled him. He did not want to live in poverty and slavery, and in that moment he wondered if he truly could relate to his people. They had suffered while he had not. What did that say about him?

The sound of bleating sheep came to him in the distance. He shaded his eyes against the sun's glare and spotted a flock some distance away. He was going to have a long walk to make it back to the palace before nightfall. He hurried his pace.

Several men came into view, and one waved in his direction. They thought him a Hebrew, of course, but he waved back and continued his trek toward them.

"I'm looking for Aaron and Jephunneh," he said. "Have you seen them?"

"My father and uncle are beyond that line of trees. They went after a couple of wayward sheep." One of the young men looked at him closely. "I haven't seen you before."

Moses nodded. "I am not from this area. But I know your father and uncle."

The young men gave him a skeptical look, then pointed in the direction of the tree line. Moses thanked them and hurried on. He couldn't look like much of a threat, a lone man without a staff. He should have found one, but he'd been in a hurry and hadn't thought he would need one. Now, for his own protection, he questioned the wisdom of coming alone without a weapon.

He shook the worry aside. He would have to use his wits and trust that God watched over him. He moved through the trees, grateful it was not a wide forest where he could lose his way.

He stepped onto lush grass on the other side and spotted Aaron not far from him, a lamb draped over his shoulders. "Aaron!" He moved slowly forward and removed his beard. "It is I, Moses."

"Moses!" Aaron set the lamb on the ground to embrace him. Jephunneh came up beside him, leading another wayward lamb.

Moses embraced Jephunneh as well. "I see you have two stubborn ewes here."

Aaron laughed. "They can be. One always follows the other, and the first one is always wandering. Sometimes we lose track of them."

"I'm glad you found them in one piece." He rubbed the back of his neck and lowered his voice. "And I am very glad to see that the Egyptians do not trouble you here."

"As are we," Jephunneh said, stroking his beard. "Your presence in the palace has kept our families in better shape than our neighbors. It is hard to watch the difference, but we admit we are grateful to be free enough to tend the animals without a whip at our back."

"Egyptians despise sheep." Moses moved with them toward the trees and stopped. "Perhaps what I have to ask is better asked here." He faced them both. "I want to do something to help our people, though I do not know what. I plan to visit the fields to see how they are treated. I've already been to the cities they are building for Hatshepsut and Thutmose III, but I want to see everything. I thought first I would ask you what you know. How do our people fare?"

Aaron looked him up and down, his gaze thoughtful. "Our mother was right, then. You are meant for greatness. How wonderful it would be if you could convince the pharaoh to let us leave Egypt!"

"It is as bad as that, then? The only way to ease the burden is to leave this land?" Moses intensely doubted that he would have enough influence with his mother to get her to release them. Thutmose, perhaps. But again doubt niggled at the back of his mind.

"Leaving Egypt is the best possible solution," Jephunneh agreed. "But if the pharaoh would ease the burden, allow the people more rest, and provide time for them to harvest their own crops and build up their own houses, that would help. Perhaps a few things at a time would be a good place to start."

Moses looked at his brother-in-law and searched his expression. The man was taller than Aaron and carried himself with confidence, his bearing steady. "That is a more likely possibility than to ask to have all of us leave. Neither pharaoh would take kindly to a sudden loss of income—and unfortunately, the Hebrew slaves are income to them. They also like wielding power, and slaves give them somewhere to wield that power." He looked around, making sure they were still alone. He had said more than he'd intended. But surely he could trust family.

"Whatever you do, be careful. If you jeopardize your position in the court, it could go worse for all of us, not just your family." Jephunneh touched Moses' shoulder. "We will pray that God will direct you to do what He deems best."

"Thank you." Moses looked from one to the other a final time, then turned to walk with them through the trees. "You all have enough to eat and the necessary provisions, yes? I can have food and wine sent to you, but I will have to do so quietly. I have a few friends in the court, but I cannot trust many of them. They know I am not Egyptian."

"We are fine," Aaron said. "Many of our women are allowed to stay home and work the gardens as long as they produce fine linen for the palace. Not everyone works beneath the whip of a master."

Moses nodded. "Good. That is good to hear."

"But we still need a deliverer to get us out of Egypt," Aaron added, causing a knot of tension to begin in Moses' gut. "Perhaps that will be you. Perhaps God will choose someone else, but someday He will deliver us."

"I hope so." Moses bid them farewell and began the walk back to the palace. He couldn't say that he was the deliverer Aaron hoped for, no matter what their mother had dreamed or believed. What could one man do against the might of Egypt? He held no real power.

Still, as the palace came into view, he rolled the thoughts over and over in his mind. He would visit his people and see for himself. What he would do after that, he didn't know. But he must do something. God help him if he remained silent.

~~≈~~

"Moses came to see us today." Jephunneh sat on a cushion in their small sitting room, which they also used as an eating area. Miriam handed him a cup of water.

"He said he planned to do so." She sat beside him, weary from the day's work. How good it felt to rest with her husband in peace. With no daughters living at home anymore, the house felt strangely quiet, though it was a quiet she could get used to.

"So he stopped to see you first." His arm came around

her, and she leaned into his protective touch. She did not think of it often, but she realized that her love for this man had grown deep through the years.

She looked into his kind, dark eyes. "Yes. Elisheba and I were weaving, and he came to the door. I will say my heart beat faster when I thought he was one of the shepherds. I feared I was going to live through what happened to my father again. I thought you were hurt."

He pulled her close. "You cannot be rid of me yet." He chuckled, and she faced him, pouting.

"You toy with me."

He pushed a strand of hair from her face and looked into her eyes. "I would never make light of your fear. But I am not going anywhere, Miriam. Unless our God takes me, I am always careful. Do not fear, my love."

She relaxed against him once more. "I am glad I married you," she whispered against his ear. She loved the way he brightened a room or lightened a mood.

He kissed her and touched her cheek. She let a sigh escape, secure in his presence. But Moses still occupied her mind.

"I knew that to fear losing you was foolish, for who can control such things? It came as a flash of memory about Abba, and then suddenly Moses removed his beard and I recognized him, and all was well. I'm glad he came. It has been so long!"

"He has trouble sneaking away. We cannot blame him. If he were caught . . . I fear he is risking much to see what is going on with our people." Jephunneh stroked her forehead, sending a tingle down her spine.

"He told you his plans, then? Do you think he can do anything to help our people? Ima always thought so, and in my dreams I have seen him challenging Pharaoh or at least standing in his court, but it always seems so far away and clouded."

Jephunneh sipped his water, saying nothing for a lengthy moment. At last he looked at her. "I think that if Moses is to deliver the people, it will not happen quickly. He is young yet, at least in my estimation. He is smart, but he is quick-tempered. I could see it in his gaze. He is angry at the treatment he has already seen of the slaves in the cities. Once he visits the fields, I don't know that his anger will abate. I fear it will grow. And acting in anger or haste could cause more harm than good."

Miriam pondered his words, settling closer into his embrace. "I fear for him sometimes. I hope he doesn't act rashly."

"We must pray that he doesn't."

She nodded. She had prayed continually for her brother. He had grown into a fine man, but how could she know what went on in his thoughts and heart? How could she know what God would do through him?

"Yes," she said. "We must pray." But she wondered if praying was enough.

# SIXTEEN

*M*oses lay in bed awake, though he remained still lest his attendants fuss about him too soon. The sun had yet to rise above the horizon, but despite the dark room, he could not sleep. The conversations he'd had with Miriam, Aaron, and Jephunneh played over and over in his thoughts. And with each memory, conviction grew.

His mother had called him her hope, a name he had never forgotten despite the years in the palace, away from all things Hebrew. And Miriam had reminded him, as had Aaron, that their mother thought he would have a part in delivering their people from the Egyptians. But how was he supposed to do such a thing? He was one man, and though his adoptive mother taught him as an Egyptian, even she did not admit him into the inner circle of Egyptian leaders.

Perhaps he should convince her of his loyalty to Egypt and ask to be one of her counselors. He could plant ideas in the minds of those surrounding her, and if they thought the ideas were their own, they might be able to convince his mother or Thutmose to change their minds in favor of the Hebrews.

He rolled over onto his back and interlaced his fingers behind his head. The first grays of dawn began to lighten the room, but still he waited. He must think. Today he would go to the fields to see how the Hebrews were being treated, but he would go as himself, not in disguise, lest the Egyptian master put him to work in the fields. But after that, what would he do with his findings?

He already knew that the Egyptians treated his people cruelly. He had nearly jumped from the chariot on his trip to Rameses when he saw that slave being beaten. Would his visit to the fields make things worse for his people? Would his mother care if confronted with the cruelties?

He needed to ask someone, but he'd already spoken to his siblings and they had given him no solid advice. They did not know what it was like to live here. To have servants attend him day and night. To spend countless hours learning to speak, read, and write in Egyptian and Hebrew and some of the Canaanite tongues. Or to memorize all of the gods and goddesses and what each one represented to the Egyptian people, all the while considering the knowledge nonsense.

Pink light replaced the gray, and he could no longer lie abed. He rose, and his servant Donkor greeted him.

"Good day to you, my lord." He held out a robe for Moses, and he slipped his arms through it.

Moses moved to the window, where a low table was already spread with fruit and nuts and cheese to break his fast. He sipped from a silver cup and tasted his favorite tea. He sat and ate a handful of nuts, still pondering his day. "Donkor."

"Yes, my lord." The servant hurried to his side.

"I want you to ready my best riding clothes and call for

my chariot. I am going out today and will also require a walking stick."

"A walking stick, my lord?" The servant raised a brow.

"Yes. Make sure it is strong."

"Yes, my lord."

The servant left, and Moses continued to eat in silence. Why had he thought to bring such a thing? He had not planned to walk about the fields, only ride past them. It was safer that way. But the more he thought on it, the more sense it made. From his chariot, he would not be able to see things as easily as he would if he walked about. And this time he would not walk defenseless.

Donkor soon returned with Moses' riding clothes and helped him dress. A few moments later, Moses moved through the halls, walking stick in hand, and took the chariot reins from his driver. "I'm going alone today," he said at the man's curious look.

"Very well, my lord." The man stepped away from the horse, and Moses mounted the chariot. He flicked the reins, and the horse began its slow trot through the streets of Thebes.

He drove his chariot onto a barge and crossed the Nile, then turned north toward the fields near the land of Goshen. He knew his people worked Egyptian land, but by the time they finished for the day, their own fields often lay fallow for lack of time and energy to plant and harvest for themselves.

His jaw clenched at the thought. His muscles were often tense of late. His mother would tell him to visit the palace massage room and have the tension worked from his shoulders. But he felt as though that would be a betrayal to his people. How could he continue to enjoy the pleasures of Egypt while those he loved suffered?

But did he love them? His sister and brother, surely, though he barely knew them. And he did not know his nephews or any of the younger children. He should have his own children by now. But he found the thought of marrying his half sister appalling and marrying a different Egyptian nearly as bad.

What was wrong with him?

Anxiety grew along with his impatience, and he flicked the reins to go faster once he was outside of the city. The fields where slaves moved about planting crops appeared in the distance. He slowed his chariot and pulled to a sandy knoll away from the furrowed field.

The sand stretched in front of him, useless land that could hold no viable plants, yet slaves were digging as though searching for better soil beneath it. Did his mother expect the Hebrews to cultivate in sand?

He pulled up to a copse of trees and tied his horse to a large branch. He patted its nose. "Wait here," he whispered, though he wondered why he bothered to talk to a horse that couldn't respond.

He took his walking stick and moved closer to the sand. As he neared the rise, he saw an Egyptian beating a Hebrew slave. He glanced about, but the other slaves were working the sand and the soil some distance away. Why was the Egyptian beating this man so far from the others?

He drew around behind the Egyptian, careful not to catch his eye, glancing about as he went. His nerves heightened and a trickle of sweat beaded his brow. His face flushed, and he knew it was not from the sun.

The man's cries filled the air as the whip came down hard

on his bare back. Welts appeared on his brown skin, blood spurting from open wounds. But the Egyptian did not stop. And the man could do nothing but cover his head and kneel in the sand, wincing and writhing in pain with every blow.

Moses felt his blood boil, a slow burn within him. He looked about again, but the other slaves and taskmasters were too far away to see what was happening. Would a fellow Egyptian have stopped him?

*You can stop him. Just shout and tell the Egyptian who you are. You can control this.*

Moses heard the words in his head, but his heart pounded and his anger grew as he slowly moved toward the man. He stopped just behind him, drew a breath, and thought again about speaking, but fear that the Egyptian would turn on him before realizing who he was stopped his words.

In a heartbeat, without thinking, he lifted his stick and struck the Egyptian hard on the head. The whip fell out of his hands, and the man fell sideways to the ground. Moses cautiously knelt at his side, but by the glazed look in his eyes, he knew he had killed him.

The Hebrew man crouched low as though awaiting the next blow, despite the sound he must have heard. The crack of Moses' stick as it had connected with the man's head still rang in his own ears.

What had he done?

He glanced around again, saw that the Hebrew still knelt unmoving. Was he also dead?

Moses dragged the Egyptian away until they were on the other side of the rise, out of sight. Heart pounding faster now, he tossed the stick aside and quickly burrowed into the sand with both hands, digging deeper, deeper. Sweat poured down his back, and he kept looking up and around him. No one in sight except the dead Egyptian.

He dug faster. Was it deep enough to cover him yet? He dragged the body toward the shallow pit and sighed. He would have to leave a mound of sand over him. He longed for help, or at least a bucket to lift the sand, but he had no tools in the chariot. He had not intended to kill a man today.

He covered the last bit of the Egyptian's skin, stood, and looked about once again. Dare he check on the Hebrew? He should help the man if he was hurt badly enough—take him to Miriam. But he dared not even step over the rise lest someone see him and question him.

He turned about, satisfied that he was alone, and walked back to the waiting chariot. He left the bloodied stick in the sand.

# SEVENTEEN

Moses slept fitfully that night. How was it possible? Had he truly killed that man? *Oh, God in heaven, what have I done?* Had anyone seen him? But no. He had made sure that no one was near. Surely no Egyptian noticed. The other overseers had been with the other slaves. This one was off by himself with the Hebrew he'd been beating.

What had the Hebrew done? He turned that thought over in his mind. Probably nothing. One thing he had noticed over the years in Pharaoh's court was that everything seemed to provoke these Egyptians to hate the Hebrews. They could be beaten for any reason. And that shouldn't be.

He rose quickly, tossing the covers aside, and dressed without aid. He would go out again and visit his brothers and see more. Maybe he could speak to the Egyptians in the fields. Command them to be kinder. Would they listen to him? He *was* Pharaoh's son, after all. He should have some authority, whether they knew it or not. He didn't have his mother's approval, but he did not care. She did not need to know. And if he could keep Thutmose from finding out as well, all the better.

He strode from his rooms, called for his chariot, and headed to the same fields he had been at the day before. He would avoid the place where he'd buried the Egyptian. He couldn't bear to look on it again. As it was, he would long have nightmares over his actions.

Miriam moved through the city of Goshen, jar atop her head. Elisheba walked at her side, sometimes falling behind her as they maneuvered through the narrow streets.

"Aaron is worried about Moses," Elisheba said as they broke from the crowded houses onto the road that led to the Nile.

Miriam looked at her sister-in-law, then focused again on the road. "How so?"

"He heard a rumor on his way in from the fields yesterday." She shook her head. "Aaron believes Moses will be our leader one day, but he still feels responsible for the people and even for Moses."

Miriam stopped, holding the jar in place, and faced Elisheba. "What rumor?" She knew Aaron felt the need to protect and lead, despite the fact that she'd been doing that for him since the loss of their parents.

"Some of the men say they saw an Egyptian kill another Egyptian—one of the taskmasters who was beating a Hebrew. The Hebrew caught glimpses of the man, but he didn't know him. He remained crouched in the sand, afraid for his life. As it is, he barely survived the beating."

Miriam stifled a gasp. "What Egyptian would kill another

Egyptian? Unless they had words with one another. Perhaps these barbarians act that way sometimes."

Elisheba shook her head. "The Hebrew who was beaten said there were no words spoken. The one Egyptian came up behind the other and hit him over the head with a stick. It killed him instantly."

"He saw a lot for burying his head in the sand."

"I think he heard a lot. Aaron believes him, but no one actually saw it happen." Elisheba started forward again. They needed water, and the day's chores would not wait for them to gossip in the road.

"What does Aaron think of it all?" Miriam's mind churned as she tried to process such a thing. Then a sudden realization hit her. "Moses was going to inspect the fields yesterday to see how things were going with our people."

Elisheba nodded. "Uh-huh. That's what Aaron fears."

"Why didn't he come to us last night and tell us this? He should have told Jephunneh right away." Irritation spiked. Sometimes having a sister-in-law was like having a friend, and other times she felt displaced by her.

"He intended to talk to him today when they are with the sheep. He didn't want to assume without thinking it over." How defensive Elisheba sounded.

Miriam shrugged her sister-in-law's tone aside. Of course she would defend her husband. Miriam would like to take him to task, but his wife was the protective sort. A good trait, but sometimes, when Miriam watched her with her sons, she wondered if Elisheba was too protective. Nadab and Abihu were spoiled, and she feared Eliezer and Ithamar would follow in their footsteps.

"If Moses was the one who killed the man, he could

be in danger if word gets out. If the palace gets word of it . . ." Fear crept up her spine. She could not protect Moses in the palace. She could do nothing. He was old enough to know better, and he would be the one to answer for his actions.

But if he had killed an Egyptian, how could God ever use him to lead their people away from this awful place of slavery? Had he just ruined his chances to make any real change in the land?

They reached the river, and she dipped her jar into the water and lifted it again to her head. *Oh, Moses, my brother, what have you done?*

⚊⚊⚊

He stopped near a different line of trees and tied his horse to a large branch. Hebrew slaves were spread out over the field, with Egyptian overseers moving up and down the rows, watching with waiting whips. He moved away from them toward the back of the field. He glanced behind him. The Egyptians were at the other end. Good.

He looked about, seeing the men and women hoeing the ground. Backbreaking work at the pace they kept. No doubt a pace set by Egypt. The thought caused anger to flare within him again. When had he grown so angry with the very people who had saved his life?

He could not think about that now. He was not of Egypt. He was Hebrew. And somehow he needed to gain the trust of the Hebrews, not only that of his brother and sister.

He turned at the sound of struggling to see two men fighting without a word. No doubt if they yelled, they would draw attention to themselves. He stepped closer. Clearly, one man had the upper hand and continually struck the other with his fist.

Moses came nearer, wishing he had his stick to protect himself from an accidental blow. He raised his voice just loud enough to be heard. "Why do you strike your companion?" he asked the man beating the other.

The man whirled about. Stopped short. But his right hand still clung to the collar of the other man's tunic. He looked Moses up and down, recognition filling his gaze. "Who made you a prince and a judge over us?" He sneered. "Do you mean to kill me as you killed the Egyptian?"

Moses stared at the man, his fellow Hebrew. But it was not concern for his people he felt in that moment. Fear snaked through him, a living thing. Surely if this man had seen and recognized him, it would not be long before everyone in Pharaoh's palace knew what he'd done.

If they didn't already know.

He stood unmoving as the other man tried to break free. The one who seemed to be in the wrong, the one who'd identified him, stared him down, not speaking. Finally, he darted a glance toward the end of the field where the overseers had gone. He dropped his hold and returned to work, and Moses turned to see two Egyptians heading in his direction.

He slowly moved in the direction from which he had come, careful not to show haste lest they see his guilt. He was dressed as a prince, so surely they would respect that. But when he drew near his chariot, he sprinted the rest of the way, untied the horse from the tree branch, hopped into the cart, and sped over the sands toward the palace.

He could not stay here. Could he even return to his rooms?

Should he go to Miriam and Aaron for provisions? No. His presence there would put them in danger. The less Hatshepsut remembered his family, the better.

As he approached the palace and left his chariot and horse at the stables, Rashida, his mother's aging servant, met him on the way to his rooms. "Moses, come with me." She motioned with her head toward a private chamber near the cooking rooms. He followed like a young child.

She closed the door but did not have a lamp with her. Darkness enveloped them except for slits of light coming through the sides of the door. "You must go, my boy. Thutmose has heard what you did to the Egyptian yesterday. He is seeking to kill you."

Moses swallowed hard. He would need provisions. His robe at least and a staff for walking. He should have kept his horse.

"And my mother?" The thought that Thutmose might kill him did not surprise him, for his half brother had always hated his relationship to Hatshepsut. Though Moses suspected that he hated Hatshepsut's co-regency with him more. Rumors abounded that Thutmose wanted full rights to ruling the kingdom.

"As far as I can tell, she does not know. She would not allow Thutmose to harm you. But Thutmose knows, and he will do all he can to find you and kill you before your mother can stop him." Rashida touched his hand. "She is very fond of you, Moses, as are all who have served her. But now you must go. Do not go to your people, or Thutmose will find you and kill not only you but them as well. You must flee far away where he will not travel. To the hill country or beyond. And do not return as long as Thutmose lives. It is not safe."

"I need provisions."

"I have made a sack of food for you. It is here." She handed it to him.

"And my robe? A staff? A horse?"

She handed him a robe that was not Egyptian, something she must have gotten from one of the Hebrews long ago. "Wear it over your princely garb for now. There is a tunic in the bottom of the sack. You can change on the way."

He slipped his arms into the sleeves, hefted the sack onto his shoulders, and took the staff she handed him. She had thought of everything. Except a horse. Would this journey be on foot, then?

"I do not recommend you try to take a horse," she said as if reading his thoughts. "It is not safe to return to the stables. Word is spreading fast among the servants. This is why I gathered what I could. I will check to see if anyone is about. Then you must go out the back way and follow the path of the Nile until you are well past Memphis. Once you are away from both major cities, cross over the Nile and hurry as quickly as you can through Goshen and leave Egypt. But stay to the shadows. If you are seen in this cloak, you may be mistaken for a slave who is running away, and that will be no better for you." She cupped his cheek. "You are a dear boy." Though he was forty years old, she still considered him like a son. "I will miss you terribly."

Emotion filled his throat, and for a moment he could not speak. "And I you." He swallowed. "Please get word to my brother and sister that I am gone. I may never see them again."

Rashida nodded. "I will do what I can."

She opened the door a crack, peered out, and motioned for him to follow. He did so without a word. When they stood at the door that led to the road away from Thebes, he kissed her cheek in parting, fighting a host of emotions, and fled.

# EIGHTEEN

Ten Years Later
1476 BC

Miriam bent over the clay pot and lost what little food she had eaten the night before. She wiped her mouth with a piece of linen and lay again on her pallet, one hand covering the slight rise in her middle. The fact of her pregnancy still baffled her. It had been so many years since her girls were born that she'd given up any thought of having another. She was already a grandmother! How was it possible?

And yet like the matriarch Sarah, though she was not nearly as old as Sarah, here she carried another child. *Please, Adonai, let it be a boy this time.* Jephunneh needed a son. Though he had never complained about having daughters, she still wanted to give him a son. She just never expected that such a thing could be a possibility again.

She closed her eyes, willing her mind to accept the fact that it was past dawn and she must rise. She glanced beside her. Jephunneh had already risen and likely left for the day. He had taken to allowing her to sleep. How she loved this gentle, godly man! He shared her love for and faith in the

God of their fathers. He even believed in her dreams, though she often doubted herself.

She slowly rose and silently thanked Elisheba for making enough bread for Jephunneh and herself. She would begin grinding for the evening meal, but for now, she ate the left-over bread that Jephunneh had placed in a clay pot on a high shelf, where mice could not reach it, and had a bit of cheese to go with it.

A knock sounded on the side door that joined their house with Aaron and Elisheba's.

"Come in," Miriam called around a mouthful of bread. She took a drink from a goatskin flask and tied it shut again.

Elisheba entered with her water jar and set it on the ground. "Good, you are up. Are you able to gather water today?" She had taken to making two trips to the river, one on Miriam's behalf, something for which Miriam felt continual gratitude mingled with a dose of guilt.

"Yes. I cannot allow you to continue to do my work for me." Her stomach would eventually settle. It had to.

"If you are sure." Elisheba looked unconvinced.

"I am sure." Miriam swallowed the last soft round of cheese and took one more sip of water, then stood. She grabbed her jar from the floor, where it still held some of yesterday's water. She poured what was left into another jar, then followed El-isheba to the door. A bit of queasiness made her pause, but she fell into step with her sister-in-law, determined to ignore it.

They walked along in silence for a few moments, then stopped abruptly as they rounded a bend and heard the sound of running feet approaching. They glanced at each other and hurried to the side of the road, attempting to hide in the shadows.

"Who could it be?" Elisheba whispered.

Miriam shook her head. "Whoever it is, they are coming from the palace. No one has come to us from that direction since Rashida told us of Moses' escape from Egypt." How long ago that seemed. Ten years had passed since word had come to them that Thutmose wanted to kill her brother for killing an Egyptian slave master.

An ache that wouldn't leave settled in her chest as the person running drew closer. She peered at the young man, an Egyptian, and felt her stomach sicken again. Was he alone?

Hiding seemed like the best thing to do, but a moment later she stepped into the road, suddenly braver than she'd thought. Elisheba gasped behind her and did not follow.

"You there!" Miriam called. "Why are you running?"

The young man skidded to a stop. He looked at her boldly but not without a hint of respect. "I am the son of Rashida. She sent me to find Miriam, sister of Moses."

Miriam stared at him, not sure whether to believe him. It was possible that Rashida had a family, but she had never spoken of them. "How do I know you are Rashida's son?"

The young man bowed. "My mother is the one who helped Moses escape many years ago. She is too old to run from the palace to tell the news, but she wanted Miriam to know."

"I am Miriam," she said, deciding to believe him.

"To know what?" Elisheba asked, coming up beside her. So now she had courage?

Miriam tamped down the urge for sarcasm. Her sister-in-law had done much for her over the past number of weeks. That she was more timid than Miriam was not a surprise. That she was suddenly bolder was.

"To know that Queen Hatshepsut has passed into the underworld."

"What?" Miriam's head felt light.

"They found her in her room before dawn. My mother suspects . . ." He glanced around. "She suspects that the queen may have been poisoned."

Miriam put a hand to her mouth. She would not be surprised if the man's words were true. Thutmose had resented Hatshepsut's co-regency ever since he came of age. Now with Moses gone these ten years, he had no rival. Had he been behind her death?

"Have they any proof?" Miriam pulled the jar from her head and held it between them like a shield.

The man shook his head. "None that I'm yet aware of. My mother has her suspicions, but she dares not say. It was a risk for her to send me to you. But your people will hear of it eventually, so she wanted you to know of the queen's passing . . . especially given your family's relationship to her."

"Thank you. Please, thank her as well for me." Miriam gave him a slight nod.

He turned to head back toward the palace. "I will."

As they watched him run in the opposite direction, Miriam turned to Elisheba. "I wonder if Thutmose will make things harder for us now. Without Hatshepsut to protect our family, we may find ourselves and our children treated as all of the other slaves."

Elisheba's face paled as they walked toward the river. "I don't think I can handle working the fields or making bricks."

Miriam pressed a hand to her middle. "Nor I." But she could not think about that now. There would be a time of mourning for the queen, the embalming, and the many details involved in an Egyptian burial before they laid her to rest in the Valley of the Kings.

There was some comfort in that thought, little though it was.

―※―

Miriam rubbed her lower back and stood for a moment to stretch. In the six months since Hatshepsut's death, Thutmose had taken no time to mourn for her, and he had quickly put an end to the privileges Moses' family had enjoyed while she lived.

Now the field stretched before Miriam, an endless row of rocks that needed moving out of the way in order for planting to begin. Memories of her days in the fields with her mother as a young child surfaced, and she placed a protective hand on her middle, where the babe had grown large. She would deliver soon, but she would not be allowed to rest long afterward. She wiped her brow with her sleeve, caught sight of the taskmaster beating a woman in the distance, and bent forward once again, forcing back the urge to weep.

*Oh, Adonai, how long?* They had suffered for generations in this land, but she had not fully realized how privileged she had been to weave for the queen rather than lift rocks in the blazing sun.

She hefted one in her arms and carried it to the dip in the land just before the tree line. Rocks were piled high enough to make half a wall, and yet the ground was still filled with them. She walked back as quickly as she could, glancing at Elisheba, whose youngest son, Ithamar, helped her with the same work. How were they supposed to grind grain to feed their families or weave cloth for clothes? Very few of the women were allowed to remain in the city during the day, the time when most of the chores must be done.

Miriam sighed as she lifted another rock, the grit of dirt and sweat filling her face and dripping into her eyes. Again she swiped at the sweat. How she wished her daughters could work beside her with their little ones, but they were working a different field, and she had no way of knowing whether or not they were safe. Would they feel the tip of the taskmasters' leather whips? Or their abuse?

Fear grew within her, and her heart pounded. There had been rumors—too many of late—that some of the Egyptians had ruined some of their women. Because the men were separated from the women, there was nothing the female slaves could do against them, even though they cried out from the ditches, where the men did what they wanted with them.

Could such a thing happen to her daughters? Her granddaughters? She looked at her swollen belly. What of her once the child was born? Would they abuse a nursing mother?

She shuddered, keeping her head down as she continued to work. *How long, O Lord?* Her prayers had become constant, her despair deepening. Even at night, she didn't dream as she once did of deliverance. All hope that Moses would somehow play a part in setting them free had vanished with him, and the only dream she had had since then told her he was living in the land of Midian.

Midian. The land of Abraham's descendants through his concubine Keturah. A land so far from Egypt, she wondered if her brother even remembered them. Had he found a wife among their people? Would he tell his children of his people left to die in this cursed land?

Oh, to flee as he had and never return! One man alone

might have a chance, as Moses did, but to take a large family or a tribe would be noticed. Even if they tried to leave one or two at a time to escape to the hills, the Egyptians would soon be wise to their actions and pursue them.

A fierce pain in her back made her gasp, and she stood again, rubbing it, looking here and there to be sure she was not seen taking a break. Water breaks were allowed at certain times, but little else.

The babe did not like this labor and was protesting loudly with his or her kicks to Miriam's back. Her girls had kicked her most harshly in her middle, but this child seemed determined to ignite pain along her spine.

She glanced toward the sky, praying the day was almost done, but the sun was still too close to the middle of the sky. Several more hours of agony awaited her. Then she could go home and lie upon her pallet or perhaps sit upon the birthing stool. Something told her it would not be long now. The thought brought both terror and relief, for to be done carrying the child meant a few days of respite, but the upcoming delivery would not be without suffering.

# NINETEEN

The house lamps remained lit long into the night while Elisheba, Janese, and Lysia kept water and blankets warm and coaxed Miriam to bear down on the birthing stones when the time was right. Jephunneh had remained with Aaron and his sons, leaving the women to attend Miriam.

"I see the head," Elisheba said, kneeling in front of Miriam. "One or two more good pushes."

Miriam bore down as Janese swabbed her forehead with a cool cloth. "You're almost there, Ima." She touched Miriam's shoulder and squeezed.

Miriam stifled a scream lest she disturb the neighbors, who desperately needed their sleep, or any Egyptian who might be near. Fears of a resurgence of killing baby boys niggled at the back of her mind, and she almost prayed for another girl, but she so longed for a son for Jephunneh.

A baby's cry broke through her thoughts.

"It's a boy!" Elisheba said, holding the child for her to see. "Lysia, please clean him up while I tend to your mother."

Lysia took her baby brother and washed him in warm

water, careful to salt his limbs, then swaddled him in the soft linen Miriam had managed to weave in the night when sleep eluded her. Elisheba encouraged her to lie on her pallet. Lysia brought the baby to her, and she placed him at her breast.

"What will you name him, Ima?" Janese asked, kneeling beside her. "He's beautiful."

Miriam beamed, the sense of pride and mother love filling her as it had the first time she had given birth. Did a mother ever lose such a feeling? She glanced at her daughters. No. A mother never stopped loving her children, no matter their age.

"His name is Caleb," she said, bending forward to plant a kiss on his downy forehead.

"It is a good name," Lysia said. "Abba will be pleased."

Miriam smiled at them. "You both should return to your homes and get some rest before dawn. Work will not wait for you. Thank you for helping me."

"We would not have missed it." Janese bent to kiss her, followed by Lysia. "We will stop by again tomorrow."

"I will sleep here tonight," Elisheba said. "I do not wish to wake the men." She had pulled Jephunneh's pallet to another side of the room, and once the girls left, she lay upon it. Miriam heard her soft snores come sooner than she expected, but working as hard as they did, few of them had trouble falling and staying asleep.

Miriam looked into Caleb's perfect face and felt the soft tug of his mouth against her breast. Her milk released, and she relaxed into the cushions, closing her eyes. Both of them would sleep, and she would lay him beside her in the basket she had prepared.

She would treasure these moments, for they would flee

too quickly. That was always the way of life. Birth seemed to take forever to come, but then life swept by in the blink of an eye and soon death's shadows fell upon them all. The cycle could not be broken, and the realization that she could not keep this child small forever brought a pang of sadness to her heart. How she had missed this!

And she would miss it even more once he was weaned and went off to the fields with his father. She would have so little time to train him before Jephunneh would take over his learning. It would not be the same as it had been with the girls. She missed him already! Tears filmed her eyes and she blinked them away. How silly to grow so sentimental when he was so new! She had several years to enjoy him, to spend time with only him. No one could take this time from her, and she thanked God for the way he had created women and given them this blessing.

Birthing was hard, but the child who came from the suffering brought great joy. She smiled, grateful. Despite all of the hardships of slavery, this one thing was a gift to be treasured.

＊

Jephunneh returned to their home the following week, on the eighth day after Caleb's birth. In privacy he circumcised the boy, and Miriam quickly bandaged the area and nursed him to keep him quiet. Jephunneh knew enough of Abraham's covenant to keep what they had been taught, but Miriam had not seen a circumcision since her father had done it for Moses.

She would remain unclean for Jephunneh to touch for a time yet, but she could no longer stay away from working the fields, so the day after Caleb's circumcision, with him strapped to her back, Miriam headed to the fields. She carried the basket as well, in case he grew too heavy, and moved through the rows, this time planting grain. How glad she was to know this field had been cleared. She had arrived in time to plant instead of lift heavy weight that could cause her problems, for she was not yet healed from the birth.

She lifted her gaze heavenward, thankful for this small grace, such as it was. *I only wish there was grace enough for all of us to be free of this harsh labor.* It was a prayer, but was she the only one doing the praying? Were there no others who cried out to God because of this captivity?

Jephunneh prayed with her every chance he could. She knew Aaron and Elisheba prayed, and her daughters had been taught to do the same, but did the rest of the people even know how to talk to the Almighty One? Was she praying as she ought?

*Do You hear my prayers?*

Guilt filled her for even asking. Jephunneh trusted God to hear. But when year after year went by and God did not act on their behalf, she struggled to believe. Abraham had talked to God, and He had appeared to Isaac and Jacob as well. But since the days of Joseph and the deaths of their fathers, God had been silent.

How did one believe in a God they could not see? The Egyptians worshiped and prayed to all kinds of gods made of wood and stone, covered in fine gold, and they prospered at every turn. While the Hebrews, whose God was unseen, suffered terrible cruelty.

*Why, Adonai? Why do Your people suffer and You do not see? Why do You not act?* Why did she bother to ask Him?

She plucked another handful of seed from the sack at her

side and tossed it into the groove that had been made in the dirt, then stomped dirt over it with her foot. Caleb nestled against her back.

Her prayers, which had become like breath, suddenly tasted like dust in her mouth. What actual good did it do to pray to the Unseen One? If He did not answer, why should she keep asking?

Abraham had waited twenty-five years for the answer to God's promise, and Joseph had waited twenty-two years to be reunited with his family.

Her thoughts betrayed her, but a moment later she pushed them away. Abraham and Joseph had not waited through over four hundred years of slavery. They had not been born slaves, though Joseph had been one for a time. Still, he had not lived and died a slave as her newborn son would.

The thought brought a pang to her middle as she continued working amidst her tumultuous thoughts. How she longed for God to act. If only prayer would truly move Him to do just that.

# TWENTY

### Three Months Later

Miriam rose early to grind grain while Caleb slept. Jephunneh had already left to tend the sheep along with the other men who had headed to the fields. The sound of the grindstone filled the predawn air, and a knock sounded softly on her door.

Miriam stopped, listening. The knock came again, so she rose, checked on Caleb, and hurried to answer. "Hava!" Her surprise came in a whisper as her very pregnant friend, who was also about to bear a belated child, waddled into the room. Miriam closed the door and led Hava to the bench. "Is everything all right?"

Hava shook her head. "I am expected in the fields, but I fear labor began in the night. The pains are closer together now, and I had to come before I needed the birthing stones. I need your help, Miriam."

"Of course. But why did you not send someone for me? I would have come to you." Miriam searched her friend's pained expression, then glanced again at Caleb. He would sleep a little longer, but she would need help if she were to deliver Hava and watch him too. "Let me send for one of my girls or Elisheba."

Hava nodded but said nothing.

"I will get Elisheba. She is closer." Miriam stood and walked to the door that joined their house with Aaron's.

Elisheba was thankfully still at home and came to kneel at Hava's side. "You are farther along than I thought," she said after a quick examination. "Let me get the stones."

"You will both be late for the fields." Fear filled Hava's gaze. "I couldn't ask my sister for the same reason. With our parents gone, there is no one else to watch our youngest children. So I left her to watch them and came here. I hoped . . . that is, I know things have changed for you, but perhaps this one time Adonai will smile on us because of your family and not let the Egyptians notice our absence."

Miriam took hold of Hava's arm and walked her around the small room, stopping when a contraction overtook her. There was no sense in sitting on the stones too soon, and Hava still had a little time. "You need not fear. Our God will watch over you. And we will stay until the little one is safely born."

Elisheba assured Hava of the same, then went to finish grinding the grain and hurriedly set the bread in the oven. Birth took energy, and when she was done, Hava would need food. Miriam sent Elisheba a look of thanks as they paced the room in silence.

How different life would be if families could celebrate a birth with singing and laughter. But the town of Goshen lay in ghostly quiet now as the Hebrews took their places in the cities and fields of Pharaoh long before the sun fully rose in the sky. Except for a handful of the sick or injured or women in labor, no one roamed the streets or occupied the houses.

"Ohhh!" Hava's soft groan and urgent nod sent Miriam for the birthing stones. Hava settled upon them, and within the hour another son was born in Miriam's home.

"A boy," Miriam said, holding the child up for Hava to see.

"Joshua," Hava said, her smile thin, exhaustion heavy upon her brow. She leaned back against the cushions that Elisheba had placed behind her, and Miriam took the boy while Elisheba tended to Hava.

"Joshua and Caleb will grow up together and become good friends," Miriam predicted as she swaddled the child. No one answered her, and as she lifted the tiny form in her arms, she turned to see Elisheba's face blanch white. "What's wrong?" Her words were a soft hiss.

"She struggled to finish the delivery, and she's bleeding too much. I think we're losing her." Elisheba pointed to a pool of blood, more than should normally accompany a birthing.

Miriam placed the baby on her pallet and rushed to find whatever linens she could. But no amount of effort would stop Hava's bleeding or bring a smile to her drawn face.

"Is she breathing?" Miriam's heart pounded. They couldn't lose her. Hava had been her friend forever. Even before she'd lost her baby brother to the Nile and Egypt's wrath.

"Barely." Elisheba held Miriam's gaze. "This is what, her fourth child?"

"Her fifth. Like mine, the others are grown. She thought she was done bearing, but when her first husband died and she married Nun, he wanted a son." As any man would.

No one would expect a woman who had birthed many children to die in childbirth with her last. How had life

143

changed so much? Hava was still young. But when her husband had died at the hands of a taskmaster, she had never recovered. Even marriage to Nun, kind as he was, could not awaken her from her grief.

"Her breath sounds too shallow," Elisheba said.

"I can't get the bleeding to stop. I've run out of linens." Miriam pushed harder, trying to stop the life from flowing out of Hava. She exchanged a worried look with Elisheba.

"Let me run home to get mine." Elisheba left her alone.

Miriam moved closer to Hava's ear. "Don't leave us, Hava. You have a beautiful son. He will grow up to be a fine man with your teaching and love." *Please, Adonai.*

Hava groaned, and Miriam took that as a sign of hope.

Elisheba returned, and she took care of the food and Hava while Miriam nursed both boys. Hours passed, and Miriam felt the exhaustion weigh on her.

"You must eat more if you are going to nurse two." Elisheba handed her a piece of bread.

"Hopefully not for long." But she knew with one look that Hava had not awakened, nor had her pallor improved.

"We should send for her husband and Jephunneh," Elisheba said, taking Joshua from Miriam's arms.

"What can they do? The bleeding has slowed, but she is not awake for Nun to speak with her." Besides the fact that both men could get into trouble if they slipped away too soon.

"Her family should be here." Elisheba's insistence increased.

Miriam stepped closer to Hava. She bent low, listening for breath. Hava's chest barely rose and fell beneath her thin tunic. "We should clean her up and make a place for her family to see her."

Elisheba set the sleeping Joshua beside Caleb, who had already awakened twice and returned to nap again. "I have a fresh tunic we can dress her in."

"There is water in the barrel outside. I can't go to the river, but we can use some of the water to soak these." She pulled the soiled garments away, and the two of them hurried to cleanse the area and Hava as best they could.

"She looks like she is sleeping." Elisheba lifted Joshua and brought him to lie at his mother's side.

"Hava, look. Your son." Miriam spoke louder, wondering if Hava could hear them at all in her place between earth and Sheol. How long would she linger? Or would God heal her?

The door opened, surprising them both. Aaron stepped inside, Jephunneh close behind.

Miriam rushed into Jephunneh's arms and clung to him. "You are home."

"And glad of it," he said, smiling into her eyes.

"Earlier than normal," Aaron said. "For some reason they sent us home. It makes no sense."

Jephunneh kept one arm around her shoulders and glanced about. "What is this?"

"Hava came to me this morning. I fear she is dying, my husband," Miriam said, holding back a sob. "She has a beautiful new son, and she has not even been awake enough to hold him."

Jephunneh seemed to assess the situation. They all knew that men should not be here, but there was nothing to be done about it. They had entered without knowing a birth had taken place that day.

"I will go and get Nun and Hava's children." Jephunneh kissed the top of Miriam's head.

Aaron nodded to Elisheba, then followed Jephunneh out the door.

"Perhaps they will try to take her home." Elisheba sank onto the bench, her expression weary. "We must get food for them."

Miriam sat beside her, glancing at the two infants who would need her soon. "I don't know what to do first." She was so tired. How was it possible that just this morning her best friend stood at her door in labor, and now she lay dying on her cushions?

*Where are You, Lord?*

But as the night waned and Hava's family surrounded her, God remained silent. And Hava slipped into Sheol.

# PART THREE

Years passed, and the king of Egypt died. But the Israelites continued to groan under their burden of slavery. They cried out for help, and their cry rose up to
God. God heard their groaning, and he remembered
his covenant promise to Abraham, Isaac, and Jacob.
He looked down on the people of Israel and knew it
was time to act.

Exodus 2:23–25

# TWENTY-ONE

## THIRTY YEARS LATER
### 1446 BC

Zipporah walked to the well, her sister at her side. Dawn had brought with it the scent of rain, and clouds darkened as they hurried to draw water.

"We probably should have waited to come," Aida shouted above the rising wind. "Maybe we should turn back."

Zipporah glanced at the sky as she tightened her grip on the jar atop her head. "We need the water now." She would get it herself if Aida decided to go back. But she was not going to let a storm stop her from completing her daily tasks.

Aida quickened her pace. They arrived at the ancient well where she and her sisters had met Moses so many years before. Memories surfaced of the Egyptian who had chased away the male shepherds who always made watering their father's sheep hard for them. How long had it been?

"Are your boys with Moses today?" Aida's interruption brought her up short.

She shook her head and set the jar on the ground. The two of them pushed the stone aside and lowered their jars.

"They went off with the goats while Moses kept the sheep. Moses likes to keep them apart." Zipporah strained at the rope she had secured to the jar. Why did it seem heavier today? The wind battering her did not help.

Aida raised her jar, then waited as Zipporah lifted the full jar to her head.

"Hobab tells me that Father intends to put him in charge of all of the harvest. It is becoming too hard for Father to do everything, and with our sisters gone, he has only us."

"He is fortunate that Moses and Hobab had no family to take us to. I would not have wanted to leave Father alone." Zipporah's robe whipped about her, and she pushed into the wind. "We can talk more later." It was taking all of her strength to walk without dropping the jar. Why hadn't she waited until the wind died down?

But she liked routine, and if she was going to bake bread or make stew for their dinner tonight, water was necessary. If they postponed this daily trip, she would be behind on everything.

She squinted as they neared their father's tents and glanced at her sister as they parted ways. Inside the tent at last, she set the jar on the ground and released a deep sigh. She looked around at the large tent, moved about to straighten pillows and cushions, and fought the fear that the wind would grow too strong. Would the tent hold? Would Moses be near a cave to keep the sheep safe? Were Gershom and Eliezer far or near? They had left only yesterday, but Zipporah always hated those nights when her men did not come home.

She moved to the cooking area and sat with the grind-stone. Though no one was home to eat except her, she would make the morning bread and grind enough to make flat cakes to go with the stew this evening. Do the same things every day, she told herself. It was what she had always known.

Until Moses had entered her life.

Such a strange yet fascinating man she had married. She had not regretted her father's choice. She only wished she better understood Moses and his mysterious ways.

She moved the millstone around the grain, its grating sound drowning out the whistle of the wind. Moses had shown strength that day when they first met, and he surely knew how to defend her father's sheep. But in their marriage he had seemed too willing to acquiesce and had only opposed her once—eight days after Gershom's birth.

"You want to do what?" Zipporah had stared at Moses where he stood at the door of their tent. He could not sleep with her while she was unclean from childbirth, but he could speak.

"The boy will be named and circumcised on the eighth day after his birth. That is today." Moses shifted from foot to foot and dug his staff into the ground.

"You want to take my son and cut him? He's a baby!" Zipporah heard the pitch of her voice rise even as she lowered its volume. She did not wish to wake the boy, as he'd only been asleep a few moments.

"*Our* son," he corrected her. "It is necessary, Zipporah. It proves that our son is one of my people. It is part of the covenant God made with Abraham." His mouth twitched, and she sensed his impatience, though she knew he would not act on it. He would wait on her as he always did. Surely he would listen to reason!

"But in our clan we do not practice such a thing. I know

your father included you in the covenant, but we are not living among your people. Why does it matter?" She glanced
at her son in the basket beside her. If it wouldn't wake him,
she would pick him up and hold him close, a barrier between
them. She grabbed a pillow instead. "Please, Moses. Do not
do this."

"I have no choice." His look held resolve and a hint of
determination. And though she had argued with him a little
longer, she sensed that this was not a fight she would win.
The first time her husband wouldn't listen to her and it
would hurt their son? How could she bear it?

Zipporah shook herself. Remembering that day only
brought to mind the fact that she *had* insisted on her way
where Eliezer was concerned. Moses could circumcise their
firstborn, but she would not allow him to touch their second. Not after she had waited so long. Twenty years before
Gershom had come along and another seven before Eliezer.
Her youngest was still a child as far as she was concerned,
though Moses insisted he work alongside Gershom or himself to tend the sheep.

A sigh escaped her. She missed Eliezer's presence. She
had babied him longer than she had his brother, for she
sensed he would be her last. To bear only two sons in forty
years of marriage did not bode well for having more. She
was not old yet, but she was in no mood to bear another.
Not if it meant another argument with Moses should it be
a boy. Though it would have been nice to have a daughter
to work beside.

She rose and dipped a cup into the water jar and carried
it to the ground flour. A cutting from the souring dough
would make it rise, and when the wind died down, she would

bake it over the coals in the yard and take some to her boys and Moses in the fields, if she could find them. Though she should be weaving instead.

Suddenly she wanted to be near her family. But the wind picked up and the tent walls shuddered. Zipporah moved to the center of the tent and knelt among the cushions. And prayed.

# TWENTY-TWO

Miriam woke with a start, the dream too real. It was always the same when God spoke to her in dreams. She saw the future unfolding and then suddenly woke. She pushed up on one elbow and glanced at Jephunneh snoring at her side. There was no use in waking him, and yet . . . the dream had been so exciting, as though God was telling her that all of her prayers were about to be answered. Her mother's tikvah was about to come true.

She rose softly and tiptoed toward the window. Caleb and his wife, Netanya, slept behind a curtain in the part of the room where Aaron used to sleep, and she did not wish to disturb them either. Their family had just expanded, as Netanya had birthed Iru, their son, only three months ago.

Would Iru grow up in the Promised Land after all? Was God truly sending Moses back to them? She closed her eyes, the dream still vivid in her mind and heart. Moses walking toward Egypt, staff in hand, and Aaron rushing to meet him. Then Moses standing before Pharaoh with Aaron at his side. "Let my people go," he said to Pharaoh.

*Oh, Adonai, are You really about to set Your people free?* How could the dream mean anything else? Every other dream like this that she'd had, though it had been years since the last one, had been proven true. She had no reason to doubt that this one would be as well.

She glanced at the sky, longing for dawn's pink light so she could share her hope, her good news, with Jephunneh.

Aaron opened the front door to their small house just after dawn. Miriam and Netanya were clearing away the clay bowls from the morning's porridge, and Jephunneh and Caleb were tying their sandals.

Miriam set a bowl down and walked over to greet her brother. She stopped as he drew near, her heart beating faster at the light shining in his eyes. "You have had a vision." Didn't she know it as well as she knew her own dream?

He nodded. "And you have dreamed again."

She smiled. "He is coming home."

"Yes." Aaron took her hand and squeezed it. "God has heard our prayers."

Jephunneh joined them and gripped Aaron in a welcoming hold. "What did God tell you, my brother? We have a few moments to hear it before we leave." He glanced at Caleb, who came closer, Netanya beside him. They stood waiting, joy seeming to spread over the room.

"I had just awakened when I saw the angel of the Lord standing in the room. No one else saw him, as Elisheba assures me I was staring beyond her and did not seem to see that she stood near." He ran a hand along the back of his neck. "He told me to head toward Midian to meet Moses."

155

Netanya released a soft gasp. She and Caleb had never met Moses, but with everything Aaron and Miriam had told of him over the years, all of their children thought him a hero. But would the older members of their people remember him? Was forty years enough time for them to forget the murder he had committed and the privilege he had enjoyed in Pharaoh's house? Would they accept him?

"When do you leave?" Miriam asked, longing to hold tight to this younger brother before he headed off alone.

"I don't think our God wants me to wait. Elisheba is packing some things for me. I'm going now. I came to tell you so you would not wonder or worry." He touched Miriam's arm. "I know you don't think you do, but you worry about us too much, my sister."

She shook her head. "I do not worry." What a ridiculous thing to say of her. She grew anxious sometimes, but it never lasted. She simply cared to know that everyone she loved was well. That no one suffered under the whip of the taskmaster. That they were still safe.

"I will be careful," Aaron said, as if assuring her as well as himself. "And will trust that Moses is happy to see me. I am assuming that if God spoke to you and to me that He will also speak to our brother. Perhaps He has already done so and I will not have far to go to meet him."

Miriam searched her mind, pulling at the memory of the dream. "I think you may have farther to walk than you'd like. Moses is not likely to come willingly."

Everyone looked at her.

She raised a hand. "I didn't say he would not come. But our brother is stubborn, and I'm not sure that even God can convince him to return to us. Not after forty years away."

"But he will come, Ima? You are sure of this?" Caleb asked.

"He will come," Aaron answered for her. "Your mother and I have both seen it." He leaned forward to kiss her cheek, embraced each one of them, and opened the door. "I must get my things from Elisheba and go. Hopefully my presence will not be missed."

"We will make sure no one notices you are gone." Jephunneh placed a hand on his shoulder. "Go in peace and return quickly."

"I will."

Miriam watched him until he disappeared from sight, anxious to see what God was about to do.

# TWENTY-THREE

Moses led his father-in-law's sheep three days' journey from camp into the wilderness, looking for green pasture. To be away this long from Zipporah would not make her happy, but he had no choice. This was the life of a shepherd, which she should well know. Why, then, did she always want to argue with him? He shook his head. He would never understand her. And her insistence not to make Eliezer a son of the covenant still troubled him. Was he disobeying the Lord by ignoring this even now? Should he do as Abraham had done with Ishmael when he was grown?

He pushed the staff into the earth as the land sloped upward and led the sheep up the side of Sinai, the mountain of God. There on the first rise, a lush, grassy knoll spread before him. He led the sheep to feast and turned to survey the area. Perhaps water was not far, and surely he could find a cave big enough to shelter them should a storm begin.

He glanced behind him, making sure the sheep were not wandering, and walked a little distance away, where he caught sight of an orange glow. Was something on fire?

He drew nearer but stopped suddenly. A bush burned, yet

the fire did not consume it. Amazed, he moved slowly closer. "Why isn't the bush burning up?" he muttered to himself. He moved one step at a time, examining the bush.

"Moses! Moses!"

Moses' heart nearly stopped at the sudden realization that he was not alone. He looked around but saw no one. Was someone hiding behind the fire?

"Here I am!" Moses called out.

"Do not come any closer," the voice said. "Take off your sandals, for you are standing on holy ground."

The voice held strength and authority, unlike any human voice that he had ever heard. He quickly untied his sandals and set them aside. *Who are you?* He could not say the words aloud.

"I am the God of your fathers—the God of Abraham, the God of Isaac, and the God of Jacob."

Fear snaked up Moses' spine, and he pulled his turban down to cover his face. He was speaking to God? Had God heard his silent question?

"I have certainly seen the oppression of My people in Egypt," the Lord continued. "I have heard their cries of distress because of their harsh slave drivers. Yes, I am aware of their suffering. So I have come down to rescue them from the power of the Egyptians and lead them out of Egypt into their own fertile and spacious land. It is a land flowing with milk and honey—the land where the Canaanites, Hittites, Amorites, Perizzites, Hivites, and Jebusites now live. Look! The cry of the people of Israel has reached Me, and I have seen how harshly the Egyptians abuse them. Now go, for I am sending you to Pharaoh. You must lead My people Israel out of Egypt."

Moses trembled from head to foot at the command. His fear grew stronger at the mention of Egypt. At the memories of his life there. A life he had no desire to return to. He dared not look at the fire, but he did open his mouth, for surely God expected an answer.

"Who am I to appear before Pharaoh? Who am I to lead the people of Israel out of Egypt?" *Please, don't ask this of me.*

The Lord seemed to pause a moment, then the voice gentled as if to reassure him. "I will be with you. And this is your sign that I am the one who has sent you: when you have brought the people out of Egypt, you will worship God at this very mountain."

Everything within Moses balked at the thought of returning to his people. To Pharaoh. Was Thutmose III still Pharaoh of Egypt? Would he recognize Moses? He would surely kill him if he did.

"If I go to the people of Israel and tell them, 'The God of your ancestors has sent me to you,' they will ask me, 'What is His name?' Then what should I tell them?"

"I am who I am. Say this to the people of Israel: 'I Am has sent me to you.'"

Moses' breath stilled at the mention of God's name. I Am. The eternal one. I Am—who had no beginning or end.

"Say this to the people of Israel," the voice continued. "'Yahweh, the God of your ancestors—the God of Abraham, the God of Isaac, and the God of Jacob—has sent me to you.' This is My eternal name, My name to remember for all generations.

"Go and call together all the elders of Israel. Tell them, 'Yahweh, the God of your ancestors—the God of Abraham,

Isaac, and Jacob—has appeared to me. He told me, "I have been watching closely, and I see how the Egyptians are treating you. I have promised to rescue you from your oppression in Egypt. I will lead you to a land flowing with milk and honey—the land where the Canaanites, Hittites, Amorites, Perizzites, Hivites, and Jebusites now live."'"

Moses' lungs burned with the need to release a breath. Slowly, he finally did.

God was still speaking. "The elders of Israel will accept your message. Then you and the elders must go to the king of Egypt and tell him, 'The Lord, the God of the Hebrews, has met with us. So please let us take a three-day journey into the wilderness to offer sacrifices to the Lord our God.'

"But I know that the king of Egypt will not let you go unless a mighty hand forces him. So I will raise My hand and strike the Egyptians, performing all kinds of miracles among them. Then at last he will let you go. And I will cause the Egyptians to look favorably on you. They will give you gifts when you go so you will not leave empty-handed. Every Israelite woman will ask for articles of silver and gold and fine clothing from her Egyptian neighbors and from the foreign women in their houses. You will dress your sons and daughters with these, stripping the Egyptians of their wealth."

The task was too much. Despite his desperate fear of the Lord, he couldn't go back. He was a murderer, and he was afraid. He drew a deep breath and risked a glance at the flames. "What if they won't believe me or listen to me? What if they say, 'The Lord never appeared to you'?"

"What is that in your hand?" The Lord's voice was stronger, less gentle now. Had he angered his God?

"A shepherd's staff," Moses said, his voice barely above a whisper.

"Throw it down on the ground."

Moses obeyed and immediately jumped back from a writhing, deadly looking snake.

"Reach out and grab its tail."

Moses moved away from its head and grabbed its tail. Only a shepherd's staff remained in his hand.

"Perform this sign. Then they will believe that the Lord, the God of their ancestors—the God of Abraham, the God of Isaac, and the God of Jacob—really has appeared to you. Now put your hand inside your cloak."

Moses could not help the dubious look he directed toward the fire. But he obeyed just the same, and the moment he pulled his hand from his cloak, it was as white as snow with leprosy.

"Now put your hand back into your cloak," the Lord said, as though the leprosy meant nothing.

Moses felt his fear growing instead of abating. He hurriedly put his hand back in his cloak and removed it again. Relief filled him that his hand looked as healthy as the rest of his skin.

"If they do not believe you and are not convinced by the first miraculous sign, they will be convinced by the second sign," the Lord told him. "And if they don't believe you or listen to you even after these two signs, then take some water from the Nile River and pour it out on the dry ground. When you do, the water from the Nile will turn to blood on the ground."

Moses' heart thumped hard, and his fear would not abate despite the signs. Despite everything. He could not tell whether he feared the Lord more than he feared Egypt. He simply knew that he did not want to do this.

He risked honesty. "O Lord, I'm not very good with words. I never have been, and I'm not now, even though You have spoken to me. I get tongue-tied, and my words get tangled."

"Who makes a person's mouth? Who decides whether people speak or do not speak, hear or do not hear, see or do not see? Is it not I, the Lord? Now go! I will be with you as you speak, and I will instruct you in what to say." The voice of the Lord was firm, though Moses sensed kindness in His tone.

Why couldn't he just say yes to God? But he fought the assignment God had given him with every fiber of his being. He could not do this. "Lord, please!" he begged. "Send anyone else."

The voice of the Lord grew silent a moment, and Moses knew he had gone too far. *You are angry with me.*

"All right," God spoke, the anger Moses suspected definitely in His voice. "What about your brother, Aaron the Levite? I know he speaks well. And look! He is on his way to meet you now. He will be delighted to see you. Talk to him, and put the words in his mouth. I will be with both of you as you speak, and I will instruct you both in what to do. Aaron will be your spokesman to the people. He will be your mouthpiece, and you will stand in the place of God for him, telling him what to say. And take your shepherd's staff with you, and use it to perform the miraculous signs I have shown you."

The flames engulfing the bush disappeared, leaving Moses no chance to argue again. Or to even respond. He looked at his sandals on the ground beside him, then at the bush, fully alive and fine. Yet he knew that God had spoken to him as a man speaks with a friend. Only, Moses had been no friend. He had argued with God!

But God had given him no choice. He was to return to Egypt, like it or not. Aaron would help him, which gave him some comfort. But knowing that he was leaving his home of forty years to obey God in an unknown future did not leave him comforted. He wondered if God would continue to speak to him. Why should He? Who in their right mind argued with the God of the universe?

He shook his head and picked up his sandals, walking barefoot to gather the sheep. He was every kind of fool there was. But he would obey. He'd seen the leprosy. He'd seen the snake. He didn't need further proof that he was no match for the One who had made him.

# TWENTY-FOUR

Zipporah entered her father's main tent, stew pot in her arms. She set about preparing the rest of the meal for her men and her sister's family. Aida joined her with pressed raisin cakes and sticky pistachio treats to end the meal.

"They should be home soon," Aida said, glancing at the tent door. "Father said he would inspect the fields with Hobab today. They are taking longer than I expected."

Zipporah strode to the tent's opening and lifted a hand to shade her eyes, looking in both directions that her men had gone. Dust swirled in the distance, and she heard the bleating of goats. Her boys were back!

She hurried to meet them and helped as they herded the goats into the pen. "Did you find good pasture today?" They'd been gone three days, and she drank in the sight of them.

"We did," Eliezer said, coming to hug her. He smelled of the earth and goats, familiar scents that warmed her. She missed her days as a shepherdess. "We saw Abba rounding a bend not far behind us, though he approaches the well from the opposite direction."

"Well, the food is ready, so as soon as you can, meet us in your grandfather's tent." She tousled her youngest son's hair, touched Gershom's arm in greeting, and moved past them to greet her husband.

She sat near the well, waiting for his approach. When he saw her, he slowed. The sheep continued toward her. She jumped up to greet him, but at the look in his eyes, she paused. Something had happened. He drew closer and bent to shove the stone from the well. She helped him water the sheep in silence, saying nothing even as they took the animals to their pen.

When he had inspected each animal and closed the latch of the gate, she held her arms akimbo and met his gaze. "Why so silent, my husband? What has happened to you?"

He looked at her then, but his gaze did not linger. He studied the mountains beyond them. "I will tell you all when I speak to your father."

Irritation spiked at his lack of response. "Tell my father? I am your wife. Should you not be telling me first?"

He shook his head. "No. This must be told to your father. If he approves, then I will know it is from the Lord."

He stepped around her and headed to her father's tent as she followed, dumbstruck. He had never acted this way in their entire forty years of marriage. She picked up her skirts as his pace quickened. Angry words were on the tip of her tongue, but she held back at the sight of Gershom and Eliezer entering the tent ahead of them.

The rest of the men had already arrived, and Moses greeted her father. They would talk after they ate, which infuriated her further. Why would he not tell her? They'd had plenty of time as they inspected the sheep. There was no reason to keep anything from her. Was her father's blessing or whatever he sought from him so important? Why?

After the meal, Zipporah cleared the food away along with Aida, who seemed oblivious to her anger. Moses lingered in the seat he always occupied, and her father sat opposite him. Hobab and the boys made up the circle in the center of the tent, while she and Aida took up their spindles in the corners.

"I can tell you have something to say to me," her father said, accepting his evening pipe from Aida. He drew in the sweet scent before exhaling in a cloud of smoke.

"I met God today." Moses' words caused both of her sons to gasp, but they did not speak.

"Did you now?" Her father's gaze seemed to bore into Moses. "What did He say to you?"

"He wants me to return to my people. To Egypt." Moses cleared his throat.

"Did you see Him in a vision?" Jethro asked.

Zipporah leaned closer, all interest in her spindle lost.

"He appeared to me in a bush that burned but did not burn up." The look of awe on her husband's face was unlike anything she had ever seen from him. "I did not see Him, but I heard His voice."

"And He asked you to return to Egypt." Jethro drew on his pipe. "Or should I say, you have been given a command?"

Moses nodded. "Please let me return to my relatives there. I don't even know if they are still alive." He paused. "He did not give me a choice."

Her father pondered the matter, though he never moved his gaze from assessing Moses. Zipporah stared at her husband, unable to move. She waited, her breath drawn tight within her.

"Go in peace," her father said. "This is obviously of the Lord."

Moses released a deep sigh. "Thank you, my father."

Jethro nodded in silence. Moses stood and left the tent. Zipporah hurried after him.

Inside their own tent moments later, Zipporah confronted Moses. "How could you keep this from me? Just because my father is a priest doesn't mean he should make our decisions! You dishonor me!" One look at his face and she knew her words were louder than she'd intended.

Moses faced her and lightly gripped her arms. He released a deep sigh. "Do not argue with me, wife. I have spent the entire day in an argument with God. I do not need another one with you." He released her and moved to his pallet. "You will need to pack enough to travel to Egypt. The boys will go with us." He untied his sandals and removed them. "You can begin packing in the morning. We will leave the next day."

"Are you out of your mind?" Zipporah stood above him, shaking. This could not possibly be happening.

Moses lifted his head, rubbed a hand over his beard. "I told you. God gave me no choice."

"You told my father, not me."

"You heard me say it. Why should I have to say it twice? The whole family heard it together." He removed his robe and lay down, his face to the tent wall. "Let it be, Zipporah. I'm tired and I am done talking."

Zipporah huffed. "Well, I'm not!" But she did not press him further. She had lived with him long enough to know that she would get no more from him tonight.

Still, she would not give him the satisfaction of her body

heat. She picked up the cushions where they normally gathered as a family and dragged them to the opposite side of the tent. She pretended to sleep when Gershom and Eliezer entered to find their own pallets. Soon her men all snored, but Zipporah lay awake long into the night.

# TWENTY-FIVE

oses awoke before dawn and headed to the sheep pens before Zipporah rose from her bed. He knew she was irked with him, but he dare not reveal to her how much it had shaken him to hear God speak. Or to admit what a fool he was for arguing with the Creator! Such audacity. Why on earth did God think him capable of approaching Pharaoh when he couldn't even say the right words to his wife? And most especially to God!

He moved closer, seeing the sheep had already wakened, waiting for him. He would miss this flock. They'd become like children to him, but they were Jethro's. He could not expect to take any of them with him.

As he unlatched the gate, he moved to touch the head of a lamb when a voice spoke behind him. "Moses."

He whirled about. He knew that voice! He fell to his knees, though he saw nothing but the whisper of a cloud near the gate. "I am here."

"Return to Egypt, for all those who wanted to kill you have died."

Hadn't God just told him yesterday to return? Why must He repeat the command?

In the next moment, Moses felt enveloped by warmth and an emotion that clogged his throat. The feeling was so clearly love that he could not deny or run from it. It was as though God held him in loving arms—as his father had done so long ago.

"I will leave first thing tomorrow." They had things to pack. Surely God would know that.

But the cloud dispersed, and the presence left him without responding. Had God come simply to assure him that the Egyptians, particularly Thutmose III, were dead?

He shook himself and inspected the sheep. He would not take them out today. He would seek Jethro's permission and go to the village to find another shepherd to take his place. Hopefully Zipporah and their sons would have packed their belongings by then.

Suddenly he could not move fast enough.

⌇

Zipporah stood beside the loaded donkey, waiting as her father spoke to Moses and her sons. Aida hurried across the camp and fell into Zipporah's arms, her children trailing behind her. They had said their goodbyes the night before, but Aida was her closest sister, and parting was hard for both of them.

"I wish you were not leaving," Aida said, holding tightly to her. "I will miss you so much!"

Zipporah pulled back and swiped at a tear that had slipped down her cheek. "I can't imagine living in Egypt with people I do not know. I wish you were joining us."

They both knew such a thing was impossible. Aida glanced at her sons, who were conversing with their cousins one last time. Dawn had barely crested the eastern ridge, but by the tapping of Moses' staff against the ground, Zipporah felt his impatience to be on their way.

"Perhaps we will see each other again soon." Zipporah inclined her head toward her husband. "I think he is anxious to be off."

"I know. I just had to see you one more time. Last night wasn't enough." Aida's expression held longing and sadness, and Zipporah fought the urge to weep. She could not afford to let emotion rule her now. She had no choice but to follow Moses, and his God had told him to go.

Her father moved away from Moses and came to her. Aida stepped back as he pulled Zipporah into his arms. "My Zipporah. My firstborn. You are a child no longer that I can protect." His voice carried a hint of nostalgia, and he held her at arm's length. "Go with your husband and children. Follow the God of your husband and obey His laws. Then all will be well with you." He kissed each of her cheeks and slowly released her.

"I love you, Abba," she whispered as he pulled away. He nodded but did not seem able to say the same. His lack did not surprise her. That he'd held her close did. Her father was not a man who easily showed his feelings, much like her husband.

Why was she not used to this by now? To feel intimacy with her husband—was that too much to desire? She did not linger over the thought.

Moses stepped close and lifted her onto the donkey, whose sides bulged with sacks of their belongings. Gershom and

Eliezer walked beside her, while Moses led them, the staff in his hand. She looked back and waved to her family, taking in the sight of the camp as the light of dawn spilled over the tents. How she would miss the only home she had ever known. How could she bear to leave?

But as her home slipped from view and they descended to the valley floor between the mountains, she settled into accepting the rhythm of the donkey's strides and watched her sons, with staffs of their own, pick their way through the rocky terrain. This would be a long journey. One she was not entirely sure she was going to like.

❧

Moses walked several paces ahead of his family, feeling the urgency in each step closer to Egypt. Where only two days ago he had resisted, and even now he felt a sense of unease, he also carried the knowledge that he was returning to fulfill a mission. Perhaps even his life's true calling.

They stopped midday to rest from the sun's brilliance, and Moses sheltered his family in one of the nearby caves before assessing the landscape.

"Can I go with you, Father?" Gershom asked. He was eager, and Moses longed to oblige him, but he shook his head. "Not this time, my son. Soon."

He turned before Gershom could argue and walked several paces down an embankment where a stream trickled from the hills. They would water the donkey and eat here soon, but first he looked about, making sure no wild animals roamed near.

Satisfied that all was well, he turned to head up the slope when a wisp of cloud cover blocked his view of the cave. He stopped, hair tingling along the back of his neck.

"When you arrive in Egypt," the unmistakable voice of God said, "go to Pharaoh and perform all the miracles I have empowered you to do. But I will harden his heart so he will refuse to let the people go. Then you will tell him, 'This is what the Lord says: Israel is my firstborn son. I commanded you, "Let my son go, so he can worship me." But since you have refused, I will now kill your firstborn son!'"

Moses stared as the cloud disappeared from sight. He stood unmoving, pondering the words. So he would go to Pharaoh, whoever he was—probably Thutmose III's son or grandson—and perform the miracles of the snake, the leprosy, and the water turning into blood. God would harden Pharaoh's heart and then would kill the man's firstborn son. How long would such a thing take? A week? A month?

And how easily would he be able to get an audience with Pharaoh? He couldn't just walk into his audience chamber and demand to be heard. If everyone who wanted to kill him was dead, then everyone who once knew him was likely dead as well. He would have no advantage, no way to garner any type of favor.

Was that what God wanted? For Moses to be completely dependent on Him to work things out? Had his forty years in Midian been God's way of removing Moses' dependency on himself? He'd thought he could make a difference by killing the Egyptian, but his way had done nothing to help his people.

The thought reminded him of the shame he had carried and the pride he had fought hard to release during his years with the sheep and living in Jethro's camp. Who was he to be Israel's leader or deliverer? His mother had been wrong. He was not their tikvah. God would have to take that place in their hearts if Moses was to have any hope of leading the people out of Egypt.

But what would he find among his own people when he arrived? By God's own word, Aaron still lived. Did Miriam? What of his nephews and other relatives? And after over four hundred years of slavery, would the people follow their God out of Egypt? Did they still believe in God alone? Or had they adopted the gods of the Egyptians as the objects of their worship?

He glanced up the incline and saw Gershom watching him. Too many questions flooded his mind, but now was not the time to answer them. He motioned to his son to bring his family to drink of the water and continue on. To what end? He could not answer.

# TWENTY-SIX

Miriam squatted beside the clay oven in the courtyard they shared with Aaron's family and pulled the day's bread from it.

Elisheba opened the door from her adjoining home and entered. "The stew smells good," she said. "Though I do miss the days when we could add lamb or goat to it."

"Barley makes a good replacement though." Miriam pushed to her feet, the loaves in her hands. "At least the Egyptians allow us to eat whatever we grow. The labor is hard, but I am grateful we are not hungry."

"On that we can agree." Elisheba sank onto a crude bench while Miriam set the loaves to cool on a long, level stone nearby. "I wonder how long Aaron is going to be gone." A hint of anxiety filled her voice.

"As long as it takes to find Moses." Miriam sat beside her. "If our God told Aaron to go, then He will be with Aaron along the way. I suspect God told Moses to come home the same way He told Aaron to meet him. Perhaps they are meeting even now."

"Perhaps." Elisheba sounded unconvinced.

Miriam patted her sister-in-law's knee. "Don't fret, my sister. We must be strong for the other women of the camp. If God is bringing Moses home, then perhaps our deliverance is not far off. We must prepare our hearts to accept this momentous change, for it will not be like anything we have ever known."

Elisheba offered Miriam a smile. "You are right, as always. Do you think Moses is bringing a family with him? Where will we put them? Our space has grown more crowded with each passing year. If Moses comes alone, we could manage, but what if he has a wife and children? In forty years a lot could have changed."

Miriam looked up at the heavens, pondering the thought. She had had no dream or vision or insight into Moses' life. All she knew was that God was sending him back to them. "We shall make room somehow," she said, pushing herself up as well as her aging legs would allow. "Come. Let us look at the area that belongs to our families and see where we might add extra pallets. What do you think—maybe four or five, six even? Moses could have many children by now!"

"Would they all return with him though? They could all be married with children of their own. Perhaps they will remain behind." Elisheba followed Miriam into the house, and the two moved from room to room, assessing the space.

"I wonder if we could add another room. I will ask Jephunneh and Caleb when they return tonight. Perhaps they could have something built before the men return." Miriam lifted a cushion and rearranged it.

"Where would we possibly put another room? There is barely space for a donkey between our house and the neighbor next to us." Elisheba, ever the practical one, crossed her arms over her chest. "I could see if my parents could take them in."

Miriam shook her head. After all of these years, she did not want her brother living with Elisheba's parents, though they likely had more room. She wanted him here, even if it meant she had to give up her pallet.

"Let us see if we can find a solution closer to our houses." She fought the excitement that talk of Moses brought to her heart. They had time. And they would be ready for him when he came, with or without a family. She wouldn't let him live far away. Not again. Not ever again.

⚒

The last rays of the sun gave up their fight to illumine the sky as Zipporah spread their blankets before a fire at the mouth of a cave. The boys sat near the cave's wall, talking quietly, while Moses stood at the entrance, looking up at the night sky. Zipporah watched the way he tilted his head and leaned on his staff. At eighty, her husband was still as virile and strong as a man of thirty. How was it that his strength had not ebbed, though sometimes she felt as though time was creeping up on her, weakening her?

The day's journey was their third, and Egypt's proud cities were still off somewhere in the distance. She wondered often what life would be like in this new land. Would they be forced to live as slaves, as Moses' people were? What if they took Gershom and Eliezer from her? What if some slave master ravaged her? Could even Moses protect her from Egypt's power?

She continued to stare at Moses' back, her body shaking

with a chill that was not coming from the night air. The urge to go to him, try to reason with him again, warred with the knowledge that it would do no good. But shouldn't she try?

She stood, smoothed her robe, and took a step closer, then stopped short at the sight of a stranger approaching Moses. Where had he come from? While she reasoned that he could be a traveler like they were, something about him caused fear to curl in her middle. She shivered again, this time from something she could not define.

Suddenly the man grabbed Moses, flung him to the earth, and stood over him with a blade that shone like silver in the starlit night. Panic swept over Zipporah as she watched, but she could not scream. Was this real?

Moses lay still, as though either unable or unwilling to move. The man could have killed him already, but the blade of the sword still hovered above Moses' neck.

This was no ordinary person. And such a weapon she had never seen. Why did he not kill Moses?

*"Follow the God of your husband and obey His laws. Then all will be well with you."*

Her father's words returned to her, and suddenly she knew. This was the Lord, and Moses' life was in danger because he had not kept all of the laws of his God. He had not circumcised Eliezer because she had not let him.

*If I don't act, Moses will die.* Her own thoughts betrayed her, and she knew she must do what God commanded if her husband was to live through the night.

*Would You really kill him?*

The man's gaze shifted to hers, and the fear she had felt at first grew to sheer panic. Yes, He would. God would absolutely kill her husband if she did not obey this ridiculous law.

She whirled about, dug through the saddlebag for a flint knife, and marched over to Gershom and Eliezer. "Lay down," she commanded Eliezer.

Eliezer stared at the knife in her hand, and Gershom, wide-eyed, seemed to sense the severity of the scene. He backed away. Eliezer remained unmoving, as if frozen in place.

"I said lay down. If you don't, I will do what I must, and it will cause you greater pain." Zipporah barely recognized her own voice. How could she possibly do this? Yet how could she not?

Eliezer obeyed, and she took the knife and swiftly did the deed, ignoring his cries of pain. Angry that she had been forced to hurt her own son, she marched across the small encampment and tossed the foreskin at Moses' feet.

"Now you are a bridegroom of blood to me." She glared at Moses but did not even attempt a look at the Lord, whose blade stood gleaming between them. She had obeyed. She hoped He was satisfied.

She stalked away, too afraid to look back, but she sensed the man had gone. When Moses lay down across from the fire moments later and Eliezer groaned nearby, Zipporah turned her back on all of them and wept.

⤡

Moses' heart pounded, and even when he tried to close his eyes and curl up near the fire, the silvery, shining blade still stood above him, white-hot and almost touching the skin of his neck. He drew in a breath. Reminded himself that the man—the angel of God, for surely He could have been no other—hadn't harmed him. He had disappeared, like the fire from the burning bush, the moment Eliezer was circumcised.

Yet the knowledge did nothing to calm Moses' racing heart or bring peace to his mind. Fear snaked through him. He had argued with God! And God had come within a hair of spilling his life's blood.

Would God truly have killed him? Or would He have intervened at the last moment and provided a different way, as He'd done for Abraham and Isaac?

Perhaps this had been a test. If Moses had insisted, obeyed the covenant when Eliezer was eight days old, would this have happened? He drew another breath and rolled onto his side. Zipporah's face was to the wall of the cave, and the boys no doubt slept nearby. He should see how Eliezer was feeling. But he could do little more than roll from one side to the other.

*I am not worthy, Adonai.* No other thoughts surfaced, just his certainty that he was not ready or worthy to lead Israel, God's people. He couldn't turn around though. He'd been sent, and after tonight, he never wanted to disobey or argue with God again!

# TWENTY-SEVEN

Morning dawned in a glorious array of pink and gray with a hint of yellow creeping atop the mountains that stood sentinel above them. Zipporah arose, groggy, what little sleep she had gotten too fitful to consider rest. Fear of Moses' God filled her with a looming sense of dread. All these years there had been no repercussions from not circumcising Eliezer, and suddenly because Moses was headed to Egypt, God was angry enough to kill him?

Was it anger? Or was His presence merely a test? Clearly He wanted obedience, as Moses had indicated with his decision to return to the land he had fled.

A land she wanted nothing to do with. The feeling had grown within her as she heard Eliezer's whimpers and groans throughout the night. She had not even offered him salve for the wound she had inflicted. The whole business had been too gruesome, too abhorrent to her.

"You are awake?" Moses stood behind her, and she turned to face him.

"I never slept." She crossed her arms, her gaze boring into his. "I want to go home."

Moses assessed her, his look resigned. "I can't go home," he said. "I have no choice but to obey my God. You saw His power, His desire. And yet you would ask me to disobey Him again?"

Zipporah studied his face, this handsome Hebrew she had grown to love. She did love him, didn't she? And yet she could not abide some of the things he clung to and forced her to believe or obey. Not when it came to her sons. She could not, wrong as it might be, put his God above her sons. Or risk the Egyptians turning them into slaves.

She drew in a long breath and slowly released it. "I would not ask you to disobey Him." She uncrossed her arms and held them out to him in entreaty. "I would ask you to send us back to my father. Don't take us with you. How could I bear to live as a slave? How could you or I bear to watch the Egyptians beat our sons? We have no way to protect them once we enter the black land. Eliezer is hurting enough. He is young and he will recover, but I do not understand your God, Moses. And I cannot put my sons at risk."

"They are my sons too," Moses said softly.

She looked at her feet, her arms falling to her sides. "I know that." She moved the dust with her toe. "But you are the one God called. You are the one who will stand before Pharaoh. You are the one who will do what God told you to do. He didn't call us, Moses. He called you."

"You are part of me. His call includes you and the boys as well." Moses rubbed the back of his neck, a frown furrowing his brow.

"How can you know that? Did God mention us when He

spoke with you?" She stared at him, her gaze intent. She had to win this battle. She could *not* go to Egypt!

"You are my wife. God made a husband and wife to live together. He didn't call me to walk away from you or our family." He turned and paced away from her. He would need time to think, but she didn't want him to take that time.

She followed after him. "Don't walk away from me, Moses. You know I am right in this. You know you cannot protect us, and you also know that the boys could become slaves along with the rest of the Hebrews. They *are* circumcised, after all! Your God requires too much, and I can't follow His rules the way you can. I would be a hindrance to you."

He whirled about. "I thought you took our vows seriously. From the time we wed, you have belonged to me, not your father."

"I know that! But my father can protect us in Midian. When you finally get the people out of Egypt, he can bring us back to you. But if you take us with you now, you risk our lives. You cannot even be sure the pharaoh will not kill you." She was shouting now, and she shut her mouth tight, tamping down her rising emotion.

"God has assured me that those who once sought my life are dead. They will not kill me." His voice was so calm it unnerved and annoyed her.

"But you cannot say the same about me or the boys."

"They will not kill you either." How sure he sounded!

This was not going the way she'd intended. She turned to look out over the winding river below them. They would need to eat soon, and in the distance, she heard the boys stirring.

"Moses, please. It is not for lack of love that I ask this. I do not want to cause a rift between us or disobey your God.

I just don't want to take our sons to Egypt. I want to feel safe, and out here, after last night, I do not feel safe." The image of God standing over her husband still sent a shiver down her spine.

Moses clasped his hands together and looked beyond her. He remained silent for so long, she wondered what was going on in his mind. But she should be used to his silences by now. She waited, watching him.

At last he lifted both hands in a gesture of defeat and sighed. "Fine. Go home to your father. We have not traveled far enough that Gershom and Eliezer cannot find the way."

"Eliezer will not be able to walk for days." Her voice held contempt.

"He will heal soon enough. This is why we carry out the covenant promise on the eighth day after birth. We don't remember the pain."

His mild rebuke stung, but she pushed the guilt aside. They both knew it was her fault that their youngest had not been made a son of the covenant at birth. She would make that choice again if she had to. The whole thing still made no sense to her.

"Wait two days, then take the path back the way we came. Send word, if you can, when you have safely arrived." Moses moved past her and picked up his staff. He rummaged through the donkey's sacks, removed a few food items, and stuffed them into his robe.

"Are you leaving before we can go? Would you not even protect us until then?" She didn't mean for him to go now! After Eliezer healed they could go their separate ways. She didn't want things to end this way.

"You said that I couldn't protect you. And I can't take the

time to return you to your father. This is a journey you and the boys will have to take alone. They are men. You have all been alone with the sheep or goats in the wilderness. The boys can protect you. I daresay you could protect them as well." His words were not said with even a hint of anger, but the truth of them hurt just the same.

"I don't want you to go." The words were out before she could stop them. How could she let him go? She wanted all of them to be together, just not in Egypt. She ran a hand over her eyes. How tired she felt!

His expression softened. He laid the staff on the ground and pulled her close. "Zipporah, I know we have not always agreed. But you are my wife and I am committed to you for as long as we live. I love our family. I even asked God to send someone else for fear of losing you and facing a life I thought I had left behind. But He would not take no for an answer. I argued with *God*, Zipporah! And I lost the argument." He gave her a rare wry grin. "Much like I often lose arguments with you."

She smiled. "I never mean to be difficult."

"You just like to win." He cupped her cheek and sighed. "I want to take all of you with me. But . . . I think this is an argument you may win again. You are right. I do not know what lies ahead of me. I do not know how my family, if they are still alive, are being treated in Egypt. I do not know where I will live while I am there or what would become of any of you. So this is wise and best. Go home, Zipporah. Take our sons. Let Eliezer ride the donkey until he heals, but go today. You will be back with your father before I arrive in Egypt." He kissed her cheek and held her head in his hands. "Be safe."

A feeling of sadness suddenly enveloped her, and she fell

into his arms, weeping. He held her close and patted her back. She knew he struggled with tears, never knowing how to react to them.

"It will be all right. Perhaps our God will cause us to leave Egypt sooner than we think and we will soon be reunited. How long can it take to convince the pharaoh once he loses his own son?" Moses spoke low against her ear.

She lifted her head. "The pharaoh is going to lose his son?"

Moses nodded. "Say nothing of this to anyone, but yes. It is what God told me. So go. Do not fret. Our release will likely come quickly once I get there, but I must go now."

Zipporah dried her eyes on the sleeve of her robe. "All right. I will make us something to eat first. Then we will go in our opposite directions."

Moses nodded, seemingly willing to at least spend one last meal with them. Zipporah hurried to mix the flour and water into flatbread, dug into their stash of raisins, and cut into a round of cheese.

Later, as she helped Eliezer onto the donkey and made sure the fire was out, she glimpsed Moses heading down into the ravine, staff in hand, and wondered if she would ever see him again.

# TWENTY-EIGHT

Miriam lit the evening lamp and moved about the house, straightening cushions, double-checking that food had been stored, and pacing. Her emotions were a mixture of worry and faith. Moses would come. God had told her so in her dreams. But where were they?

Aaron had left over a week ago. Was the trip to the wilderness really so far? Had he found Moses, or were they still moving toward each other? Surely God would guide their steps. Wouldn't He?

"Miriam. You will wear a path in the floor, and I have no time to repair such a groove. Come to bed." Jephunneh already rested on his pallet, and when she turned to face him, he motioned her closer. "They will come when they come. Since you cannot know the day or hour, there is no sense in worrying."

"I'm not worried." She walked toward him and forced herself to lie beside him.

"Yes, you are." Jephunneh pulled her close and spoke softly into her ear. Caleb and Netanya were murmuring behind the curtain, and her restlessness certainly was not allowing them to sleep. Jephunneh was right.

"Perhaps a little." She nestled into the curve of his body, but her heart still pounded as though it wanted her to jump up and run to the hills. How would she ever relax, husband beside her or not?

"They will come when they come. If they come in the night, Aaron will probably take Moses to his home. They aren't likely to come here first." He yawned and pulled her closer. "Relax, beloved. God will work all things out for us soon. Perhaps waiting is just to test our patience."

"Bah! I'm patient. I've waited for years for this moment. But to taste that freedom could be near . . . it is hard to keep waiting," she whispered lest she wake the baby.

"Miriam, my love. We can all learn more patience. Get some rest. They could come in the morning, and you will not want to be sleeping when they get here."

She knew he spoke wisdom, but she lay awake just the same.

The light tap on the door came to her—another dream, no doubt. But at its persistence, she could not understand why no one went to answer the knock. She felt a touch on her shoulder. No one touched her in her dreams.

*Lord? What is this?*

"Miriam. Wake up." Jephunneh touched her again, and she jolted upright.

"What is it?" She blinked at the three lamps that sat along the table. Men stood near the door, and she blinked against what she thought was a dream at the truth standing before her.

"They have come?" She scrambled to her feet and took Jephunneh's hand. "But it is not yet morn." She shook herself. Starlight came through the small window, and she knew she could not have been asleep long. "Moses?" She hurried to greet him.

"Miriam!" His arms came about her so fast she nearly gasped. "How good it is to see you!"

She looked him up and down. "You have not changed at all—except for the beard. You look Hebrew now."

He laughed. "I *am* Hebrew, my sister. And Egyptians do not fare well in Midian, so I accepted my rightful heritage while I was there."

She glanced at Aaron. "I thought you would have taken him to your home first, since it is so late." Her gaze quickly shifted to Moses again. "But I am so glad you didn't!" She motioned to the cushions, offering them a place to sit while she hurried to get water to drink.

"Tell me everything," she said the moment they were all settled. Caleb had joined them now, but Netanya stayed abed with the child. "But keep your voices low lest you wake the baby . . . and the neighbors."

Moses yawned and ran a hand over his beard. She should let him rest, but now that he was here, there would be no more sleep tonight.

"I have lived in Midian for forty years. I have a wife, Zipporah, and two sons, Gershom and Eliezer. They were headed this way with me, but on the way it seemed prudent to send them back to Zipporah's father, Jethro, for I do not know what will happen to me here. I am not certain that I could have protected them. But once we are settled outside of Egypt, I will send word for them to join me again."

Miriam nodded, grateful that they would have Moses to themselves without having to meet his entire family. Though a part of her felt a sense of loss that she would not meet her sister-in-law or nephews for some time.

"What made you decide to return?" Jephunneh asked him.

Moses glanced at Aaron, who apparently had already been told the story. "Simply put," Moses said, "God met me in the guise of a burning bush. He spoke to me and told me to return to Pharaoh and tell him to let our people go to worship Him. He assured me that those who sought my life were dead."

"That is true," Miriam interjected. "Thutmose III died some time ago. His son, Amenhotep II, now rules in his stead. Even Rashida has gone the way of all the earth. I daresay no one in the palace remembers you now."

Moses studied her as she spoke, a sense of acceptance in his gaze. "Our God spoke this to me along the way and assured me that He would go before me. He has heard the cry of our people and is planning to punish the Egyptians for enslaving us. In the end, Pharaoh will let us leave Egypt for good."

Miriam glanced around, seeing joy light the faces of her men.

"God has given me miraculous signs to perform before Pharaoh, and when they are completed with the death of his firstborn, then we will leave."

Miriam's heart thumped at the severity of the punishment. "Must it come to that?" She cared not for the Egyptians, but a part of her still felt some small allegiance to Hatshepsut and Rashida and struggled to wish such harm to their people, despite everything.

"Pharaoh is going to harden his heart against our God, Miriam. So God is going to show His power against the gods of Egypt. When that day comes, all of Israel and all of Egypt will know who the true God is."

"We will call the elders of the people together today and give them this good news." Aaron stifled a yawn, which all of them were fighting.

"You can call them to meet here." Miriam looked about the room, hoping it was big enough. She would move things to the farthest walls to make sure of it.

"I think it would be better to meet in the courtyard in front of the house. Some of the signs Moses will show them, you would not want in the house." Aaron smiled at her, his look telling her that he had already seen everything Moses would do.

Jealousy filled her that she had not been privy to what went on between the brothers. She would not have the privilege of standing with them when they met with Pharaoh. She could only remain in Goshen and help the women prepare to leave. It seemed like such an unimportant task.

"We will need you too, Miriam," Moses said, as if reading her thoughts. "You have always been there to help me, to watch over me, and now, without Zipporah at my side, I will count on you and Elisheba to prepare the women and children to be ready to move out when God says it is time. They will have to continue to serve the Egyptians for a little while longer. I do not know how long."

"Hopefully your miraculous signs will convince the pharaoh to let us go soon. I am ready to leave today if God will allow it." Her anxiety and restlessness returned with a rush.

"It will not be today, my sister. It may be a week, a month, even a year. Only God knows when Pharaoh's heart will give in." Moses ran a hand over his eyes, and Miriam sensed he needed to sleep, if only for a few hours.

"Aaron, go home to your wife. Caleb, go back to bed. Moses, you may sleep on the cushions while Jephunneh and I rest on our pallets. There is still time before dawn. We will help no one if we do not take our rest."

Aaron nodded and stood, bid them good night, and slipped through the door. Caleb did not object and returned to his privacy behind the curtain.

"Thank you, Sister." Moses lay down and closed his eyes. Miriam had no desire to sleep again and longed to ply him with questions about his life in Midian, his family, the work he'd done. But she held her tongue and followed her husband to their curtained room. Tomorrow—no, later today—would bring time enough to ask more questions.

But Miriam did not sleep again. She rose quietly and listened to the snores of her men. Her men. How grateful she was to have Moses back under the roof where he had been born. Memories surfaced of Ima swaddling him and nursing him and faithfully making the basket that saved him from the sword and the crocodiles.

This was good. This day would be one she would long remember. She moved to the window and stood watching as the dawn broke through at last.

# TWENTY-NINE

Miriam stood near the door later that evening as the elders of Israel gathered in the small courtyard between her house and Aaron's. The men—including Joshua, who had become like family to them since his mother's death at his birth—stood in a half circle, listening to Aaron tell the men everything Moses had shared the night before and during the day. She noted the fire in Caleb's and Joshua's eyes as they gazed at Moses, though it was Aaron who did the speaking.

"Men of Israel," Aaron said, pointing at Moses, "long ago, Pharaoh Thutmose I ordered the deaths of all infant boys at the moment of birth. Our mother and father, peace be upon them, saw something special about Moses when he was born and hid him from the taskmasters until he could no longer be hidden. So they set Moses adrift in a basket in the Nile, and the princess Hatshepsut found him. Our sister, Miriam, watched over him and brought our mother to the princess, who allowed Moses to live with us until he was weaned. It was here in this very house that Moses learned of our God, and though he grew up in Pharaoh's palace and later fled to Midian, he did not forget who he was. And God did not let him forget that he was saved for a purpose."

Miriam listened as Aaron talked about their history and how God had brought Moses back now. The introduction was probably necessary, but when Moses did not even speak about what God had told him but rather allowed Aaron to continue to speak for him, she looked at him, curious. Was he self-conscious? Or did he allow Aaron to tell the tale because he knew these men while Moses was foreign to them?

"Show them the sign of the staff," Aaron told Moses, catching her attention again. Aaron's explanation of Moses' experience with God was apparently at an end.

Miriam glanced at her husband and son and did not miss the excitement written on Joshua's face. His allegiance to Moses seemed immediate. But one look around and she could see the rest of the elders needed convincing.

Moses took the staff in his hand and tossed it on the ground between him and the men. Immediately the staff turned into a snake, writhing and hissing. Gasps filled the small crowd as the men backed away, nearly tripping over each other. Moses grabbed the snake by the tail. In an instant the snake became a staff in his hand.

Miriam released a deep sigh, which joined the collective sigh of the men around her. How on earth? She glanced heavenward. Hearing God speak to her in dreams was one thing, but to see this! A piece of wood turn into a living being? Impossible!

The men had barely regained their composure when Moses

placed his hand inside his cloak and pulled it out. It was leprous, white as mountaintop snow. Miriam swallowed hard. *Moses. No!* Leprosy was the most dreaded of all diseases among her people. She could think of nothing worse than the slow death that came with this skin disease.

But when he placed his hand back in his cloak and removed it again, the leprosy had disappeared as if it had never been. Moses' hand was as strong as the other, and he took the staff in it and squeezed the wood to prove it.

"Lastly," Aaron said, drawing the men's attention once more, "God has given Moses one more miracle to perform." He looked at Miriam. "Bring me a cup of water that you have drawn from the Nile."

Miriam hurried into the house, grabbed a clay cup, and handed it to Aaron, who passed it to Moses. "Pour the water on the ground," Aaron said.

Moses tipped the water slowly so all could see. The clear liquid turned bloodred on the ground. Moses caught some on his finger and moved through the crowd, allowing each man to sniff the liquid. All of them turned away, disgust in their eyes. Moses shook the blood from his finger.

"As you can see, God is able to turn water to blood, and He will do the same to the Egyptians if they refuse to let our people go." Aaron smiled at Moses, and the men of Israel stared at her brothers, awe filling their faces.

"God has surely sent Moses to deliver us," one of the men said.

"Yes, truly. You are sent to us from God Himself," said another.

The word spread throughout the group until one by one each man fell to his knees. Miriam watched, amazed, then joined them as they bowed their faces to the ground, grateful that God had finally heard the cries of His people.

⸺◈⸺

The next day, Miriam and Netanya prepared a quick meal for Caleb and Jephunneh and watched them hurry to care for the flocks. Moses remained behind, and Miriam longed to keep him with her, to hear about the forty years they'd been apart. But a knock sounded, and Aaron entered the house before she could begin to ask Moses of Zipporah, his sons, his life in Midian—anything!

"Are you ready to go?" Aaron met Moses where he sat finishing a last bite of porridge.

Elisheba entered after Aaron, holding a sack. "You forgot this. In case you are hungry and you await an audience with Pharaoh." She attempted to give it to him, but he refused it.

"I do not expect this to take long. Keep it, my love. I will return soon." Aaron patted her arm, then faced Moses. "Ready?"

Moses stood and walked with Aaron to the door. He grabbed his staff from where it leaned against the wall, then took one look back at Miriam, Elisheba, and Netanya. "Pray for us."

"We will," Miriam said quickly. She stepped closer and watched them leave, her feet itching to follow them. "I wonder what Pharaoh will say."

Elisheba joined her. "He will not give in, according to Aaron. I do not think this is going to be an easy process. But I've been wrong before. Let us pray I am wrong this time."

Miriam nodded. She joined her sister-in-law and daughter-in-law at the table, where they entreated God to go with

Moses and Aaron. Surely God would answer quickly. Hadn't He finally heard their cries for deliverance? Now all He had to do was to convince Pharaoh that He had more power than some earthly king and make him let them go. How hard could that possibly be?

# THIRTY

Moses looked up at the giant doors of the palace, wondering how he had ever considered this place home. Somehow when Hatshepsut lived, he had managed to cope and spent so much time with his tutors that he didn't really think about being royalty or having privileges his people were denied.

But now . . . would anyone recognize him? He touched his beard. Doubtful. Even if a servant or an old tutor still lived, they would be ancient, and none of his peers would recognize an Egyptian beneath Hebrew robes.

"Are you ready?" Aaron stood at his side as they looked up at the grand steps leading to Pharaoh's audience chamber.

"If it were up to me, I would never be ready, Brother. But we are here now. Let's go." Moses climbed the steps, pausing at each one, but when they reached the last few, he no longer hesitated.

A scribe sat at a table under the portico, and guards flanked the wide doors. "Name and business," the scribe said, looking

Moses and Aaron up and down. "Hebrews." He spat onto the limestone steps.

"Moses and Aaron, sons of Amram, of the tribe of Levi," Aaron said, straightening, seemingly undaunted by the scribe's hostility. "We have a message for Pharaoh Amenhotep II from the Lord."

The scribe lifted a brow, his gaze skeptical, almost mocking. But he recorded their names on the scroll and handed it to one of the guards. "Wait here. If he will see you, you will know soon."

Moses stepped back a pace, and Aaron followed suit. The sun had moved halfway to the middle of the sky before the palace doors opened and they were beckoned to enter. Sweat trickled down Moses' back as he took in the familiar surroundings. The ornamental trappings had changed, but the basic format of the room, even down to the throne where Pharaoh sat, was the same.

"You grew up here," Aaron whispered with a hint of awe. "I cannot imagine what it was like for you."

"Not as pleasant as you might think." Moses stopped at the place indicated by the blue line in the tiles and bowed low. Aaron followed his example.

"Stand tall and speak," the pharaoh said. "You have a word of wisdom for me from some god? Let me hear it, then."

Both men rose as one, but Moses deferred to Aaron to speak. He had no stomach for this man or this place, and he had already given Aaron the words. But he held his head high, watching the king's reaction.

"This is what the Lord, the God of Israel, says," Aaron said, his voice firm and loud enough to carry throughout the entire room. "'Let My people go so they may hold a festival in My honor in the wilderness.'"

"Is that so?" Pharaoh's tone ridiculed them. "And who is the Lord? Why should I listen to him and let Israel go? I don't know the Lord, and I will not let Israel go."

"The God of the Hebrews has met with us," Moses interjected. "So let us take a three-day journey into the wilderness so we can offer sacrifices to the Lord our God. If we don't, He will kill us with a plague or with the sword."

Pharaoh Amenhotep laughed. "Moses and Aaron, why are you distracting the people from their tasks? Get back to work! Look, there are many of your people in the land, and you are stopping them from their work."

"We have not interfered with their work," Aaron said. But Moses touched his arm to stop him from saying more.

"Get out of my sight," Pharaoh said. He waved his hand in dismissal.

Without another word, Moses and Aaron bowed again, turned, and left the palace.

"We didn't really expect him to listen, did we?" Aaron asked once they were back on the road toward Goshen.

Moses' laugh held no mirth. "No, I did not expect him to. Not yet." Though he did hope that it would not take too much time. He was not sure how long he could continue to confront the man who reminded him too much of Thutmose III, who had tried to have him killed. The sooner the Israelites could leave this place, the better.

~≈~

Miriam greeted Jephunneh and Caleb and Joshua later that night as they arrived home from the fields. Leaders of

Israel also filled their courtyard once again. They pounded on the door until Moses and Aaron met them in front of the house.

"What have you done to us?" they demanded.

"What are you talking about?" Aaron asked, holding up a hand for silence since the men were all speaking at once.

One of the elders spoke for the others. "Pharaoh sent an order to the Egyptian slave masters and Israelite foremen to stop supplying us with straw to make bricks. But we are still required to make the same amount! How are we supposed to do that? They will beat us—some already have—if we do not meet their quota."

"They claim we are lazy," another said. "Where are we supposed to find enough straw? Have you come here to kill us?"

Miriam's stomach knotted with the news. *No! Oh, Adonai, why?*

"Perhaps it will not be as bad as it sounds." Aaron's words were meant to placate, but none of the men, even her men, looked convinced. "Give it a few days and see whether Pharaoh changes his mind."

Grumbling persisted among the gathered men. Would they attack Moses and Aaron for trying to do what God commanded? Fear of her own people slithered through her.

"We will do what we must, but if this does not improve, it's on you." One man pointed to Moses.

"We will approach Pharaoh ourselves next time," said a man at the back of the crowd. "Perhaps he will listen and have mercy."

They dispersed then, but Miriam doubted very much that this pharaoh was capable of mercy. If one visit from her brothers could cause such a change, what would he do when they demanded more?

⸗

As the days passed, news from Jephunneh and Caleb—and Joshua when he managed to stop by—remained the same. The people were desperate, and straw, even stubble, was nearly impossible to find. More Israelites were beaten for being unable to meet the quota of bricks, and the Egyptians' mood toward Israel had grown worse. Even the Israelite foremen were beaten when the workers under them failed.

Miriam poured tea for her men and sat in a corner as Caleb told Moses and Aaron what he had heard. "I watched an Egyptian beating a foreman today. I had chased a wayward lamb and could hear the man's screams. The sight was impossible to continue watching." He paused, and the room grew silent. "As we headed home for the day, I saw the foremen gather. They were headed for Thebes."

"Did you hear what they planned to do there?" Moses asked.

"Only that there have been rumors and grumblings for days that they planned to speak with Pharaoh and beg him to have mercy, to be lenient. Only God knows whether they will succeed." Caleb rubbed a hand over his weary face.

"Let us hope they do." Miriam spoke softly, but each man looked at her, obviously hearing her words.

"We must go and meet them." Moses stood, and Aaron joined him. "When they leave Pharaoh's presence, we must hear what they have to say."

Miriam watched them go, then looked at her husband and son. "What will you do?"

Jephunneh lifted his gaze and met hers. "What is left to us but to pray? There is nothing we can do. Pray God will do something, because if He does not, there is no hope."

Miriam's heart sank at the despair in his voice. But he was right. Moses had returned and things had only gotten worse. If God truly cared about their plight, why was He so silent?

Moses stood as the sun nearly set the Nile ablaze in its descent into the underworld. But no, the sun did not die and rise each dawn. That was Egyptian teaching. Hadn't God shown him differently during his years in the desert? The sun merely disappeared to lighten a different part of the earth.

Aaron shifted from foot to foot beside him, his nerves obvious. At last the great doors opened and the foremen descended the steps. They stopped at the sight of Moses and Aaron.

"What did he say to you?" Aaron asked.

"He refused to change anything. He said we are lazy!"

Spite and anger pulsed through the crowd of men, aimed at Moses and Aaron.

"May the Lord judge and punish you for making us stink before Pharaoh and his officials. You have put a sword into their hands, an excuse to kill us!"

They stalked off, cursing Moses as they went.

Moses stood still, feeling the weight of their curses. Aaron touched his arm, but he brushed it off. "Go home, Aaron. I'm going for a walk."

Aaron offered him a questioning look but said nothing. He walked slowly back toward Goshen while Moses walked toward the path he'd taken to Midian. When he was a good distance from the palace, he knelt near a protrusion of rocks, anger and hurt moving through him.

"Why have You brought all this trouble on Your own people, Lord? Why did You send me? Ever since I came to Pharaoh as Your spokesman, he has been even more brutal to Your people. And You have done nothing to rescue them!"

A soft breeze brushed the hair along the back of his neck. He sat back on his heels and looked toward the distant mountains. Light streamed toward him, and a voice, low and whisper-like, spoke.

"Now you will see what I will do to Pharaoh. When he feels the force of My strong hand, he will let the people go. In fact, he will force them to leave his land!"

Moses bowed low again, unsettled.

"I am Yahweh—'the Lord.' I appeared to Abraham, to Isaac, and to Jacob as El-Shaddai—'God Almighty'—but I did not reveal My name, Yahweh, to them. And I reaffirmed My covenant with them. Under its terms, I promised to give them the land of Canaan, where they were living as foreigners. You can be sure that I have heard the groans of the people of Israel, who are now slaves to the Egyptians. And I am well aware of My covenant with them.

"Therefore, say to the people of Israel: 'I am the Lord. I will free you from your oppression and will rescue you from your slavery in Egypt. I will redeem you with a powerful arm and great acts of judgment. I will claim you as My own people, and I will be your God. Then you will know that I am the Lord your God, who has freed you from your oppression in Egypt. I will bring you into the land I swore to give to Abraham, Isaac, and Jacob. I will give it to you as your very own possession. I am the Lord!'"

The light was extinguished, the voice gone, but Moses still lingered, the words gripping his soul. *Yahweh*.

He rose slowly and leaned heavily on his staff as he made his way back to Miriam's house. I Am That I Am, the source of all being, had spoken to him. Unworthy as he was.

He was weak and had no strength to do what God had required of him. And yet . . . if God remained his stronghold, his purpose, he would trust Him for the power and the words to say to Pharaoh. But first he must convince his people that they would not suffer under the Egyptians much longer.

# THIRTY-ONE

Miriam hurried to the house of one of the Israelite women, her midwifery bag in hand. So much had changed in the few weeks since Moses and Aaron first attempted to speak to Pharaoh. She and Elisheba had taken to helping the women deliver, as they had done for Hava long ago, but the Egyptians had grown harsher with each passing day. Even Caleb and Joshua and Miriam's daughters were forced to make bricks. No longer did anyone work the fields, and few handled the flocks, Jephunneh and even Moses among them.

But without straw to make the bricks, the people grew quiet, discouraged. Most were too tired to even grumble, though Miriam heard plenty of grumbling as the babies were delivered.

She met Elisheba, who had arrived before her, and the two of them worked in near silence as they helped one of their neighbors deliver a boy.

"How handsome he is," Miriam said as she cleaned and salted his small body and wrapped him in bits of cloth. The grandmother sat nearby and reached for the baby before they placed him in his mother's arms.

"Thank you," she said, though her hardened gaze held little gratitude. "I know my girl could not have delivered without help, and I am too old to provide it. I cannot say we are grateful for your brother's attempt to help us though. This boy will grow up without a father if he is beaten one more time. He will not survive it." Her words held scorn, and she looked at her grandson with tears in her eyes. "It would have been better if Moses had not returned."

Miriam's exhaustion did not help as the woman's words brought a knot to her middle. A knot that had perpetually lingered since word of Pharaoh's decree about the bricks had come down. The people were discouraged, and how could she blame them? Her Caleb showed strength, but even he and Joshua were worn down by the change in work.

"Do not lose hope," Miriam said, as much for herself as for the woman. "Our God sees our mistreatment at the hands of the Egyptians. He will act and rescue us. We must not lose heart because it is taking longer than we expected."

"That's easy for you to say, Miriam. You do not feel the same effects of our slavery. Because of Moses, your family has always been treated better than most." This from the young mother who now held her son in her arms.

"My son makes bricks like any other. As do my daughters. We are not exempt from cruelty any longer." She felt her defenses rise, wanting to defend her brothers and cling to hope in the God who had spoken to her in dreams.

"Well, they didn't in the past. You cannot deny that." The old woman shifted to better see her grandson.

"No, you are right. They were shepherds until this decree. But all of us have suffered. You cannot deny that." She lifted her chin and turned to gather her things. "If you need anything, please do not hesitate to call for us." Without another glance at either woman, she moved through the door, Elisheba at her heels.

"They are right, you know," Elisheba said. "Some of the women resent us. And all of the people resent Moses and Aaron. How are we to help the women if they see us with such disdain?" She looked at Miriam as they stopped in a patch of moonlight several paces from their homes.

"We can only do what God allows. We cannot make them see. Hopefully our God will act, and then they will listen to us again." Miriam continued walking, too hurt and angry to discuss it further. If she was called of God to help lead the people, most assuredly the women, how could she possibly do so if they would not listen? And if they would not listen to her, whom they had known all of her life, how would they listen to Moses, whom they barely knew?

She stopped at her door and bid Elisheba good night, then glanced heavenward. *What would You have us do, Lord?*

⌒⌒

Another day passed with no change in routine or harsh labor, though Miriam could not help the anticipation rushing through her, knowing that Aaron and Moses stood again before Pharaoh to demand that he let their people go. Would God give their words enough weight to sway the stubborn heart of the king?

She bustled about the garden and ground the grain, Elisheba working beside her, and watched the sun slowly move in its path to the west. She intended this meal to be one of her best to feed her men while she heard all that they had to say.

The door burst open long before the food was ready or

Jephunneh and Caleb had returned from their work. Moses and Aaron stood in the open doorway, then came in and shut the door.

"What happened?" Miriam asked, her heart pounding with a sudden sense of hope. "Did he say we could go?"

Aaron shook his head. "Not even close. Not even when my staff became a snake and devoured the staffs of the magicians, which also turned to snakes. Pharaoh remains as hard-hearted as ever."

Moses sat on the bench near where Miriam stood, a pile of vegetables cut in front of her. "God told me that Pharaoh would continue to harden his heart. He is using Pharaoh's stubbornness to show more and more miracles in this land. He is going to show them that He alone is God, and not the many gods they worship."

"Do you think all of these signs and miracles will take long?" She was so weary of waiting. They had waited as a people for over four hundred years. Why was God so slow to act? They'd been groaning under their slavery for too long.

"I don't know," Moses said, interrupting her thoughts. "But tomorrow we are to meet Pharaoh at the Nile and turn the water to blood."

Miriam remembered the stench from the small cup Moses had used to demonstrate this sign.

"I want you to go to the women and have them gather water tonight, enough to last for several days. For God is going to turn the Egyptians' water to blood, not only in the Nile but in the canals and streams and even the pots where they store it."

Moses looked at her, and she saw the strength in his gaze. Her timid brother was beginning to believe that he had the strength to do as God asked, though she knew he would still rely on Aaron to help him.

"The water will remain as blood for seven days, so you will need to go to some of the lakes to the north or south, for I know you cannot possibly store enough to last that long." He rubbed a hand along his jaw as if to ease the tension.

"How will the Egyptians survive without water for so long?" Miriam asked. How would they, for that matter? She knew the women could not possibly carry enough after the exhaustion of making bricks alongside their men. "And we are going to need our men to help us, if we can even travel so far after such harsh labor." In that moment, she thanked God that she was old enough to stay home and care for those who needed her. Any younger and she would be like her daughters, who, like her own mother, had their children helping them with the impossible work.

"The Egyptians will manage. This is judgment on them, Miriam. Do you think God is happy with the way they have treated our people all of these years? While they've lived in prosperity and luxury, we've lived in poverty and slavery. God is exacting the judgment He had planned long ago."

Moses' words rang true, matching some of the things God had revealed to her in dreams.

"I know our God is not happy with them. I have seen this judgment in my dreams, though not all of it." How much more would there be?

"Some of the Egyptians may come to see the truth and join our ranks," Aaron said, sitting next to Moses on the bench and resting his elbows against the table. "If they do, we must be cautious. Some could cause us trouble."

Moses' face grew sober. "I do not think that will happen

right away. If they join us, it will be later. After Pharaoh has suffered the might of God's power against him."

"Some of the Egyptians have been kind to us," Miriam said. "Hatshepsut and Rashida among them."

Moses nodded, his gaze distant, as if remembering. "Yes. And some will come to believe our God, but right now, they do not know Him. Let us pray that when they see our God's power, they will repent and join us as true people of God and not cause us trouble."

Miriam nodded her agreement.

Elisheba said, "Yes, we must pray."

But they did not pray together as Miriam would have liked. Later, when her men returned, she prayed alone with Jephunneh, while Moses left the house to speak alone with God.

What was it like to hear from God as Moses did? She would never know. No one had heard from Him in hundreds of years. Only Aaron's visions and her dreams had come of late. This was a different time, and Moses had been chosen to be their leader. Miriam only prayed that the people would see him the way she did. Because right now, they were still too discouraged to believe a word he said.

# THIRTY-TWO

S even days later, the blood turned back to water and the stench of dead fish slowly abated. As darkness fell on that seventh day, Miriam called the women together. They overflowed the small courtyard and spilled into the streets, quietly listening to her.

"This plague of water into blood was to show our Egyptian neighbors that our God, Yahweh, has power over their god of the underworld, Osiris, whose lifeblood is the Nile. I want you to all be prepared, for more plagues are coming against the Egyptian gods. Moses has warned us that the next god to be put in its place is Heqt, the frog-headed Egyptian goddess of fertility. If any of you have kept an image of this goddess to aid you in childbirth, you must destroy it now, lest we suffer the same plague that is about to come upon the Egyptians."

Miriam searched the faces before her and noted the look of guilt in many expressions. Moses had said that Yahweh would send frogs to cover the land. Would the Hebrews also suffer this plague because the women had purchased the amulets of this fertility goddess or kept her image beside their beds?

"Will you do as I say?" Her voice boomed over the area, but no one spoke in response. A few heads nodded, though Miriam saw a hint of defiance on some faces. "Be warned. If Goshen suffers this next plague, it will be because you did not obey the Lord your God. We are to be separate and distinct from those around us. We have the only truth to offer them. If we fail to act in obedience to Yahweh, why should the Egyptians do so? They think us no different than they are except that we have no power as slaves. But we have a powerful God. We must trust Him and obey."

Her words carried the passion and fire she felt for her God. He was indeed powerful, and she *must* convince their women to believe. But how? They had not seen Him work except for the bloody water. What would it take for God to separate His people from those He had come to judge?

She dismissed the women with another warning but was not convinced they would all act.

"Tomorrow we will know," Elisheba said, coming up beside her. "Tomorrow if our God sends the frogs to Goshen as well as Egypt, then the women will be sorry for their stubborn hearts."

"I hope it doesn't come to that." The passion in Miriam's heart turned into an ache that came from longing to help others believe as she did. Why couldn't they understand? They were Abraham's offspring!

"I hope not too," Elisheba said. "I'm going home."

Miriam watched her enter the door to her house and waited a moment, glancing at the stars. *Oh, Lord, please let them see the truth. Let them come to obey You so that we do not suffer along with the Egyptians. Surely we have suffered enough at their hands. Haven't we?*

But the air held no whisper of God's voice. Miriam returned to the house, wondering.

※

Moses and Aaron entered Miriam's home the next afternoon, kicking frogs away from the door. Miriam, Elisheba, and Netanya had spent the day killing the horrible-looking amphibians and shoving them from their houses, but more continued to come.

Miriam approached her brothers, arms crossed. "Can you not ask the Lord to keep the frogs from Goshen? Why must we suffer with the Egyptians?" Though she knew in her heart that the women of Israel had something to do with this judgment, she had never worshiped an idol.

Moses stopped a frog from jumping onto his robe and tossed it through the window. The *splat* was one of too many Miriam had heard that day. "It is because Israel has worshiped this goddess that we suffer too," he said. "You know this."

"I entreated the women to rid the town of those images, but I suspect they did not listen. At least not all of them."

"Even one is enough to incur God's wrath on the people. We will never be in unity with our God if there are rebels among us." He took a broom and pushed a dozen more frogs from the house, while Elisheba handed Aaron their broom to do the same.

"Call all of the people to meet in the town square. I know it is not large enough, but we cannot meet in the fields where the Egyptians might still wander. We will warn the people again.

215

If they will not listen, we will continue to suffer along with the Egyptians." Moses glanced at her, his expression grave.

"How can we possibly lead these people out if they continue to want to live like the Egyptians? We've lived in this land too long." Miriam felt a frog crawl up her back. She shook it off, despair filling her. *Adonai?* Had her own sins caused Him to include them in this plague?

"I will go and speak to the Lord for us," Moses said when most of the frogs were out of the house and the windows were shut tight. "Perhaps He will relent here. But we must remove the sin from among us."

"If only we could offer a sacrifice." Aaron looked at Moses. "Of course, that is precisely what we are trying to get Pharaoh to let us do."

Moses said nothing but gave Aaron a slight nod. He slipped from the house, preventing more frogs from entering.

Miriam sank onto the bench, exhausted, the smell of the dead frogs already seeping through the walls. Outside, she could still hear the sounds of their croaking and hopping throughout the town.

"How are we going to call the people to repent and to meet tonight if we cannot walk without an onslaught of frogs?" She released a deep sigh. "I wonder if they are landing on the sheep as well. The poor animals will run with fright." She could picture the mess facing Jephunneh, Caleb, Joshua, and the other shepherds.

"I will go and see how they fare," Aaron said, heading toward the door. "And do not worry. Stay here for a while. I will spread the word to meet as I make my way to the hills."

"Please, God, have mercy on us," Miriam said quietly as Aaron left the house.

Elisheba sat next to her, and Netanya moved behind her curtain to check on her son. "We can be thankful that it isn't worse here," Elisheba said, touching Miriam's arm. "The way Moses talked, the frogs are going to be in the kneading bowls and the beds of the Egyptians. At least your house is clear for now."

"I hope yours is as well." Miriam met Elisheba's gaze. "We could go over there and check."

Elisheba shook her head. "Let us wait to see if God responds to Moses' plea. And let us rest a moment. The frogs can't do much damage there since I brought our food over here, remember?"

"Let us hope they stay out of our beds." Miriam shivered at the thought of one of them sleeping with her —or a whole horde of them. "They are a living nightmare."

As night descended and Moses returned to meet with the people, Miriam noted that the frogs had left Goshen. By the sounds coming from the nearby storage city of Rameses, however, and the call from Pharaoh's servants to Moses and Aaron, Miriam knew Egypt's fate was not the same as Israel's. She sent a silent prayer heavenward that they would not suffer with Egypt again.

<hr>

The town square seemed to hold all of Israel, though Miriam knew only the men had come. She stood behind her family, farthest from her brothers yet close enough to hear Aaron's words.

"Our God sent this plague on Egypt to punish their god Heqt. The reason He did not make a distinction between them and us is because our hearts have not been faithful to

Him. We cannot have divided loyalty between their gods and ours. There is only one God, and He has shown you His power. You will see more of that power in the days to come, but I entreat you to rid yourselves of any idols you still possess because another plague is coming, and we cannot promise it will not affect our people if our hearts are not obedient to Yahweh."

"We have already done as you asked," one of the elders said. "We serve no God but the God of Abraham, Isaac, and Jacob."

"Yet some of your wives have kept idols of Heqt. You must rid yourselves of all idolatry, even if you keep no symbols but simply believe the Egyptian lies in your hearts." Aaron's voice rang in the stillness.

"Our God is going to attack the Egyptian god Set tomorrow," Moses said, surprising Miriam, for he almost never spoke when Aaron was with him. "Aaron is going to strike the dust of the earth, for Set is god of the desert, chaos, and overall evil. Our God is greater than any evil that any god of any nation can contrive. Is His arm too short to save us? Is there anyone here who believes that evil is stronger than our God?"

Silence was his only answer, but Miriam saw a myriad of expressions cross the faces of the men who stood before him. After four hundred and thirty years of her people being enslaved, after watching babies murdered simply for being male, after seeing people beaten and their conditions worsen year after year, did *she* believe their God was stronger than the god of evil and chaos? Set was not one they thought of much, but the evil they suffered had caused some of their people to cry out even to him to leave them alone.

"Go home," Aaron said when no one responded to Moses. "Repent of your beliefs in the false, useless gods of Egypt and know that Yahweh is the only God who has power over the dust of the earth, the wind, the chaos, even the evil one. Tomorrow you will see the truth."

Aaron and Moses turned and walked toward the house, Miriam hurrying to keep up. Jephunneh and Caleb were two steps ahead of her, and she cinched her scarf tighter over her head. She'd been the only woman among them, but was she not a leader in Israel—at least among the women? She must know what was to come to prepare her own heart for what God would do.

They entered the house as the sun dipped fully below the horizon. Aaron left for his own house, and Miriam turned to Moses as Caleb slipped behind the curtain to join his wife and son. Jephunneh rested a hand on her shoulder.

"Will we feel the effect of tomorrow's plague?" She searched Moses' dark eyes and noted the small streaks of silver in his beard. Despite their ages, her brothers, especially Moses, still seemed as young and vigorous as Caleb.

"I fear it is possible." Moses looked from her to Jephunneh. "God has not told me to go to Pharaoh. Aaron is simply going to strike the dust. Then we will see what God will do."

"Pharaoh will feel the effects of whatever God does, no doubt." Jephunneh pulled Miriam close and rubbed her tight shoulders.

"No doubt. I am certain I will hear from him again. But he will not soften his heart, for God has told me he will not do so until he loses his son." A distant look crossed Moses' face, and Miriam thought of his two sons, whom he'd sent back to Midian. For his sake, she was glad they were not here to witness this.

"I hope God spares us that one," Miriam said, her mind drifting to her firstborn daughter and Caleb's only son.

"He will." Moses moved to his pallet, fighting a yawn. "But I do not think we will be spared tomorrow's unpleasant judgment. After that, the people will come to see God's power. I have prayed that God will soon make a distinction between them and us, but until hearts are changed, we are only different because of our ancestors. It is that covenant with them that God is keeping. We are His people, but we are not an obedient people. Pray that we soon will be."

Miriam pondered his words as she attempted to sleep that night, but her mind would not rest. She had never considered that God would judge His own people as well as their oppressors. But sin was sin, and she knew deep within her that no sin went unnoticed by their God. She spent the night praying for forgiveness for her own disobedient heart.

# THIRTY-THREE

The gnats filled the air soon after Moses and Aaron had left the house to walk the distance toward Thebes. They would not cross the river to stand before Pharaoh this time, but Miriam felt the air darken as if the gnats had appeared the moment Aaron struck the ground. She and Elisheba fought to keep them from landing on the water in their jars, but even a linen cloth could not keep them out. And though they veiled their faces, they could barely see through the gnats on their way back from the river to draw fresh water.

Cries from the women returning with their own jars went up from Goshen, and that day they crowded into Miriam's house and courtyard.

"What can we do?" one woman asked. "Please have Moses pray to God for us to make them go away."

"We do not need Moses to pray for us," Miriam said, her arms lifted in entreaty. "We need to fall on our faces before our God and repent ourselves. Have all of you removed the idols from your houses?"

Nods and yeses filled the courtyard and the small house.

"Every last one of them? Don't think our God will not see if you do not speak truth." She searched the faces before her, each one veiled and each woman swatting at the air, futilely trying to keep the gnats away. Though she could not see their expressions, she sensed they spoke truth. "All right. Then fall on your faces with me and repent of your sins. I will ask Moses to pray for us." Though she knew that Moses was the only one God truly spoke to, God had given her a role as well, and she must help her people the only way she knew how.

Elisheba, Netanya, and Joshua's wife, Eliana, circled closest to Miriam, and they all knelt and placed their hands on the ground, then bowed low. One by one the women did the same. Prayers and petitions floated in the air until the sounds turned to weeping, not the bitter cries of oppression but the sorrowful tears of repentance.

Silence slowly descended, and as the women rose, Miriam noticed that the gnats no longer filled the room or even the courtyard beyond. Did the men notice the difference in the fields or where they worked to make bricks? She would ask Jephunneh when he returned home tonight.

"They're gone," Netanya said softly.

Murmurs of agreement followed. As the women departed, thanking Miriam, she moved into the streets, discovering that the plague of gnats appeared to have left Goshen early. Or at least part of it.

She lifted her gaze to the billowy clouds overhead and spoke. "Thank You, Adonai, for hearing the prayers of Your unworthy people. May our hearts always remain true to You from this day forward." She couldn't know what would happen tomorrow, of course. But she knew her own heart had been and still was sincere. Her repentance came from a need for God's touch.

She returned home with a spring in her step and a song of praise on her lips.

~

Moses knelt by the protrusion of rocks away from Goshen, where he had become accustomed to praying. *What next, Adonai? Pharaoh still hardens his heart against You. I know You are mighty in power and wonder, but please tell Your servant what I should do now that Pharaoh has rebuffed yet another of Your plagues.*

A light wind blew the hair from his neck, and the softest whisper spoke into his ear. "Get up early in the morning and confront Pharaoh as he goes to the river and say to him, 'This is what the Lord says: Let My people go, so that they may worship Me. If you do not let My people go, I will send swarms of flies on you and your officials, on your people, and into your houses. The houses of the Egyptians will be full of flies. Even the ground will be covered with them.

"'But on that day I will deal differently with the land of Goshen, where My people live. No swarms of flies will be there, so that you will know that I, the Lord, am in this land. I will make a distinction between My people and your people. This sign will occur tomorrow.'"

Moses waited a moment longer, yearning to hear the voice again. How had he ever lived without hearing the sound of God's voice? Even His whisper carried such a musical beauty that Moses wanted to weep from the longing of hearing Him always. But the Lord spoke no more, so Moses arose, brushed the dirt from his knees, and looked into the night sky.

The people had repented. Miriam had told him the women had done so, and Jephunneh had confirmed that the Egyptians stayed away from the fields while the gnats swarmed, giving the men time to fall on their faces and confess their sins to Yahweh. So now God could make the distinction that Moses sensed He had always intended to make. The people hadn't been ready when the plagues first began. They hadn't believed. But now . . . now they saw God's great power in their own homes. Now there was no denying His mighty hand in this.

He returned to Miriam's home, his heart lighter than it had been since he'd arrived in Goshen. There was no telling how many more judgments God would exact on the Egyptians, but Moses sensed that the time of their departure was soon. Very soon.

He glanced at the starlit sky. *I'm not sure I can lead this vast number of people out of here. But I will go where You lead.*

Peace settled over him. God would go with him, for this was His plan. As long as he obeyed God's voice, surely the people would obey as well.

⤗

The next day, toward dusk, Moses heard a knock on Miriam's door. Egyptian guards stood there, their painted eyes haunted. "Pharaoh asks that you come."

Moses called Aaron from his home, and the two followed the soldiers down the familiar path to the palace. Thick swarms of flies filled the air the moment they left the boundary of Goshen all the way into Pharaoh's gilded throne room.

"The flies have ruined us!" Pharaoh shouted as the two

stepped over the threshold toward his throne. "Go, sacrifice to your God here in the land."

"That would not be right," Moses said. "The sacrifices we offer the Lord our God would be detestable to the Egyptians. And if we offer sacrifices that are detestable in their eyes, will they not stone us? We must take a three-day journey into the wilderness to offer sacrifices to the Lord our God, as He commands us."

Pharaoh looked hard at Moses, his brows furrowed beneath his heavy headdress. "I will let you go to offer sacrifices to the Lord your God in the wilderness, but you must not go very far. Now pray for me."

"As soon as I leave you, I will pray to the Lord, and tomorrow the flies will leave Pharaoh and his officials and his people," Moses said. "Only let Pharaoh be sure that he does not act deceitfully again by not letting the people go to offer sacrifices to the Lord."

Moses turned without a backward glance, Aaron at his side, and did not stop until they reached Goshen. "I will go and pray." He motioned for Aaron to go on without him.

"I can wait for you here," Aaron said, as though he did not want to leave.

Moses nodded. "I may be some time."

"I'll wait."

Moses walked on ahead to his place of prayer. "Oh, Lord, please hear my prayer on behalf of Egypt, and lift this plague of flies that has devastated their land. If not for Pharaoh, please hear the cries of the Egyptian people who are suffering under his hardness of heart." He knew even the people did not deserve such mercy for the way they had treated Israel, but a part of him, the part that knew there were some

Egyptians who did not approve of Pharaoh's decrees, caused him to want to seek mercy for them.

Moses returned to Aaron a short time later.

"The flies will go, then?" Aaron pointed toward the border between their lands.

"Yes. Tomorrow." Moses looked toward the palace far in the distance, which gleamed in the starlight and from the many lamps illuminating the halls. "But he will change his mind again."

Aaron's shoulders slumped as they turned to walk back to Goshen and their homes. "I should have known."

"But you hoped."

"I did hope."

"Keep hoping. The time is coming, but it is not yet."

# THIRTY-FOUR

Miriam set bowls of lentil stew before Jephunneh and Caleb, Aaron and Moses, Aaron's sons, and Joshua. Four months had passed since Moses had returned to Goshen, and since then God had sent eight devastating plagues over the land of Egypt, destroying nearly everything belonging to them. Though livestock in the fields died early on, those in the stalls birthed more, and Egypt continued to survive until another plague hit to devastate another part of their land. When the boils hit, the people themselves seemed to take the God of Israel more seriously, for they listened to Moses when he predicted the plague of hail to come. And yet Pharaoh continued to refuse to let Israel go to worship their God.

"How much longer?" Joshua asked as he dipped his bread into the stew. The women had retreated to the far corners of the room, and those with small children remained at home. The meeting was not one for all of the elders of Israel but the few who belonged to the families of Moses and Joshua.

"Not long now," Moses said, tearing a strip of bread from the loaf they passed among them. "Our God will defeat the two remaining and most worshiped gods among the Egyptians—the sun god, Ra, and Pharaoh himself. Then Pharaoh will know that the God of Israel is the only true God. Only then will he let us leave Egypt."

"Then it would be wise for us to choose leaders among the people to be heads of families and tribes, to help as we follow you out." Aaron met Moses' gaze. Miriam noted Moses' furrowed brow, as though he was pondering the thought.

"Do we not already have elders over each tribe?" Moses searched the faces of the men.

Jephunneh nodded. "We do."

"Then that is enough." Moses chewed a morsel of stew-soaked bread in silence.

"But what about leaders who can go out to fight our enemies?" Caleb asked. "We are not trained in warfare. We do not even know how to live in freedom. How are we going to enter the Promised Land and defeat the nations living there if we are not trained?"

Moses picked up his cup and drank, then sat back and studied the men.

"Caleb makes a good point, my brother," Miriam said, despite her promise to herself to simply listen. How could she remain silent when Moses seemed uninterested in the future beyond setting them free? Someone needed to plan, to be ready to take the land they'd been promised.

Moses glanced at her, then looked at Caleb. "God will teach us to fight, and once we are free, I will pray and ask

Him whom to appoint to lead. He alone knows each heart and can give us that wisdom."

"Forgive me, Brother, but doesn't God expect us to also learn and study the techniques of war? Who among us understands such things? We have known nothing but slavery." Aaron rested his elbows on the table and leaned forward. "Surely God would not be against our desire to train and prepare ourselves."

Moses stroked his beard as he so often did and briefly closed his eyes. When he opened them again, Miriam noted a softening in his gaze. "I have lived free all of my life. I know you have not, but except for the rules in the palace, I was free to come and go and not fear a beating. When I fled to Midian, I lived in freedom tending sheep for forty years. I answered only to my father-in-law, who kept an account of his sheep, which I tended. So you are right. Our people do need training. But they will first need to learn to obey the Lord and follow where He alone leads them. They will not know what to do with their freedom from slavery, and that freedom can lead them into great sin if they do not obey the Lord." He paused as if remembering something, and Miriam yearned to understand what, but she knew he would not reveal it to her.

"I do not know how long God will take to teach us to learn to live in freedom. A lot depends on our people. We can all do our part to encourage them to trust our God, but we cannot make them trust. It may take more time for them to learn trust than it will take for Pharaoh to let us go." Moses released a deep sigh as though the thought of leading a free people was a great burden to him already.

"I will be happy to help in any way you deem best," Joshua

said, looking intently at Moses. "If God trains my hands for war, I would lead the people to war. If peace, then I would lead the people to learn to live in peace. I am His servant . . . and yours if you need me."

Moses smiled, and Miriam felt a sense of pride in this man who was like a son to her.

"I agree," Caleb said quickly. "Whatever you need, Uncle, please ask." Caleb and Joshua exchanged a look.

Moses nodded. "First, let us get out of Egypt. God still has two more plagues to visit upon this land, and we will see His power in a way never seen before. Tomorrow darkness will fall upon the land of Egypt. Darkness so dark it will be felt. They will not be able to see each other or move from their beds. It will last for three days. After that, when Ra is vanquished, one last plague remains. Gather the elders to meet here in three days, and I will give you instructions to pass to all of the people. Then we must be ready to move, for the Lord our God is going to go ahead of us, and we must follow quickly."

Miriam cleared the bowls as the men rose and left the house, speaking quietly among themselves. Moses left as well, no doubt to go and pray. But Miriam had heard what she needed to. She must go through their things and pack what they needed. Soon, very soon, they would leave this place for good. And she would not look back.

✦

Miriam walked with Elisheba to the edge of the Nile, where the light ended and only the bank of the river was visible enough for them to draw water. Beyond the bank, the river was as black as the land beyond. They dipped their jars in the water and hurriedly backed away. Tomorrow the darkness would lift, according to Moses, but today they felt as they had the past two days.

"I can't shake the feeling of dread I sense coming from the dark." Elisheba visibly trembled, gripping her jar in front of her as if she feared it would fall from her head.

"If it is this palpable to us, and we do not feel its deep effects, what is it like to the people in their homes? They cannot see to do anything." Miriam felt a sense of pity for those Egyptians who had listened to Moses' warning about the hail and saved themselves, their servants, and their livestock that remained from the other punishing plagues. "Do you feel sorry for them?" She faced Elisheba. "I know they have oppressed us, but this . . . I fear our God. I should not wish to ever face His displeasure as they are now."

Elisheba nodded. "I waver between a longing to escape and fear of what is coming next. I am very glad God is making a distinction between our lands." She sighed. "But yes, I pity them."

"Pray God has mercy on their souls. Perhaps some of them will turn to Him. Even now I think somehow His judgments are His way to show them that if they repent He will grant them mercy."

"Do you think so? They are not of Israel." Elisheba lifted the jar to her head as they drew farther away from Rameses and the Nile.

Miriam pondered the thought as she kicked a stone along the dirt path. "I think so. Didn't Joseph marry an Egyptian? Surely our God had mercy on Joseph's sons, for they are counted among our tribes."

"This is true. Perhaps He is making a way for all people

to one day know Him. Perhaps . . ." She stopped to face Miriam and glanced behind them again at the dark land where eeriness crept. "Perhaps He will even now save some of the Egyptians out of this land, and they will go with us to the Promised Land."

Miriam wrinkled her nose at the thought. She might pity them, but could she really bear the thought of even one of them joining the exodus from Egypt?

"You do not think so." Elisheba continued walking but gave Miriam a sideways glance.

"I only hope that if any join us, they come because they believe our God, not because they want to harm us. We have suffered enough from them. And yet . . . there were those who were kind to us." She could not forget Rashida or Hatshepsut, especially in their younger days.

"Surely Moses and Aaron will keep troublemakers from joining us. Our men will not want Egyptians among us." Elisheba seemed quite sure of their men. Miriam hoped she was right as far as the rest of the Hebrews were concerned.

"Of course they will stop such a thing," Miriam said. But she knew Moses was concerned as well. She must keep watch so no woman not of Israel entered their ranks unnoticed.

❧

The darkness lifted the next day, and Miriam found a small crowd of Egyptians walking through Goshen as she made her way through the town square. Most of them were women with children, so she gathered her courage and spoke to those who had stopped and were looking around as if they were lost.

"What are you doing in Goshen?" She searched the gaunt faces. Had they eaten during the days of darkness? Was there any food left in Egypt to eat?

"We want to go with you," one woman said, her voice cracking with emotion. "We believe your God is the only true God, and we cannot abide Pharaoh's decision to keep you here. We know he will soon let you go, and we want to go with you."

Elisheba's words came to mind as Miriam looked from one woman to another. "Where are your husbands?"

"Some are dead, killed by the hail. Others work for Pharaoh, but they want to join us. They asked us to come and appeal to you to let us become one of you." The women before her were mostly Egyptian, but some were of other races. Had some of them been slaves themselves at one time? Egyptians did not normally mingle with people not their own. But she noted darker-skinned people among them, some with wide features, some narrow.

"Tell me where you are from, for surely you are not all of Egypt." She needed more if she was going to make a case for them to Moses.

"We are mostly of Egyptian birth. Some are from Ethiopia. Others from Cush. Some have intermarried with people from foreign lands." The woman doing most of the speaking looked Egyptian and reminded Miriam slightly of Rashida.

"I cannot tell you whether you can join us. I must speak to our leader. Go to your homes and come again tomorrow. Then I will tell you." Miriam turned to go back to her house but was stopped by a hand on her arm.

"No, please. If another plague comes tonight, we do not

want to be there. Please let us stay. Send one of us to tell the men, and they will slip away as soon as they can."

"What is your name?"

The woman stood close but released Miriam's arm. "Calanthe," she said, lowering her chin in deference to Miriam. "Please."

Miriam wished in that moment that even one of her men or Elisheba were with her. Someone with whom to share this burden and discuss the matter. But apparently she would have to decide on her own.

"All right," she said. "I will see if some of the families will take you in. You cannot remain together, but if the people will allow you to stay with them, then you may stay. But if Moses tells me you must go, then you will have to leave. Agreed?"

Every woman nodded, and Calanthe said, "We agree. We trust Moses. He is regarded highly in Egypt. You may not think so because Pharaoh does not listen to him, but the people respect him. And many of us respect your God. He is greater than the gods of Egypt or He would not have been able to do the things He has done."

Convinced by the woman's words and the sincerity in her gaze, Miriam motioned for them to follow her. She spent the rest of the morning finding homes that would take each family group in. Calanthe and her two children were the last.

"You will come with me," she said. "If Moses, who stays in my house, will not have you, then we will know."

The woman looked at her, tears in her dark eyes. "Thank you."

Miriam gave her a slight smile. What could she say? She

could not possibly send them back to that land of destruction. Not when she knew what was coming. *Please, Adonai. Speak to my brother. Let those who believe in You stay and escape Your final judgment.*

But as dusk fell and her men returned to find Calanthe and her children sitting quietly in a corner of the house, Miriam wondered if she had made a huge mistake.

# THIRTY-FIVE

Upon his summons, Moses and Aaron entered Pharaoh's palace the day after the darkness lifted.

"Go and worship the Lord," Pharaoh said before they had reached his throne. "But leave your flocks and herds here. You may even take your little ones with you."

"No." Moses met Pharaoh's hardened gaze, unflinching. "You must provide us with animals for sacrifices and burnt offerings to the Lord our God. All our livestock must go with us too. Not a hoof can be left behind. We must choose our sacrifices for the Lord our God from among these animals. And we won't know how we are to worship the Lord until we get there."

The veins stood out in Pharaoh's forehead, and his face purpled with rage. He leaned forward on his gilded throne and slammed the crook and flail onto the tiled floor. "Get out of here!" he shouted. "I'm warning you. Never come back to see me again! The day you see my face, you will die!"

Moses straightened and held his staff at his side, unmoving. "Very well," he said, his voice low yet commanding. "I will never see your face again. But know this, Pharaoh. Thus says the Lord: 'I am going out into the midst of Egypt, and all the firstborn in the land of Egypt shall die, from the firstborn of the pharaoh who sits on his throne to the firstborn of the slave girl who is behind the millstones, and all the firstborn of the cattle as well. Moreover, there shall be a great cry in all the land of Egypt, such as there has not been before and such as shall never be again. But against any of the sons of Israel a dog will not even bark, whether against man or beast, that you may understand how the Lord makes a distinction between Egypt and Israel.' All these your servants will come down to me and bow themselves before me, saying, 'Go out, you and all the people who follow you,' and after that I will go out."

Moses turned on his heel and stormed out of the palace, his face like fire. He and Aaron walked on without a pause, not even to draw a ragged breath, until their feet left Thebes.

The moment they crossed into the territory where Israel resided, Moses heard the Lord's voice, though Aaron did not show any sign that he heard it as well.

"Pharaoh will not listen to you," the Lord said, "so that My wonders will be multiplied in the land of Egypt."

Moses waited to hear more, but the Lord did not speak again.

Aaron had stopped in his tracks, studying him. "Did you hear from Him?"

"Yes." Moses glanced heavenward, longing for a glimpse of his God who spoke so clearly. But he saw nothing.

"What did He say?" Aaron rested both hands on the top of his staff, a wistful look in his dark eyes.

"He said that Pharaoh would not listen to me. But we already know this. God will harden Pharaoh's heart so that he will not even believe the word that his son will die."

"I do not pity the man." Aaron looked back from Rameses toward Thebes, then walked on toward their homes.

Moses followed. Pity was not an emotion he felt either. But he was angry that the man could be so stubborn he would sacrifice his firstborn son for his pride. What kind of a father would do such a thing?

"There is much for us to still do. God gave me instructions for what our people must do when this day came, and now it is here," he said to Aaron, who slowed his step to walk in line with Moses.

"What would you have me do?" Aaron lifted his gray head, his look determined.

"Come with me to speak to the people tonight. They must be ready, for when the angel of the Lord strikes, we do not want a single person to suffer the fate of the Egyptians."

❧

Moses entered Miriam's house as the sun neared the west. The people would soon be in from the fields. "We must gather the people," he said, then stopped short. He looked from Miriam to an Egyptian woman and her children standing beside her, holding on to her legs. "What is she doing here?"

Miriam stepped closer to him. "I went to the town square this morning and found a group of women and children seeking to join our ranks. They want to leave Egypt with us."

Moses rubbed the back of his neck. While he knew the servants of Pharaoh would look on them with favor and even bow before the Lord, this he had not expected. "How many?" he asked in the Egyptian tongue.

"There are about one hundred of us, my lord," the woman responded. "We are from the same community and have suffered because of Pharaoh's stubborn decisions. We can no longer bear your God's wrath. We want to become one of you and go with you when your God leads you out."

Moses rubbed his beard, holding the woman's gaze. "Where are your husbands?"

She lowered her head as if to study her feet. "They hope to come as soon as they can get away from Pharaoh."

Moses glanced toward the window. Dusk hung over the horizon, and he sensed the need to seek the Lord. Did God want these people joining them? Yet how could he keep them from following once God killed the firstborns of Egypt? Even now Aaron was calling the people together. He silently prayed for wisdom as he spoke to Miriam.

"They may stay here tonight," he said. "But right now we need to meet—all of the people. God has directions for us, and we must quickly obey. Go and gather your children and tell everyone to join us in the field beyond the houses near the sheep pens. I will meet you momentarily." Whether there was time or not, he needed to hear from the Lord.

Miriam nodded, and he turned and walked into the gathering dusk. He leaned heavily on his staff as he climbed the hill to his place of prayer. He would miss this spot once God moved them out. Yet he knew there was nowhere God did not see. One day God would show him another place to meet with Him. And Moses sensed it would be better, far better, than this secluded place in Egypt.

He knelt in the dirt near the rock, where he laid his burdens.

*This one is heavy, Lord. What do I do with these extra people who know nothing of You? Do I let them come out of Egypt with us?*

He waited, but God did not answer his question.

"When he lets you go," the Lord said, "he will surely drive you out from here completely. Speak now in the hearing of the people that each man ask from his neighbor and each woman from her neighbor articles of silver and articles of gold."

As he listened, God gave him detailed instructions for the people to protect themselves from the death that would befall the Egyptians.

The light and the voice left him then, and he did not linger, though he longed to stay. There were so many things he longed to understand about the Most High. But he stood, knowing that to ask more would do no good until he obeyed the directions he'd been given. Perhaps these women who had joined them would lead the way into Egypt and help them plunder the Egyptians of their gold and silver and jewels as God had directed. If they helped Israel, then Moses would know that they were serious about joining them. He would have the men circumcised once they were far from Egypt, and accept them and their women and children to live in their midst.

This time using his staff to help balance his long strides, he hurried to the field where he knew the people waited. One more plague and then he would lead this vast host out of Egypt. Change was coming, and he sensed that the future would be bright, despite the challenges they were sure to face.

# THIRTY-SIX

Miriam stood silent as she watched Jephunneh slit the throat of a spotless one-year-old lamb taken from their flock. A lamb they would share with Aaron's family and Moses, along with Calanthe and her family, who had come to reside in their small home. The women had already prepared the house, ridding it of all yeast these past seven days, and the lamb had been chosen two weeks earlier, the first day of the month of Abib.

These actions were to be a permanent ordinance, Moses had told the people. They were to be remembered among their people for generations throughout time.

She glanced at Elisheba as Jephunneh and Aaron dipped the hyssop into the blood of the lamb and brushed the blood over the top and side beams of the door of each house. Inside the house, packs sat on the floor near the door, filled with gold, silver, and jewels from the Egyptians who resided nearby in Rameses in Pithon. Even those as far away as Memphis had willingly given the Hebrews anything they asked for. These Egyptians did not know what was coming this night, except for those few who had joined their ranks after the plague of darkness.

Words failed Miriam as she helped Elisheba lift the lamb's carcass and put it over the open fire. All of it was to be roasted and eaten in haste, Moses had said. With their sandals on and staffs in hand. The bitter greens waited in a bowl on the table and the bread in another bowl beside it. They would burn every part of the animal that they could not eat, then carry their kneading troughs and packs with them as they led their flocks and herds out of Egypt.

Were they really leaving this very night?

A sense of anticipation and fear mingled together in Miriam's heart. The last of the blood now covered the door frames, and Moses spoke loud enough to be heard in the houses closest to them.

"Go inside now, and when the lamb is ready, get it and eat. Once you have removed the lamb and burned its flesh, do not come outside of your houses again. You must remain inside until the death angel passes us by." He walked throughout the town, repeating his words. Words he had already commanded every elder to follow. All of the people had been preparing since their meeting near the sheep pens.

Miriam slipped into the house, Elisheba and Netanya behind her. Calanthe and her family had not moved from the corner of the room, shivering and wide-eyed. Would God spare them because the blood covered them? Or did they have to be Hebrew by birth?

Miriam did not voice her thoughts. She sat at the small table, watching the bitter herbs and bread as if they might somehow move, waiting for Caleb and Aaron and Jephunneh to bring the lamb into the house. She looked at Elisheba, whose eyes showed the whites, her fear palpable. Netanya picked up Iru and held him close.

At last the men entered, the smell of roasted lamb causing Miriam's stomach to growl. Moses came in after them and shut the door. "It is time. Let us eat in haste. Come, all of you." He motioned for them to gather around the food.

The men broke off portions of the meat, the women did the same with the bread, and they passed the food among each other. The bitter herbs reminded Miriam of the life she had lived here. Despite the few moments of good, most of her life had been hard, and for most of the Hebrews it had been especially bitter.

All of that was about to end. Why could she not feel joy? But anxiety and fear of what would happen this night stole every positive emotion.

As the last bite was eaten, darkness grew deeper outside their window. Miriam longed to curl up on her pallet, knees to her chest, but she forced herself to stand with the men, waiting.

The eerie sound of wind, like wings flapping, passed over their house, shaking the walls. The children stifled their cries, and Miriam bit her lower lip. She must be strong. She must.

Silence fell like a heavy pall throughout Goshen. Not even the cry of a wild animal could be heard.

And then she heard it. In the distance, from the direction of Rameses and, if it were possible, even as far away as Thebes, came first one wail, then another. The wails were so loud, the cries so bitter and inconsolable, Miriam felt her knees weaken. The earth shook with the noise as the night waned, until a knock on the door made them jump.

Moses went to the door and opened it.

"Pharaoh asks you to come." An Egyptian guard stood before them, his expression desperate and pained.

Moses and Aaron followed the guard in silence.

Miriam looked at her men, her family still waiting for the word to go. "Gather the bread dough and the kneading boards. Put the packs on your shoulders and be ready. Moses will not be long now," she said. She knew it as she had known the truth when God spoke to her in dreams.

Everyone stood, including the Egyptians, who remained untouched by the plague of death. Apparently the blood covered anyone who believed. They gathered what they needed and stood near the door, waiting.

⤳

Moses and Aaron did not even have to enter the palace. Pharaoh stood on the steps, his finger pointed at them. "Get out!" he ordered. "Leave my people—and take the rest of the Israelites with you! Go and worship the Lord as you have requested. Take your flocks and herds, as you said, and be gone. Go, but bless me as you leave."

Moses did not respond but turned and walked with Aaron out of Pharaoh's sight. He did not bless Pharaoh, but he did not curse him either. *He is in Your hands, Lord.* Let God deal with the man.

Both men hurried back to Goshen and found the people had already gathered outside of their homes, which must have been Miriam's doing.

Moses climbed on a rock and called out to them, "Tonight we leave Egypt. Pharaoh has commanded that we leave, and we will not disappoint him."

A cheer went up from the six hundred thousand men plus

women and children as Moses jumped down from the rock and led them toward Succoth.

⟞⟝

On the way to Succoth, before leaving Goshen and Rameses, Moses stopped at a small pyramid that housed the bones of Joseph. Joshua and Caleb and several other younger men dug open the tomb and placed the sarcophagus on a cart, then continued on their journey. As they moved forward, Joshua came up beside Moses.

"Forgive me, my lord. I was wondering something," Joshua said, dipping his turbaned head in respect. He carried his own shepherd's staff, using it like a walking stick as Moses did.

"Speak." Moses walked on ahead of the throng, Aaron and his sons several paces behind. He glanced at Joshua, then looked at the pillar of fire that guided them.

"Why do we take this path? We are headed toward Etham, a city on the edge of the wilderness. But the straighter path toward the Promised Land of Canaan leads toward Philistine territory. Wouldn't God want us to engage our enemies and push on to what He has promised us?"

Moses rubbed his beard and studied Joshua. "The Lord chose this path," he said. "God knows that if the people are faced with a battle, they might turn back to Egypt." He offered the younger man an understanding smile. "We are not ready, son. Israel has been in slavery for so long that if we were faced with a foe to fight so soon, the people would flee in terror. We need time to prepare for the battles we will surely face in the future."

Joshua nodded and turned his face slightly away, as if ashamed of his question. "I suppose I am simply anxious to take the land our God has promised for so long. It is hard to wait."

Moses sensed the zeal of youth in him and, by his acceptance, also a willingness to obey the Lord. "You understand much already, Joshua. It is hard to wait on the Lord, for He sees far beyond what we can see. My parents thought me chosen when I was born and did all they could to protect me from an evil pharaoh at that time. I thought it was my place to turn things around for our people near my fortieth birthday when I saw how we were treated. But God did not call me to return to Egypt to lead us out for another forty years. So you see, His timing is not ours. His ways can be hard to understand."

Joshua faced Moses. "I have tried to understand Him all of my life. I will admit I want to know Him. But to understand His ways—they are unsearchable."

"Perhaps one day He will reveal more of Himself to us. Then we will know better than we do today."

They walked on in silence, and Moses wondered if this young man held the promise of leadership that he had rarely seen among the elders of Israel. He liked what he saw in him. But he would wait on God to show him who should be among the leaders of this vast company of people. Would the people listen to one so young? It had taken months for them to trust Moses, and that was only after the many signs and wonders God had performed against Egypt. Without God's mighty hand, Moses could never have led them this far.

He glanced again at the fire. Joshua was right in that it was leading them toward Etham. Were they to go to the Promised Land by way of the wilderness, then? He would seek the Lord and ask.

❦

Miriam spread her mat on the mixture of sand and dirt and lay beside Jephunneh, gazing on the angel of God and the pillar of fire that stood at the head of their troop. "So this is how God is going to lead us?" She twisted her head in the crook of her husband's arm and looked at him. "By fire?"

Jephunneh pulled her closer. "It would seem so. Is Moses back yet from seeking the Lord?"

Miriam sat up and looked over their tribe, where many people already slept. Some mothers sat up nursing children, and a number of their men tended to the animals and settled everyone in this wide area of land outside of the city of Etham. "I don't see him yet."

Jephunneh pulled her back down and tugged the rough blanket over them. "It can get cold in the desert at night, and this is as close to desert as I have seen."

"We need to build tents as soon as possible." Sleeping in the open wasn't bad near a fire, but she missed her privacy, as she was certain all of her countrymen and women did as well.

"Yes, after we are well away from Egypt. When we are safe."

Jephunneh's words made her sit up again. She studied her husband's drawn but handsome face, grateful for his protective arms, thankful all over again that her father had given her to this quiet yet wise man. "Do you think we are not?" she asked. A niggling sense of fear crawled up her back. God would not lead them this far only to have Egypt chase after them to make them return. Would He?

"I do not think we will ever *feel* safe until we are far from Egypt. You remember they have chariots and horses. We have women and children and livestock that cannot be pressed to move too fast. We are vulnerable until we are farther away."

He was right, of course. She rested beside him again, gazing up at the pillar of fire, silently begging God for mercy and grace to trust Him. The glory of God seemed to come from its center, and she felt herself enveloped by the security it represented. Surely God was watching over them. He would not have brought them out with such a mighty hand only to send them back again. But Jephunneh's concern suddenly became hers, and she wondered if they would ever feel truly free.

Moses would know. But he had gone off to talk with the Lord, something she wished she could do as well. *Why do I no longer hear from You in dreams?* She missed the way she felt when she heard from Him. When she knew her dreams were truly from the Holy One.

If only He would speak to her now and assure her that her husband's fears were false. Soon they would be past this place and enter the Promised Land, and all would be well.

But despite the fire of God shining down on her, her sleep was fitful that night.

# THIRTY-SEVEN

W e're going where?" Miriam asked as Moses joined their family group the next morning. "We just got here."

Aaron nodded in agreement, his look as confused as Miriam felt. "Truly, Moses, you're taking us backward from the way we just came!"

Moses drew in a ragged breath. "The Lord told me, 'Order the Israelites to turn back and camp by Pi-hahiroth between Migdol and the sea. Camp there along the shore across from Baal-zephon. Then Pharaoh will think, "The Israelites are confused. They are trapped in the wilderness!" And once again I will harden Pharaoh's heart, and he will chase after you. I have planned this in order to display My glory through Pharaoh and his whole army. After this the Egyptians will know that I am the Lord!'"

Miriam stared at her brother, could sense the baffled looks of her men as they stood near.

"Hasn't the Lord already proven to Pharaoh His power? Was not the death of his firstborn enough to keep him away from us?" The question from Caleb echoed the thoughts in Miriam's heart.

"Pharaoh is a proud man. Our God has devastated his land and taken everything from him that he counted of value. Including us. Why do you think Hatshepsut would never release us? Israelite slavery was an economic advantage to them. They didn't have to pay us to work. Can you imagine what it would have cost Egypt to pay workers to do what we did for them for nothing? Now that we are gone, it is going to hit Pharaoh that he has lost his economy along with everything else. He has no way to rebuild without us. So he is going to want us back." Moses ran a hand over the back of his neck, releasing a sigh.

"But God is sending us to a place where we will have nowhere to go." Jephunneh's words were said quietly lest the rest of the camp hear. Miriam knew her husband would never question Moses' decisions in such a way that people would turn against her brother.

"Do we trust our God or not?" Moses looked from Aaron to Jephunneh to Caleb to Joshua to her. Very few were in this trusted meeting, and Miriam felt a measure of pride knowing that she was allowed to be privy to her brother's thoughts. God had spoken to her, after all.

"We do," she said when the men merely nodded. "We will follow you. If the women complain, Elisheba and I will keep them quiet." Though how they would do so with thousands of women, she couldn't say. She wanted to believe the people would simply obey what God had said, even though her own family questioned.

"The men will follow," Joshua asserted, moving closer to Moses. "If God is leading us to a place where we are trapped by wilderness and sea, He must have a reason. Look." He pointed at the cloud, which led them by day in place of the fire that watched over them by night. "Even now God is moving."

Moses took his staff in hand and nodded. "Let us follow."

They hurried to pick up everything they had unpacked the night before as Moses commanded Israel to follow the cloud toward Pi-hahiroth. The fear Miriam had felt the night before, with Jephunneh's prediction that Pharaoh would follow them, now grew to full-blown anxiety. Despite her fine words and her obedient following, her heart feared. She'd been a slave too long. One more act of God against Pharaoh seemed unnecessary to her. But she kept her thoughts to herself and walked with Elisheba behind the men. It was going to be a long, anxious day.

~

They camped the next night at Pi-hahiroth between Migdol and the sea, near the shore across from Baal-zephon. A sense of confusion and fear rose among the people as first one day passed, then another day and night, but the angel of God and the pillar of cloud and fire did not move. Were they truly going to stay here until Pharaoh overtook them?

Miriam walked throughout the camp, hearing murmurs among the women and noting the fear in the eyes of the men. "Why aren't we going anywhere?" The question was raised over and over, but she could do little but shrug.

"We move when God moves the pillar," she said until her voice grew hoarse.

She returned to the area where her family camped and watched Moses standing on a rock protrusion, his gaze toward the billowing dust behind the camp. The ground rumbled with the sound of approaching horses, and moments later cries of panic spread among the people.

Some cried out, "Lord, save us!" while a contingent of men rushed through the encampment straight toward Moses.

"Why did you bring us out here to die in the wilderness?" one of the men shouted. "Weren't there enough graves for us in Egypt? What have you done to us? Why did you make us leave Egypt?"

Another then another shouted at her brother until they all seemed to be yelling at once. "Didn't we tell you this would happen while we were still in Egypt? We said, 'Leave us alone! Let us be slaves to the Egyptians. It's better to be a slave in Egypt than a corpse in the wilderness!'"

Miriam's knees grew weak, and she felt a sudden sense of fear. Where was her bravery now? She wanted to drown out the sound of the angry crowd, but worse, she wanted to run from the oncoming army. *Oh, Adonai, what will we do?*

She heard Moses' voice rise above the ruckus. "Don't be afraid. Just stand still and watch the Lord rescue you today. The Egyptians you see today will never be seen again. The Lord Himself will fight for you. Just stay calm."

The men closest to Moses quieted quickly, though Miriam could still hear soft grumbling throughout the camp. Everyone turned to face the coming chariots, and the mass of people drew closer together. Cries to the Lord still filled the air around her.

She looked to her brother, whose gaze had shifted from the people to the heavens. His hands were raised high, but no words came from his lips. Was God speaking to him in silence like He did with her in dreams?

Moments passed, and Miriam's heart filled with the same panic she heard coming from the tribes of Israel. *Oh, Lord, help us!* She glanced at Jephunneh and Caleb and the rest of her family, but no one moved, as though their feet were baked to the dust beneath them.

Suddenly the cloud and the angel of God who had been leading them moved from before them, blocking their view of the Egyptians and revealing the writhing sea behind them.

Moses jumped down from the rock and walked toward the huddled masses. "Be ready to cross the sea," he called to the people. "Tonight, do not unpack any more than you must. By dawn you will see what God will do."

The people quieted as Moses continued to speak. "God is going to cause a wind to divide the sea, and we will walk through it on dry ground. Return to your tribes and be ready to walk in order of your tribes. Ephraim will carry the bones of Joseph. Not one of you will be left behind, so there will be no need to hurry, even though it may seem that the Egyptians are going to catch up to us. Trust our God. Watch and see what He will do."

He dismissed them, and Miriam returned to her camp. She rolled up their pallets and packed everything they had carried with them out of Egypt. Tonight they would eat flatbread and cheese and sleep on the ground.

As dusk fell, the cloud pillar became a blazing fire once more, and the wind picked up, blowing steadily throughout the night. Miriam crept to the bank of the sea and found Moses standing there with his hand stretched out over the sea.

"The waters are separating," she said, unable to keep the awe from her voice. As though water could become a wall!

"They will remain walls on either side of the wide path of

ground until we have all reached the other side." He sounded so confident, boosting her courage.

"Will the ground truly be dry?" It seemed so impossible. She'd seen how long it took for a puddle to dry. One night hardly seemed enough without the hot sun to bake the ground into clay.

"It will be dry. For us." Moses looked at her. "Get some rest, my sister. I will need you tomorrow to help me lead these people once and for all out of Egypt."

She touched his arm. "Ima was right about you. You are our tikvah."

He looked away as though her words embarrassed him. "Only God is our true tikvah, Miriam."

She knew that. Ima had known it too. But God always seemed to use a human deliverer to display His power. Abraham had rescued Lot. Joseph had rescued the sons of Israel. God gave the victory, but He still used men and women to lead the way.

"Good night, Brother." She walked away, slightly troubled that he could not accept her compliment. But she pushed the thought aside. He was just too humble to accept the truth.

"Good night, Sister," he said, a smile in his voice. Perhaps he appreciated her words after all.

⸙

Long before dawn, Moses called to the people who had heard the wind and drawn closer to the sea in their eagerness to see what God would do. Cries of delight replaced the cries of despair that had filled the air the night before. The cloud remained behind them, blocking the Egyptians from view, and what stretched before them was what Miriam had glimpsed the night before. Two walls of water banked a bone-dry seabed.

"Move forward and cross to the other side," Moses commanded. Instead of leading them, he stretched out his hand toward Aaron, Joshua, Jephunneh, and Caleb, who led the tribes of Levi and Judah first, followed by the rest of Israel's twelve tribes.

Miriam joined her family, feeling a mixture of excitement and fear. Would the wall hold? Of course it would. If God could do this, He could also carry them safely through to the other side.

Men, women, children, flocks and herds, and the many carts carrying supplies along with Joseph's bones moved down the embankment and crossed through the sea behind her. She glanced back several times, straining to see Moses, but he stood high above the bank until the last of Israel's people had stepped onto the seabed. At last he made his way down the embankment into the sea.

Joy filled Miriam's heart as she watched little children skipping and running, some touching the water. Her grandchildren joined the younger ones, though her daughters attempted to restrain them. If the people all began to run, they would topple each other and could end up with injuries or worse.

"Calm down," she called to some of the young ones as they rushed past her. "Don't run!"

Other men and women joined the chorus of voices, some grabbing hold of little hands to keep the children from getting too far ahead. The sea before them was large, the shore still impossible to see in the darkness. Dawn had yet to fully rise, and when it did, would they have reached the other side?

Miriam picked up her pace as she tried to keep up with the men and women who were much younger.

*Please, Adonai, help us make it through.* But it was a prayer she need not have prayed. God was clearly with them in the pillar, which was now both fire and cloud.

The distant shore grew closer while dawn slowly crept over the horizon, as if God had held back the sun from breaking through to reveal where they were. Miriam glanced behind her again. All of the people were well past the middle of the sea. The shore ahead drew closer, and within another hundred steps or more, Aaron set foot on the opposite bank.

This time the tribes of Levi and Judah could not be held back, and the little ones ran up the slope. The young men and women hurried the flocks along, and even the donkeys seemed eager to climb the bank. Not a single foot slipped, despite their pace and the many warnings to take care and be calm. One by one, tribe by tribe, they drew closer and closer to Baal-zephon.

Miriam looked for Moses, who still came at the last. Behind him she could see clearly now as dawn broke free. The Egyptians slapped their horses' flanks, and both horses and chariots with their riders rushed into the sea after them.

Cries of alarm came from some of the trailing tribes, and they moved faster, some running full tilt, others limping along as quickly as their aged feet would allow. The last of the tribes were only a quarter of the way from the shore when the Egyptian army attempted to close in on them.

Suddenly the chariot wheels twisted and the chariots tipped sideways. The people of Israel continued to walk unhindered, but the Egyptian chariots seemed unable to get past the middle of the seabed.

"The chariots aren't moving," Miriam said to Jephunneh, who stood at her side, hand on her shoulder. "They are falling over, and the men are struggling to get the horses to move."

"Perhaps the horses are afraid of the wall of water."

"Their wheels don't seem to be turning correctly."

The people of Israel moved ever closer to the shore. Miriam spotted Moses bringing up the rear of the crowd. When her brother's foot touched the shore, he turned and raised his hand over the sea. The people stood mesmerized as the waters crashed against each other like two giant walls falling together. Chariots and horses lifted with their force.

"Look." Joshua pointed. "They can't escape."

"God is fighting against them," Moses said softly. "I could hear them say so as they tried to follow us. They knew our God was against them, and they tried to escape but couldn't."

The chariots and Egyptians and horses were swept away toward the farthest reaches of the sea.

"Truly the Lord is God Almighty, who has saved His people this day," Aaron said to the crowd that had gathered around Moses. "He has used His servant Moses to lead us here. And at last, at long last, we are free!"

A loud cheer went up from the people, Miriam's voice among them. She looked at the Red Sea again and could hardly see the bank on the other side. They had crossed a great body of water on dry ground, and God had truly and finally delivered them from the hands of the people who had oppressed them for all of her life and much more—for four hundred and thirty years. This was a day to celebrate. And a day to worship their God.

Later that night, Moses gathered the people around him and led them to sing a song of deliverance that brought tears of joy to Miriam's eyes.

"I will sing to the Lord, for He has triumphed gloriously. He has hurled both horse and rider into the sea. The Lord is my strength and my song. He has given me victory. This is my God, and I will praise Him—my father's God, and I will exalt Him!

"The Lord is a warrior—Yahweh is His name! Pharaoh's chariots and army He has hurled into the sea. The finest of Pharaoh's officers are drowned in the Red Sea. The deep waters gushed over them, and they sank to the bottom like a stone.

"Your right hand, O Lord, is glorious in power. Your right hand, O Lord, smashes the enemy. In the greatness of Your majesty, You overthrow those who rise against You. You unleash Your blazing fury, and it consumes them like straw. At the blast of Your breath, the waters piled up! The surging waters stood straight like a wall. In the heart of the sea the deep waters became hard. The enemy boasted, 'I will chase them and catch up with them. I will plunder them and consume them. I will flash my sword, and my powerful hand will destroy them.' But You blew with your breath, and the sea covered them. They sank like lead in the mighty waters.

"Who is like You among the gods, O Lord—glorious in holiness, awesome in splendor, performing great wonders? You raised Your right hand, and the earth swallowed our enemies.

"With Your unfailing love You lead the people You have redeemed. In Your might, You guide them to Your sacred home. The peoples hear and tremble. You will bring them in and plant them on Your own mountain—the place, O Lord, reserved for Your own dwelling, the sanctuary, O Lord, that Your hands have established. The Lord will reign forever and ever!"

As his song ended, Miriam stood and called to the women. "Gather your tambourines and dance with me!" She moved to the middle of the crowd as they made way for her. She took up her tambourine, an instrument that had been used far too little during their years of slavery, and looked heavenward. "Sing to the Lord," she sang, her voice carrying far with the help of the water, "for he has triumphed gloriously. He has hurled both horse and rider into the sea."

Where they would stay.

# PART FOUR

Then Moses led the people of Israel away from the Red Sea.

Exodus 15:22

# THIRTY-EIGHT

## TWO MONTHS LATER

Miriam sat on the ground near the fire, grinding what little was left of the grain they had brought from Egypt. Had it really been two months since they had crossed through the Red Sea?

Netanya emerged from the goat's-hair tent behind her, one that Miriam, her girls, Netanya, Elisheba, and Joshua's wife, Eliana, had sewn together every night during their stay in the oasis of Elim. How pleasant life had been there, a respite from Marah, the spring of bitter waters, and a kinder terrain than they had followed to this wilderness of Sin.

"Can I help you?" Netanya said, settling onto the ground beside her.

Miriam handed her the sieve. "You can sift stones from the grain." She had already done so for this first batch, but they needed more food to feed a household that had grown large. To save effort, they had created one big tent with several rooms to house her family, Aaron's family, her girls and their husbands, Joshua and his family, and Moses.

The sounds of the other women in the Levite camp could

263

be heard as they worked. Though Jephunneh was of the tribe of Judah, they lived among the Levites. The men had dispersed to explore the wilderness to find food for the flocks, and Moses had no doubt gone off to seek the Lord.

"I thought by now we would have reached the Promised Land," Elisheba said, joining them around the fire pit. Miriam's girls followed, carrying a jar of water to pour into the pot hanging over the unlit fire. "We have a few leeks and lentils left from our hurried departure, but soon we will run out of food." Her brows drew together, and the lines around her mouth formed a frown. "How does Moses expect to feed all of us?"

"She's right, Ima," Janese said. "How will we feed our families with only a day or two left of the provisions we brought with us?"

Murmurs of agreement moved about the fire, adding to the doubts Miriam had been fighting the longer the journey became. She looked at her family, then glanced up at the sound of more women from her tribe coming closer.

"We heard what you said. We are also worried. Has Moses told you anything? We cannot go on like this," one woman said.

"She's right," another said. "This wilderness stretches on and on, and I see no towns nearby, nor even the oasis we first came to where dates were easy to pick from the palm trees and there was fresh water to drink. Here there is water, but our men can barely find enough scrub grasses to feed the sheep and other animals. Will we have to kill our flocks and herds to survive?"

"It would have been better to have died in Egypt," said a third.

Miriam held up a hand for silence. "Please," she said, looking from one irritated face to another. "Let me talk to my brother tonight and see what he knows. Perhaps the Lord has spoken to him and already told him what to do. We must trust him." She straightened, setting the grindstone aside.

"Why should we trust him?" This from a woman who appeared to be looking for an argument. "What good has that gotten us? He brought us out here to die!"

"We were better off as slaves in Egypt!" came another voice from the back of a growing crowd.

Miriam stood, alarm rising within her. She glanced at Elisheba, who also stood. They had to keep the women calm or the men would also rise up against Moses and Aaron.

"Please," Miriam said again. "We still have food today and enough for tomorrow, perhaps even for a third day. We may move on by then. You may not trust Moses right now, but please trust our God. Didn't He give us good water for bitter at Marah? Didn't He give us the oasis at Elim? Are we going to trust Him to care for our needs or not?" She straightened to her full height and crossed her arms over her chest.

"Miriam's right," Elisheba said. "Moses and Aaron have simply been following God's leading, and did He not bring us out of Egypt with a great and powerful hand? Would you really rather have died as slaves in Egypt?"

The women exchanged chagrined looks, but Miriam spotted some among the group who still seemed irritated. "Go back to your tents and prepare your meals. Wait to see what our God will do." She motioned them away and breathed a deep sigh when they did as she asked.

"What are we going to do when they come back? And what is Moses going to do if their husbands are with them the next time?" Elisheba's words caused a flutter of fear in Miriam's middle.

"I don't know," she said after no positive answer came to her. *Oh, Adonai, what are we to do with these people? What are we to do to help ourselves?*

&#8764;

Two days later, Miriam's fears had been verified. And her prayers for calm from the people went unanswered. The assembly of men and women had complained to Moses and Aaron in a similar way the women had complained to Miriam and Elisheba, until the Lord spoke to Moses and provided bread from heaven. Had a month truly passed since that time? Yet the memory of that dispute and grumbling remained. It was as though they always lived within a breath of the next argument and frustration from the people.

A sigh escaped as she walked from the area where the dispute had taken place. Food came to them daily now, raining down from heaven. But some of the people still grumbled.

She continued walking and happened upon Moses as he came from a grassy knoll where the sheep grazed. "Good day to you, my brother," she said, for she had not seen him that morning.

"Miriam. I expected you to be back at the camp." He wiped sweat from his brow, as the sun was nearly to the midpoint of the sky and burned down on them. "It is time for a midday rest."

She looked at him, searching his gaze for signs of weariness or frustration. "Are you not in need of rest as well? The people are wearing you out."

Moses walked with her toward the camp, their steps slow.

"The people take out their frustration on me, it is true. But their grumbling is against the Lord, as you well know."

"It feels personal," she said, keeping her voice low. She glanced around them. "Where is your new assistant, our Joshua?"

"I have sent him on a mission. As you said, I too need rest and was about to seek it." He glanced toward the encampment but stopped where the trail led toward the mountain. "The people are not ready for the Promised Land, Miriam." He held her gaze. "Though God has rained down manna, the bread of heaven, and given us water whenever we cannot find it, they will not trust Him. They still act like slaves."

"I feel as though I have failed you, Brother. I tried to keep the women from grumbling, but they would not listen. I am certain if they had trusted, the men would have listened to them, for what man doesn't listen to his wife?" She touched his arm, and a lopsided grin appeared on his face, a sight she rarely saw.

"I know of none," he said.

"Was your wife also one to give you her opinion?" How often she had wished Zipporah and his sons had joined him in Egypt. Would she ever meet them?

Moses laughed softly. "Zipporah definitely has a mind of her own. But she might have complained along with the women you could not control. Trust me, Miriam, when a wife and mother cannot care for her family, she will not be happy. Men protect, but it is a woman who protects more. She protects with her heart."

"How wise you are for a man married only forty years!" Miriam smiled, pleased with this rare exchange. "Seriously, Moses, the people asked for bread and God has blessed, but now that you have moved us to Rephidim and the water was not good . . ."

He held up a hand. Much had passed since the women had first complained. But at Rephidim it was mostly the men who argued with Moses, until God had commanded him to strike a rock at a place they now called Meribah. "Has our God not met every one of our needs? Even our flocks have food, and despite the people's grumblings, God has blessed. But, Miriam." He paused until she looked from the distant herds to meet his gaze. "God is testing us, and I don't think we are going to enter the Promised Land until the people begin to pass the tests."

"What tests? Surely we as a people have already suffered so much! Why would God bring us out here to suffer hunger and thirst and uncertainty? And now I hear rumblings that a foreign nation is making threats against us?" Though she was expressing the fears of the women, some of the thoughts were her own.

Moses glanced toward the hills and sighed. "We still don't trust our God to care for us. Look at the people, Miriam. Think about your own questions. Have we suffered? Yes. Absolutely. Has God delivered us from our worst enemy, Egypt?"

She nodded.

"But you do realize, don't you, my sister, that Egypt was not really our worst enemy?" He stroked his graying beard. The people were taking a toll on him, for when he first came to them his hair was as dark as a young man's.

"Our worst enemy is ourselves," she said softly. "You knew it all along, didn't you?"

"I was my worst enemy when I lived in Egypt. It is not

hard to think as a victim of suffering when that is exactly what you are. And though I did not suffer in the palace, I saw what they were doing to you. I ran away from the pain and the fear of it all. After I killed a man, of course." His expression held deep regret.

"Will it take us long to learn all that God wants to teach us?" She longed so much to see the Promised Land. "How can I help you?"

Moses took her hand and held it palm up. "You already do much. You can no more make the women listen to you than I can make the entire throng listen to me. It has only been because of God stepping in with more miracles that the men haven't already stoned me."

Her eyes widened. "Do you think they would really do that?"

"I think they would like to. But my God would not let them."

His trust sounded so simple. Why did she find it hard to trust their God as he did? Why was this the one thing her people could not seem to do?

"I feel like a failure," she admitted as he released her hand. "I have heard from God in dreams for years. He has spoken to me. I should trust Him implicitly and be able to give my faith to the women of Israel. My example should be able to spark them to follow. If I wasn't so bad at keeping the faith myself."

He suddenly pulled her close. "You fret too much, Sister. God will take care of us, and if the people continue to rebel, well . . . I do not know what God will do. What I do know is what you have seen. We have food and water and a place to camp. Very soon, however, you are right. We will face

Amalek. They are already forming their military camp not far from here."

Alarm shot through her. "So soon? We are not ready to fight."

"I have instructed Joshua to pull together enough men to form an army. He has been working with some of them now for weeks, but tonight he will command them to prepare for battle." He glanced at the hill.

"What will you do during this time? Please tell me you and Aaron are not going to try to battle these people." Her brothers were much too old to consider wielding a sword or shooting an arrow. "Do we even have any weapons among us?"

"The men have flint knives, and we made bows during the journey. And no, I am not going with them. I will go up to the top of that hill." He pointed to the place high above where they stood. "I will hold up my hands to help give Joshua the victory."

"Your arms will grow tired if they do not win quickly."

"Aaron and Hur will help me." He started walking again and pointed to the camp. "Go and rest, Miriam. Then tell the women to gather their tents and move them around the mountain, away from where Joshua will engage the Amalekites in battle. You will be safe there."

She nodded but did not immediately leave. "I will do my best to not be part of the problem, Moses. If God will help us, Elisheba and I will do our best to continue to calm the people. And I will pray. Other than that, I do not know what else I can do."

"That is the best thing you can do. Do not worry about the rest, my sister. God will fight for us as He always has."

"Yes, He has." She walked away, pondering all they had been through.

*Oh, Adonai, help me to trust You more. It is so easy to doubt when there is no clear way before us, when obstacles cross our path. We are a fickle people, Lord. Help me to be strong for You.*

# THIRTY-NINE

The battle with Amalek went exactly as Moses had told her it would. By the following evening Joshua returned victorious, and all of the people heard that God would make war against Amalek throughout all generations. The thought sobered the people, and for once, to Miriam's delight, they did not grumble but returned to their tents humbled at the victory God had given.

Days passed, and Moses again called the people to move from Rephidim to the wilderness of Sinai near the mountain of God. Miriam walked with Elisheba and her daughters and daughter-in-law toward the stream to gather water, a daily task that simply changed locations, and peered up at the great mountain.

"Do you ever wonder where God is taking us? The Promised Land seems a long way off, yet I thought it was only about a month's journey." Elisheba's comment sounded much like a complaint, but Miriam did not say so.

"Sometimes I wonder, but we have to trust that He knows what He is doing." She glanced toward the path they had come from and saw in the distance a small group of people riding donkeys toward the camp of Israel. "Do you see them?" She pointed, and all of the women turned, squinting to see.

"They would not be riding donkeys if they were part of Israel. We are not moving yet again," Lysia said.

"No, they would not." Miriam lifted her water jar from her head, looking from the stream still a distance away to the visitors. "Let us hurry and gather the water. If they have come to visit, we will need to prepare food for them." She was finding it difficult to come up with new ways to serve manna, the bread God rained down on them each day and night except for the Sabbath.

The women turned and quickened their pace, the younger ones outpacing Miriam and Elisheba.

"I wonder who they are," Elisheba said, her breath coming faster.

"You wonder a lot these days, my sister." She smiled, for she also wondered what a new day would bring. What was God doing? And why were these people here now? Were they friend or foe?

She drew her water and hurried back to camp, not willing to be the last to find out what they all wanted to know.

⬿

Miriam arrived at the camp, deposited her water jar inside the tent, and hurried toward the people coming their way. But before she could get close enough to see their features, she glimpsed Moses many strides ahead, using his staff to hasten his steps. Did he know these people?

Since moving to the mountain of God, Moses had pitched a tent of his own, separate from the others. He had asked her and Elisheba to make it for him. People came and went from him, and Miriam no longer knew his daily routine. Had someone sent word ahead to these people that Israel was headed this way? How else would Moses know to greet them?

Irritation moved through her, but she tamped it down. There was no sense in growing upset when Moses was the one who *should* greet outsiders. She would simply be a good hostess for him once they entered the camp.

She continued forward, eager to see who had come. Moses reached them first. When he bowed down before the older man and kissed him, she sensed that he knew the man. He would not act so before a stranger, would he?

Moses rose, and she could hear the men speaking, though she could not understand what they were saying. Then, without a glimpse at her, Moses led the man and those with him toward his newly raised tent.

Miriam stopped and turned to Elisheba, who had come up behind her. "I suppose we should still plan to prepare enough food to feed them. Even if we aren't invited to hear what they are saying."

Elisheba turned about, and Miriam walked with her back toward their tent. "We will have to pray about how to make the manna stretch to feed more bellies. We don't have enough."

Miriam nodded. "If they have come to see Moses, surely God will help us figure out a way." She moved toward her tent, trying to come up with a solution. Sometimes she longed for more to add to their food, though God had given them a substance that reminded her of coriander seeds, which could be ground or beaten or made into cakes. It tasted like pastry with oil when water was the only thing they had to add to it. She wouldn't mind a different taste in her mouth. But in the wilderness there was no place to grow or harvest food. They simply had to work with what God had given them.

She glanced once more toward Moses' tent, this time noting two young men and a woman closer to Moses' age. Could this be his wife and sons?

Suddenly Miriam wanted to fix the food to please them. She would need Moses' portion of manna. But God only gave them enough for each family's needs. What were they to do with so many more mouths to feed?

Zipporah followed her father inside Moses' tent, her gaze fixed on the husband she had not seen in months. It would be unlike him to greet her and their sons until he had spoken at length with her father. So she waited to be told where to put their things and what to do.

"Have a seat over here, Jethro." Moses motioned to some cushions that were nothing like the plush cushions in her father's house. Moses' tent looked new, but his furnishings were sparse. He turned and nodded at her and their sons. "Welcome to your new home." He quickly showed Zipporah where they would sleep and eat, then returned to talk with her father.

Was there no place to prepare food? And what of sleeping mats and more cushions to rest upon? Obviously Moses had been sorely in need of a wife, and it was time she took up where they had left off.

But would he still want her as he once did?

She sank onto a mat on the floor where she could listen to Moses speak.

"Our God did amazing things to free us from the Egyptians," he said, his eyes alight with remembering. "One plague after another fell upon the land, ten of them for ten of Egypt's gods. The last was the worst, for every firstborn in Egypt died that night." He glanced at Gershom, then returned his attention to her father. "But God spared every Israelite who remained in their house and had the blood of a lamb on the doorposts. It is the Lord's Passover to us so that we never forget what He did to rescue us from slavery in Egypt."

"You had to kill lambs to be spared?" Zipporah could not stop herself from joining the conversation.

Moses barely looked her way. "A spotless year-old lamb or goat spilled its blood for us. God has always required blood to cover sin."

"This is true," Jethro said. "As a priest, I have often offered lambs upon God's altar." He glanced at Zipporah. "You know this, Daughter."

All she could think of was the man who must have been God who had tried to kill her husband and forced her to make her son bleed. Animal sacrifice she understood, though she did not like it. She smiled at her father lest her thoughts betray her. "I know."

"So once God took the lives of the firstborn—men and animals—Pharaoh finally let us go. But then God led us toward the Red Sea, and we were trapped between Egypt and the sea. Pharaoh regretted his decision and pursued us."

A little gasp escaped Zipporah. "I am glad we were not there."

"But God parted the waters of the sea, and we walked through on dry ground. The Egyptian army tried to follow us, but the sea swallowed them. None escaped."

Jethro clapped his hands and laughed. "This is wonderful news! Blessed be the Lord, who has delivered you out of the hand of Pharaoh and has delivered the people from under the hand of the Egyptians. Now I know that the Lord is greater than all gods, because in this affair they dealt arrogantly with the people.

"Come," he continued. "I have brought animals to sacrifice to our God. Call your family to join us along with the elders of Israel. We will offer Yahweh a burnt sacrifice."

"We have yet to build an altar here, as we have only recently come to the mountain of God." Moses' cheeks darkened as though he was embarrassed by his lack. "We have not taken from the flocks yet as we should have. I fear I have allowed myself to become too easily distracted."

Jethro studied Moses for a lengthy breath. "Then it is time to remedy that. You have flocks and herds to choose from, yes?"

"Yes. We do not eat of their meat, as our God provides bread from heaven each day."

"Then tonight we will sacrifice because of our gratitude to God and celebrate with a greater feast. We brought vegetables enough to feed your family."

"Enough to feed us for a month, Abba," Eliezer said. "Ima did not know how many members there were in your family."

Moses stood. "Let me call Aaron and send Joshua to gather the elders of Israel. Zipporah, I will bring Miriam and Aaron's wife to help you prepare the bread while we build an altar and offer a sacrifice."

They were the first words he had truly said to her since she arrived, and for a brief moment he smiled into her eyes. She released a shaky breath. Perhaps he had missed her. She saw no other signs that he had taken another wife, which also relieved her.

"I will gather our supplies," she said as Moses led Jethro out of the tent. "Boys, go help your father."

It was time they learned the ways of Israel if they were going to stay here. And her father, once he had heard that Moses escaped Egypt, was unwilling to keep her another day.

"I guess we are Israelites, like it or not," she murmured as she searched her bags for the food she had brought. Perhaps Miriam had a place to chop the vegetables, because it was clear Moses had very little a woman could use. Once they were settled, she would see what she could do to change that.

# FORTY

Miriam watched as Moses left his tent with his sons and Jethro, but Zipporah did not follow. Curious, she pinned the scarf better about her hair and face and beckoned Elisheba to join her.

"Where are we going?" Elisheba brushed the dust of the manna from her hands. "I am not finished with the bread."

"Moses has left his tent and Zipporah did not follow. We are going to meet her." Miriam lifted her chin. "The bread can wait."

"But . . . I don't know how I'm going to stretch it to feed more."

"We will find a way," Miriam said, dismissing Elisheba's concerns. She stopped near Moses' tent and looked in the direction her brother had gone. The men had stopped near the foot of the mountain and were gathering large stones. What were they doing? She glanced at Elisheba and shrugged, then tapped on the tent post where Zipporah had stayed behind.

A Midianite woman with hair the color of a raven lifted the flap. "Yes?"

"You are Zipporah?" Miriam asked.

"I am." The woman looked her up and down, then took Elisheba's measure as well. "And you are?"

"Moses' sister, Miriam. And this is Elisheba, Aaron's wife. Aaron is our brother." How much did the woman know of their family?

"I have heard of you. Please, come in." She stepped back and offered a smile. Eyes as dark as the Nile gazed at Miriam as Zipporah motioned for both women to sit on the few cushions Moses had taken from her home. She must sew more for him.

They sat, and Zipporah did as well. "We have come from Midian to join Moses. We thought it best not to join him in Egypt, but now that you are free of that place, my father thought it time to bring us back."

"We are happy to have you," Miriam said, hoping the woman did not see the skepticism she felt. Why now? Of course, as Moses' wife, Zipporah belonged with her husband. Perhaps Miriam had gotten too used to Moses living with them. She could not picture him as a husband and father.

"I have brought food," Zipporah said, pulling Miriam's thoughts from her foolish jealousy.

"Food?" Elisheba's eyes lit. "We have had only manna since our food from Egypt ran out."

"We thought we would be to the Promised Land by now," Miriam added. "But our God has delayed our entrance there and feeds us with the bread of heaven."

Zipporah tilted her head. "What is manna?"

Miriam laughed. "Exactly what we said when we saw it! Manna sounds like 'what is it?' No one knows, but we can use it in many ways or eat it as it is. It looks a little like coriander seeds and tastes a little like honey."

Zipporah lifted a brow. "I would like to taste it, then. But I have brought vegetables and lentils with me to feed all of us. I didn't know what you would have. My father has come to offer a sacrifice, and tonight the men will feast." She looked toward the tent door. "I wonder, though, do you have a place to chop the vegetables? I brought cooking pots, but I expected Moses would have an area where food is prepared."

"He didn't think he needed one, as he takes his meals with us. And manna does not take much preparation unless we want it to. But I do have an area outside of our tent where we can grind or beat the manna into cakes, and a board to chop and a board to knead the bread—when we are able to do so again. I don't dare part with it, for we don't know how long our God will supply our food. If it runs out because we harvest in the Promised Land, then I will knead wheat again." Miriam smiled, her heartbeat picking up at the thought of crossing into that land of promise. How long they had waited! Surely soon.

"Come with us to our tent," Elisheba said. "Once you are settled, you can make Moses' tent more agreeable to you. But you are always welcome to share our meals."

The invitation didn't surprise Miriam, but she felt a pinch of irritation that Elisheba had spoken up before she could.

"Yes, please consider our family yours. We are used to taking meals together." Miriam stood.

Zipporah stood as well and moved outside of the tent to a donkey tied to a nearby tree. Miriam and Elisheba followed her. Zipporah filled their arms with vegetables and carried a jar of lentils with her. This would be a good evening. At least for now, they could eat something other than manna.

Miriam denied the kick of guilt she felt that because of Zipporah, her family would eat well tonight. The elders would eat of the sacrifice and taste some of the foods they had enjoyed in Egypt. Would they miss the taste of onions, leeks, and melons?

The rest of the people would surely complain. She glanced at Zipporah. Would *she* complain once her store of food was gone? Or would she return to her father rather than follow their God?

Miriam was not sure which choice she wanted most.

The evening sacrifice lifted dark smoke high into the clouds. Miriam watched, mesmerized. The sun was at an angle, ready to dip into the west for its circle around the earth. Is this what God had wanted from them? To offer the blood of an animal to Him, just as He had asked them to kill the young lamb they had tended for two weeks so the blood could protect them?

She searched the heavens, but no answer came to her. She looked back at the altar, smelled the burning meat. She swallowed hard. *What does it mean, Adonai?* Why did it please God to smell the fat of lambs as though He had an appetite like any man or woman? Or was there more to sacrifice than she understood?

Though she had heard of altars built by her ancestors, no one in Egypt had burnt an offering to the Lord lest the Egyptians stone them. The Egyptians hated shepherds, and if they found out that the Israelites had offered one of their sheep on an altar, they would not have understood why. She wasn't sure she did either.

She released a long-held breath. She had only heard of these things because her father had been a Levite who remembered the traditions of their fathers and passed them on to his children. As she had done with hers. But this was the first time she had seen an actual sacrifice. Was this what Moses had intended when he demanded that Pharaoh let them go to offer a sacrifice to God in the desert?

Blood had been shed from the beginning. She recalled the stories of Adam and Eve. Even then God shed blood to cover their nakedness. Why, then, couldn't she grasp the deeper meaning behind this need?

Elisheba touched Miriam's arm, drawing her thoughts back to the moment. The men were kneeling before the Lord, and Jethro stood to bless and pray for them. Miriam slipped to her knees, catching sight of Zipporah opposite Elisheba, already kneeling with her face to the ground.

She exchanged a look with Elisheba. Zipporah would be used to such things. Her father was a priest and could sacrifice to God as often as he needed, whereas they could not.

Miriam told herself that it was a good thing for Moses' wife to be used to such customs. She listened as Jethro prayed for Israel and blessed Moses and Aaron.

When the prayer ended, the men stood, and Miriam hurried with Elisheba and Zipporah to tend to the rest of the food. Once the men brought the meat, they would not get up again until they had eaten their fill. And it was Miriam's job to make sure they enjoyed it all.

The next morning, Moses rose early and left the tent before Zipporah expected. She rose quickly and dressed. Her father was also gone, as were the boys. Had she overslept? As she lifted the tent flap, she saw the gray light just now turning to pink and the earliest part of dawn. And covering the ground at her feet was a blanket of white.

"What is it?" she spoke aloud. Was this the manna Miriam had spoken of? She bent low, picked up a handful of seeds, and touched a few with her tongue. Sweet like honey, as Miriam had said.

She shivered, returned quickly to her tent, and grabbed a shawl to wrap around her, then tied on her sandals. Was she supposed to gather the manna? And how much?

She took the jar she would need to draw water and hurried to Miriam's tent. She was about to knock when the flap lifted. Miriam stood there, Elisheba behind her.

"Zipporah! I did not expect to see you so soon." Miriam looked her up and down. "We do not draw water until we gather the manna." She gave the jar Zipporah carried a pointed look.

"I see. I did not know what to do. So you gather the manna into bowls? How much do you gather?" She felt her defenses rise with being beholden to ask so many questions, but she had little choice.

"Enough for each of us to eat for one day. So you would gather enough for you, Moses, your sons, your father, and the servants you brought with you. But only gather enough for one day or it will turn rancid and draw worms. Our God provides for us daily bread, except on the day before the Sabbath. Then we gather twice as much and the manna does not spoil."

It was then that Zipporah noticed a large clay jar in Miriam's hand and one in Elisheba's. "You came out to gather manna, then. I will return home and gather what is around our tent." She hurried away before Miriam could respond, suddenly feeling foolish to have come.

She slipped inside Moses' tent again and leaned against the post. Breathing deeply, she pushed aside her embarrassment and moved to find a clay jar large enough but settled on two smaller ones. She should have asked Miriam how much was the right amount for an entire day. What if she had too much or not enough?

She hurried outside again and nearly bumped into Miriam.

"I am sorry I did not tell you more about this yesterday, Zipporah. You should gather about two quarts per person each day and twice as much on the day before the Sabbath."

Zipporah released a breath. "Thank you. I was just wondering how much to gather and realized I should have asked you. When the men left before the dew lifted and I saw this yellowish-white mass covering the ground, I did not know what it was until I remembered what you said of it yesterday."

"Moses and the others will likely eat right from the ground. He has gone to judge the people and rarely takes time for food. There are so many needs, I fear he doesn't take care of his own needs to meet theirs." Miriam handed Zipporah an empty jar. "In case you need more. Perhaps now that you are here, Moses will start taking better care of himself. The people are such a burden to him sometimes."

Zipporah didn't know how she felt about hearing this information from her husband's sister instead of her own husband. Why was it so hard to get information out of Moses? Yet Miriam had lived among these people, and she had likely been his confidante in addition to Aaron since Moses had arrived back in Egypt. Would he continue to run to his sister or brother for advice or to share his burdens instead of confiding in her?

The thought did not settle well. She thanked Miriam for the jar but did not invite her to stay.

"Perhaps later I can show you where we draw water," Miriam said as she turned to leave. "Come by my tent when you are finished if you would like to join us."

Zipporah nodded and thanked her. But as she scooped up handfuls of the seeds into the jars, she felt a sense of irritation and confusion fill her. Moses had been difficult enough when they lived in Midian. What kind of a husband would he be now that he had his sister and brother and his people? Would he care about his own family anymore?

The thought left a bitter taste in her mouth.

# FORTY-ONE

*L*ater that evening, the family gathered in Miriam and Jephunneh's tent, the largest among them, and Miriam served her brother and his new-to-her family.

Jethro finished a last bite of the leftover vegetables and manna and wiped his hands on a piece of linen. He cleared his throat. "I watched you today, my son. What you are doing is not good." His gaze held Moses' while Miriam looked around at the reaction of her men. To reprimand her brother in front of his entire family seemed strange. Could the man not have waited for time alone with him?

She caught Caleb's and Joshua's intent expressions and met Jephunneh's gaze above the heads of the men seated on cushions. She ventured a look at Zipporah, who did not seem troubled in the least by her father's outspoken words. No wonder the woman was difficult for her to accept. She had learned from her father to speak her mind, and he should use better discretion.

But Moses did not seem to notice that he had been put on the spot. He bowed his head toward his father-in-law and then met his gaze. "How is that, my father? What am I doing that is not good?"

"It is what you are doing for the people. Why do you sit alone while all the people stand around you from morning till evening?" Jethro leaned forward, his dark eyes probing Moses'.

"Because the people come to me to inquire of God. When they have a dispute, they come to me and I decide between one person and another, and I make them know the statutes of God and His laws."

*But how do you know God's laws and statutes?* The thought troubled Miriam, for though Moses spent much time with their God, he had not yet spoken to the people as a whole to explain all that their God required of them. Had He told Moses something that Moses had kept from her and Aaron?

Jethro's deep voice pulled her out of her musings. "You and the people with you will certainly wear yourselves out, for this thing is too heavy for you. You are not able to do it alone. Now obey my voice. I will give you advice, and God be with you! You shall represent the people before God and bring their cases to Him, and you shall warn them about the statutes and the laws and make them know the way in which they must walk and what they must do. Moreover, look for able men from all the people—men who fear God, who are trustworthy and hate a bribe—and place such men over the people as chiefs of thousands, of hundreds, of fifties, and of tens. And let them judge the people at all times. Every great matter they shall bring to you, but any small matter they shall decide themselves. So it will be easier for you, and they will bear the burden with you. If you do this, God will direct you, you will be able to endure, and all the people also will go to their place in peace."

Moses nodded and bowed low before his father-in-law, something Miriam wondered if he had even done before Pharaoh. "Thank you, my father. It is wise advice that you give. I will do as you suggest."

"Very good. You are a good man, Moses. I can see that my daughter and her sons will be safe with you, so in the morning I will return to my own country." Jethro did not even glance at Zipporah, but Miriam understood. He would say his goodbyes to them in private.

The men stood as Jethro moved to the door of the tent. He embraced Jephunneh, Caleb, and Joshua, then followed Moses to his tent. Miriam watched her nephews fall into step behind Moses, Zipporah coming at the last. By Zipporah's thin-lipped expression, Miriam could not decide whether her sister-in-law was happy to be staying or not.

⬧

Zipporah accepted her father's kiss on each cheek, then stood in a field of manna yet to be gathered, watching his donkey disappear into the morning mist around the mountain. Moses had said his goodbyes the night before and had already left to gather Aaron, Joshua, Caleb, and Jephunneh to help him choose the leaders her father had suggested he put in charge of the sons of Israel.

She felt the sting of emotion and blinked, blaming the mist and the rising sun for her watery eyes. She turned back into her tent. Even her boys had left early to help their father. Apparently they had missed him more than she realized. They would soon be shepherding flocks or doing something

Moses would want them to do. If only she could get used to living among this strange people.

She pondered the thought as she gathered the manna again and later walked with Miriam and Elisheba to draw water. At least they had given her a variety of ways to prepare this bread from God. Was this the food of angels? Her father had said as much. Perhaps he knew.

She left the water jar in a niche in the ground, set the manna aside after eating a handful to assuage her hunger, then set off to walk through the camp in search of her husband. Perhaps he would be pleased to have her company. But he would probably ask why she hadn't remained with the women. A sigh escaped. *Please, God of the Hebrews, let him allow me to stay with him today.*

She didn't pray often, but it seemed like a good idea given where she walked. The God of her husband had certainly performed great miracles for His people. Could He not answer one woman's simple prayer?

She came upon Moses near the base of the mountain some distance from the tents and the flocks. She hurried over to him. "Moses."

He turned at her call, glanced at the mountain, then came to her.

"Zipporah. What are you doing here?" He touched her arm and drew her away from the foothills.

"Looking for you. Are you planning to climb this thing?" She pointed upward.

He nodded. "My God has called me to come up to Him there. I will not be gone long. Though you probably should not plan to see me tonight." His look held apology.

"Why did you not warn me of this? I would have worried

when you did not return." Was this how he was always going to treat her? As if she wasn't there?

"I'm sorry. These past months I have not been used to having you near." He rubbed his beard. "I have heard from our God just now, and He wants me to climb the mountain to hear what He has to say to the people."

"Then you should go," she said, defeat settling over her. She already knew she was no match for Moses' God.

He leaned closer and kissed her cheek. "I will be back soon."

She watched him turn toward the base of the mountain and begin his climb, wondering exactly what "soon" meant to him and to his God.

# FORTY-TWO

Miriam slipped in at the back of the crowd of elders three days after Jethro had left their camp to return to his own land. Zipporah had brought the news that God had called Moses to climb up the mountain. His return signaled a word from the Lord, and Miriam did not plan to miss anything he said.

Moses stood above them on a rocky ledge so they could better see him. "Men of Israel," he called to the group, "this is what the Lord says." He paused as though making sure he had everyone's attention, then continued. "'You have seen what I did to the Egyptians. You know how I carried you on eagles' wings and brought you to Myself. Now if you will obey Me and keep My covenant, you will be My own special treasure from among all the peoples on earth, for all the earth belongs to Me. And you will be My kingdom of priests, My holy nation.'"

The elders spoke as one. "We will do everything the Lord has commanded."

Murmurs of agreement and a feeling of acceptance moved

through the crowd. Miriam's heart felt light, and her body longed to respond—if only she could lift her arms and feel her feet rise to the heavens. God considered them, her people, His own special possession! They would be His kingdom of priests. His holy nation! The thought overwhelmed her. She had dreamed of things He told her would happen, but to hear what He thought of Israel . . . She lifted her eyes to the top of the mountain, where Moses had met with God. What would it be like? Did Moses see God's face?

She did a little dance, not caring who saw her twirl about. Around her, men were singing praises to Adonai, and as she watched, Moses began to climb the mountain once again. So soon?

She glanced about, but Zipporah and Elisheba and the other women in her clan had not joined the men. She must tell Zipporah that Moses would not be coming home yet again tonight.

Why must he return without a chance to go home? But the thought quickly slipped away as she turned toward her tent, leaving the men to celebrate without her. It was a heady day for them, and soon all of the people would know how much God valued them. Perhaps such knowledge would keep them from grumbling and complaining against her brothers and against their God.

But as she neared Moses' tent, where she expected to find Zipporah, a shudder worked through her. The people were fickle. This good knowledge of their God's love for them wouldn't last. And all of the promises of obedience in the world would be too easily broken.

Moses descended the mountain the following day and entered the camp. Joshua met him at the base. "You are back," he said, smiling.

"Yes. And you were waiting." Moses looked deeply into the younger man's eyes. "Your heart yearns for Yahweh." He could see it in the look on Joshua's face and the light in his smile.

Joshua lowered his head a moment, then held Moses' gaze. "Yes. I long to assist you and obey Him."

"Good." Moses looked beyond them. "Go and gather the people—all of them. Bring them to the valley floor, but do not allow them to come near the mountain. I will speak with them there."

Joshua nodded, turned, and ran off to do Moses' bidding. Moses headed toward his tent. Zipporah would not be happy with his absence or with his words when he told her that he would be making more visits to the top of the mountain to talk with God.

His heart felt heavy at the thought of disappointing her, but when his mind turned to the memory of God's voice in his ear, there was no difficulty in the decision he must make. He yearned for Yahweh as one yearns for the deepest kind of love, even greater than that of a man for his wife or for his firstborn son. How was it possible to feel the way he did when he could not adequately describe it? And Zipporah would never understand, for she wanted him to be her husband as he once was, before God called him.

But the call of his God was stronger. And though his mind could not find the words, his soul sang with the beauty of the purest kind of friendship and love.

He rolled that idea through his thoughts. Was he God's friend? Moses did not deserve to be called that.

He attempted to shake the notion aside, but as he entered his tent, he felt as though he wasn't truly home. Home was near God. He longed to hear the call to return to the mountain to be with Him.

A few hours later, Moses stood again at the base of the mountain, but this time, Miriam was not the only woman there. All of Israel stood in the valley before him, waiting. A sense of excitement filled her. Something profound was going to happen. She sensed it the moment she spotted Moses enter their camp and visit his tent. There was a slight glow about him, and he walked as a man many years younger.

The crowd grew quiet as Moses lifted his hands for silence. "This is what the Lord says," he began. "'Consecrate yourselves today and tomorrow, and wash your clothes. Be sure you are ready on the third day, for on that day the Lord will come down on Mount Sinai as all of you watch.

"'But be careful! Do not go up on the mountain or even touch its boundaries. Anyone who touches the mountain will certainly be put to death. No hand may touch the person or animal that crosses the boundary. Instead, stone them or shoot them with arrows. They must be put to death. However, when the ram's horn sounds a long blast, then the people may go up on the mountain.' So get ready for the third day, and until then abstain from having sexual relations."

Miriam listened, her heart beating fast. God was going to come down on the mountain! They would hear His voice! She glanced around at the rest of the people, but instead of the joy she felt bubbling within her, she saw fear, even terror, on the faces of most.

"Why are they so afraid?" she whispered to Elisheba, who stood beside her.

Elisheba met her gaze. "Are you not? Moses said if anyone so much as touches the boundary, they would die! They're afraid for good reason, Miriam."

"They just need to stay back and obey the boundary God sets up." How hard could that be?

"But even an unknowing animal could wander past. To touch the beast would mean the death of that person. Does that not cause you to worry? What if one of your grandsons escapes his mother and reaches the boundary?" She shook her head, her eyes dark with the same fear Miriam had seen in the expressions of all those around her. "I am surprised you are not frightened as well."

"Perhaps I should be." Miriam turned and walked back to her tent to gather the clothes of her household. As she pondered Moses' words on her walk with Elisheba and Zipporah to the river to wash the clothes, she realized that the people had only the plagues and the miracles as evidence of their God's care for them. They didn't have the dreams she'd had or the visions Aaron had had. And no one else had the privilege Moses had of speaking to God as a man does to a friend.

They had good reason to fear a God who had displayed such might against the Egyptians. Though He loved them and considered Israel His special possession, He was still a consuming fire. A God they must learn to obey.

She scrubbed the dirt from Jephunneh's tunic in silence. Despite all of those good reasons, she simply could not fear that God would hurt her or those she loved.

On the third day, Miriam and Elisheba quickly gathered the manna, then joined Zipporah and her sons and hurried with their families to the valley floor just outside of the camp, far from the base of the mountain of God. Moses already awaited the people and stood well outside of the boundary he had instructed the men to build to keep the people from coming too close.

Clouds darkened above them as the people drew together, their gazes lifted upward. Thunder roared like a lion emerging from its den, and lightning flashed from one end of the sky to the other. A dark, dense cloud descended on the top of the mountain, and a long, loud blast sounded from a ram's horn.

Miriam felt fear she did not expect move in a deep inner tremble throughout her body. She looked at her husband and the others around her. Everyone seemed to be shaking, their knees knocking, some falling on their faces, others looking away from the vision above them.

"Come," Moses called to the entire group. He moved away from the camp to the foot of the mountain. To meet with God.

Smoke billowed upward, and the entire mountain was encased in the smoldering fire that was their God. It shook with such violence that Miriam nearly fell backward. She clung to Jephunneh's arm.

The ram's horn blasted again, louder this time. And again. And louder still. Moses spoke, but she could not hear him above the noise of the blasts. When God thundered His reply, the people fell to their knees and covered their faces.

When Miriam lifted her head to look for her brother, she saw him climbing the mountain, past the barrier that kept everyone else out. God must have called him to come up to Him. The people waited in silence.

Sometime later, Moses called Aaron to join him. "Do not come near the boundary I have set up," Moses said to the people, nearly shouting to be heard. "If you do, you risk God breaking out against you and consuming you. Do not risk it."

He turned and motioned for Aaron to follow. Miriam watched both of her brothers climb the mountain, wishing in that moment that she too had been singled out to meet with God.

# FORTY-THREE

*M*iriam fluffed cushions in her tent and walked about the large room, putting things her grandchildren had moved back into their proper places. She glanced at the jars of manna sitting on her chopping board held up by two large rocks. Someday, perhaps, she would live in a house again and have a bench and table to work at. For now, she must live with what was, though she could not deny her restlessness.

Moses had remained on the mountain after Aaron returned, and every day Joshua returned to report that there was still no sign of her brother. How long would God keep him on the mountain? Three days seemed sufficient, but as evening and morning came and went, the days stretched to seven.

What was taking so long?

No longer able to remain confined to her tent, she pushed the flap out of the way and walked to Zipporah's tent, where she found Elisheba already sitting with their sister-in-law, spinning wool.

"Welcome, Miriam. Do you bring news?" Zipporah's

brows drew closer together, her concern evident. "He's been gone longer than in times past."

"Yes, I know. And I'm restless with wondering how long. How much time does God need with him when we need him here?" She hadn't expected to express her frustration, but she couldn't stop herself.

"Imagine how we feel." Zipporah glanced toward the sleeping mats of her sons, empty now, as they were off tending the flocks. "I rarely see him, and he is so busy with the people that his family suffers."

"And now the people suffer for lack of his leadership, though Aaron is still able to handle some of the complaints. And the elders Moses appointed help. Still . . ." Miriam did not complete the thought. She should go about the camp to make sure the women were not as restless as she felt. But she longed to know what Moses was hearing from God and could not seem to bring herself to do what she should.

A commotion in the courtyard caused them to stop their spinning. Miriam had yet to sit, so she hurried to the door and stepped outside.

"Moses is coming down the mountain." Joshua's voice came from a distance, but his words were repeated throughout the camp.

The people streamed from their tents and hurried to the edge of the camp, though they kept a healthy distance from the foothills. Miriam looked up and released a long-held breath. Moses was indeed coming down the mountain with a speed that surprised her. Where did her brother get such energy?

She was too anxious to see him to care. She moved to the front, where Aaron stood with the elders. Elisheba and Zipporah came up behind her.

"So he is finally returning," Zipporah said softly. "I wonder if he will come home or climb the mountain again."

Miriam glanced at her, then returned her gaze to her brother. "I guess we will know soon." She dearly hoped Moses would sit with them at the evening meal and share the details of his visit with the Lord.

The crowd grew quiet as Moses reached the base of the mountain and held his hands high. "I have instructions from the Lord." His voice carried to the edge of the crowd, amplified either by the Lord or by the place where he stood, Miriam couldn't tell. "Listen to the instructions from the Lord your God," he continued.

The people grew quieter, if that were possible. Moses lowered his arms and drew in a breath. Then he spoke as though quoting every word from God's mouth.

"This is what the Lord says: 'I am the Lord your God, who rescued you from the land of Egypt, the place of your slavery. You must not have any other god but Me. You must not make for yourself an idol of any kind or an image of anything in the heavens or on the earth or in the sea. You must not bow down to them or worship them, for I, the Lord your God, am a jealous God who will not tolerate your affection for any other gods. I lay the sins of the parents upon their children; the entire family is affected—even children in the third and fourth generations of those who reject Me. But I lavish unfailing love for a thousand generations on those who love Me and obey My commands.

"'You must not misuse the name of the Lord your God. The Lord will not let you go unpunished if you misuse His name.

"'Remember to observe the Sabbath day by keeping it

301

holy. You have six days each week for your ordinary work, but the seventh day is a Sabbath day of rest dedicated to the Lord your God. On that day no one in your household may do any work. This includes you, your sons and daughters, your male and female servants, your livestock, and any foreigners living among you. For in six days the Lord made the heavens, the earth, the sea, and everything in them, but on the seventh day He rested. That is why the Lord blessed the Sabbath day and set it apart as holy.

"'Honor your father and mother. Then you will live a long, full life in the land the Lord your God is giving you.

"'You must not murder.

"'You must not commit adultery.

"'You must not steal.

"'You must not testify falsely against your neighbor.

"'You must not covet your neighbor's house. You must not covet your neighbor's wife, male or female servant, ox or donkey, or anything else that belongs to your neighbor.'"

When Moses finished his speech, thunder rumbled at the top of the mountain. There was a loud blast from what sounded like a ram's horn, only clearer, like the ring of a long, loud, silver song. Lightning flashed as it had days earlier, and smoke billowed upward as if from a huge furnace.

Miriam, along with the rest of the people, stepped back a pace, fear and trembling coursing through her body. How was it that Moses could even speak to a God so powerful as to shake the heavens and earth with His voice? She fought the urge but could not stop her teeth from rattling.

One of the elders shouted from a distance, "You speak to us, and we will listen. But don't let God speak directly to us, or we will die!"

Miriam started to nod in agreement, for wasn't it God's voice that thundered and blared above them? Her earlier wish to climb the mountain abated with this second display of God's presence. She preferred the God who met her in dreams. But she could not let the people know that she feared as they did. Surely God was with them and no harm would come to them if they obeyed.

"Don't be afraid," Moses called back to the people, "for God has come in this way to test you, and so that your fear of Him will keep you from sinning!"

Miriam could not pull her gaze from her brother, longing to call out to him to come home so that they could hear more from him away from the crowd. But as the people stood watching, Moses turned and climbed the mountain, approaching the dark cloud that had descended again. The cloud where God was.

Zipporah let out a frustrated sound behind her, and Miriam turned. "So he is not coming home again."

"No. Not yet." Miriam's frustration matched Zipporah's, but she kept it hidden. There was nothing they could do. God wanted her brother, and her brother seemed to want God more than he wanted anything else.

# FORTY-FOUR

*T*hree days later, Moses descended the mountain of God yet again and met Joshua, who was waiting for him. He crossed the boundary and walked with the younger man toward the camp of the Levites where his tent stood. "The Lord has given you to me to be my assistant," Moses said, stopping to take Joshua's measure. He studied the man's clear gaze and saw acceptance, even joy, in his dark eyes.

"I am honored, my lord." Joshua bowed. "And grateful."

"As am I," Moses said. "I have instructions again from the Lord, and then we will take Aaron, Nadab, Abihu, Hur, and the seventy elders with us to a place God has prepared for us to meet Him. But first we must build an altar, call the people together, and sacrifice to the Lord."

"I will do whatever you say." Joshua girded his robe into his belt. "Shall I go now and call the men and the assembly together?"

"Yes. Go." Moses nodded, and Joshua took off running like a gazelle in the opposite direction. Moses moved toward his tent and stopped on the way to call Aaron and Miriam to join him there.

⧽

"Aaron will come with me, along with his two oldest sons, after I have written down the Lord's instructions and built an altar to Him," Moses said. He sat among the circle of cushions in Miriam's tent, his face radiant.

Miriam watched him closely as she, Elisheba, Zipporah, and the younger women served manna to their men. But Moses barely touched his portion.

"Is he not hungry?" Zipporah whispered in Miriam's ear. "Everyone else has already finished, yet his food remains."

Miriam glanced at the bowl in front of Moses, then looked again at him, drawn to the light in his eyes. Was this what happened when a man talked with God? She longed to ask so many questions, but the men were talking. She would have to wait.

"Did you actually see God?" Caleb asked, putting his arms around his young daughter, who had crawled onto his lap. "I am both intrigued and terrified by the thought. Our God is a consuming fire, and it seems to me that He must favor you greatly to want to speak with you so freely, Uncle."

Moses shook his head. "I do not actually see Him. That is, I see the part of His character He chooses to show me. I am not sure anyone can truly look on God and live."

"And yet He continues to call you to come to Him. Perhaps one day you will see Him more clearly." Jephunneh's words caused the yearning in Miriam to begin again.

She slipped out of the tent as the conversation picked up once more. Moses would return to his tent soon to write the

305

laws of God for the people. She should stay and listen, but she found herself drawn to the night sky.

She looked toward the mountain. The cloud above it had turned to burnished gold, like fire blazing. A shiver worked through her. Caleb was right to fear a God like theirs. Why were her dreams of Him so different?

*Adonai?* Her heart yearned heavenward, her gaze drawn to the fiery billows on the mountain's heights. *Moses says You are testing us. I know You want obedience, and I would give it to You with all my heart. I only wish I could see You as Moses does. I wish my gaze carried the light that comes from his.*

She waited, not certain her prayer was heard. If God spoke to her in a dream again, she would know. But since Moses had returned, her dreams had grown infrequent. Though she knew God had called her to help Moses lead, she had lost some of the connection she once felt to Him—as if He had given it to Moses and no one else.

But that was foolish. Moses himself had just told them that God wanted more than seventy of their men to come to Him with Moses on the mountain.

*If I am to lead the women, why are only Moses and Aaron and the men called to be with You there?*

Again she waited for some answer in her spirit. The clouds near the mountain blocked the moon from view until her eyes could see only the fire in the cloud of God. In that moment, she knew she would never have the same privilege her brothers had. Yet she did not believe God loved her less. He had rescued all of His people, young, old, male, female—all.

She turned to enter her tent once more when she felt the slightest touch on her shoulder. She whirled about, but no one was there. Her gaze lifted again toward the mountain, and her heart surged with sudden joy. Had God somehow touched her? No wind whispered in the nearby trees or lifted the hair from her face. The night was totally still. Yet she was not mistaken, was she? Something or someone had touched her.

As she watched the fire of God move and breathe like a spirit ablaze, somehow she knew. He cared for her. She might never see His face, but she had felt His touch. And that was enough.

⁓

The next day Moses arose early despite staying up late to write the Lord's instructions on clay tablets. Zipporah stopped him at the tent's door. "Will you be gone long again?" There was a note of despair in her tone.

He touched her cheek. "I do not know. First the people will gather and we will offer sacrifices to the Lord—after I build the altar." He reached for the tent flap, but Zipporah clung to his arm.

"I cannot bear you being gone a week or more at a time. You are allowed to come home, and then God calls you right back again. I need you, Husband. I feel as though I should have stayed with my father if I'm never to spend time with you."

He caught the glint of tears on her lashes and felt guilty that he had neglected her. "I am sorry, beloved." He cupped her face and kissed her. "But I must obey my God. Would you have me do otherwise?"

She leaned against him, then pulled away. "No. Of course not." She crossed her arms over her chest. "Go. If you don't get started soon, you won't complete the work today."

He lifted the flap and looked back at her. "You will be all right?"

"Yes," she said.

As he moved into the camp where the manna coated the ground and women were just beginning to gather it for the day, he wondered if his wife spoke truth.

The thoughts of Zipporah, however, did not linger. He had instructions from the Lord that he dared not ignore.

"Joshua," he called softly as he neared the man's tent. "Are you up?"

Joshua opened the door, sandals on his feet and staff in hand. "Coming." He kissed his wife and fell into step with Moses.

"Good. I want you to sound the ram's horn to call the people to the foot of the mountain. When they arrive, choose some of the young men to pick some of the perfect lambs and bulls from our flocks and bring them to the mountain. I will build an altar there."

"What else can I do?" He glanced at Moses, who picked up the pace as they walked.

"Help me to find twelve large stones to set up as pillars for the twelve tribes of Israel. We will stand them near the altar at the foot of the mountain."

"I will do as you have said." Joshua hurried with him, both men silent now.

Moses looked up at the mountain. The dark cloud had returned to a simple white cloud, its fiery presence hidden as the sun rose. His heart beat faster at the thought of going again to spend time in the presence of Yahweh. There were joy and love in His presence, despite the awe and wonder and fear He evoked. Could the people ever understand that all their God had done for them, bringing them out of Egypt and preparing them to enter the Promised Land, was because of His great love for them?

Moses had not known how to give voice to a word that could describe God's love the first time he encountered it, but as he spent more and more time on the mountain, listening to God's words, the more he recognized what love felt like. It reminded him of the way his true mother had looked at him as she held him in her arms, before she gave him to the palace to raise. And yet, even his mother's love did not compare to this.

He struggled even now to comprehend how to describe it, yet he knew the reality of it—as if love came through from God's very being. That didn't diminish the terrifying presence of His power and justice, but on those who came to Him in love and obedience, He showered His great, all-encompassing love and compassion.

Somehow Moses needed the people to understand this. Yet he knew in the deepest part of his being he could never make them see as he did.

$$\iff$$

After Moses had drained the blood and sacrificed the animals, Miriam listened as he read from the Book of the Covenant. He stood again on the base of the mountain so that his voice would carry to the ends of the camp.

When he finished speaking, the people responded as if with one voice. "We will do everything the Lord has commanded. We will obey." Miriam's own voice lifted to blend with those around her.

Moses stepped closer to the people and picked up a basin of blood that sat on the ground near the altar. He moved into the crowd and splattered the blood over the people in sweeping motions. Blood hit Miriam's robe, and she caught Moses' words as he moved past her. "This blood confirms the covenant the Lord has made with you in giving you these instructions."

By the time Moses finished going through the crowd, dusk had blanketed the sky and the dark cloud of God's presence had mixed again with orange and yellow fire.

Miriam turned to Elisheba. "It looks like you will only have Eleazar and Ithamar to eat with you tonight. You will join us, of course?"

Aaron had moved his family to a tent of their own soon after Moses had done the same. Still, they often gathered in Miriam's larger tent to take their meals or discuss the business of the camp.

"We will be glad to join you," Elisheba said, glancing toward the mountain. "I am glad Aaron and our oldest sons were called to meet with God. It is good for others besides Moses to glimpse our God."

Miriam agreed. She moved toward her tent, Elisheba at her side. How she longed to be among the men who were called! But Elisheba was right. It was good that others might have the ability to speak with God or at least be allowed on His mountain.

Perhaps someday all of the people would be able to make their home with their God. It was a foolish dream, she supposed, but one she carried in her heart nonetheless.

⁓

Moses led Aaron, Nadab, Abihu, and the seventy elders up the mountain, though they stopped before they could reach the summit. About halfway to the top, the cloud descended. Suddenly a place to break bread and a meal of meat, bread, and vegetables was spread before them.

Moses looked above the table and saw a surface of brilliant blue lapis lazuli, as clear as the sky. Above the surface, a throne rested, and one like that of a man wearing a long robe sat upon it. A gold sash fell across His chest, and His head and hair were like white wool or new-fallen snow. His eyes were flames of fire, and His feet looked like polished bronze. When He spoke and bid them to eat, His voice thundered as it had when He'd descended the mount and caused it to shake so violently.

Moses motioned the stunned men to sit at the places prepared for them. They did as he said, though no one spoke. "Sit and eat and drink before our God. He is inviting us to come and enjoy His bounty."

Moses sat first, for he wasn't sure the others would do so if he did not set the example. As he took up the bread and passed it to the men, he felt as though they were all in a dream. Were they really eating and drinking before their God? Though they saw His presence in the form of a man, He did not destroy them. He had never appeared in this form to Moses in times past, not even when they spoke on the mountain. Was this the only way they could ever see Him? As a man?

He lifted his gaze to drink in the experience, to memorize this moment and hold it close to his heart. *Ah, Adonai.* Had there ever been a God as great as their God?

The men about him murmured among themselves, each one periodically glancing upward, but while Moses noticed their actions, he could not take his eyes from the beauty before him.

They finished eating, and the thunder roared again. The men with him shrank back, fear etching their faces.

"Come up to Me on the mountain." Moses heard the voice in his ear. "Stay there, and I will give you the tablets of stone on which I have inscribed the instructions and commands so you can teach the people."

Moses tore his gaze away from the vision of God, and a moment later it disappeared from their sight. "The Lord has called me to come up to Him on the mountain. Joshua will accompany me. Stay here and wait for us until we come back. Aaron and Hur are here with you. If anyone has a dispute while I am gone, consult with them."

He turned and hurried up the mountain toward the beckoning cloud, his heart beating faster with every anxious step.

# FORTY-FIVE

Miriam held the scarf closer to her neck to keep the wind from pulling her hair from its bindings. Elisheba and Zipporah walked beside her as the three of them moved through the camp to check on the women. This marked the thirtieth day since Moses had climbed the mountain with Joshua, and neither one had returned.

"Aaron said the men grew weary of waiting on the mountain," Elisheba said. "I would have felt the same after seven days and no sign of Moses or Joshua. Do you think God killed them?"

Miriam gave her a sharp look. "No! Don't even say such a thing. Moses is called of God to lead us, and he will return as he always does."

"He's been gone a long time," Zipporah said, her voice soft, her tone discouraged. "I don't know what good I am to him. He is never there for our sons or me. They should be wed by now, but their father is too busy to look for wives for them."

"Perhaps we can give you some suggestions to propose to

him once he returns," Miriam said. "Right now, we need to find out the mood of the camp. I've heard grumbling from some of the women when I've drawn water—surely you have both heard it too. If they will complain around me, they will complain around anyone." She looked from one to the other, saw the scowl on Elisheba's face, and lifted a brow. "What?"

"You act as if you are so above us. You think they would grumble around us any more than you? We are all Moses and Aaron's kin. Why should the women trust us with their complaints any more than you?"

Miriam's stomach clenched as though she had been struck. Never had Elisheba lashed out at her like this. Had she truly acted so above them? "I didn't mean to offend," she said when she found her voice again. "If that's the way you truly feel."

Elisheba turned her head away and lifted her chin. "I think I will check on the women in another part of the camp." She stalked off, leaving Miriam alone with Zipporah.

Stunned, Miriam stared after her sister-in-law, her friend. She looked at Zipporah. "Do you feel the same way?"

Zipporah shook her head. "I am too new to your people to know what either of you thinks or what has gone on between you. But I see her point. She feels inferior to you. As do I."

Miriam took a step back and would have looked for a place to sit if there had been one. Up ahead of them, women sat on the ground grinding manna or stood shaking out the rugs they had woven from the sheep's wool. "I never meant to make you feel that way."

"I know you didn't." Zipporah moved closer and touched

Miriam's arm. "But you must understand that we both know—all of the women do—that God speaks to you in dreams. He may not call you to come speak with Him on the mountain, and He may not have allowed you to see Him as Aaron and the elders did, but He considers you differently than He does us. Special somehow."

The knot in Miriam's stomach released a little as she saw the truth in Zipporah's words and the kindness in her eyes. "I don't feel special," she admitted. "I long to be favored as Moses is, or even Aaron."

"I think all of us feel that way. But we only get to glimpse God's power or hear His thunderous voice. We only see what causes fear. Moses sees much more." She looked at her feet. "I only wish he would share his experiences with me."

Miriam studied this sister-in-law, a foreigner yet accepted by God into Israel, respecting her in a new light. "I wish he did too. My brother has always kept his thoughts close to his heart. He did not grow up as we did, and I don't think he ever felt close to anyone."

"Except God."

"Yes. Except our God." Miriam adjusted her headscarf and glanced at the tents where the women worked. "We should really go and see what they are thinking. If they are complaining against Moses, maybe we can stop it before it gets out of hand."

Zipporah nodded. "Though I doubt we will have much success if the women are already riled. He's been gone a month. Much longer and I don't know what we will do."

"We will do our best." Miriam walked beside Zipporah toward the group of women who had gathered in the center of the tribe of Levi. She did not like the scowls greeting her.

And her heart still grieved Elisheba's outburst and the rift she felt between them. But she smiled as she approached the group.

~

Later that night, she filled Jephunneh in on what she had learned. "The women are agitated, and I have no doubt the men feel the same. What are we going to do?" She looked into his dark eyes, feeling the same warmth she had always felt from the first day she had learned to love him.

He broke bread and gave some to her. "Some of the men came to Aaron today," he said. By his look, she knew his news was worse than hers. Thoughts of Elisheba surfaced, and the guilt and hurt returned.

"What did they say?" She straightened, bracing herself.

They were alone, as Caleb and his wife had a tent of their own next to theirs now. How strange it felt to have so much room and only share it on occasions when the whole family came together.

Jephunneh cleared his throat and lowered his voice. "The men came to Aaron and said, 'Come on, make us some gods who can lead us. We don't know what happened to this fellow Moses, who brought us here from the land of Egypt.'"

Miriam gasped, put a hand to her throat. "They didn't."

"They did." Sorrow filled her husband's eyes, and in that moment she felt her deep love for and kinship with him grow. That he loved Adonai, even though He had never spoken to him in dreams or visions, drew her. Such faith he had. How she wished hers were as unwavering.

She drew in a slow breath. "What did Aaron do?"

A scowl appeared where his mustache nearly touched his beard. "That's just it. I couldn't believe his next words."

Miriam felt the same awful punch in her middle that she had felt earlier with Elisheba. "Tell me."

He released a heavy sigh. "Aaron told them to take the gold rings from the ears of their wives and sons and daughters and bring them to him."

Miriam stared at her husband, dumbstruck. "He's going to make an idol for them?"

"It looks that way. The men went to do as Aaron asked, and Aaron took the gold to his tent. What he will do won't happen today. Perhaps he is hoping Moses will return tomorrow and he can return the items."

"Why didn't he just tell them to be patient and trust our God? Why did he give in so easily?" Anger flared that her brother seemed so weak.

Jephunneh held up a hand. "Don't take it out on me, beloved. I did not get the opportunity to ask his intentions."

Miriam sat back, defeat washing over her. "And if Moses does not return in the next day or so, does he plan to go through with their preposterous request?"

"I don't know. I hope not."

"Do you plan to speak to him?"

Jephunneh nodded. "Tomorrow Caleb and I will go to him and plead with him to wait."

"Remind him that he was one of the few who actually saw our God. He knows, as do the people, His fierce power and even His wrath. Do they so easily forget Egypt?"

"It is Egypt that they have false memories of. I think some of them want to go back. Or at least they want to return to the customs they knew in Egypt and have physical gods they can see." Jephunneh ran a hand over his beard and stifled a yawn.

"They can see the pillar of fire and cloud by night and day. What more do they need to prove our God is with us, guiding us?" Frustration rose within her, and she felt a strange fear crawl up her spine. What would happen if Aaron gave in to the people? "You must stop them, my husband. You must convince Aaron not to give in to them."

"Aaron is powerful, almost as much so as your other brother," he said. "I will do my best, but Aaron may think God will not turn against him after the encounter he had with Him on the mountain. I don't know."

Miriam stood and came over to her husband. He pulled her onto his lap.

"We must stand strong as a family, even if that family is shattered and smaller than it was. Moses will return and set things right again. Hopefully sooner than later," Miriam said. She leaned her head against his cheek. "After the way Elisheba spoke to me today, I don't know if Aaron will listen to you. I think he's grown proud, and pride, as I realized today, can destroy good things."

Jephunneh kissed the top of her head. "Very true, my love. But let us pray tonight and see what the morrow brings. Perhaps Moses will return and this will all be a worry for nothing."

"I hope you are right." She followed him to their pallet, but she slept little. God did not speak to her even in her fitful dreams.

～

The next day Miriam accompanied her husband and son to Aaron's tent. Jephunneh knocked on the pole and called out Aaron's name. Her brother lifted the flap and stepped outside. He did not invite them in.

Miriam studied her brother, saw the way he listened to Jephunneh and even Caleb, but he did not even look in her direction. Had Elisheba's anger turned her brother against her?

"You can't possibly think that making an idol of gold just because the men are worried is a good thing, my brother." Jephunneh lifted his hands in supplication. "Surely you know that God will not allow anything to happen to Moses. He would not leave us without our leader."

"May I remind you that God called Moses *and me* to lead the people? When Moses first returned to Egypt, he was too afraid to speak. So God called me to act with him." Aaron lifted his chin in the slightest gesture of authority—or pride.

"Yes, of course, but it is Moses God speaks to alone. Our God will send him back to us. We must simply be patient." Jephunneh locked gazes with Aaron until Aaron finally looked away.

A moment later he spoke. "I will wait a few more days, but then I must obey the voice of the people or they will riot. How will we defend ourselves against their wrath?"

Caleb moved closer to Jephunneh, but it was Jephunneh who spoke. "Who would you prefer to obey—our God or the people? Whose wrath is greater and harder to bear—our God's or the people's? I think you should consider what you are saying, Aaron. If you listen to the people, you risk bringing God's wrath down on all Israel."

Aaron turned without responding and entered his tent. Jephunneh whirled about, took Miriam's hand, and headed home.

"Whatever will we do?" Miriam said, fear falling on her like the dense cloud of God's wrath.

"Obviously he did not want to listen," Caleb said. "Father could not have said it better or been more persuasive. For some reason Aaron fears the people more than he does our God."

"I'm going for a walk," Jephunneh said. "I need to check on the sheep." He kissed Miriam.

Caleb followed. "I'm going too. Do not fret, Ima. Surely God will send Moses back before the people cause Aaron to sin so grievously."

Miriam watched them go, longing to follow, yet in that moment she felt as though she could shrivel into herself and cry. Her bed beckoned, but she looked at the bowl of manna instead, wondering how to prepare it tonight. Why hadn't Aaron even looked her way? They had shared so much. God had called all of them to lead. Did he think her advice or that of her husband held no value? Or had Elisheba poisoned his thinking against her? Was she truly so much of a failure that people thought she considered herself above them?

She fell to her knees. *Oh, Adonai, please send Moses back to us. Please don't let Aaron and the people sin against You in this way.*

She stood after swiping away her tears and walked outside to gaze at the mountain and the cloud resting atop it. *Do You hear my prayer? Please rescue Your people from themselves.*

But the cloud did not move, as though God were so intent on speaking to her brother that He was not focused on what went on down in the valley. But surely God could see everyone everywhere. Was He aware of the people's attitudes and what Aaron had already done?

A puff of dark, smoky cloud escaped the larger, denser cloud that engulfed the mountain. Had God heard her? She couldn't tell, but her heart sensed that He had. Surely now He would act and send Moses home before it was too late.

# FORTY-SIX

*D*ays passed and there was still no sign of Moses. The people crowded around Aaron near the river, away from the mountain. He built a fire and hung a kettle over it. Miriam stood with her family, along with Zipporah and her sons, and watched from a distance as Aaron melted the gold the people had brought to him.

"He didn't listen to you," Miriam said, leaning close to her husband. She reached up to speak into his ear above the noise of the crowd. "I don't know what to do."

Jephunneh's arm came around her. "We wait," he said, his tone resigned. What could he do against such a crowd? Especially when they were far outnumbered and Aaron had sided with the people?

Aaron leaned over, stirring the pot. He took tools and pulled it from the fire, shaping the hot metal as the people watched. The sun rose, and still he worked, carving and reheating the parts that had cooled, then applying them to the idol taking shape before him. At last, as late afternoon shadows fell on the people, Aaron finished his creation and raised it high for all to see.

"It's a calf," Miriam said, unable to keep disgust and fear from curdling in her belly. "Like they worshiped in Egypt. One of their many gods."

"The bull represented creation to our captors," Jephunneh agreed. "Aaron is making a representation of our Creator, but this is far from the God of heaven." He pointed to the mountain behind them and the cloud that still hovered above it. "We need to go home," he said, motioning to their family to follow.

A moment later, the crowd erupted in a cheer. "O Israel, these are the gods who brought you out of the land of Egypt!"

Miriam watched her brother, saw his lips curve in a pleased, if not elated, expression. He was proud of what his hands had made! But how could he be? He knew this was not *their* God!

"We cannot leave yet," she said in Jephunneh's ear. "Let us see what Aaron will do."

Surely he would reprimand them. But Aaron raised his hands for quiet, then motioned to Nadab and Abihu to help him, and within the hour they had built an altar in front of the golden calf.

Aaron turned to face the people. "Tomorrow will be a festival to the Lord!" He dismissed the people to return to their tents, and Jephunneh ushered their family away before Aaron or his sons had the chance to approach them.

"We are not going back tomorrow," Jephunneh said once he and Miriam were inside their tent, their family surrounding them. "We must not take part in this sin against the Lord."

"Your father is right," Miriam agreed. "My brother has committed a grievous sin against our God. I fear greatly for what God will do once Moses returns."

"We will stay with you tonight, then," Caleb said, looking at his sisters and their families.

Miriam released a low sigh when each one nodded or offered words of agreement.

Caleb looked again at his father. "Should we attempt one more time to speak to Uncle Aaron to stop this before it goes any further?"

Jephunneh lifted obviously tense shoulders, and his brows knit in a frown. "Aaron has already committed himself by making that calf. He has traded the invisible God for an object like that found in Egypt. He will not go back on his promise now."

"Uncle Aaron has grown proud in Moses' absence." Caleb glanced at the door at the sound of a knock.

Miriam hurried to see who it was and found Zipporah and her sons standing there. "May we stay with you tonight?" she asked, seeming uncertain when she saw the crowded tent. "Perhaps we should not ask. You are already full."

Miriam waved a dismissive hand. "Nonsense. Come in. Join us. I assume that you too are unhappy with Aaron's choices?"

She nodded, her expression like that of a frightened doe. "I do not know what has happened to my husband, but I do know that he will not be pleased with his brother. And my tent is closer to Aaron's. I do not like what I am hearing from them this night."

"What are you hearing?" Miriam could not stop her curiosity. She sensed that everyone was looking at Zipporah.

Zipporah's cheeks flushed as she stepped away from the tent door. "Sounds of celebration are coming from Aaron's tent. I think all of his sons and their families are with him. They think what he has done is a good thing for Israel."

Miriam motioned Zipporah and her sons farther into the room. The words hit hard, for until this moment, she assumed that Aaron was simply doing what the people wanted to appease them. Deep down, she hadn't thought he really believed a word he said. But as she showed everyone where to sleep and the mothers calmed her grandchildren, who complained because they could not return to their own beds, she felt an ache in her soul. Her brother, leader in Israel, spokesman for God, had broken the first and greatest commandment that Moses had given them before he ascended the mountain again.

She sat on the floor and pulled her knees to her chest, longing to go outside and pray to God as she gazed at the pillar of fire, which would have replaced the cloud by now. But she feared the people who had followed or led her brother on this foolhardy path. And there was nothing she could do about it.

⌘

Miriam and her family remained in their tent, listening as the crowd of Israelites gathered. The sound traveled from the river where they had been yesterday, where the calf stood and the altar waited before it.

"I dreamed in the night that Moses saw all that is going on." Miriam directed her words to her husband and son, but others in the room quieted at her remark. "I believe God is telling me that He sees what Aaron has done and is sending Moses back to deal with it." A shiver worked through her at the thought.

A loud cheer coming from the distance interrupted the silence that followed her remarks.

"They are celebrating," Caleb said, scowling. "No doubt Uncle Aaron has already offered sacrifices to the 'god' he has made."

"No doubt," Jephunneh agreed.

"Should we go and see?" Zipporah asked, her eyes large and showing her fear.

"No." Jephunneh's firm command caused Miriam to look at him. He met her gaze. "What else did God show you in your dream?"

"Only images really. Moses on the mountain. Aaron offering sacrifices. The people indulging in the kind of revelry we saw from the Egyptians in Egypt. The kind that would displease Yahweh." She crossed her arms to ward off another chill that she knew was not coming from the air around them.

"Then we will stay here until Moses returns. God sees and He will act. Moses will know what to do once he comes down to look on what Aaron has done." Jephunneh turned to Caleb, and the two began a different discussion, though the tension in their tent did not abate.

No one could drown out the chaos outside, even though their tent was not near the revelry. Surely the sound was loud enough to reach the heart of heaven. The question remained of what God would do once Moses discovered that the people could not even obey their God for forty days, after they'd promised to do just that.

⤮

Moses hurried down the mountain, Joshua on his heels. The stone tablets God had inscribed with His own finger were in Moses' hands, and the words God had spoken rang in his ears as he made his way over the craggy rock surface.

How was it possible that the people had already broken their promise to Yahweh and worshiped before a calf of gold? Why hadn't Aaron stopped them?

*Leave Me alone so My fierce anger can blaze against them, and I will destroy them. Then I will make you, Moses, into a great nation.*

The hair on Moses' neck bristled with every step. How angry God had been! Moses felt the heat of the flames even through the cloud, as though the fire and the cloud comingled in that moment. How could he stop God from breaking out against His people when they were so stubborn and disobedient?

But He couldn't destroy them! To do so would be to go against everything He had promised to Abraham, Isaac, and Jacob. In that moment, Moses had tried to pacify the Lord.

"O Lord! Why are You so angry with Your own people whom You brought from the land of Egypt with such great power and such a strong hand? Why let the Egyptians say, 'Their God rescued them with the evil intention of slaughtering them in the mountains and wiping them from the face of the earth'? Turn away from Your fierce anger. Change Your mind about this terrible disaster You have threatened against Your people! Remember Your servants Abraham, Isaac, and Jacob. You bound Yourself with an oath to them, saying, 'I will make your descendants as numerous as the stars of heaven. And I will give them all of this land that I have promised to your descendants, and they will possess it forever.'"

That God had listened to his plea still filled him with awe, but the knowledge that the people were involved in pagan worship galled him. "We must hurry," he said to Joshua.

His young assistant did not argue but kept pace with Moses. As they neared the base of the mountain, a loud cry came from below, startling them both.

"It sounds like war in the camp!" Joshua said.

Moses felt defeat threaten, but in the next instant, his anger flared. He need not have doubted God, who would be justified to do exactly as He wanted to do. How did God put up with these people? A heavy sigh escaped. "No," he said, "it's not a shout of victory nor the wailing of defeat. I hear the sound of a celebration."

Their feet touched the base of the mountain, and they ran toward the camp near the foothills. A river ran nearby, where the people congregated.

"It looks like all of Israel is there. And they are dancing before the calf." Joshua looked at Moses, incredulous. "How can they do such a thing?"

"My thought exactly." Moses' anger grew to a pulsating rage as he drew closer. The stones of God's law felt weighted in his hands, and he threw them to the ground at the foot of the mountain.

The crowd grew instantly quiet as Moses stomped over to the calf, smashed it, and beat it into a powder. He threw the whole of it into the river and stood before the people. "Drink it, every one of you. Now!" He raised his arms as though he carried a weapon in them, realizing that he had destroyed the tablets God had given him in his fit of rage. "Go on now, drink from the river of the god you have made."

The people, surprisingly, moved to the water and knelt, lapping water from their hands to their mouths, scowling at the bitter taste. Moses watched them, searching the crowd for his family. When he didn't see Miriam's family or Zipporah and his sons, a small sense of relief rushed through him. But the sight of Aaron, his wife, and his sons caused the anger to return.

He put Joshua in charge of making every last person drink the water and then walked over to Aaron. "What did these people do to you to make you bring such terrible sin upon them?"

Aaron gave him a half shrug as if the whole thing had nothing to do with him, causing Moses' face to burn hot.

Aaron held up a hand as if to stave off a blow. "Don't get so upset, my lord," he said. "You yourself know how evil these people are. They said to me, 'Make us gods who will lead us. We don't know what happened to this fellow Moses, who brought us here from the land of Egypt.' So I told them, 'Whoever has gold jewelry, take it off.' When they brought it to me, I simply threw it into the fire—and out came this calf!"

At that moment, Moses glimpsed Miriam and Jephunneh walking toward him from the area where their tent stood. All of their children followed behind them, and Zipporah and his sons as well. He silently thanked God for sparing them a part in this sin. But it became all too obvious that Aaron had not listened to them if they'd tried to stop him, and he had allowed the people's actions to grow completely out of control.

"You have done a very foolish thing, Aaron," he said, his voice low. Then he walked to the entrance of the camp and raised his voice above the crowd. "All of you who are on the Lord's side, come here and join me."

Slowly, one by one, his entire tribe of Levi joined him.

"This is what the Lord, the God of Israel, says," he said, looking over the large group surrounding him. "Each of you, take your swords and go back and forth from one end of the camp to the other. Kill everyone who has partaken in the idol worship—even your brothers, friends, and neighbors."

He stepped back, arms crossed, barely able to contain his fury. And his fear. Would his prayers be enough to stop the Lord from destroying His people?

Shouts and screams and guttural cries came from the people who had started to run away from the river the moment Moses gave the Levites his command. Moses briefly closed his eyes, then opened them again to glance at Aaron. Would God listen to his prayers for his brother? How could Aaron have done such a thing after being chosen of God to lead?

He looked out over the camp once more, sorrow slowly replacing the anger that still pulsed through him. The Levites were overtaking their fellow Israelites, and men were falling to the earth with such force and outcry that even the heavens darkened as though showing God's displeasure. Such stubborn, stiff-necked people!

And yet, Moses knew that God loved each one. He simply could not abide such disobedience.

The sun, blotted mostly by clouds, had slowly moved toward the west when at last the Levites returned to Moses.

Joshua came up beside him. "They've killed three thousand of the people, my lord."

The number felt like exacting justice and a kick in his gut at the same time. He took no pleasure in the death of his people any more than he sensed God did. God wanted to fellowship with these people, to tabernacle among them, as

He had shown Moses these past forty days on the mountain. But they could not see God the way he did. They didn't sense the love behind His holiness.

A deep sense of loss filled him, but he looked to the Levites who had obeyed his command. "Today you have ordained yourselves for the service of the Lord, for you obeyed Him even though it meant killing your own sons and brothers. Today you have earned a blessing. Now all of you go home."

He moved to join Zipporah and the rest of his family who had not followed Aaron. He would deal with Aaron another day. Right now he didn't even want to speak to his brother. The brother who had walked with him every step of this path and even eaten a meal with their God. How could he?

He shook the thought aside and put his arm around Zipporah's shoulders. "I'm sorry you were witness to this," he whispered.

She leaned into him but did not respond, though he could feel her tears wetting his robe the entire walk home.

~❧~

"Don't go back up there," Zipporah pleaded the next morning. "You are gone so long that I wonder if you will ever return."

"I must go back to plead for forgiveness for the people." He looked into her eyes and grasped her hand as he spoke. "I am sorry it is so hard for you, Zipporah. If I could change things, make it easier for you somehow, you know I would."

"Do I know that?" She searched his face. "I'm sorry. It does not seem so, and I do not know. How can I know a God who keeps you from me? Am I not included in the people of Israel? I am your wife. Does He not want all of His people, including me and Miriam and the rest of those who did not sin against Him with Aaron's calf?"

Moses stroked her cheek with his other hand. "The Lord loves all of His people, beloved. But He cannot look at our sin, so when the people are not faithful, it causes His anger to rise because they are forcing Him to act against them."

"I don't understand. Surely He can do as He pleases. How does what they do force Him to do anything?" She gave him a quizzical look.

He released his grip on her hand and ran his hand over the back of his neck. "Our God longs to live among us, to dwell with us, but His holiness will not allow Him to do so because of our sinful nature. Holiness and sin cannot dwell together, which is why no one can look on Him and live. When we sin against Him so blatantly, we grieve Him and bring on His holy wrath. His love keeps Him from destroying us utterly, but only because He restrains His anger. He forgives, but His forgiveness is not without cost. Just what it costs Him, who can say? He has told me much, but I will not fully understand Him in my lifetime. He is too far above me."

"And yet you talk to Him face-to-face."

"I do not see His face. But yes, He speaks to me." He sighed, and she sank onto a cushion, defeat filling her.

"So you will go back again."

"If I do not, I cannot plead with Him to forgive the people, and He might destroy them. Do you want that?" He seemed torn, and she suddenly wanted to comfort him.

"No. I don't want that." She released a deep sigh. "Go back tomorrow if you must. But please do not stay away so long."

"I will pitch a tent outside the camp where He can meet

with me. Perhaps He will allow it and I will not have to climb the mountain so often." He sat beside her and pulled her into his arms. "I miss you."

"And I you."

He kissed her then, and they remained still, holding each other, while she wondered how long God would keep Moses from her the next time He called.

# FORTY-SEVEN

Miriam walked with Zipporah to gather water in a different area than where Moses had forced the people to drink the water mixed with gold. She shivered in the post-dawn light, though more from the fear of what God would do next than the cool temperature. Moses had gone to the mountain to plead for forgiveness for the people, but he'd returned with a solemn warning for them. Then he set up a Tent of Meeting outside the camp.

The tent came within sight of the river, and Miriam glanced at it. "Moses has gone to speak with the Lord again." She looked at Zipporah, whose gaze also rested on the tent and the cloud that had descended on it to show the Lord's presence. "At least he is home more than he used to be."

Zipporah did not immediately answer but stared at the cloud as they continued to walk toward the river. "He goes there often," she said. "Though he comes home at night, it still feels as though he is gone from me." She glanced at Miriam. "His mind is filled with the problems of the people and consumed with longing for Yahweh. Even the men he set over the people, as my father once suggested, do not ease his burden. The seventy elders help some, but it is the overall rebellion of the people that Moses cannot erase from his heart. I can see it wearing him down, but he rarely speaks of it."

Miriam stopped at the river's edge and lowered her jar. "Sometimes he speaks to Jephunneh and Caleb, but you are right, he says little other than to relay what the Lord has told him."

"Joshua has his ear even more than his sons do. They watch the sheep, and he instructs them when to keep the flocks from the mountain, but he spends so little time with them now. I miss life in Midian." Zipporah's admission caused Miriam to regard her sister-in-law in a new light.

"I am sorry this has happened to you." She lifted the jar to her head, a task that grew weightier with each passing year, and walked back to their camp with Zipporah. "Your family would have been happy if God had not stepped in and called my brother. But our God called Moses from birth. He was destined for this whether he wanted it or not, and I am fairly certain he resisted it."

Zipporah's smile was sad. "I am certain he resisted as well. But as I have seen with my own eyes, no one wins a fight with God."

Miriam nodded. How true her words. Hadn't she tried to control things that only God could handle? Hadn't God shown her in dreams that His way would come to pass whether Israel liked His plan or not? Oh, they could rebel, as they often did, and they could complain, which they did even more, but they could not stand against the Almighty's power. And she sensed, as they returned to their tents, that there was something more than power behind the Almighty's actions. She had felt His touch. She had sensed His love. If only the people would realize that to obey was freedom. To rebel only brought heartache and loss.

"When Moses returns tonight, why don't you join us for the evening meal?" Miriam met Zipporah's hesitant gaze. "I know it's only manna, but I've learned a new way to prepare it. I'd like to try it out and see if everyone likes it." The yellow coriander-like seed had proven very versatile, despite the fact that it was also always the same.

"If Moses agrees, we will join you." Zipporah stepped toward her tent while Miriam did the same.

Miriam set the water in a niche in the ground and then went outside her tent once more to gaze at the cloud hovering above the Tent of Meeting in the distance. *How long, Adonai, until You move us to the Promised Land? Will this people ever be ready to obey and follow wherever You lead?*

Though she heard no answer as Moses would have, she knew in that moment that the time was not yet. They still had much to learn to be ready to inhabit a new land. Too much rebellion still filled the camp. Was that what Moses spoke of when he talked to God—the rebellion he struggled with every day? Would God forgive His stubborn people?

The thought troubled her as she moved through the camp, checking on the women, helping where she could. She needed to keep a better presence among them, even if she had to go alone, for Elisheba still stayed away. *Soon, Lord?* But she couldn't know when Elisheba would forgive her any more than she could know when God would lead His people toward all He had promised them.

Moses, Zipporah, and their sons entered Miriam's tent that evening and settled in a circle with Miriam's family and Joshua and his wife. Miriam served her new baked manna and then settled beside her daughter Lysia as all eyes turned to Moses.

"You met with the Lord today," Joshua said, his expression bright with longing. "What did He say to you?" Joshua had been known to remain at the Tent of Meeting even after Moses had left, yet God had not spoken to the young man, only to Moses.

"He told me to chisel out two new stone tablets like the ones I smashed at the foot of the mountain and return to Him on the mountain tomorrow. He is going to give me the law again." Moses wiped his mouth on a piece of linen fabric. "This is good," he said, directing his gaze to Miriam. "Thank you."

Miriam nodded. "Do you need help chiseling the stones?" She knew any one of the men sitting around them would volunteer to help, but Moses shook his head.

"I will do it as soon as I leave here." He took in every face as though memorizing them. "I do not know how long I will be gone."

"Well, we know that if forty days passes again, we will not worry or allow the people to be unfaithful again." Miriam met her brother's gaze. "If I have to hold Aaron down myself, we won't disobey if you are delayed."

Moses chuckled, as did the rest of her men.

"Now that is something I would almost like to see, Ima," Caleb said. "Uncle Aaron is not a small man."

"Perhaps," she said, an edge of defiance creeping into her tone. "But I am sure all of you would help me."

Moses stroked his beard. "Aaron will not disobey again. You need not fear."

Miriam nodded. She had also seen a change in their brother since the incident with the calf and God's reprimanding words. But the loss of so many Israelites probably had the greatest effect on him. If only Elisheba would change her attitude as well. Why must there be rifts in their family?

The thought pained Miriam as she got up to pour water and offer more manna cakes to anyone who wanted them, listening to the discussions going on around her. Her girls talked with Caleb's wife about their children, while the men talked about how long it might be before God moved them closer to the land of promise.

Moses excused himself earlier than she'd hoped, and Zipporah and their sons quickly followed. Miriam bid them farewell as Jephunneh came up behind her and put an arm around her shoulders. "He will be safe on the mountain," he whispered against her ear. "He is safer with our God than he is here among the people. Though I daresay that God will not allow harm to come to His servant Moses." He turned her to face him. "Nor will God allow you or Aaron to be harmed, as He has also chosen you to lead."

"Will He also protect you, my husband, and our families from the stubborn people and the foreigners living among us? I could not bear to lose a single one of you." When had that fear begun to take hold? They had survived slavery in Egypt. Why did she fear loss here in the wilderness of Sinai? Was not God's power on display night and day in fire and cloud? Why, then, should she fear her neighbors when she knew she could trust her God?

"We cannot know how long we will live, beloved. But

we are safe from the punishment of our God and the rebels among the people as long as we are staying true to Him." Jephunneh kissed her cheek.

Their son and daughters gathered up their children to return to their own tents, and Miriam hugged each one as they left. When only she and Jephunneh remained, she sank down beside him and rested her head against his chest. "Every new day is the same, and yet the shadow of uncertainty also fills it. Sometimes I do not know how to act or react." She looked at him. "But I do my best."

"Our best is all we can ever do." He pulled her close again, and she wondered, was their best enough for God? Or did He want something more?

The next morning Moses trudged up the rocky path, higher and higher to the summit of Sinai, two new stone tablets in his hands. The weight of the stones was nothing compared to the burden he had for the people of Israel. He carried no doubt that he was privileged to speak with God in a way none of them could. Would he be as prone to rebellion as they were, as he had been in his youth, if not for the grace he'd known from his God? Oh, that his people would know that same grace and be given a taste of the Spirit God allowed to rest on him.

His breath came out in puffs the higher he climbed, until he reached the flatter surface of the familiar summit. If he looked in any direction, he saw a range of mountains similar in size and equally as time-consuming to climb. But God was here, and the difference His presence made caused Moses to again feel unworthy of His grace.

As he stood there, the cloud of God descended and stopped next to him. A voice from the cloud called out God's own name.

"Yahweh! The Lord! The God of compassion and mercy! I am slow to anger and filled with unfailing love and faithfulness. I lavish unfailing love to a thousand generations. I forgive iniquity, rebellion, and sin. But I do not excuse the guilty. I lay the sins of the parents upon their children and grandchildren; the entire family is affected—even children in the third and fourth generations."

The voice and the words penetrated deep into Moses' soul, and he fell to the ground, hands outstretched, palms up. *Holy, holy, holy are You, Lord God Almighty.* He sang the words in his heart as though led by a source outside of himself. Yearning for his God grew, and he could not stop the deep awe and respect he felt overtake him. *You are good.*

How long he worshiped, he could not say, but when at last he lifted his head, the cloud remained as if focused on him. He dared to speak. "O Lord, if it is true that I have found favor with You, then please travel with us. Yes, this is a stubborn and rebellious people, but please forgive our iniquity and our sins. Claim us as Your own special possession." He had pleaded for their forgiveness before and had even gone so far as to ask to see God's glory, a sight he would never forget. But he still did not have the assurance that God would continue to go with them and forgive His rebellious people.

"Listen," the Lord said, interrupting his thoughts. "I am making a covenant with you in the presence of all your people. I will perform miracles that have never been performed anywhere in all the earth or in any nation. And all the people around you will see the power of the Lord—the awesome power I will display for you."

Moses sat back on his heels as God continued to tell him what He would do and what the people must do to obey Him. Eventually he stood, still listening. The Lord finished giving His instructions and said, "Write down all these instructions, for they represent the terms of the covenant I am making with you and with Israel."

Moses found soft stones near the place where God waited, as though they'd been left for him. He then found a stick with which to write and did as God asked. In the meantime, God Himself wrote His commands on the two stone tablets Moses had brought to Him.

It took forty days and nights to complete the task, and Moses basked in the Lord's presence. If he'd stopped to think about manna, he would have realized there had been no food provided for him. Yet he did not hunger or thirst when in God's presence.

As he made his way down the mountain with the instructions and tablets of God, he wondered if the reason he ever hungered or thirsted was because he was not sustained in those moments by God's ultimate sustenance. Was the Creator bread and water enough for men and women? Would there come a time when all they needed was Him?

⁓

Miriam followed the elders and Aaron along with the rest of the people to the base of the mountain to meet Moses at the first sighting of his return. Joshua had barely left the mountain's foothills to go home at night to his wife. But as Moses came into view, even Aaron stopped in his tracks and would go no farther. Moses' face glowed like the sun.

Miriam leaned closer and whispered to Zipporah, "That is Moses, isn't it?" She glimpsed Elisheba with her sons some distance away, behind Aaron. A sigh lifted her chest. Still there had been no change in their relationship. No matter what Miriam did to fix things, Elisheba refused to speak to her.

"It looks like Moses in his bearing, but I cannot see his face," Zipporah said, drawing Miriam's attention back to Moses.

He called out to Aaron and the elders, "Don't be afraid. Come closer." He continued down the mountain and stepped onto the foothills where most of the camp waited. "I have the instructions from the Lord."

Aaron took a cautious step closer. "Can you veil your face, my brother? It is too bright for us to look upon." He looked behind him to Elisheba. She removed her head covering and handed it to him. He closed the distance and handed the head covering to Moses. It wasn't a perfect veil, but it blocked the blinding light from searing their vision.

"I will have to make him a veil if the brightness does not go away." Zipporah spoke softly, and Miriam nodded her agreement.

She watched her brother with renewed awe and listened to every word he had received from the Lord. There was so much to do. A Tabernacle? Priests? Feasts? Laws for everything a person could name. Her mind spun with the enormity of it all.

The crowd listened, and though the speech grew long, they did not become restless, not even the children among them. When Miriam glanced about, she saw excitement on the faces of the people. At last they would have purpose. Something to do with their time as they waited for God to lead them onward.

Was this what God had intended all along? To set up a governing body of priests and Levites, a place to worship Him, and laws to obey Him so they would know how to act once they possessed the beautiful land of promise?

Miriam smiled. This was good. God was good.

As Moses dismissed the people to their tents to begin gathering what they would need for the work, she wondered how she could continue to be of use to Adonai. Surely He still had a purpose for her as a woman, as a leader of the women of Israel. Perhaps He would tell her in a dream. Or perhaps Moses had received a word just for her.

She would know soon enough. In the meantime, she walked in silence with her family, pondering the enormity of Moses' words. No wonder he had remained for forty days and nights. The work of God was exact and immense. She couldn't wait to see it begin.

# PART FIVE

Then the cloud covered the Tabernacle, and the glory of the LORD filled the Tabernacle. Moses could no longer enter the Tabernacle because the cloud had settled down over it, and the glory of the LORD filled the Tabernacle.

Now whenever the cloud lifted from the Tabernacle, the people of Israel would set out on their journey, following it. But if the cloud did not rise, they remained where they were until it lifted. The cloud of the LORD hovered over the Tabernacle during the day, and at night fire glowed inside the cloud so the whole family of Israel could see it. This continued throughout all their journeys.

Exodus 40:34–38

# FORTY-EIGHT

**1445 BC**

The work began on the Tabernacle as soon as Moses could call the craftsmen and gather the materials. Within nine months the work was complete. Aaron and his sons were consecrated to do the work of the priesthood, with Aaron consecrated as high priest. The people had come together to offer sacrifices as the Lord had prescribed. The resulting shouts of joy and adoration of humble worship filled the camp. Miriam could not recall a more festive and yet solemn time.

After the people had confessed their sins and the work of the Tabernacle continued, while they still resided in the wilderness of Sinai, Miriam and Zipporah settled into a rhythm of spinning and weaving together after they had gathered the manna and the water they needed each day.

"I wish Elisheba would join us," Miriam said one day, her thoughts still troubled that Aaron's appointment as high priest had only continued to keep Elisheba away from them. Instead of showing the humility she had accused Miriam of not possessing, she herself had grown proud, her head lifted high as she watched her husband and sons anointed to the work of the priests.

"She does seem more distant than ever," Zipporah agreed. "It's like Aaron's elevation to the priesthood has made her feel superior."

"She did seem to want that," Miriam said, remembering a similar accusation made against her. "She's probably more pleased that Moses also consecrated all of her sons." Miriam had long pondered why God had chosen Aaron's sons for this role instead of Moses'. Perhaps because Zipporah was not of Israel, so they were not fully from the Levitical tribe.

"That's true." Zipporah's tone held a hint of sadness, and when Miriam searched her face, she saw dark shadows under her eyes. Had she not slept?

"Do you wish the honor had gone to Gershom and Eliezer?" She didn't want to pry, but Zipporah didn't say much unless she was asked.

Zipporah shook her head. "No. I am not bothered by that. Actually, I'm relieved. The priests hold much responsibility and carry a heavy burden. I am glad our sons can marry and live the lives of shepherds instead of priests." She let the spindle come to a stop to tie a different color of thread to the device, stifling a yawn. "I will be glad when Moses can finally take time to find wives for them though."

Miriam continued to work her spindle in silence a moment, then looked again at this sister-in-law whom she had come to love. "I notice you seem very tired. Is there anything I can do?" She knew some herbs that might help aid sleep.

"Can you bring my husband to my tent and keep him there?" She gave Miriam a pointed look. "Do not tell him, but I have not slept well in some time. I feel as though my whole body is stretched thin like parchment." She released a heavy sigh. "I suspect my time is not long in this world."

Her words caused Miriam's heart to beat faster. Zipporah was still young. Surely she was mistaken. "Why don't you let me make you an herbal tea? It may help you sleep, and then you will feel better."

Zipporah nodded, as though to refuse took too much energy. What would Miriam do if Zipporah was right and her time was shorter than anyone thought? What would Moses do? Or their sons? Miriam could not explore the realization that she would also have no friends unless something changed between her and Elisheba.

"I will make it now." She let the spindle slow and set it aside, then rose to pull from her small supply of medicinal herbs she had brought with her from Egypt. The spices she used sparingly in the manna, but these herbs she saved for times such as this. But what kind of time was this? Should she tell Moses? Could he plead with God to spare his wife?

When she glanced at Zipporah, she dismissed the idea. Zipporah was simply overwrought and worn out. Once she started sleeping well again, all would be fine. She would live many more years on the earth. Miriam would make sure of it.

⁘

A week later, the camp gathered before the Tabernacle while the priests offered incense to the Lord and the evening sacrifice was given. Miriam stayed near the back with the rest of the women, kneeling and bowing before the Lord. The singers took up a song of praise to Adonai as the bulls were offered and the scent of burning flesh filled the air.

Miriam's stomach rumbled at the smell. How rare it was for them to eat meat, and she realized how much she missed it. But manna was enough, as she had often told the other women. They must be grateful and not complain.

The men rose and the women followed. Aaron's sons Nadab and Abihu approached the altar of the Lord, carrying their incense burners. Silence fell over the camp as the men took coals from the altar and placed them in their incense burners. Then they each took a handful of incense powder, which they were to carry into the Tabernacle and pour over the coals before the Lord.

Miriam waited for them to enter the tent to finish offering their incense, but in a heartbeat they poured it over the coals for all to see. What were they doing? The incense was to be poured before the Lord, not in front of the people.

Miriam's breath caught as she watched. Did it really matter that they chose to do this step ahead of the normal God-given plan? But a weight settled on her and fear crawled up her spine as she waited to see if God would respond.

Nadab and Abihu had turned to enter the Tabernacle when a sudden rush of fire blazed forth from the pillar of cloud above it. Both men were caught in the flames and instantly consumed.

Shock nearly caused Miriam to fall to her knees, but Zipporah leaned against her, clinging to her arm. "What happened?" she asked.

Miriam craned her neck to better see. "Fire from the Lord came down and killed Nadab and Abihu." Her words were a whisper, and even as she spoke, she could not believe what she had seen.

Moses emerged from the head of the tribe of Levi and approached Aaron, who stood outside the Tabernacle, staring at the bodies of his sons. "Your sons are dead," Moses said, loud enough for those who couldn't see to hear him. He faced Aaron, his expression stern. He cleared his throat and met Aaron's wide-eyed gaze. "This is what the Lord meant when He said, 'I will display My holiness through those who come near Me. I will display My glory before all the people.'"

The grave consequences of shunning God's holiness hit Miriam with such force she fought to remain steady, helping Zipporah do the same. The crowd grew silent, and in the stillness she could tell that Aaron had not yet spoken.

Moses turned to the men and called out, "Mishael and Elzaphan, come forward and carry away the bodies of your relatives from in front of the sanctuary to a place outside the camp." Uncle Uzziel's sons approached Moses and entered the court near the altar in front of the curtained Tabernacle. Moments later they pushed through the crowd, carrying the bodies of Nadab and Abihu, and walked toward the outskirts of the camp.

Miriam heard Elisheba cry out, her voice deep and guttural, but she did not run after the men, and a look from Moses silenced her.

Moses looked again at Aaron and his two remaining sons, Eleazar and Ithamar. "Do not show grief by leaving your hair uncombed or by tearing your clothes. If you do, you will die, and the Lord's anger will strike the whole community of Israel. However, the rest of the Israelites, your relatives, may mourn because of the Lord's fiery destruction of Nadab and Abihu. But you must not leave the entrance of the Tabernacle or you will die, for you have been anointed with the Lord's anointing oil."

All three men nodded without a word. But Elisheba fell to her knees, rocking back and forth in silent grief for all she had just lost.

# FORTY-NINE

Zipporah lifted her head from the pillow and felt the room spin. She lay down again and closed her eyes. What was wrong with her? She'd not slept well until Miriam had given her the sleeping herbs, but now she found herself troubled by headaches and a whirling world.

Footsteps caused her to open her eyes again, and a moment later she watched Moses kneel at her side. "You are ill?" His brow furrowed, and she knew the burden he carried would not be helped if he thought she could not care for her family, for him.

"I'm just a little dizzy. I will be fine once I rise." She couldn't let him know. He was with her so infrequently. She wanted him to enjoy every moment he could in peace while in her presence. She wanted him to long for her the way he longed for his God. But she could not tell him that.

"Let me get you something. Can I help you up?" His concern did not lessen, and she saw the anxiety in his dark eyes.

"Yes, that would help." She forced herself not to grit her teeth as he took her hand and slowly pulled her up. The spinning continued and she felt a little sick, but she drew in a deep breath and slowly felt herself return to normal. "I think I'm all right now."

. He helped her to stand and continued to hold on to her until she nodded. He led her to a small bench Jephunneh had crafted for them and then left her side to gather some of the manna. He returned and offered it to her. She ate, though she was not hungry. To please him mattered. He was about to leave to inspect the people and divide them into fighting men, and he did not need to worry about her in the process.

"It's been a year," he said as she took another small bite of the raw manna, which was surprisingly good despite her lack of cooking it. They could never eat flour in the same way. "We left Egypt a year ago."

"It is hard to believe God has kept us in the wilderness for so long. I think my father expected us to move into the Promised Land rather soon, since the distance is not far." She took a sip of the water he gave her and smiled.

"We are not yet ready," Moses said, looking beyond her as though remembering something. "God has been testing the people's willingness to obey Him. He wants to walk among us, Zipporah." He looked at her then. "He wants to tabernacle among us, but He can't when there is rebellion and sin in the camp. So He gave us the law and the sacrificial system and all of the rules for holy living. He needed to give us a government, laws He Himself has created and will enforce until we learn to abide by them and enforce them ourselves."

Zipporah traced a line in the wood of the bench, unable to look into his passionate gaze. He grew so enthusiastic when he spoke of God, as though He were his friend. If only she could feel the same, but God felt like her competitor, like her husband would choose God over his love for her. It was wrong to feel thus, but she could not stop herself.

"But are we not ready now? Since the death of Aaron's sons and the continual practice of sacrifice and observance of a few of the feasts, surely the people are ready to obey." She looked at him again. "Will God move us out soon?" He'd never said, and she wanted to know why it was taking so long to have the life she longed to live.

"We will number the fighting men first and train them for battle. God will fight for us, but we must know how to fight for ourselves as well. God may save us the trouble of war and give us the land without us lifting a bow or raising a sword, but He may ask us to fight with His guidance and help. We cannot know." Moses touched her arm. "Gershom and Eliezer will not be among those counted since they are Levites, so you need not worry. The Levites are set apart for God in place of every firstborn. They will serve our God, but not in that way."

She released a soft sigh. "I'm glad." She longed to say more, but a moment later he stood. "If you are all right, I must go." He kissed her cheek and searched her face. "You will be fine?"

She nodded. "I will go to spin with Miriam as usual today. Perhaps Elisheba will finally join us."

He frowned and rubbed his beard. "She is still staying away from the two of you?"

Zipporah slowly stood to walk him to the door. The dizziness had left her, and hope rose that perhaps she was not ill after all. "Sometimes she will speak to me, but she accuses Miriam of pride. She does not see that she carries her own pride. I wish they could talk things out."

He pulled her close. "As I wish we could talk about things more, my love. But I do not want to burden you with things even I find too great to bear." His kiss on the top of her head signaled his going. He released her and left the tent.

She watched him traipse through the sea of manna that lay before their tent, something she must gather quickly before it burned away with the late morning sun.

Perhaps she would stop at Elisheba's tent on the way to see Miriam. The woman had spent weeks grieving her sons. Maybe their deaths had softened her toward the rest of her family.

She picked up a clay bowl to gather the manna, ignoring the slight headache that began as she bent low to scoop the yellowish-white substance from the ground. She would not allow herself to grow ill. She was simply tired of living without Moses and of sharing him with everyone else, including his God.

⌐≥⌐

Miriam emerged from her tent, water jar in hand, and nearly bumped into Zipporah and Elisheba. "Elisheba! How good of you to come." She hid her surprise with a smile of welcome. The woman had just lost her two oldest sons. She must tread lightly to show understanding and her own grief at losing her nephews.

Elisheba nodded, though she withheld a returning smile. "Zipporah asked me to come. I did not want to."

Silence followed her remark until at last Miriam spoke. "You are grieving your sons. I grieve them too. I remember when they were small. We had such fun watching them play, even in the midst of our slavery. They were always showing us new things." Had she said the right thing? She watched Elisheba, but the woman did not meet her gaze.

"I remember," she said softly. "I'm glad you do too."

It was a peace offering, Miriam decided. There was no need to expect her to apologize or discuss the past if Elisheba would let it go. Miriam had forgiven her long ago. Though a discussion would help make things smooth and right between them, now was not the time.

"I could never forget them," Miriam said. "You were having boys while I bore girls. I wondered if I would ever be so blessed with sons as you were, but I considered your children as close as my own. I loved them, Elisheba. I hope you know that."

Tears filmed Elisheba's eyes, and Zipporah stifled a cough Miriam had not heard from her before. She gave Zipporah a sharp look, assessing her. Was she ill as Miriam had long suspected, or was it a passing reaction to something in the air?

"Thank you," Elisheba whispered, and Miriam strained to catch her words. Would Elisheba allow an embrace?

She set her water jar on the ground and walked slowly closer. When Elisheba set her jar aside as well and did not back away, Miriam pulled her sister-in-law into her arms. "We will not let them be forgotten," she promised.

"Aaron is not allowed to speak of them," Elisheba said, nearly choking on her words. "He fears disobeying God in the same way they did or some other way. So my other sons and husband do not speak of them. It is as if they never existed. Only our distant relatives grieve with me."

Miriam nodded, not knowing what to say. Nadab and Abihu *had* sinned against the Lord. It was a grievous thing to do after they had seen and eaten in the presence of God.

What made them think they could do as they pleased instead of offering to God what He had prescribed?

"I grieve too," she said. "Though I could not tell you then, I want you to know now. Thank you for coming today." She released her hold on Elisheba's arms and stepped back.

Elisheba picked up her water jar. "I am sorry for the rift between us. I would like to be friends again."

Miriam smiled. "I would like that as well." She took up her own jar and glanced at Zipporah. "Are you feeling well enough to gather water with us?"

Zipporah nodded, looking away from Miriam's scrutiny. "I can gather my own water." She offered a weak smile. "But if you have some herbs to help a headache I can't seem to get rid of, I would be grateful."

"I will mix you a tonic as soon as we return."

They set off for the river, passing the crowd of Israel's leaders as they listened to Moses tell them how to number the men for fighting. Warring emotions tugged at Miriam's heart—a longing to sing that Elisheba had been restored to them, and concern for Zipporah's health, which stopped her from fully embracing joy. Life was full of trouble, and the longer she lived, the more she realized that even in the good times, trouble could meet them around the next bend.

*Be grateful for today, this moment*, she told herself. She forced herself to thank God for small favors. One day they would see Him as Moses did, when they stepped from this world into the next. Still, she longed for joy and His glory and good things now, not then. Now was all she knew.

# FIFTY

Two weeks later, Miriam prepared the manna into flatbread while Jephunneh and Caleb killed the Passover lamb to share with their growing family. Just as on the night of their flight from Egypt, the lamb was roasted in the small area in front of their tent, and the family gathered inside, waiting to share the unleavened bread and the bitter herbs they found growing among the scrubs near the mountain's foothills.

"Are Moses and Zipporah joining us?" Lysia asked Miriam as they stood at the tent's door, watching the men turn the lamb evenly over the fire.

Miriam gave her daughter a sidelong glance and looked toward Moses' tent. "They are eating with Aaron's family this time." She didn't expect the sadness in her voice and hoped Lysia hadn't noticed. She longed for all of her family to share in this celebration together, but one lamb was only enough for her family. Aaron's family was missing two sons, so Moses had chosen to spend Passover with them.

"I wish Nadab and Abihu were still with us," Lysia said, her voice barely above a whisper. "Aunt Elisheba rarely smiles anymore."

Miriam agreed. She had also noticed Elisheba's continual sadness. Between that and Zipporah's failing health, Miriam worried. Often.

She looked at her daughter again and smiled, thankful that all of her children lived. She touched Lysia's cheek. "We must pray for them. It is not an easy task to be chosen by God. The demands of obedience are strict, especially for the priests. I am glad your father is not in Aaron's place."

Janese joined them in that moment. "What are we talking about? Is the lamb almost done cooking?"

Miriam put her arms around both girls. "No, the lamb is not ready, and we were just talking. Come, let's rest for a moment while we wait."

"And listen to our children squabble," Janese said.

Miriam laughed. "Just as both of you did nearly every day."

Her girls gave her playful scowls. "We were just keeping you from growing too used to motherhood," Lysia said, laughing.

The banter between them continued until the lamb was ready, and then the mood took a somber turn. This was a day to remember. Had it truly been a year since God had set them free from Egypt?

"We must never forget," Miriam said as they gathered around the food to eat.

"Never," the rest of her family echoed. She hoped they would long remember their words.

Months passed after Passover, and Miriam fell into a regular daily routine, which now included the morning and evening sacrifices. The work of the priesthood seemed firmly established, and Elisheba no longer grieved as publicly for her sons, though Miriam had no doubt she would never stop mourning their loss.

On one of their trips to visit the women of the camp, only Miriam and Elisheba were together, as Zipporah had taken to her bed. Worry sat upon Miriam's chest like a millstone at the thought that Zipporah's illness might be worse than any of them had realized. But she did not speak of it. She glanced at Elisheba and smiled through the heaviness.

"Shall we start with the tribe of Judah?" She knew Jephunneh's kinsmen would be easiest to meet with, as the women of that tribe were usually less likely to complain.

"I would save the best for last," Elisheba said, "but I will go wherever you think we should." Her tone held the slightest hint of defeat, but Miriam chose to ignore it. She could not handle more sadness today.

"Then let us do that. End our journey with a happy visit." She moved in the direction of Dan instead, the tribe slated to move last whenever the Lord moved them out of Sinai. Assuming He would one of these days.

As they walked, they met a woman Miriam had seen now and then but rarely spoken to. She was not hard to miss, as her skin color was many shades darker than even the darkest Israelite, and she did not have Hebrew features.

Miriam stopped and glanced at Elisheba. "Let's introduce ourselves," she whispered.

Elisheba gave a slight nod.

"Greetings," Miriam said, causing the woman to turn toward them instead of passing them by on the wide path.

"Are you speaking to me?" The woman looked around. No one else was within hearing distance.

"Yes," Miriam said, taking a step closer. "I have seen you many times, but we have never met or learned your name. We are going through the camp to encourage the women, and it seemed a good time to meet you as well. I am Miriam, Moses' sister. And this is Elisheba, Aaron's wife."

The woman dipped her head and then lifted it, but her dark eyes remained downcast. "I am Liya, a Cushite of Ethiopia. I am not one of your people, but I know who you are."

"How is it that you came to live among us, Liya?" Elisheba stepped closer as well, looking the woman up and down.

"I came with you out of Egypt." She lifted her head to meet their curious gazes. "My husband and I came to Egypt with our parents many years ago. We were both children then, and after we married and they died, we decided to stay in Egypt rather than return to Ethiopia. But when the plagues came, the hail killed my husband. It was then that I took my children, who were nearly grown, and fled to Goshen. We found a place in the city to stay hidden from the hand of your God against Egypt."

"Where did you find this place? We had Egyptians and other races join us, but few came to live among us to escape the plagues. Did someone take you in?" Miriam's brows drew together as she tried to decide whether she believed the woman.

"One of the families from the tribe of Dan. At least that's what they told us. I hope it is not a problem for us to be with you. We have come to fear and believe in your God. I am told that God accepts foreigners who follow Him." A glimmer of uncertainty appeared in Liya's eyes.

Miriam was quick to dispel it. "Yes. Foreigners may join us. If they believe and the men are circumcised, they may participate in our festivals."

Relief settled over her dark features. "Oh, good. I would not wish to offend your God. We want to be part of your people if you will have us." Uncertainty swept through her gaze again, as if she needed reassuring.

"Moses has heard from our God that foreigners are to be treated with respect and included if they are willing to obey our laws, so you have nothing to fear. Welcome, Liya. I hope we will be able to get to know you better in days to come."

A big smile filled her face, and relief showed in her expression. "Thank you! Moses told me we were welcome, but I feared . . . It is easy to fear."

*Yes, it is.* "You spoke to Moses?" The thought of fear fled at her brother's name.

She nodded. "He saw us during one of the gatherings and asked our origin, much as you did. When I explained it all to him, he said we were welcome. But until you said so as well, I doubted. I am not always sure how the women of the rest of the tribes, besides the small family that took us in, will accept us."

Miriam's pulse quickened. Moses had said nothing of this or of any other foreigners to her. She had introduced Calanthe to him in the days before the first Passover, but he had failed to give her the courtesy of welcoming her in more than a cursory way. But then, Miriam couldn't know everything her brother said or did when she was not around. Still, the woman's words troubled her the slightest bit, and she held Liya's gaze a moment too long. "Well, if Moses welcomed you, how can we not?"

"Of course you are welcome," Elisheba said, coming to her rescue. "I hope you will visit us in the tribe of Levi now and then."

"I would like that," Liya said, suddenly preoccupied with the sash at her waist. Even her clothes were slightly different from those of the children of Israel, all stripes and bolder colors.

"You will have to show us where you find such vibrant dyes for your clothes." Elisheba must have noticed too, but at this point Miriam had wearied of the conversation. Something about the woman made her uncomfortable, though she didn't know why. Was it because she was not of Israel, or because she dressed differently and seemed to already have Moses' ear? Why hadn't Moses mentioned that he'd met her? And why on earth did she care? Was she so unfeeling that she would turn away a foreigner when their God had accepted all those who trusted Him?

"We should be going," Miriam said, realizing that she was too distracted to continue paying attention to the woman. She didn't want to offend her.

Liya bowed. "It was my pleasure to meet you both."

Miriam nodded. "The pleasure was ours." She touched Elisheba's arm and nudged her forward. "Excuse us. We must see to the other women."

Liya stepped aside and let them pass, and Miriam hurried Elisheba away from the tribe of Dan, where she feared she might find more Egyptian or other refugees. Why she felt so strange about foreigners troubled her, for she had not felt so when they lived in Egypt and Calanthe and her children had come to them. But perhaps it was simply worry for Zipporah that put her on edge.

"Where are we going now?" Elisheba interrupted her frantic musings.

"To Judah. I decided I do not want to wait for happiness."

# FIFTY-ONE

**1444 BC**

Another year had passed, another Passover celebrated, when in the second month, the twentieth day, the cloud rose from above the Tabernacle and the tribes fell into their assigned places to follow where God would lead. Miriam found Moses before he left his tent the morning of their move and walked with him as he headed toward the foothills where the Tabernacle stood.

"Has God told you where we are going?" It was so nice to finally be leaving Sinai. "Will He lead us to the land of promise?" She could not keep the excitement from her voice. How long it had been since God had spoken to her in dreams, and it galled her to have to ask her brother, but the truth was, he seemed to be the only person who heard from God these days. Even Aaron admitted that he did not hear from the Lord apart from Moses giving him instructions.

Moses glanced at her, and she hurried to keep pace with him. "He has not told me. All I know is that we will follow the cloud, stop when it stops, and move when it moves. We will know when it is time to rest."

A mild sense of defeat came at her brother's words, but she did not leave his side. "Are you aware that your wife has been ill?" He should know, as he spent most evenings in their tent, but was he oblivious to what Miriam had seen for the past year? She had not spoken of it with Moses in recent days, and she did not know how observant he had been.

Moses stopped to face her. "I know she has not been as well as she was when Jethro returned her to me. She has headaches and dizziness, but she does not complain of any other ailment. What are you saying, Miriam?"

"Only that she often does not join Elisheba and me when we visit the women, and even if we are just working in our tents, she stays alone in yours. I have given her herbs to ease her headaches, but I think there is more that she is not saying. Though she did tell me almost a year ago that she does not expect to live long on the earth." Miriam searched her brother's gaze, hating that she had just added to his burden.

A deep sigh left his lips. He adjusted his turban and suddenly didn't seem sure where to put his hands. "I have suspected. But when I ask, she does not tell me. I fear she does not want to give me cause to worry about her. But what can I do? I cannot heal her."

"Couldn't our God heal her? For your sake? You are His favored one. Surely if you asked Him . . ." Miriam left the thought unfinished.

Moses shifted his feet and kicked a stone away. "Who am I that God should grant me this favor? I am not better than any of you, Miriam. I am God's servant, that is all. I cannot ask Him for special kindnesses."

Miriam stared at him. "Not even for your wife?"

Moses shook his head. "If He heals my wife, what of your

husband or Aaron's wife? When one of us falls ill, is He to heal all of us? Eventually we all die, Miriam. Our years are seventy, perhaps eighty, but they are all filled with pain and trouble. Soon they disappear and we fly away. We cannot stop what happens to every person who walks the earth."

"You and I and Aaron are all past eighty. Zipporah is only in her early seventies. We should be the ones who fall ill and die. Not her. Not yet." She heard the tremor in her voice and read the pain in Moses' eyes. Neither one of them wanted to lose Zipporah.

"We can pray for her," Moses said, touching her arm. "But we cannot expect God to give her more years than He has already ordained for her. It is not ours to choose."

She knew that. But she wasn't ready. Zipporah had become a friend and confidante. "Maybe I am wrong," she said, mostly to give him hope, for she knew her words had worried him. "Maybe she will be better soon and we will laugh about this conversation."

"She may recover, but we will all eventually die. I hope she lives to see the Promised Land. I have always hoped for that." A wistful look crossed his face. "But I must go now." He pointed to the cloud rising in the distance. "The tribes need to follow God's exact orders to gather the Tabernacle, its utensils, and all that goes into it, and move out exactly as God instructed. I must make sure they do not fail."

She nodded and touched his arm as he was about to walk away. "The burden is too great for you, Moses. Do not let it destroy you."

He gave her a brisk nod and hurried away while she returned to check on Zipporah, wishing she had kept her fears about the woman to herself.

Miriam walked with the rest of her tribe until the cloud settled for the night and turned to a pillar of fire. But the next day the cloud rose again, and the people walked all day until they grew utterly weary.

Miriam frequently checked on Zipporah, who had taken to riding in a cart while Miriam and Elisheba walked beside her. The woman's cheeks were hollow, and her eyes grew vacant the longer they traveled. She slept on cushions in the back of the cart and did not rouse even when Moses and her sons spoke to her.

By the evening of the first week of travel, Moses came to Miriam's tent. "You must come," he said, his voice choked.

Miriam hurried after him and entered the tent, dark now except for a few oil lamps. "I can't rouse her," he said once they both knelt at Zipporah's side.

Miriam leaned close to listen for breath, then placed a hand on Zipporah's chest. But there was no movement or sound coming from her, and her eyes stared at the tent's ceiling, unseeing. Miriam leaned back on her heels, stifling the urge to let out a bitter cry. She looked at her brother, tears streaming down her face. "She is gone, Moses."

Moses knelt, burying his face in the blanket next to his wife. He would be unclean for touching her body but could purify himself after they buried her. His sobs came, broken and soft, and Miriam put a hand on his back, ever the older sister wanting to comfort him. But what comfort could there be in death? Death was final until God resurrected their bodies on some future promised day.

"She is no longer in pain," Miriam said, rubbing circles

along his back. "She wouldn't want you to grieve overmuch." Though everything inside of Miriam screamed to grieve as anyone would for a sister or brother.

Moses lifted his head and pulled Miriam close. "I was not good to her. I should have been here more."

Miriam swiped at her tears. "You had no choice. Our God called you and you answered. Do not blame yourself, Brother."

He held her at arm's length. "Will you gather the others to help me find a place to bury her outside of the camp? We should also send word to her father and sisters and brothers-in-law."

"We will stay here, then, until they arrive? Will our God wait for us to grieve?" Miriam had no sense of God's will in this.

"I will ask Him." He stood and pulled her to her feet. "First I will tell the boys." His sons had married in the past year and lived next to him in tents their wives had made.

Miriam nodded. "I will tell Jephunneh and Caleb. They will gather our relatives to help you bury your dead."

Moses kissed her forehead and thanked her, then left the tent to find his sons. Miriam looked one last time at Zipporah lying still, seemingly at peace. They would need to wash and bind the body for burial, and Elisheba and her girls would help with that. But for a moment, she simply stood there, allowing her tears to fall unhindered. Death held no hope outside of a vague understanding of the future. The ancient patriarch Job had believed he would see God's face—had believed in a coming resurrection. Wasn't it the hope of Israel? And yet death was so final now. She dared not hope for a tomorrow she could not see.

The caravan from Midian came within a week, though Zipporah's body lay in a nearby cave long before its arrival. Moses greeted his brother-in-law Hobab along with Zipporah's sister Aida and several servants. He looked beyond them, but there was no sign of anyone else.

"Jethro is ill, and the daughters that remained close by stayed in case he passes while we are away. But at your summons, we could not disregard our sister's passing." Hobab kissed Moses on each cheek and embraced him. "I am deeply sorry for your loss, my brother. Zipporah will be missed by us all."

"Thank you for coming." He glanced at Aida and nodded his welcome. She and Zipporah had been close all of the years they had lived in Midian. "You will want to see where we laid her." He led them through the camp and to the outskirts, where a line of caves filled the mountainsides.

He pointed to the one where Zipporah now rested. Though Joseph's bones remained with them to be buried in Shechem once they entered the Promised Land, Moses could not do the same with Zipporah or any of the other Israelites who had died along the way, for there was no way to preserve their bodies as Joseph's had been.

Aida released a loud cry and fell to her knees, weeping. Hobab stood beside her and also lifted his voice in a loud cry. Moses could not keep the tears from again slipping down his cheeks. So many memories filled him at the sight of Zipporah's family. And to know that Jethro's life was coming to an end on the earth filled him with additional grief.

*Oh, Adonai, I ache for my loss. Please comfort me somehow.* But how did one find comfort in death? He needed time alone with God. Perhaps it was time for a visit to the Tent of Meeting, now that he had purified himself from touching the dead. Perhaps God could fill what Hobab and Aida and even his sons could not. A void Zipporah had left that he could never refill. Did God heal broken hearts?

# FIFTY-TWO

Another week passed, and Moses' heart did feel lighter after he met with God in the Tent of Meeting. Joshua had followed him there every time he could and waited outside. Moses had felt God's reassuring love in that place and knew Zipporah would not decay forever. One day God would defeat even death. Though Moses could not see how, he knew He would.

The mystery of it all caused him to fall into periods of deep silence as he pondered his God. If he could, he would never leave His presence, but the people would never allow that.

One day, about the time Hobab indicated they should return to Midian, the cloud lifted, telling them to move on.

Moses entered Hobab's tent and called him outside. "We are on our way to the place the Lord promised us, for He said, 'I will give it to you.' Come with us and we will treat you well, for the Lord has promised wonderful blessings for Israel!"

Hobab twisted his hands in the belt of his robe and studied the ground. At last he met Moses' gaze. "No, I will not go. I must return to my own land and family."

Moses did not want to accept Hobab's response. "Please." He heard the pleading in his voice. "Don't leave us. You know the places in the wilderness where we should camp. Come, be our guide. If you do, we'll share with you all the blessings the Lord gives us."

Hobab stroked the length of his beard as though he was considering Moses' request. But a moment later he said, "I'm sorry, my brother. As I told you, Jethro is not well, and even now he could rest in Sheol. I am the oldest brother-in-law left to lead the family. I would love to help you, but I rather think that your God can do a better job of leading you than I can." Hobab's gentle rebuke made Moses' cheeks flush, and he realized he felt the way he had in Midian, as though he wanted someone else to lead.

"You are right, of course. I will miss you." He embraced Hobab and bid Aida farewell. "Be safe as you travel."

"And you as well. Until we meet again." Hobab waved as Moses turned toward the camp, where the tribes had lined up to move to their next destination. They had stayed there long enough to bury Zipporah and grieve her loss. At least God had given them that.

Moses glanced up at the cloud, which was moving toward the wilderness of Paran. How long would it take to get there? And would they enter the Promised Land soon after they arrived? God had not told him.

They marched for three days before coming to rest again. Moses returned to his tent alone each night, wishing life was not so painful.

Months passed as the glory of the Lord moved them onward with the pillar of cloud. At night they would settle, never knowing whether they would move again the next day or remain where they were for a time.

Miriam shoved the last tent peg into the dry earth and straightened, rubbing the small of her back. She was going to have to admit her age to her children soon enough and ask them to help raise her tent. Jephunneh would have done it, but he was busy herding their flocks. She gazed about, wondering when life had lost its joy.

Elisheba knelt in the area in front of her tent a few paces away to grind the manna, but Miriam had no energy to help her. She'd grown weary of traveling here and there with no end in sight. When would God be satisfied that they were ready to enter the land He'd promised? They'd been away from Egypt for two years now, fought a war with Amalek, and come close to the edges of the towns of unfriendly neighbors as they followed the cloud, forever trailing God's lead.

Her arms felt weighted, as if she could sleep for a week. She moved to pull the cushions from the saddlebags and spread them out on the ground. Would tomorrow see them pulling up their stakes and moving forward again?

She sank onto the cushions, feeding the grief she still carried for Zipporah. Even Moses seemed different, defeated somehow. She couldn't blame him. The people were a burden even she grew tired of dealing with. The women were beginning to complain again, and now she had only Elisheba to help her. Perhaps her daughters should be taught to help guide the other women, to take her place when her days were at an end.

A rattle of the tent's door drew her attention from her melancholy thoughts. "Miriam? Are you in here?" Elisheba stepped inside and waited, probably letting her eyes adjust to the darkness.

Miriam had yet to light the lamp, but she stood and greeted Elisheba. "I'm glad you came," she said, reaching for the lamp she had already set in its niche against one of the tent poles.

"I thought you could use some company. Besides, I need water for the manna and wondered if you would walk with me to the stream."

Miriam noticed the jar in Elisheba's arms and nodded. She searched about for her own, plucked it from the ground, and followed Elisheba out of the tent.

"I've heard a rumor," Elisheba said when they were out of earshot of other women outside of their tents. "Please tell me if it's true."

Miriam lifted a brow and glanced at Elisheba. "If I know the answer, I will surely tell you, but I have heard no rumors that would interest us. Tell me, what have you heard?"

Elisheba drew in a deep breath, her expression one of uncertainty, even concern. "Do you remember the Cushite woman Liya we met many months ago when we headed to the tribe of Dan?"

Miriam stopped walking to search Elisheba's face. "I remember her well. What have you heard? Has she caused trouble in the camp?"

Elisheba shrugged. "I don't know if I would call it trouble . . . but Aaron said that he has seen Moses speaking with her. More than once."

Miriam grew suddenly still. Liya was not of their tribe, even of their race. *Neither was Zipporah*, she reminded herself.

But that was different. Moses had wed Zipporah when he was living in a different land. Why would he speak with a foreign woman here? He rarely spoke to the women at all. He spoke to the elders and let Miriam and Elisheba handle the women.

"What did he want with her?" The words came out in a frustrated rush.

"Aaron thinks he is interested in her. He saw Moses laugh with her." Elisheba lifted the jar from her head and set it on the ground. "What if he marries her?"

The thought hit Miriam hard, and she forced herself to keep from reeling. Zipporah was barely gone, buried only a few months before. How could Moses think of such a thing so soon? Had he not loved Zipporah? And how could he even think of marrying someone outside of Israel?

"I must speak to him." Miriam started walking again, and Elisheba followed.

"What will you say? Do you really think we should say something to him? He is God's man, after all. Isn't he grown, one who can make his own decisions?" She prattled on, but Miriam barely heard her above her own anger rising in defense of Zipporah.

"He may be a grown man, but I am still his older sister. At the very least, he should consider someone in Israel. But should he marry again at all? Whoever he marries will be as lonely as Zipporah was." She whirled about, holding tight to the water jar. "He can't do this!"

Elisheba held her tongue, but after they had filled their jars and were walking back toward their tents, she finally spoke. "He can do this, Miriam. You know he can. Even if you speak to him, do you really want to face his anger? He carries the weight of all of Israel on his shoulders. What if Liya can lift some of that burden? When is the last time you heard Moses laugh?"

Miriam bit her lip lest she lash out and ruin what still felt tentative in her relationship with her sister-in-law. He couldn't marry a Cushite. He couldn't! But one glance at Elisheba told her she would not understand Miriam's protectiveness of a woman now gone from them.

"He rarely laughs," she admitted. "But he is still wiser to marry a woman of Israel than a woman half his age from a foreign land, believer in Adonai or not."

Elisheba said nothing, and Miriam quickened her step, her anger carrying her to her tent. She must do something about this. But as they prepared manna for the evening meal, she still had no idea how to broach the subject with her brother.

⁓

Days passed with no sign of the cloud leaving its resting place. Miriam felt herself continually sighing in relief every morning when the cloud did not move. But every time she attempted to catch Moses leaving his tent, he had already gone to wherever it was he went each day. Sometimes to the Tabernacle, other times to the Tent of Meeting or to the sheepfolds with his sons. She never knew for sure.

She watched lines of people attempt to speak with him when he sat in judgment, and her heart softened at the sight. Why shouldn't he marry again? Was she stubbornly against this because Liya was not of their people? Or was it her grief for Zipporah? Or could it be something more?

She examined her heart, even prayed for her brother, but

she felt nothing but weariness overtake her. The anger that had burned that first day had abated. Perhaps she should visit Liya and find out Moses' intentions. But Moses was the person to speak with, and he was becoming impossible to reach. Was he avoiding her on purpose? Was he keeping his distance so that she would not offer her advice?

Sadness settled over her at the thought that she was losing a relationship she had valued all of her life. Before Zipporah came, Moses had confided in her and Aaron. After Zipporah came, Miriam could still talk with him about trouble in the camp. But since Zipporah's death, he rarely came to family meals, didn't confide in her or Jephunneh. Perhaps he spoke to Aaron? But from what Elisheba indicated, Aaron had simply observed or overheard Moses and Liya. It seemed that neither one of them had their brother's ear as they once did.

Miriam stepped out of her tent as dusk settled. She gazed on the beauty of the cloud-enveloped fire. *Oh, Adonai, I don't like this new season of my life. I thought so much would be different than it is. I've lost a friend, and worse, I've lost connection to my brother. I'm weary of so many things, yet I don't want to be among those who complain to You, for I know You do not abide the complaints of Your people.* Hadn't a number of them recently died because they had angered the Lord with whining over their hardships? Wandering in the wilderness to prepare for a better day was not hardship. Had they forgotten their slavery in Egypt so soon?

*Please help me to see what I cannot see. My heart yearns to hear from You as in days of old. Won't You speak to me again as You once did?*

She waited, hoping, longing. Perhaps this night He would come to her in a dream. *Oh, please!* But she would have to wait until the morrow to know whether God had heard her prayer. Perhaps then He would tell her what to do about Moses or how to ease her grief.

# FIFTY-THREE

Miriam woke with a start the next morning, her mind whirling. She sat up, jerking the covers from Jephunneh in the process.

He roused, rubbing his eyes, and slowly rose. "What is it?"

"I had a dream." The wonder of God's answering so quickly left her feeling a little stunned. "God hasn't spoken to me in months, even years, but last night I saw Caleb and Joshua returning with joy from the Promised Land. Other men were with them, but I could not make out their faces. I only know that our son and Joshua will get to see God's chosen land, and soon!"

Jephunneh took her hand in his. "That's wonderful news, beloved. I wonder why they were returning from the land and not leading us into it?"

Miriam looked into his eyes, her mind searching for anything else the dream might have held. "I don't know. All I know is that they entered and then came back. Perhaps they went to scout out what is there. But they were smiling." She grabbed her husband's arm. "This is good news!"

He laughed and pulled her close, kissing her forehead. "Yes, indeed. It is good news. But let us not share it until it comes to pass. It is not a message for you to share, is it?"

Miriam tilted her head, thinking. "No. It is a message for us. To give us hope. But we will wait until God brings it to pass."

~≈~

The barest hint of predawn light woke Moses alone in his tent, robbing him of sleep. He knew this feeling too well, and he could not keep himself from lying abed any more than he could force sleep to come. He sat up and rubbed the grit from his eyes. Months had passed since Zipporah's death and burial, and with his sons married, despite how close they lived, no one could fill the need he felt for a female companion.

He knew he was not a young man who needed sons, but he did need someone he could share his life with—what was left of this trying life God had given to him. Why he had been chosen was a question he could not answer. He longed for God every single day and didn't want to leave the Tent of Meeting after God spoke with him there. But in the times when evening fell and he sat alone in his bed, he wanted human touch.

Liya's face filled his thoughts, and he felt himself smiling. True, she was a Cushite, but she was beautiful and smart and loved Yahweh. Her children were grown and married, and though she was half his age, she was alone in the camp. As he was.

Would she marry him if he asked? Would remarriage be a slight against the mother of his sons, who was so soon in the grave?

He ran a hand through his tangled hair and stood. Though dawn had not yet risen, he would inquire of the Lord at the Tent of Meeting. Then he would know.

~

Moses entered the tent and bowed with his face to the ground. His heart yearned heavenward, and he wished he could go again to the top of Mount Sinai and spend time with just Yahweh. But Sinai was in their past, and they were not likely to return there. He waited as he prayed, hands lifted, palms up, his heart beating an anxious rhythm.

When the cloud descended from above the camp and the Lord's glory filled the tent, he looked up, still kneeling. "Do I have Your favor to marry Liya, a woman not of Israel? I will not ask her if You do not approve."

He waited, expectant, but God did not speak as He usually did. Instead, Moses felt a sense of peace and rightness about his desire settle over him. He searched his heart to be sure he was not simply following his own selfish longings. When he found no fault and the peace remained, he lifted his arms and praised the Lord.

"Thank You, Adonai, for looking on Your servant with favor. Please continue to go with us and bless Your people, despite our many sins. Forgive us, Lord, as only You can do."

Again he received no response, only a feeling that God would not be displeased if he married Liya. Now he needed to ask her and see if she would say yes.

~

Miriam stepped out of her tent several days later and looked toward Moses'. Should she speak to him even now?

She'd waited more than a week, and he'd been impossible to talk to.

Dawn had coated the sky in brilliant yellow and pink, and the pillar of fire had returned to a cumulous pillar of cloud. The contrast always struck her as strange, but there was no mistaking God's cloud for the others that naturally surrounded it.

She picked up her bowl to gather the manna coating the ground and looked up every now and then, hoping for some sign of Moses. When she saw Liya emerge from his tent with a bowl to gather her own manna, her heart fairly stopped.

Moses had married the woman and not told anyone? It was not like they had to go through a ceremony to pledge their lives to each other as she had done when she married Jephunneh. Most couples wed by simply agreeing or by their fathers agreeing, and they moved into the tent of the husband or husband's family. But why didn't Moses tell his family? Was he ashamed to tell her and Aaron of his plans for fear they would not approve?

Heat filled her face as she continued scooping up handfuls of the coriander-like seeds. He should have warned them. Told them his plans. Even asked their opinions! Didn't God speak to them as He did to him?

She let that thought linger, remembering her dream of a short time ago. God had spoken to her, and she should have been consulted. It was not right for Moses to just marry a woman without telling anyone.

She hurried through her gathering chore and burst into her tent, fuming. She must do something about this. Moses couldn't just do whatever he wanted. He was not so special that he was above the law of God. Surely God would have wanted him to make a better choice. Wouldn't He?

⧟

The cloud lifted again, and the silver trumpets Moses had made blew twice, telling which tribes to move first. The Ark of the Covenant led the way, and Moses shouted, "Arise, O Lord, and let Your enemies be scattered! Let them flee before You!"

This move to another place took away any chance Miriam might have had to speak to Moses. He was too busy making sure the tribes all followed the same protocol they always did.

When they arrived at the place God intended them to rest for the night, Moses shouted again, "Return, O Lord, to the countless thousands of Israel!"

Miriam went about her tasks, setting up camp. Elisheba came to her side. "Let me help you, then you can help me."

Miriam nodded, grateful.

As they worked, Elisheba lowered her voice and leaned close to Miriam's ear. "What do you make of Liya sharing Moses' tent? I assume he married her, for I can't imagine him breaking the law of our God when he is the one who gave us the law in the first place. He knows the penalty for adultery."

"He married her," Miriam said, feeling defeated. "I found Gershom as we walked and asked him. Moses took Liya before one of the Levites to bless them before he took her to his tent."

"One of the Levites? Why not his own brother? Aaron is high priest in Israel. He should have blessed the marriage."

Miriam agreed, meeting Elisheba's scowl with one of her own. "I doubt he trusted either of us to bless his choice.

Why else would he keep his desire a secret? We are family! He should have told us."

"Yes, he should have. But his children knew?"

"Yes."

"Are they happy about it?" Elisheba used a mallet to pound the peg into the hard ground.

"Gershom accepts it. Eliezer knows his father was lonely. I don't know whether they like her or not." Miriam straightened and rubbed the small of her back.

"Well, I don't like her. I don't think Aaron does either." She stood up as well. "Come, let's get my tent up now. Then we can sit for a moment."

"And grind the manna. Our men will want to eat soon."

Nothing changed day after day, and Miriam wondered if her dream would ever come true. Were they close to the Promised Land? They had already wandered for two years. They had a governing law, a God to follow, and a military to fight for them. What more did they need? But she did not ask the Lord. All she could think of was how she felt about Liya, and she didn't like the direction of her thoughts.

Two weeks after his marriage to Liya, Moses walked through the camp and came near a group of foreigners who had also left Egypt with them. They did not appear to be from Cush or Ethiopia—perhaps Syria or one of the bordering Egyptian towns. Some were even Egyptian by the looks of them, but none of them were smiling. As he passed the tents and saw the men and women standing in the doorways, the same refrain came from their lips.

"Oh, for some meat!" they cried. "We remember the fish

we used to eat for free in Egypt. And we had all the cucumbers, melons, leeks, onions, and garlic we wanted. But now our appetites are gone. All we ever see is this manna!"

He moved on, ignoring them, though a sinking feeling settled in his gut. When he came to the tents of the tribes of Israel and heard the same complaint, his frustration grew. He whirled on his heel and headed to the Tent of Meeting.

He entered the tent and fell on his knees, his face to the ground. "Why are You treating me, Your servant, so harshly?" he asked the Lord. "Have mercy on me! What did I do to deserve the burden of all these people? Did I give birth to them? Did I bring them into the world? Why did You tell me to carry them in my arms like a mother carries a nursing baby? How can I carry them to the land You swore to give their ancestors? Where am I supposed to get meat for all these people? They keep whining to me, saying, 'Give us meat to eat!' I can't carry all these people by myself. The load is far too heavy. If this is how You intend to treat me, just go ahead and kill me. Do me a favor and spare me this misery!"

The words came out in a heated rush, and when he finished speaking, his energy drained from him. He covered his face, ashamed, yet he could not bear the burden any longer. Life was too hard, and he was too weary.

A soft rumble fell from the glory that surrounded him. "Gather before Me seventy men who are recognized as elders and leaders of Israel," the Lord said, His voice like soft thunder. "Bring them to the Tabernacle to stand there with you. I will come down and talk to you there. I will take some of the Spirit that is upon you, and I will put the Spirit upon them also. They will bear the burden of the people along with you, so you will not have to carry it alone."

A sense of relief washed over Moses.

"And say to the people, 'Purify yourselves, for tomorrow you will have meat to eat. You were whining, and the Lord heard you when you cried, "Oh, for some meat! We were better off in Egypt!" Now the Lord will give you meat, and you will have to eat it. And it won't be for just a day or two, or for five or ten or even twenty. You will eat it for a whole month until you gag and are sick of it. For you have rejected the Lord, who is here among you, and you have whined to Him, saying, "Why did we ever leave Egypt?"'"

Moses sat back on his heels and gazed into the dense cloud. "But, Lord, there are six hundred thousand foot soldiers here with me, and yet You say, 'I will give them meat for a whole month!' Even if we butchered all our flocks and herds, would that satisfy them? Even if we caught all the fish in the sea, would that be enough?" How could God possibly feed so many with meat? Try as he might, Moses could not fathom it.

"Has My arm lost its power?" The words of the Lord rang loud in the tent, and Moses wondered if His thunderous voice had carried to the ends of the earth. He did not miss the rebuke for not having trusted. "Now you will see whether or not My word comes true!"

With that the cloud lifted, and Moses sat for a moment, stunned and humbled. He should not have questioned God's ability to feed the people with meat. If He could give them manna, surely He could provide anything they needed.

He stood, chastened, and left the tent. He called one of the priests to blow the silver trumpet to gather all of the people together, and Moses repeated God's words to them. Then he dismissed them and told the seventy elders to meet him at the Tabernacle.

Once there, the Lord did as He had promised and gave the seventy elders the same Spirit that rested on Moses. Prophetic praise came from their lips, and they proclaimed the Lord's goodness throughout the camp. Moses lifted his eyes toward the cloud and whispered his thanks. The Spirit of God remained with him, and he felt a sense of profound gratitude to now have others to share his burden.

In that moment, he realized that God never meant for men or women to walk with Him alone or bear the burdens of life alone. He had made them to live in families, clans, tribes, and communities. And one day His Spirit would rest on many more than these seventy men. One day all would have the chance to know the Lord as he did.

Moses could not wait for that day.

# FIFTY-FOUR

Miriam tightened her scarf against the brisk wind coming from the direction of the sea. She looked at the sky, the sun blocked by a great horde of birds that settled above the camp, hovering low enough for the people to catch. Everywhere she looked, she could not get away from the birds, and she ducked into her tent to avoid being hit by their flapping wings. Most flew so low that she could grab them with one hand.

Was this the way God intended to give meat to the complaining people? She wrapped the scarf around her head, covering most of her face lest the birds get too close, and went out again to gather meat for their meal. If God was going to send it, she might as well feed her family too.

Jephunneh and Caleb and her girls soon joined her, and before they knew it, they had fifty bushels of birds! They gathered quail from dawn to dusk, and the next day the birds came again.

"This is too much," Miriam said as her family gathered

to eat that evening. "I think God is punishing the people for complaining against Him. We should eat only enough to satisfy us. Do not take more than you would if we killed a lamb from our flock." Somehow she sensed that this was a test. Was God speaking to her heart and not just through her dreams?

"Your mother is right," Jephunneh said. "Do not gorge yourselves, for that would be gluttony. Our God would not be pleased with us if we did so."

"Did Moses tell you that?" Miriam asked as she picked a small piece of quail from the bone.

"No. I have not spoken to him of late. But it makes sense in my heart."

Cries from a distance broke through the walls of their tent, and they stopped eating to see what the trouble was about. Miriam and Jephunneh left their tent and met Moses and Aaron and their wives nearby.

"What is it?" Jephunneh looked at Moses, who slowly shook his head.

At that moment, Joshua ran toward them and approached Moses. "My lord, the Lord has sent a plague among the people who complained. All those who spoke against Him have died, even while the quail was still in their mouths!"

Moses stood still, looking from one to another, then rested his gaze on Joshua. "Gather men to bury the dead outside the camp. This place shall be called Kibroth-hattaavah, for we have created graves of gluttony here," he said.

Miriam returned to her tent, sick at the thought that the people had angered God yet again. She was grateful for the silver trumpets calling them to leave that place the next morning.

⌘

The walk to Hazeroth felt longer than most, and Miriam had a sense of constantly searching for something she had lost. If only she understood what. God had yet to fulfill the dream about Caleb and Joshua. Liya tried to be friendly to her and Elisheba in her own foreign way, but Miriam simply could not get used to having her as part of the family. She was too young. Miriam was old enough to be her mother! How could Moses marry a child?

And yet the woman was a grandmother already and seemed to make Moses happy. Why couldn't Liya have that same effect on Miriam? On Elisheba? Both of them huddled together and tried to figure out ways to make things better, to no avail.

"Perhaps if I spoke to Aaron," Miriam said to Elisheba one day after they had finally settled and seemed to be staying in Hazeroth for a while.

"Do you think I have not already done so? He tells me to leave it be. What's done is done." Elisheba's brows wrinkled, and lines deepened across her forehead.

Neither one of them was getting any younger, and just looking at Liya's smooth, dark skin where no lines appeared made Miriam feel useless. Moses didn't need her anymore. Not like he used to. And Miriam desperately longed to be needed. Wanted. Had her brother lost concern for his family of birth?

"Yet perhaps Aaron will listen to me as his sister. We could go to Moses together and express our concerns." She warmed to the thought, and Elisheba nodded.

"If you think it will help pull this family together. Right

now we are pretty disjointed, and while I'm not sure talking to Aaron will ease your feelings or mine, it can't hurt."

No. It couldn't hurt. She would find him first thing in the morning.

~

Miriam met Aaron at his tent the next dawn and motioned for him to follow her away from Moses' tent and the camp of the Levites. They stopped near an outcropping of rocks, where Miriam sat. Aaron sat on a large rock next to her.

"What's this about?" he asked as he adjusted the turban over his gray hair.

"Liya."

"What about her?"

"He should never have married a Cushite. He should have wed someone from our tribe if he had to marry. And to wed so soon? Zipporah has not been gone long enough for the full days of mourning to be past."

Aaron stroked his beard, which came to his chest. "Well, that's not true. Months have passed, Miriam. If he wanted to marry, he didn't have to wait forever."

"But she's not of Israel!"

"True. You do have a point. He should have come to us first before just marrying her without our knowledge."

"Exactly!" Miriam said. "Has the Lord spoken only through Moses? Hasn't He spoken through us too?" Memories of the dream surfaced, and she wondered how long it had been since God had spoken directly to Aaron.

Aaron opened his mouth to speak, but a moment later thunder roared from the heavens—more precisely from the cloud where God's Spirit moved. They looked toward the camp and saw Moses emerge from his tent.

"Moses, Aaron, and Miriam, go out to the Tabernacle, all three of you!" The voice could not have been clearer despite the rumble that followed and enveloped it.

Miriam's heart raced. She felt chastened by the voice and the realization that she might have angered the Lord with her complaints. Didn't God hate grumbling from His people?

Guilt filled her as she trudged behind Aaron and joined Moses. The three walked in silence through the camp to the Tabernacle.

When they arrived, the Lord descended in the pillar of cloud, stopping in front of the entrance to the Tabernacle. "Aaron and Miriam!" He called.

They moved slowly forward, Miriam's whole body trembling now. She had never heard God call her this way, nor seen the cloud so focused on her. Fear settled deep within her.

"Now listen to what I say." The Lord's voice was stern, like a father to his errant children. "If there were prophets among you, I, the Lord, would reveal Myself in visions. I would speak to them in dreams. But not with My servant Moses. Of all My house, he is the one I trust. I speak to him face-to-face, clearly, and not in riddles. He sees the Lord as He is."

A pause followed His words, and Miriam realized that though God loved all of His creation, Moses *did* hold a special relationship to Him. A relationship that even she and Aaron, as leaders with him and prophets themselves, did not hold. Maybe they never would. Not after this.

"So why were you not afraid to criticize My servant

Moses?" The words carried the tone of anger, and a moment later the cloud departed, leaving the three of them alone.

"Oh, my master!" Aaron pleaded, looking at Miriam. "Please don't punish us for this sin we have so foolishly committed. Don't let her be like a stillborn baby, already decayed at birth."

Miriam looked down at her skin, and a deep, guttural cry escaped her. She was covered head to foot with leprosy, a skin disease for which there was no cure. She fell to her knees and wept bitter tears of sorrow and repentance. How could she have been so foolish? How had she not seen?

Moses' voice broke through her sobs. "O God, I beg you, please heal her!"

The Lord did not descend again, but His voice could be heard above them. "If her father had done nothing more than spit in her face, wouldn't she be defiled for seven days? So keep her outside the camp for seven days, and after that she may be accepted back."

Silence followed the remark, and slowly Miriam stood. She pulled her headscarf more fully over her face to hide her shame. Without a word to either brother, she left the Tabernacle and moved away from the camp to a place where defiled things went.

⌀

Miriam did not eat for seven days. She drew water from the spring, but most of the time she walked among the rocks and prayed. *You are right, O Lord, when You judge. You are holy and righteous and good, and You alone are God. I have sinned against You by thinking I knew better. I thought*

*Moses too privileged, and I wanted what he has. I wanted
to be close to You, but I resorted to complaining instead of
trusting You. Oh, please forgive Your servant.*

She prayed similar prayers during those seven days, confessing her sins as though it were the Day of Atonement, wishing she could offer a sacrifice for her sin and have Aaron bless it. But God did not ask that of her. And so she waited alone and prayed, though God did not answer.

Still, she felt His comfort and His protection when the wild animals called out in the night and she had no one to shelter her. She feared and then prayed. She praised and then trusted.

At the end of the seventh day, she began the long walk to see Aaron and be cleared of her disease. As she walked, she looked on in amazement as her skin returned to its normal state, even more youthful than it had been.

In that moment, she realized that though God had not verbally answered her, as He spoke to her brother, He *had* heard her prayers. She was clean again, only this time she knew she was clean both inside and out. She sang praises to the Lord all the way to Aaron's tent.

⁓

The trumpets sounded a few days later, calling the people of Israel to leave Hazeroth and journey to the wilderness of Paran. From there they would be on the very edge of the territory God had promised to give them.

Spirits were high among Miriam's clan, and the people sang as they traveled, rejoicing in the hope that their two-year-long trek through the wilderness would finally be at an end.

When they arrived in Paran, Moses selected twelve men to spy out the land for them, ahead of the troops he would send in to begin to claim what God had promised them. Caleb and Joshua were two of the chosen spies.

"So your dream is coming true," Jephunneh told Miriam the night before the spies were expected to leave for Canaan.

"Yes. God truly did speak to me, though I'm not sure I deserved anything from Him. I never did." She felt in her spirit a deeper appreciation for the fact that God had entrusted her with His thoughts in words or in dreams. She had been highly blessed all of her life and took far too much of it for granted.

"None of us deserve anything from the Lord, beloved. He chose to bless you in this way. We must simply be thankful." Jephunneh cupped her cheek and played with a strand of her hair. "I am thankful that He gave me you."

"And soon we will make one more journey across the Jordan and into the beautiful land that Abraham once knew." She couldn't wait to hear the report of the spies and to hear the silver trumpets announce that it was time to move on one last time.

"Yes, soon. Caleb is excited to be chosen. He is ready to fight anyone who might stand in our way." He chuckled.

"Yet I wonder if our God might just fight for us," she said, running her hands through his hair. "He has fought so many of our battles and met so many of our needs. I am very glad He gave me you."

"I couldn't have said it better." He kissed her as though they were a young couple newly married. She had thought she was too old for human love and too sinful for God's forgiveness, but apparently God chose to prove her wrong on both counts.

She laughed as Jephunneh kissed her neck and pulled her down beside him. "We are truly blessed," she whispered. But he didn't answer, and she said no more as she melted into the arms of her husband's love.

# EPILOGUE

*M*iriam lay on her mat, barely able to lift her head or to smile at her family gathered around her. So much had happened in the past few years, and none of it was what she had expected. Caleb and Joshua had indeed returned with a good report from Canaan, but the other ten spies had not. Instead of giving the people the joy of crossing into the Promised Land, God had exacted an even harsher punishment on them for their rebellion than she had experienced for only seven days outside the camp.

Forty years they would wander, He had promised Moses. Forty years for the forty days the spies had explored the land. And in the ensuing years, the people had rebelled and complained even more. Hardship followed hardship, until Miriam's body grew too weary to bear it any longer. She knew her time to go the way of all the earth was near.

Moses had pleaded with the Lord for the people when they complained against Him after Joshua and Caleb returned, but Miriam knew that God would not change His mind.

Nothing even Moses could say could undo all of the times Israel had tested the Lord and had not believed Him, despite the miracles and the blessing of seeing His glory.

"As surely as I live," the Lord had said, "I will do to you the very things I heard you say. You will all drop dead in this wilderness! Because you complained against Me, every one of you who is twenty years old or older and was included in the registration will die. You will not enter and occupy the land I swore to give you. The only exceptions will be Caleb son of Jephunneh and Joshua son of Nun."

Miriam sighed, and Caleb bent over her as if to see that she still breathed. Hadn't he heard her sigh? She felt the pressure of Jephunneh's hand and heard the soft weeping of her girls. She opened her eyes to take in one last look at their dear faces.

Summoning the strength to speak, she looked at Caleb. "I'm glad you were one of the exceptions. You will see the land of promise."

Tears filled his eyes at her words, and when she met Jephunneh's gaze, he also blinked back emotion.

"It has been a good life," she said so low that they all leaned closer to hear. But she had no strength to raise her voice.

The tent opened, and Moses and Aaron walked in. Elisheba had passed before, and Liya probably felt unwelcome despite Miriam's attempts to change that. Still, this was a time for family to gather.

Moses came to her side and knelt where Caleb had been. "The Lord loves you, Miriam. He always has." His voice sounded raspy from unshed tears. "When you go to Him, you will know just how much He cares for you . . . and I do too."

She blinked and opened her mouth, trying to force her

voice to work. "You have always been our tikvah." Ima would have agreed and been so proud of him, of them all.

And soon she would see those who had gone before her. What would it be like? Her soul sensed a beckoning to leave them, and the room grew dim despite the light pouring in from the open tent door. She closed her eyes but then opened them again one more time, this time in response to the call of the Lord.

Hadn't He called her name? And then she saw Him, His hand held out to her. *Adonai.* She knew it was He without Him saying a word. And as she took His hand, she felt so enveloped by love and mercy and grace that it seemed her soul had leapt from her body into His waiting arms. As they flew away to a place that she had never been but that felt like home, she wept. And then she raised her voice long and loud and sang.

# NOTE TO THE READER

There are some books that are easier to write than others. In fact, some seem to almost write themselves. This was *not* the case with Miriam's story. The truth is, I wasn't sure I wanted to write her story. You might wonder why, but the reason is simple. There is very little about her in the greater story that belongs to Moses, from Exodus to Deuteronomy in the Old Testament.

In order to understand Miriam, I had to follow Moses' journey. In doing so I found that I had to give him a point of view, and I also gave one to his wife Zipporah, because all three people saw things from completely different perspectives.

Miriam is called a prophetess, but we never read about a single thing she prophesied. We remember her as the little girl who watched her baby brother in the Nile and spoke to the Egyptian princess to save his life. We know she led the women in song after they left Egypt behind for good. We know that in her later years she complained against Moses for marrying a Cushite. And later we hear of her death.

The Bible does not tell us if she married, but most women

married in her day, so I found her a husband, Jephunneh. He was a real man of Scripture, but their marriage is from my imagination. I gave her daughters—purely fictional— and a son, Caleb, because Caleb was the son of Jephunneh in Scripture. He also had a younger brother, Kenaz, whom I left out of the story because there was too much material to cover as it was.

If you read Exodus through Numbers, you will find a lot of laws. I chose not to include them all, but I do recommend you read them for yourself. I find it fascinating how much God cared to cover so many details of the way the Israelites were to live holy lives before Him. And His laws on cleanliness and dealing with everything from mildew to sexual sins protected His people from things they could not have imagined and that we are still dealing with today.

Sometimes the Bible repeats an event in an adjoining book. We will find some of the same events expanded on or placed in a different order. This made writing Miriam's story a challenge because I needed to mesh the events together to fit a timeline. I hope I succeeded in capturing the heart of Miriam and the heart of God in these pages.

The thing this story taught me the most? The holiness of God. It was His holiness that kept Him at a distance from the people because He can't look at sin. But it was His love that made Him long to be close and to tabernacle, or live, among them—to be near them in such a way that their sin wouldn't force His holiness to punish them. Ultimately, He knew that He would not be able to truly tabernacle with them, or with us, until Jesus came and bridged the gap between God's holiness and our sin, between His love and our desperate need for that love.

I hope that helps explain the book a little better. The setting for the exodus is still debated today, and I nearly drove myself crazy in trying to figure out which pharaoh best fit the one of Moses' childhood. Hatshepsut proved to be the best fit for his Egyptian mother, though she was only seven when she found him. Her historical record seems to bear this out—at least as best as I could find.

As always, I hope you will research Miriam's story on your own, especially in Scripture. Any errors in the research are mine.

In His Grace,
Jill Eileen Smith

# ACKNOWLEDGMENTS

*I* honestly thought *Rebekah* was the hardest book I would ever write. Then I encountered *The Prophetess: Deborah's Story* and realized I was wrong. *Hers* was the toughest story. And then Miriam came along.

If you know me at all, you know I hate writing the first draft of any story, and I'm certain that every book is absolutely awful until it's completed. This is especially true when I find so little on my current subject. So here we are. My patient team at Revell has seen me through my hardest book to date, and I am forever grateful to them for easing the burden with other projects I carried as I simply tried to get this book's first draft written.

I want to thank Lonnie Hull DuPont, the editor who acquired this book and retired before it was finished but graciously chose to edit it for me freelance. Thank you also to Rachel McRae, my current acquisitions editor, and to Jessica English, my line editor, who fixes all of my errors and comma mistakes and makes the books so much better.

Thank you to the rest of the Revell team, particularly

Michele Misiak for having my back and assuring me that all I had to do was write the book, nothing more. The marketing and publicity at Revell are outstanding! Thanks to Karen Steele, who took me on my first book tour during the year of writing this book. And to Gayle Raymer for another outstanding cover.

Always, always, thanks go to Wendy Lawton, who has stayed with me through every book. We've been through much together, and I am grateful to also call her friend.

Thank you to my in-person and online friends for praying or grabbing lunch with me when I needed to stop and relax a minute. And to my family—all of you who make life a little bit better every day.

Randy, my best friend and husband extraordinaire—thank you for your faithful love. Jeff, Chris, Molly, Keaton, Ryan, Carissa, and Jade—I couldn't love you more.

Most of all, thank You, Adonai, for showing me a tiny glimpse of Your holiness as I studied this book. I do not think I will ever look at Your character or Your love the same.

Jill Eileen Smith is the bestselling, award-winning author of the Wives of King David, Wives of the Patriarchs, and Daughters of the Promised Land series, as well as *The Heart of a King, Star of Persia*, and the nonfiction books *When Life Doesn't Match Your Dreams* and *She Walked Before Us*. Her research has taken her from the Bible to Israel, and she particularly enjoys learning how women lived in Old Testament times.

When she isn't writing, she loves to spend time with her family and friends, read stories that take her away, ride her bike to the park, snag date nights with her hubby, try out new restaurants, or play with her lovable, "helpful" cat, Tiger. Jill lives with her family in southeast Michigan.

Contact Jill through email (jill@jilleileensmith.com), her website (www.jilleileensmith.com), Facebook (www.face book.com/jilleileensmith), or Twitter (www.twitter.com /JillEileenSmith).

# LOVE. DUTY. FEAR. COURAGE.
### In the court of the king,
### which will prevail?

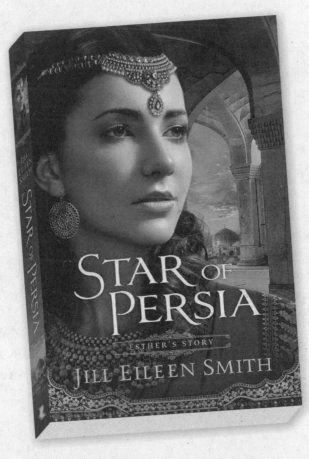

Esther is poised to save her people from annihilation. Relying on a fragile trust in a silent God, can she pit her wisdom against a vicious enemy and win? With her impeccable research and her imaginative flair, Jill Eileen Smith brings to life the romantic, suspenseful, and beloved story of Esther, queen of Persia.

Revell
a division of Baker Publishing Group
www.RevellBooks.com

Available wherever books and ebooks are sold.

# Get Swept Away by a Story of Love, Loss, and Longing

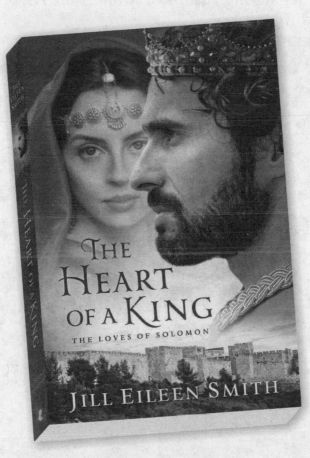

King Solomon could—and did—have anything he wanted, including many women from many lands. But for all of his wealth and wisdom, did he or the women he loved ever find what they are searching for?

**Revell**
a division of Baker Publishing Group
www.RevellBooks.com

Available wherever books and ebooks are sold.

"Jill's storytelling skills kept me reading late into the night. A beautiful tale, beautifully told."

—LIZ CURTIS HIGGS, *New York Times* bestselling author of *Mine Is the Night*

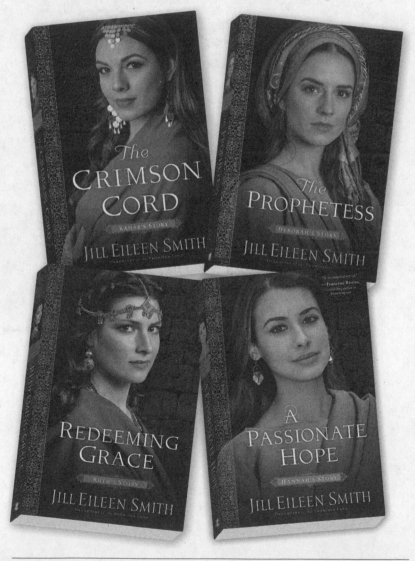

THE CRIMSON CORD
RAHAB'S STORY
JILL EILEEN SMITH

The PROPHETESS
DEBORAH'S STORY
JILL EILEEN SMITH

REDEEMING GRACE
RUTH'S STORY
JILL EILEEN SMITH

A PASSIONATE HOPE
HANNAH'S STORY
JILL EILEEN SMITH

Revell
a division of Baker Publishing Group
www.RevellBooks.com

Available wherever books and ebooks are sold.

*Against the Backdrop of*

# OPULENT PALACE LIFE, RAGING WAR, AND DARING DESERT ESCAPES
*Lived Three Women . . .*

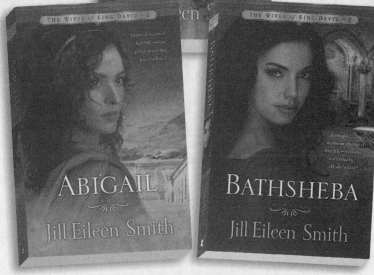

Revell
a division of Baker Publishing Group
www.RevellBooks.com

Available wherever books and ebooks are sold.

# JILL EILEEN SMITH
## Brings the Bible to Life

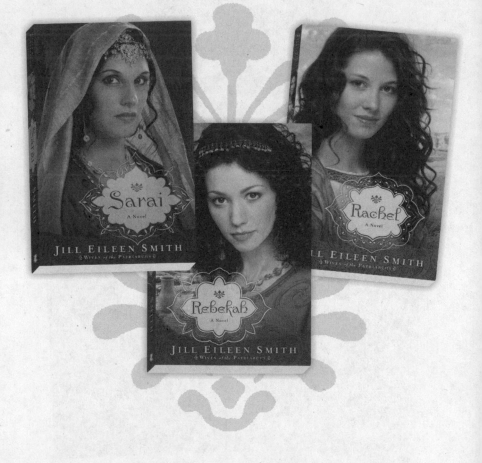

Revell
*a division of Baker Publishing Group*
www.RevellBooks.com

Available wherever books and ebooks are sold.

# Experience God's Unchanging Grace in the Challenging Seasons of Life

**She Walked Before Us**
Grace, Courage, and Strength from 12 Women of the Old Testament

JILL EILEEN SMITH

Hope *for* Today *from* 12 Women *of the* Bible

**When Life Doesn't Match Your Dreams**

JILL EILEEN SMITH

Revell
*a division of Baker Publishing Group*
www.RevellBooks.com

Available wherever books and ebooks are sold.

Meet

# Jill Eileen Smith

at **www.JillEileenSmith.com** to learn interesting facts and read her blog!

## Connect with her on

**f** **y** @JillEileenSmith